W0006376

FOREWORD

This is the first Companion novel in the Otherworld series. What is a Companion novel?

This story and all others with the "Companion" tag will be about characters in the main stories who might not have gotten a voice otherwise. These are non-royal characters given life in their own stories. They are standalone retellings and can be read in any order.

As always, I'm not a historian and as much as I wish I was, this is a work of fiction.

PROLOGUE

Once upon a time, when the world was new, a tiny seashell washed ashore. She was small and rough, for only a small snail had lived inside her. But she was strong enough to withstand the heaviest of storms and the crushing weight of the ocean.

Alone and insignificant, she rested on the sands and waited. The seashell didn't know what she was waiting for, but she was certain it was something big. The land was not quiet like the ocean. People shouted, the ground thundered, the animals were noisy, and the world was very frightening.

The brave little seashell waited in the sand, buffeted by gentle waves and softened by their wandering touch until she shone like a pearl. She waited and waited until a man stopped right beside her.

His foot came so close to crushing her that she cried out in fear! He paused—a bear of a man with so much hair she thought him an animal—stooped down and picked her up. Tossing her back and forth between his meaty fists, he stared at her shimmering surface.

"Hello," he murmured. "It's good luck to find such a pretty

seashell."

She stared up at him in awe. "You think I'm pretty?"

"I think you're beautiful."

At that moment, the tiny seashell fell in love. She decided his furry face wasn't quite so loathsome, his booming voice wasn't too loud, and the bright flash of his smile wasn't too blinding.

"Will you come home with me? I shall place you by my bed on a tiny pillow which will keep you safe from all harm," he asked.

"Yes," the tiny seashell whispered. "Yes, I will."

He placed her in his pocket which had a tiny hole at the seam. Through the opening, she peered out at the world. It was wondrous and great, far more than a seashell could comprehend.

The animal-like man placed her atop a velvet pillow and kissed her shiny surface.

"Thank you for the good luck, little shell. I must go to sea, but when I return, I promise to turn you into a necklace and keep you with me forever."

She waited—she was good at that—and waited some more.

A spider wove her web across the door. The tiny seashell watched her weave, capture food, create a family, and then die. Soon, another spider took her place and unraveled all the work she spent her entire life creating.

The tiny seashell watched dust settle on the home and on her velvet pillow. The windows cracked in a storm and tiny birds nested in the rafters. Mice tore at her pillow and pulled out the stuffing for their nests.

And still, the man did not return.

CHAPTER 1

THE MERROW AND THE PIRATE

Seagulls screamed overhead, their rasping cries echoing in the fresh salt air. The sea rolled in gentle heaves which did not disturb the ship bobbing atop its surface. A faint breeze cooled overheated skin, but it was not enough to fill the sails hanging limply from the mast.

Manus shaded his eyes staring out at the horizon. It was always the same. A small sliver of hope, the slightest glimpse of land, and a ship that wouldn't move.

Such was the life of a sailor. The sea tossed and turned, storms tore at ships and men, and dehydration tore at their bodies. They all did it for one reason.

Adventure.

Danger dogged them at every corner, yet each man returned month after month to climb atop the great ship and set sail for new horizons.

He lifted his face to the wind and breathed in the salty air. It didn't matter to Manus that they were sitting ducks on the ocean, that their water supply ran low, nor that their food was slowly disappearing.

As long as he was on the ocean, he could take any beating. Always did, even when he was a child. The old sailors used to call him the street rat born in the arms of the ocean. The boy who was meant to live on a ship.

"Manus!"

He glanced over his shoulder at the boatswain. The sturdy man was intimidating on a good day, frightening on a bad one. Oisin knew how to order the men about and get them moving without complaint. It was a talent Manus intended to learn someday.

"Get yer arse moving, sailor! The wind is bound to blow again!"

The wind wouldn't move anytime soon. Manus had always felt the weather deep in his bones. Faerie touched, some might call it, although he would never admit to having any marks on his soul. Faeries hadn't mingled with his family line in a long time.

But there was one grandmother whose tipped ears made people question how truthful he was when he denied having faerie blood. The ancient crones remembered his loving gram spending hours making certain everyone was well-fed and content. They still thought she was cursed and wanted nothing to do with her, even though she'd bent over backwards to make them happy.

Shaking his head, Manus tossed the long mane of his hair back and made his way up the netting.

"Wind," he grumbled as he climbed up the mast. "As if there will be any wind in these waters."

Not for a few more weeks, at best. He'd suggested last night they put all the men's backs to use and row. The other sailors nearly shoved him overboard for that proposition.

The ropes tugged hard, and his feet slipped from their hold. He grasped the horizontal post, glared down at the laughing shipmate, and swore under his breath.

Manus had bribed his way onto the ship, and now everyone knew because a loud-mouthed shipmate had shouted it during a drunken revelry. He laughingly revealed Manus wasn't meant to be here at all, but the Captain let him stay for a little bit of coin.

All chances of a fair trip had shattered at that moment.

No one wanted a man aboard who didn't know his way around a ship. Manus told them, time and time again, he knew how to sail. He'd known since the first moment his mother dipped his toes into the water and pressed a kiss to his head.

They didn't believe him.

There was also the slight problem of Manus's big mouth. He didn't take shit from any man and solved problems with fists rather than words. On the streets of Uí Néill, it was far easier to push and shove his way out of a bar.

On a ship? That was a different story altogether.

He heaved himself to the top of the mast, wrapping his legs around the smooth wood to anchor himself in place. His ribs protested as the stretching movement pushed against the raw bruises blooming across his dark skin.

Another beating, another day. How many had he endured so far?

He couldn't count that high.

If this was how they wanted to deal with him, then so be it. But, he would be back for the next trip, and the next. When the Captain wouldn't have any more of him, he would look for another ship.

The sea called to him like a siren. It wanted him to ride her great swells and feel the kiss of sea spray against his skin.

Manus whipped a cloth out of his waistband and scrubbed the mast. It wasn't doing anything. The boatswain kept saying how it was good to clean the mast of salt, but Manus knew it wasn't that.

They wanted to keep him away from the real work. Scrubbing the deck put him in the way of everyone. He was a big man, and a ship wasn't a place for big men. So, they sent him as high up as he could go, out of their line of sight and their hair, told him to clean, and forgot he was there.

He didn't mind too much. If anything, this was where he wanted to be. He could see every bit of the water spread out like a blanket around them. Seagulls soared above his head, dolphins leapt into the air with chattering cries, and the clouds created patterns only he could decipher.

Who wouldn't love this life?

Manus spent the rest of his day in the crow's nest, only descending when the sun dipped below the horizon.

The rest of the crew slept beneath the deck, other than a single man on watch who sat at the bow and stared out to sea. Manus recognized his face. The only man who didn't take part in the regular beatings that made Manus's ribs creak.

He silently crept up the main deck, readying himself to grab the other man.

"Don't, Manus. I don't have the humor for it tonight."

Sighing, Manus slumped next to him on deck. "And why not, Arturo? The world is a grave enough place without people losing their sense of humor. Where shall you go when you can no longer laugh?"

Arturo sighed, scraggly blonde hair dipping in front of his eyes. "I wished to be home a week ago."

"We can't all have our wishes granted."

"My wife was with child when I left. I should be by her side."

Manus stared at the dirt underneath his nails. "Why? That is women's work."

"Just because I cannot help her doesn't mean I shouldn't be there." When Manus didn't reply, the sailor leaned down and cuffed him. "Take note! Someday you'll have your own wife to tend to."

"I don't expect to marry."

"Whyever not?" Arturo exclaimed. "Women are wondrous creatures, and they give us a reason to return after a long voyage."

"Like what?"

"A warm bed at night, a willing woman after a long trip, children, food, a clean home. What more shall I tell you?"

"I can find all of that at a brothel."

Arturo rolled his eyes. "Aye, you could. But none of those women are yours. They belong to every man who presses a coin to their palm, and there's something sweet about knowing a woman is yours alone."

"Is it worth that much? I don't care if a woman stays true, as long as she's there when I return."

"You don't understand," Arturo replied, shaking his head.

Manus gestured to the sea, the ship, and the sky. "What more is there? We're all here for a reason. The ocean calls to us. She is our mistress and our wife! Why would I need another woman in my life?"

"Because the sea cannot give you sons!"

He scoffed. "I have no need of sons. I don't plan to leave anything behind and wouldn't be able to give them a comfortable life as children deserve. My father was a brute with a heavy hand. I will not continue the cycle."

"Why should you? Stop the cycle and become a good man."

"That isn't an option for me."

"Isn't it?" Arturo looked him in the eye. "Why not?"

"The same reason I just said. The sea is my mistress."

He heaved himself up and leaned over the edge of the ship. Manus reached out a hand, imagining icy spray numbing his fingertips as it did when they sped across the sea with sails full.

"The sea isn't a real woman," Arturo grumbled. "The older you get, the more you'll realize that."

"A woman deserves a faithful husband. I would run away at every chance, just to let my mistress rock me to sleep at her breast."

"You haven't slept on the right woman's breasts," Arturo said with a chuckle. "You wouldn't be saying that if you had."

They laughed, making certain the others didn't hear. The sailors would put an end to it if they knew.

Shaking his head, Manus patted the sailor's shoulder. "Why don't you get some sleep? I'll keep watch tonight."

"The captain won't like it."

"He won't know, now, will he? Go, sleep. You look like you're about to keel over, my friend."

Arturo lumbered below deck, and Manus stared out at the still sea.

He meant every word he said. The ocean was more a person to him than many he'd met in his lifetime. Frightening, consuming, and wondrous, it was his life's calling to devote himself to salt waters.

Manus stared down into the murky depths and felt a tension ease inside him.

Sometimes, in the very dead of night, he wondered what was beneath the waves. The great unknown of the ocean was baffling and frightening. There could be creatures staring up, looking right at him even as he stared down into the abyss.

Saoirse stared up at the silvery light filtering through the surface of the ocean. Its rays pierced through the depths until it was swallowed by the ocean and disappeared. She wished it didn't.

Moonlight was so beautiful and less dangerous than its sunny counterpart.

Merrows weren't supposed to go to the surface. Too many things hunted them there; humans, ships, sharks, even the occasional faerie would attack the delicate little creatures.

She nudged aside a strand of hair that floated in front of her eyes. The strand was so inky dark that no one would ever know it was green. Her father called it a shame. She would have been infinitely more beautiful if she had hair like her mother and sisters.

Saoirse much preferred her dark hair to the vibrant green of her people. She didn't like the way theirs looked like seaweed waving in the shallows, and besides, she stood out in a crowd.

The other merrow men didn't seem to mind her oddities. In fact, most found her differences thoroughly interesting. They lifted their webbed hands to touch the strands whenever she passed.

Saoirse did her best not to shiver in disgust, but the merrow-men were not attractive creatures. Their giant red noses were a beacon that attracted attention to their frog-like faces. Webbed hands and feet kept them firmly at the bottom of the ocean, though their strong tails could propel them forward when needed.

In contrast, merrow women were beautiful. Their long sleek tails came in a variety of colors, and their smooth skin shimmered in the sunlight. Rainbows danced in the slick webbing between their fingers, and the green hue of their hair mingled with vibrant fish that swam through the long locks.

She drifted on the currents, letting them drag her deeper and deeper into the abyss. That was where she lived, where her father and his many children waited for her to return.

Warmth faded from the waters. An icy chill wound around her shoulders and pulled harder, deeper, until darkness covered her vision and even her sensitive eyes were blind.

This was the part of the ocean that frightened her. Squid could tangle her in their tentacles without her ever seeing them. Saoirse had bumped into whales a few times, terrifying her so much that each time it happened, she remained in her undersea home for a very long time after.

But she always returned to the surface.

A tiny light bloomed in the darkness, small but enough that she knew precisely where she was.

Long ago, when she was very little, Saoirse had stolen a tree sapling and dragged it down with her. The scraggly, dying thing didn't stand a chance in the deep salt water. Her mother had felt such pity for the daughter who longed for a tiny piece of the land, that she wove a tapestry of magic around an abandoned grotto.

White pillars surrounded the small outcropping, the remains of a once great kingdom. A barrier held the ocean back between the pillars. Within that tiny space, her mother coaxed glowing coral to grow. She breathed life into the sapling, planted it in the center, and taught her daughter how to will the tree to stretch its roots and lift branches towards the sky.

Now, the great oak reached the ceiling of the grotto and spread wide leaves almost as large as Saoirse's head. Her mother kept saying she needed to tell the tree to slow down, but Saoirse couldn't.

It was an impossible thing growing at the bottom of the ocean. She would never tell it to change.

She didn't hesitate as she swam towards the grotto. Her shoulder slammed against the surface of the shield which made an audible pop and spat her to the ground. Landing hard on her arms, she blew out a relieved breath.

Grace certainly wasn't required to enter the grotto. She shook her head and winced as her legs tingled. Exposure to air caused an immediate reaction. The silver scales of her tail melted into a thick mucus that slid from her smooth skin.

Legs were such strange things. Saoirse didn't know how humans and merrow-men could stand having two appendages. They moved separately from each other, independent and infinitely difficult to control.

She stumbled to her feet, groaning with frustration before finding her balance.

The tree glowed in the dim light of the coral. She sighed in happiness and stepped towards the worn bark. She knew it as well as her own skin.

Its rough texture abraded her palm as she slid her hand down it. Saoirse reached up and framed the branches with her arms. They were nearly as thick as her new legs.

"Hello," she whispered.

Sometimes, she thought she heard a whispered greeting from the old tree. It would bend just so, as if a wind blew past. It was, perhaps, a rather fanciful thought, but she liked to think the tree knew her as well as she knew it.

She swayed side to side, getting used to her new body. Saoirse was fascinated by the changes merrows could undergo with little pain.

Magic was a strange thing. It allowed her to become something new and allowed this grotto to exist. It was wonderful, and fanciful, and so bright.

Saoirse closed her eyes and hummed under her breath. If she hit the right tone, faint and quiet, it almost sounded like there was wind. She could mimic birds as well.

The tree liked that. She was certain he stretched his roots deeper into the earth when she made bird sounds.

Pursing her lips, she trilled a few notes and stared up at the tree as if it were a man. She wouldn't mind kidnapping a person and bringing them down here.

Once in a great while, a ship would pass through their waters. She'd only seen a few men in her life, but they captivated her.

Their bodies were so different from her own and from the merrow-men. Humans grew hair in the strangest of places. Their arms were far stronger than she would have expected, and their bodies trim and muscular. It was a shame their skin was so strange. Pale white and faintly blue, they swelled as soon as they touched the ocean.

Granted, she'd only seen them after they were dead. The guardians wouldn't let them get too close to any ship that carried harpoons.

The great guardians, larger than most whales, traveled with the merrows when they left their homes. They escorted them from place to place, sometimes even just to stretch their tails.

They were kind, sweet, and thoughtful in a way most things under the water weren't. Saoirse loved them dearly. It was a shame her father didn't.

She glanced over her shoulder at the tree and saw instead a strong man with hair as dark as hers, reaching out his arms. Dark thoughts forgotten, she batted her eyelashes and asked, "Who? Me? Dance? Why I haven't danced in years."

She didn't really know what dancing was. A passing merrow, who had once shed her tail at the surface, spoke of humans tapping their feet to music.

Dancing wasn't the merrow way, and not likely something she would ever participate in.

Instead, merrows listened.

She had seen hundreds of females all gathering around a whale singing its haunting song. They floated, still as death with their hands pressed against their chests, listening as quietly as possible.

Why would anyone stomp their feet and not hear the music?

Still, it seemed rather interesting. She stamped her feet against the ground a few times, humming a tune that echoed the whale song. It was too slow, too simple, too quiet.

Frustrated, she shook her head and looked back at the tree. "I can't do it. You must have seen dances, even in your young life. What were they like?"

The tree seemed to sway, bowing to her.

"Oh! Were they all so polite? Did the men look at the women with their hearts in their eyes? Did the women sway?" Saoirse lifted her hands into the air and spun. "What do human women look like? Their men are quite handsome, so I cannot imagine what they must be. Are they ethereal creatures whose beauty burns?"

It was the only life she knew. Merrows were painfully more attractive than their counterparts. Humans must be the same, otherwise, what kind of creatures were they?

She bit her lip, looking the tree up and down. "Were you a handsome prince? If you were, tell me, right now. I simply must know!"

She didn't expect it to respond, not really. But there was always a bit of hope in her breast that someday she would meet a real prince. That he would sweep her off her feet, fall in love, and save her from marrying a merrow-man.

The tree didn't respond. Instead, all she heard was the sound of someone's muffled laughter.

Saoirse spun around so quickly her ankles tangled together. Tripping into a heap, she landed in the roots of the tree with her long hair wrapped around her body. She pushed the dark length away and stared between two of the closest columns.

Her brother and father hovered just beyond the border. Their ugliness made her wince in pity. Her father was covered in warts, his froggish feet so large they were longer than her arm. Her brother was slightly more attractive, for a merrow-man, at least his nose wasn't quite as bulbous as the others.

He chuckled again, bubbles frothing from between his hands pressed against his mouth. "Saoirse, really?"

"What?" she asked defensively. "Mother gave this to me to do as I wish."

Her father shook his head. "You are too old to be playing pretend."

"I am not that old."

"You are well beyond the age of marriage. I have been looking for you all day, and here I find you with this damned tree."

"It's not a damned tree!" She pressed her hand against the bark. "It's mine and it means something to me."

"I should have had your mother take these walls down a long time ago. They have made you fanciful."

"I am allowed to have something which is mine and mine alone."

"You won't for long!" he thundered. "You are going to have to accept marriage sooner or later, Saoirse. Most girls your age are already married, and still you will not pick a husband!"

She should have known that was why he was here. Her father wanted her to marry more than anyone else, although she couldn't understand why. There were other sisters for him to focus on, seventeen to be precise.

Her mother and father were prolific, desiring to be the family with the most children so they might have more bride prices. It wasn't difficult as a merrow. They had the choice to carry their children within them, or within an egg sack which was anchored to the bottom of the ocean.

Most tried to keep the babe within them. But, if one wanted many children, it was easier to place the eggs on the ground and forget until they hatched.

Saoirse helped take care of the eggs when she could. The number of her siblings were ever growing.

"I have no wish to marry," she informed her father, tight lipped and angry. "I have already told you this."

"And I have told you it is not acceptable. You *will* marry, and if you do not choose a husband soon, I will choose one for you."

Saoirse stumbled to her feet, cheeks flushed with anger. "You can't do that!"

"I can, and I will!"

"Athair!"

"Enough!" Her father held his webbed hand forward, treading water with an unreadable expression on his wart covered face. "Listen to me child and listen well. You will be married by the next turn of the tides, whether you wish it or not. I would suggest you choose a husband soon."

He swam away, frog-like legs kicking rapidly as he fled the sadness in her eyes.

Saoirse pressed her fingers to her face, the remaining short webs glistening with her tears. She had never noticed the leak when she was underwater. Tears mixed with the sea until everything tasted like salt.

Not so when she was in her little grotto. Her sorrows were all the greater when the ocean did not cradle her in its embrace.

Her brother chuckled and floated closer to the grotto. "Little sister, when are you going to learn that arguing with Athair is a waste of time? He always gets what he wants."

"Not if I can help it."

"What are you going to do? Run away?" He gestured towards the surface. "Do you think life above the sea will be any better than it is down here?"

She turned away from him, sniffing loudly. "How would we know?

"The rumors aren't true, you know. All those fanciful, romantic tales you whisper to yourself at night. Our sisters hear you, Saoirse. They listen to them and think you are foolish. Humans don't care about us, and they certainly don't care about the sea."

"You don't know that."

"I do!"

She flinched as his heavy fists struck the magical bubble holding back the ocean. The sound echoed through her head, then stilled as he pushed hard and slid through the shield.

The wet slap of his feet sent shivers down her spine. The merrow men were ugly in the water, but without the buoyancy of the salt water, they were monstrous.

Saoirse steeled herself and glanced over her shoulder. Flesh sagged from his form, dripping down his body like the slimy glow worms she'd seen in caves. Grayish green skin did little to enhance his appearance.

She swallowed hard. "What are you doing, bràthair?"

"Enjoying your little haven. Mother built it for all of us,

after all."

"You've never liked this grotto."

"I think anything from above is not worth our time." Water dripped from his shoulders to land with wet plops on the moss she had carefully cultivated. He glanced slyly over his shoulder. "You know father will pick the worst of them."

"He wouldn't do that. I'm his favorite."

"You like to think that, but he thinks you're too wild. A husband with a heavy hand is needed to control you, we all think so."

"A heavy-handed man would break me. I am more delicate than Athair knows."

"Is that so?"

Her brother padded around her, peering around the tree with unnaturally dark eyes. "Who do you think he'll pick, piuthar? Craig? His hands are large enough to crush your skull."

"He wouldn't dare."

"I always thought he would make a good match for you."

She liked Craig even less than the rest of them. He enjoyed the hunt too much. Saoirse couldn't count the number of times she had caught him floating in a blood-stained current. He liked to inhale the metallic scent.

"No, it won't be him."

Her brother arched his brow. "That almost sounds as if you're considering choosing."

She didn't like the shrewd look in her brother's gaze. He was too smart for his own good and read her too easily. He had no right to know her thoughts, but she was bound to tell him.

As a faerie, she couldn't lie. Her tongue twisted into knots the moment she tried. But, she could twist the truth. And she *was* fragile, she felt like the thinnest of shells beneath the weight of the ocean.

This world wasn't for her. She longed for the sun, for waves, for seagulls screeching above her head. The darkness and silence didn't fit the glowing light of her soul.

"You've made it perfectly clear I have no other choice."

"What are you planning?"

"Nothing at all. I am trapped, though you didn't say it in so many words. If I do not choose, I will be forced. And I will not submit to whatever brute father chooses for me."

"This is unlike you."

Saoirse sniffed. "Perhaps you do not know me as well as you think."

"No, I know you better than any of our siblings. I'll be keeping a close eye on you, Saoirse. You won't do anything foolish to compromise this family."

With a hard look, he stepped back through the bubble of magic and into the water. She waited until he disappeared into the murk before huddling against the tree. Her shoulders shook with the force of her emotions.

Married? To one of those disgusting creatures?

Her mother would say that looks weren't everything. Saoirse needed to set up her future so she would be happy and comfortable. A lone merrow in these waters didn't have the protection they all required.

She hated it. She hated them.

The mere thought of a merrow man touching her skin made her shudder. Her scales weren't thick enough to shield her from their warts and wrinkled skin. What was she to do?

A few leaves floated down from the branches above her head and gently rested against her shoulders. She plucked one off and rotated it. The weak light from the coral shone through the fine leaf and made the veins glow.

"You're right," she whispered. "There is always another way."

She stared through the bubble towards the surface. Darkness obscured her vision, but she knew it was up there. The sun would touch her skin again, and it didn't matter that her brother thought her foolish.

If they would force her to marry, then she would see the sunlight one more time.

CHAPTER 2

Of Seas and Storms

The rocking waves lulled Manus deep into sleep. Dreams danced through his head, each wilder than the last.

His mother's voice whispered in his ear, "Manus! My boy, where have you been off to?"

"The sea, mother!"

"You visited her again?"

"She told me stories."

"Stories?" his mother said with a laugh. "What stories did she tell you this time?"

"She told me stories of merrow women with seaweed hair."

"Oh!" He heard the shifting sound of fabric and the trickle of water as she washed her hands after a long day of work. "Merrow women are a strange lot. They're beautiful and kind, but their husbands are terrifying to behold."

"The merrow men can't come out of the water, though."

"No, but you must be careful to never anger them. They will tear a ship apart with their bare hands just to take back their brides."

The dream shifted, swelling and cresting with the waves. His mother's quiet voice shifted and warped, changing to a desperate cry.

"Manus! Manus, wake up!"

He jolted upright, sweat staining his brow and sticking his shirt to his chest. Nightmares weren't frequent in his life, particularly about his mother. Her soul remained in the afterlife where it belonged.

Manus blew out a sigh and wiped his forehead. It came away not sticky with sweat, but cold and gritty with dried salt.

"What?"

His groggy mind thought for a moment he was sweating seawater.

Slowly, he pulled himself from the strange dream and glanced up at the planks above his head. Water leaked through, dripping down on his forehead in solid and heavy drips.

He shook his head. "Arturo?"

The man who shared his bunk snorted and turned over in his sleep.

"Arturo," he growled. "Wake up."

"Is it time for our watch?"

Manus watched as the drops became a steady stream, pouring through the cracks on the ceiling to the floor in a quiet trickle. "The deck is leaking."

"The deck doesn't leak."

"It does now."

Arturo rolled over onto his back, stared up at the drips, and scrunched his face. "So it does."

"Doesn't seem good, does it?"

"Probably not."

"Should we go topside?" Manus questioned.

"I'm not sure that's wise." Arturo's hand flopped over the side of the bunk and waved. "It's probably just a bad storm, and if it isn't, we're safer down here."

Manus wanted to agree with him. The ship rolled over the heavy waves, but there was something strange about the way the hull moved. It shouldn't be bouncing like this.

He remembered the strange dream and his mother's voice whispering in his ear.

"Arturo?"

"Aye?"

"Where did the captain say we were headed?"

"Out into the Great Ocean. A passing tale caught his attention, that if he turned the ship into the wind when the sea grew still, that he would see the land of plenty."

Manus swore. "Fools! The land of plenty? You mean Tir na nOg?"

He watched as the sailor's eyes grew wide with fear. "That's another way to think of it."

"All you bastards should listen to the old tales," he spat as he swung his legs out and leapt onto the deck. "I'll see if I can fix this, or if we're too far gone."

"Gone?"

"We're heading straight into faerie waters!" Manus shouted as he grabbed ahold of the ladder leading out of the belly of the ship. "They'll sink the ship!"

A sudden shift sent him toppling sideways. His strong hands grasped the rungs, preventing a nasty fall. He swung himself upright and made his way to the deck.

The storm raged above them. Unnaturally colored

lightning struck the mast, flaring bright and leaving bright spots in the center of his vision. Stumbling to the side, Manus caught himself on the stairs.

"Captain!" he shouted. "Captain!"

"Get down below deck, boy!"

"No!" He pulled himself hand over hand, up the railing and stairs to the captain's side. He flung himself onto the wheel of the ship. "You don't know what it is you do!"

"I do, boy! We sail towards riches."

The rain lashed against the captain's cheeks, but he didn't seem to feel it. He stared with blank, dull eyes into the heart of the storm. His coat flapped in the wind. Fabric cracked against his side with harsh smacks, but he did not react.

It was as if he were under a spell.

White with fear, Manus held the wheel still. "You'll kill us all."

"It's just a small storm. We can get through it."

"We can't without faerie protection!"

"Who says we don't have that?" The captain's eyes moved a fraction, settling on Manus. "We have one of faerie blood to keep us alive."

"Me?" Manus shook his head. "You think they care for a drop of faerie blood in an ocean of human?"

"It's more than any of us."

"It's only enough to tempt the sharks."

Lightning cracked again, flaring so bright Manus thought he would never see again. The mast creaked in warning and fire spread across the sails.

"It's an omen!" he shouted. "We must turn back!"

"Just a bit further."

"No!"

The captain wasn't listening. He stared through Manus as if he didn't exist at all.

What had happened?

Manus let go of the wheel and raced towards the back of the ship. There were lifeboats there, he could gather as many men as possible, toss them into the dingy and....

And what? Where else could they go?

The waves swelled, spilling water over the edge, causing him to slip and slide across the boards. His heart thumped in his chest, a terrible feeling, foreboding and dark. Would they die here?

Arturo poked his head out from below deck. His eyes narrowed as saltwater sprayed in his face.

"Get out!" Manus shouted. "We have to get off the ship!"

"Why? We're safer here!"

"No one is safe in this storm!"

A deep bellow echoed, sending vibrations travelling through his feet and deep into his chest.

"What was that?" Arturo asked, his expression grim.

Manus wanted to tell his friend it was likely nothing. A whale, the groan of churning ocean waves, thunder on the horizon. But it was worse than that.

Much worse.

"Go!" he shouted, sprinting towards the lifeboats himself. "Run!"

He didn't have enough time to take even a few steps. A wave larger than the ship swelled beside them, arched overhead, and crashed down upon the deck.

Salt water pounded down on him, throwing his body to the

planks and rolling him into darkness. Wood cracked against his ribs, splintering the bones. Pain ricocheted through him until Manus couldn't tell what hurt. Everything felt shattered.

He hit the ocean with a sharp slap that ruptured his eardrums and sent his senses reeling. His lungs burned, but he didn't know which way was up and which was down. Was he even swimming?

A bolt of lightning struck the surface of the water, illuminating the carnage underneath the waves.

Men floated in the sudden silence between muffled cracks of thunder. Their arms hung limp at their sides, hair billowing in almost graceful tendrils. Manus peered at their faces, recoiling at the vacant expressions in their eyes.

They had drowned. And there were so many of them.

Lightning struck again, and this time he stared straight up into the sky. Swimming to the surface was nigh impossible. His arms ached, his lungs squeezed, and small dots of darkness obscured his vision.

He burst into the air with a gasp. Coughing and choking, he called out, "Arturo! Arturo, can you hear me?"

A groan echoed in the air, so loud that Manus was certain it was a beast of the waves. But it wasn't. He stared in horror at the burning mast of the ship which tilted down… down…

Swearing, he set his body into motion and swam. The burning wood barely missed him as it crashed into the water sending ripples and waves splashing over his body

He inhaled, coughing so hard he dipped underneath the surface again. Manus was a strong swimmer and even he was having a difficult time finding his bearings. Swimmers needed to be calm and let the ocean do the work for them.

And yet, it felt very much like the ocean was working against him.

Hands grasped his ankle, and he shuddered. Had the faeries come? He had known they wouldn't allow humans to enter their lands without retribution, but he hadn't expected them to be so cruel.

To sink a ship needed magic. And there were only a few creatures in the ocean with magic strong enough for that.

The hands clawed up to his thigh, his chest, and then a head burst out of the water. Dark hair plastered to his skull, his beard stuck over his mouth, but Arturo was alive.

Manus grabbed onto him, forcing Arturo to stay above the waves. "You're alive!"

"Not for long. Look at the ship."

He had seen the ship. The crumbling pieces, the burning sails, the hole in the side which hadn't been there before.

"What could have caused this?" Arturo asked. "What madness lives in these waters?"

"No madness," Manus replied. "Just the Fae."

"The faeries did this?"

"I tried to tell the captain to turn around. There was only one way for this to end."

And now they would all face the mercy of the sea.

He cursed the captain and his foolishness for thinking he could enter faerie lands and steal their cursed riches. What had possessed him to think he could claim it?

"Manus," Arturo gasped. "Manus, what's the plan?"

"Plan?"

He didn't have a plan. He might like the ocean as his mistress, but he didn't want to rest in her arms forever.

Manus glanced around, finding a small bit of debris within reach. The plank wouldn't float forever, but it would ease Arturo's exhaustion. He pushed the other man up onto the board and tried to grin.

"See? We'll be fine. I'll get you back to your wife in no time."

"If I don't make it—"

"I won't hear it, Arturo."

"You have to find my wife—"

"Stop talking."

"Tell her I love her and that the child would have meant more than the world—"

"Enough!" The shout was too harsh, too ragged, but he couldn't listen to his friend plan his own death. "We're going to live, Arturo."

"We're in the middle of the ocean with a ship that's slowly sinking. I'm not going anywhere." Arturo shook his head ruefully. "But you? With that faerie blood, you might stand a chance."

"You know better than to put trust in rumors."

Faeries didn't care if he was the bastard son of a bastard son. They didn't care there was a drop of their own kind in him.

Still, it wasn't the time nor the place to dash Arturo's hopes.

Manus nodded. "Aye, I'll tell her."

"Good."

"But I'm staying with you until we figure out what we're going to do."

Arturo's teeth chattered. His expression said he didn't believe Manus for a second, but he gave a firm nod all the same.

There had to be something they could do. The mistress of

the ocean took away their ship, and she would give them something in return. That's how it always worked.

Manus just had to find what she had exchanged.

"Manus?"

"Yes, Arturo?"

"Do you ever see shadows in the water?"

"Sometimes."

"Large moving shadows?"

He stilled as cold fear trailed down his spine. "How large?"

"Bigger than a ship. Bigger than a whale."

He'd only heard of such things in myths and legends. Old sailors whispered of creatures so large that the ocean could barely contain them. Creatures that patrolled the faerie waters and removed any who did not belong there.

A guardian.

Swallowing hard, he patted Arturo's shoulder. "Stay alive, sailor. I'll take a look."

"You be careful."

"Faerie blood, remember? I'll be fine."

He likely wouldn't be. Manus couldn't imagine what a guardian would do to him, the stories never went that far. The sailors always said they had seen the beast but couldn't describe what it looked like. Or even what it really was.

Just a faerie in the water who was larger than life. Not exactly helpful.

Manus took a deep breath, ducked underneath the surface, and opened his eyes. The murky darkness revealed no secrets, no oddities, no guardian. The burning sails fell and landed not too far away.

Whale oil spread across the surface of the ocean, carrying

with it orange light. Spears of fire sank beneath the waves and bounced off the surface of an ink dark hide.

He followed the line of the body that floated near the wreckage of the ship. It was like a whale in texture, smooth, supple, no scales to deter from the sleek body. A large hand shifted. It reached through the water and grabbed the remains of a lifeboat.

His stomach clenched. It was big enough to palm a lifeboat?

Smaller shadows moved all around the strange creature. Sharks? Beings it had at its beck and call?

The guardian paused, hesitating for a moment before he realized it had a head. Not just a whale head, but a *human* head. She wasn't a beautiful thing in the slightest, with hair shaved close to either side of her skull and lacking a nose. But those eyes were eerily human, and they were staring directly at him.

Manus gulped and kicked to the surface. It had seen him. The guardian had seen him, and now what was he going to do?

He looked over at Arturo with fear racing through his veins. "I'm sorry, old friend. I don't think I'll be taking that message to your wife after all."

"What is happening? Manus, what did you see?"

The image of the guardian seared into his mind for all time. What could Manus say? That he had seen a beast which lurked in the depths of the ocean? That this creature shouldn't exist, shouldn't be possible, yet it had stared back at him with eyes as black as hell?

No. He couldn't tell Arturo any of that. Not when he felt the waves lapping at his neck and knew the guardian was coming for them.

Humans had no place in faerie waters. They should never have come here, and though it hadn't been their choice, the guardian wouldn't care. There would be no reasoning with a creature meant to hold the gates of faerie oceans closed.

He gulped. "Think of your wife. Picture her face in your mind and don't let go of her image."

Arturo licked his lips. "We're going to die."

"It'll be quite a story to tell if we survive."

The wave swelled and crested over their heads. Manus tumbled beneath their weight, shoved deeper and deeper into the dark depths.

He threw his arms wide, pushing and punching against the wall of water until he stilled. Floating far beneath the surface, he stared up at the meager light. It disappeared as the guardian passed overhead.

She paused and stared down at him with an eye so large he saw his entire torso reflected in it. Spots danced in his vision as she swam by. With one flick of her tail, she pushed him even farther down into the heart of the sea.

Saoirse held her breath and watched as the ship sank. It was a rare sight for a merrow. Ships rarely traveled into faerie waters.

Especially unmarked ships.

Her heart clenched as she saw her sisters dart through the waters, grabbing the bodies of fallen sailors who hadn't known any better. The humans didn't understand that yellow was a soothing color to the guardian who then would allow them to pass. Why didn't they know to paint the hulls for smooth passage?

Another merrow swam past, her tail flicking aggressively as she swarmed with the others. They would take the bodies of the sailors to their homes. Humans made good food for the bottom feeders, and they would help keep small fish and snails alive.

She understood why they needed to die. Humans were the ones who had chased the faeries out of Uí Néill long ago. They only knew how to fight and rage at the world.

They didn't look like the rage-filled creatures of lore as their limp bodies drifted with the currents.

Saoirse could easily picture her father's livid expression when he found out she had come with the guardian. She was supposed to be searching for a husband, speaking with all the merrow men who were interested.

There were less than her father had expected.

She knew she shouldn't feel pride in that, but she did. Saoirse wanted to be an old maid. She wanted to live on her own, in peace and quiet, passing her days in the grotto with her tree.

Why was that so hard for him to understand?

The guardian sang out, her melancholy song marking the end of their battle. Not that it was ever a battle when a guardian was involved. No one could stop the sheer power her dearest friend wielded with a blithe smile.

Merrows flashed by. Their scales glimmered in the dim light, feral smiles on their faces as they dragged their prizes down into the depths. They called out for Saoirse to follow them, but her gaze caught on a dark shadow.

A silhouette hovered in the crystal-clear water, suspended above slowly sinking planks and great swaths of sails.

She bit her lip. The guardian swam overhead and traced a gentle finger down Saoirse's spine. She knew what the message was.

Go home, little merrow. Back to safety and family.

Angry thoughts bubbled in her head. If she were to marry an ugly, mean creature who wanted to beat her down with a heavy hand, then she would do as she wished while she was still free.

Casting a defiant glance at the guardian, she swam towards the man. He floated, long dark hair billowing like ink around him. It was sad he had died. He was handsome.

The current shifted his clothing, lifting his shirt to reveal ridged bumps that trailed down his stomach and disappeared under the fabric of his pants.

She cocked her head to the side. His legs weren't as repulsive as the merrow men's, although she still found it strange that he had two. They weren't as frog-like and they certainly weren't scaled.

He was handsome, in a chiseled kind of way. A long nose, strong jaw, and dark piercing eyes all melded together to create a pleasing face. His skin was burned to a dark, earthen color by the sun.

Saoirse reached up and marveled at her pale skin in comparison. She looked like the moon, silver and pale and shimmering with an inner light, whereas he was dark and swarthy, like the night sky.

Temptation's song was too much for her to ignore. She touched the high peak of his jaw, her expression softening. He felt just like she did, soft and warm.

Her brows drew down. Warm?

The man's eyes snapped open, staring directly into her dark gaze.

She flinched back, swinging her tail up to cover her face and vulnerable torso. But he did not attack as she had expected. Instead, he lifted a hand towards her. Then, his entire body jerked. The spasm rocked down his entire frame and his eyes rolled back in his head before he went limp.

Saoirse pressed her hands against her mouth. He was alive! How was it possible that the guardian had missed him?

Or had she? Perhaps the guardian hadn't wanted Saoirse to go back at all. Perhaps she wanted the tiny merrow to meet a human for the first time.

Resolve settling on her shoulders, she surged forward, slid her arms underneath his body, and swam to the surface. Her strong tail propelled them; his added weight was nothing in the water.

Would he like that? Would he be frightened of her because she could hold his weight? She knew nothing about humans.

They broke into the air with a wild splash. Saoirse tilted his head up, cupping the back and helping his body float.

He wasn't responding. Weren't they supposed to do something other than lie there?

"You're supposed to breathe," she whispered. "Humans are supposed to breathe."

She pressed her hands against his cheeks, patting gently. His head lolled to the side and dipped beneath the surface before she could grab it.

"No," she groaned. "It's not supposed to be like this. Wake

up! Please wake up."

Water bubbled between his lips, frothing over his cheeks, and then he coughed. Coughed so hard he slipped from her arms, but she quickly yanked him back to the air.

"That's it," she encouraged. "That's it!"

His body curled away from hers. Each wracking cough sounded painful to her ears. Was he hurting himself? Could humans do that with such a simple thing?

Saoirse panicked. She didn't know the first thing about human anatomy. What if he coughed himself to death?

She shivered, pulled him close to her chest, and swam. There was an island nearby. Small, nothing that would sustain a man for a lifetime, but enough he might live for a little while.

Her father would be livid if he heard about this, so she would need to keep him secret. Her human was still weak, and no one needed to fight with a merrow man when they weren't well. And her father was a very large merrow man.

The man's body scraped against her scales. Saoirse winced as a few wiggled loose and floated on top of the waves. They would grow back, but she hated the itchy feeling as they healed.

He slowly stopped coughing, but his body fell limp again. She hovered a hand over his mouth to make sure he was still breathing. Strong gusts of air buffeted her palm.

Good. He would live.

Setting her jaw, she turned her attentions to the faint outline of an island far away. It wasn't Tir na nOg, even she wasn't foolish enough to bring him to the realm of the Seelie Fae. Nor was it Hy-brasil, she didn't want to imprison him with the unruly prince.

No. It was a quaint little place with only Lesser Fae to

bother him. She would bring him food, scoop fresh water from the depths of the ocean and bring it back to him. He would stay alive.

For her.

Though her tail trembled, she pulled him through the waters. She desperately wished they could travel underneath the water. Waves splashed in her face, confusing the gills on the side of her neck as they tried to suck in air while her lungs breathed.

Soon, she was coughing as well. How did humans do this? The air was confusing. There were too many things she could inhale. The water was easy, she breathed through her gills and it filtered out anything she didn't need. Human lungs were useless.

Every gurgle from the depths sent adrenaline spiking through her veins. No one could know what she had done. Especially not the sharks, notorious gossips who had never liked her very much anyway.

Just as her tail shook in exhaustion, she felt sand brush the tips of her fin. It was enough. She relaxed and released her hold on the man in her arms.

As much as she wanted to rest, the hard part was ahead of her. He couldn't stay in the ocean.

She caught her breath for a few moments and then pushed. He would have to survive the dunks under the water as she rolled him onto the sand. Up and up he went until his torso was firmly on land.

"Just a bit more," she grunted.

Dragging herself herself onto land was far different than hauling him. Merrows were naturally graceful creatures, and far more acclimated to land than selkies. But it wasn't easy.

She coiled her tail and launched herself onto the soft white sand next to him. Saltwater slid from her scales. They softened and slid away from her pale skin. Her legs felt different above the surface with the sun stroking her limbs.

Thoughts danced through her mind, all the possibilities of the paths her life could now take. What if a ship came to find him? What if she could flee her father, her brother, all the merrow men who wanted to grasp at her flesh until it turned black and blue?

She looked at the sailor in a new light. He could be her salvation.

The remaining mucus of her tail slid off her legs as she leaned over to peer down into his face. He was still breathing. The broad expanse of his chest lifted and fell in a hypnotic rhythm.

Gently, she touched a single finger to the intriguing muscles of his chest. A necklace hung in the valley of his chest, accentuating the broad musculature. Light from the pink sunrise reflected off the round single pearl at the end of the chain.

"Who are you?" she murmured. "How did you end up in faerie waters? Didn't you know it was dangerous?"

He couldn't answer her questions, but it made her feel better to ask them. A second finger joined the first, walking up his sternum to touch the long column of his suntanned throat.

The muscles worked beneath her touch, shocking her. He was so similar to her, and yet so different. The pale skin of her hand fairly glowed against the darkness of his.

Trailing up his neck, she touched the bristly hairs that

made up his coarse beard. It was softer than she expected although still strange. The merrows who had gone to land said humans brushed their hair. Did he brush this as well?

Her fingers caught on a golden bead tangled in the long strands. Decorations? Adornments? Did it mean he was important?

"Are you a prince?" she asked.

He groaned low in his throat.

Saoirse flinched back, drawing her hand away from the beard which parted to reveal rows of blinding white teeth.

"Water," he rasped. "Water."

She didn't have water he could drink. Saoirse knew humans didn't drink saltwater. Their bodies couldn't filter it the way merrows could, which was why so many sailors died at sea when the winds fled and the ocean called for their souls.

Instead, she curled herself around him and brushed her fingers through the long, tangled snarls of his hair.

"Shh," she murmured. "Rest easy, my prince. Go to sleep and all shall be well."

He didn't seem to believe her. Delirious and blinking, he stared directly into her eyes.

Dark eyes, like hers. But the more she looked at them, the more she realized there were colors of the ocean in his eyes. They appeared brown at first, like the dirt they dug up for her tree. But flecks of yellow, green, blue, every color she had ever seen, all existed within his gaze.

Lust speared through her chest and stole her breath. He was so handsome that she couldn't even think.

"Who are you?" His voice warbled with strain. "How did you find me?"

"You should be resting."

"I have no wish to rest. I was drowning."

She hesitated, licking her lips at the harsh tones in his voice. He was frightening while awake and she much preferred him asleep. "The ocean is a cruel mistress; she wanted your soul for her own."

"Why didn't she get it?"

The question in his eyes was one she couldn't answer. Saoirse knew the sea wanted him. It wanted to drag him down into the depths so that his sailor body would feed her children and his spirit would wander the currents for all eternity.

Her expression softened, and she tentatively brushed her finger over the frown lines on his forehead.

"I did not want her to take you." She shouldn't say it, but she couldn't stop herself from blurting out the admission.

His brow wrinkled. "Why?"

"I wanted to meet you first."

His brow furrowed even more, flexing behind her fingers.

Saoirse smiled and bit her lip. "I have ever been a selfish thing. I desire that which I cannot have."

"You can have me anytime you want, beautiful." His voice shivered across her skin, deep and sensual.

Her cheeks burned red. Was she ill? She reached up and touched the pads of her fingers to the heat, realizing quickly that it was a reaction to his words. Was she embarrassed? Was this how human bodies reacted?

"I should go," she quickly replied. "Stay well, prince."

"Go?" He moved to sit up. "Where are we?"

She couldn't afford for him to sit up. He would know she was a merrow and then all her plans would be ruined. Humans didn't know what to do with faeries, let alone those that came out of the sea.

Launching herself at his chest, she pushed him back into the sand.

A warm hand pressed against her spine, holding her close to the heat that billowed from his skin in waves.

She stared down into his strange eyes and swallowed. "You almost died."

And she couldn't bear the thought of it. The lament of death was a song she knew well. It was a song she did not want to sing for him.

"I feel much better now."

"I can see that."

His fingers shifted over the bumps of her back. "I hadn't noticed you weren't wearing much."

"Much?" She wasn't wearing anything. Merrows didn't, it wasn't in their nature. Bodies were bodies, and they weren't embarrassed by them.

"It was your hair," he murmured. "I must not be as awake as I thought. Your hair was covering you and I thought it was some kind of headdress."

"I said, you should rest."

"Am I dreaming?" He leaned back slightly, lifting a strand of her wet hair to the light. "I've never seen hair such as this."

"Never?" She shook her head, dislodging his warm hand and the confusing feelings it evoked. "I should go."

Saoirse fought her way out of his arms. Her legs didn't want to listen to her orders, not surprising considering she still hadn't gotten used to the strange limbs, but they were even more unruly around him. Knees shaking, she whimpered as she stood.

Embarrassing. This entire situation had been embarrassing. He must think her a weak little thing, incapable of even standing on her own.

"Wait."

His words made her freeze just at the edge of the water. Trembling, she tucked her hands close to her heart and stared out to sea. "Yes?"

"Will you come back?"

"I want to." More than anything else in the world. Her soul already ached at the mere thought of his loss although she didn't understand why. No man had ever wiggled underneath her skin. Not like this.

"That isn't a yes," he said. Amusement warmed his voice to sweet wine.

"I don't know if I'm allowed."

"Do you always do what you're told?"

The tone of his voice made her turn, curious what this strange human could be suggesting.

He laid out on the sand, his head on his hand and his legs crossed at his ankles. The shark-like grin on his face made her shiver.

"Well?" he asked. "Do you always follow the rules, my strange female friend?"

She shook her head. "No."

"Show me."

She stooped down, grasped the rock hidden beneath the water, and tossed it as hard as she could. It struck his head with a solid thump and knocked him flat on his back. Tiny puffs of sand burst into the air.

"Oh," she muttered. "That might have been too hard."

Breath brushed her hand when she leaned down and pressed it against his mouth. He was alive, and she was still the foolish one.

Saoirse pressed her fingers firmly against his lips. "You can't know I'm a faerie. You can't know anything about who I am, or you won't take me with you when you leave."

Humans knew merrow men were dangerous to deal with. Stealing a merrow from them was as good as signing a death warrant. And though she felt guilty tricking him into stealing her away, she didn't think he would mind much.

Casting one last glance at the intriguing human, she slid beneath the waves and deep into the heart of the sea.

CHAPTER 3

EILEAN AN FHAERIE

Manus thrashed through the underbrush, cursing the leaves that stood in his way. What were these strange growths? He'd never seen a plant in the middle of the ocean grow so tall, so wide, nor so large.

But they did here.

Leaves as large as his head reached towards the sky and slammed down on him every time he tried to walk around them. It made for slow progress, and all he wanted to do was explore a little.

The isle did not want to relinquish its secrets. He had looped around it multiple times in the days since he had awoken. It took exactly half a day to come back to the same place where he'd first opened his eyes.

He knew, because he left a line of rocks from the edge of the jungle all the way to the water lapping at the pristine, white sand.

And what a lot of good it had done. All he knew was that it took half a day to round the entire isle.

Every time he tried to go into the interior, the vegetation

stopped him. From the giant leaves, to the strange flowers, and spine-chilling growls, everything seemed to work against him.

He fought with plants until the sun dipped below the horizon, and only then did he go back to his line of rocks. A small bit of food awaited him every night, along with a pitcher of fresh water.

Huffing out a frustrated breath, he turned around and stared at the waves. Nothing yet, but the sun was close to skimming the western horizon. Whoever brought him the food would reveal themselves soon, or he wouldn't eat.

Somehow, he didn't think they would let him go hungry. They had gone through a lot of trouble to keep him alive.

Then there was the mysterious woman he remembered. Her eyes haunted his dreams. Big and black like the deepest point of the ocean, but so kind it made his chest burn.

He'd never seen a woman who looked like that before. He'd never seen a woman who made him *feel* like this before.

Manus assumed she lived on the isle and spent many of his first days looking for her. It didn't take long before he realized she wasn't anywhere near him, no one living was, and that she must have come from another isle nearby.

The problem was that he didn't think there was another nearby isle. He'd scaled a palm tree and stared out at the horizon for hours. There was no land nearby, nothing but water and waves.

He glanced over his shoulder again.

No food, no water, no small platter made of gilded metal that was far too fine for the likes of him. This place was strange and his mysterious benefactor even more so.

"Let's see who you really are," he muttered.

If he had to resort to trickery, then he would. Manus punched a leaf so hard it flew up into the air. Using the opportunity, he ducked beneath the small space revealed for a split second before the it snapped back down.

The dim light made it difficult to see what might be around him. He could smell the earthy loam, the decaying plants, and the faintly sweet scent of flowers. His bare feet sunk into the wet soil where he curled his toes.

If he had to wait all night, he would. Whoever was providing food and water would arrive. He was certain of it.

Manus waited for what felt like hours. The sun froze, the waves slowed, everything hesitated with bated breath. Would the mysterious person arrive? Would it be the woman with dark eyes and hair so black it shone green like whale oil on water?

No one arrived. Darkness fell over the isle, and the moon showed its silver face.

Manus frowned. He hadn't expected them not to arrive. Why wouldn't they show up? It had been five nights, and every night someone had left food and water for him.

Strange.

His knees creaked as he stood. He'd bed down in the sand again tonight. The sun's heat didn't leave it until late into the night, and the air was strangely warm here.

Slumping to the ground, he wrapped his arms around his knees and stared at the waves lapping at the shore. Just when he thought he had it figured out, his strange circumstances changed.

Where was he?

A soft sound danced down his spine. Not the quiet sound of someone hidden moving. A whine, like that of a wounded animal.

The last thing he needed was to discover he wasn't alone here. If there were beasts that hunted, then he had little to protect himself with.

He curled his hands into fists and glanced down the shore. A white form slumped half in the ocean and half out of it.

"What?" he muttered.

It looked like a dog or some semblance of one at least. The long muzzle was familiar. He'd seen wolfhounds as a boy, used to play with them outside the butcher's who had used them as guard dogs. They were fiercely loyal and dangerous, but kind to those who treated them with respect.

Slowly standing, he approached the animal as quietly as he could.

"Easy boy." Manus poured honey into his voice, calming and peaceful. "Did you wash up on shore as well?"

The mutt whined again. It only had enough energy to turn its head towards him, then let its jaw rest against the sand.

"Let me guess. A strange woman brought you here? Hair the color of oil on water?"

An ear pricked forward.

"You're a good wee beastie, aren't you? You won't bite me."

He stepped too close, and the dog curled a lip. Manus carefully watched the dog, unsurprised that it would feel threatened.

The closer he got, the more he realized this was no normal dog. Its fur had a slightly green tint to it although he thought it might be a trick of the moonlight, and it was far too large. Almost as big as a half-grown cow, it would fit just underneath his arm if it stood up.

"Cù sìth?" Manus exclaimed.

The dogs were said to be a legend. They were faerie born, the faithful companions of only a few Fae who proved themselves worthy.

For humans, they were the harbingers of death. They walked at the sides of bean sídhes, waiting for the moment when their faerie would cry out at the taste of carrion in the air. The dogs were rumored to then steal human souls.

He shivered but shook his head. "You aren't here to kill me, are you boy? You're just as unlucky as I."

Stooping just out of the dog's reach, he hunkered down and cocked his head to the side.

It was an intelligent enough creature to know it was being watched. Manus guessed the cù sìth was male. It was larger than the legends claimed, and the growl in its throat was deep.

"Easy there, friend. What shall I call you?"

The beast snorted.

"When I was a boy, I used to be obsessed with Manannán mac Lir, god of the sea, and king of the ocean I love. I shall call you Mac Lir in honor of the Tuatha dé Danann who gave you to me."

He heard a tiny sound behind him. Something another might have missed, but Manus was a very perceptive man. He listened for the slightest of sounds which may be important—like the slight clink of a plate hitting gilded edges.

It took everything he had not to whip around. The person who had taken care of him was there, close enough he might be able to run and catch them.

Was it the woman? Did she row a boat all the way out here

just to feed him? Was she hiding from someone?

His mind drifted towards the possibility of a husband causing her to run away into the ocean. There must be a mainland somewhere.

He lifted his voice but spoke to the cù sìth. "Do you know the story of mac Lir?"

The faerie dog twitched its ear, one forward and one back. Its eyes were not focused on him, but on something behind him.

"He was a great and powerful Tuatha dé Danann. Half druid, half Fae. Some say he was more powerful than Nuada himself. Now, that is not an observation I might make, but he is an incredible figure in our mythology.

"You see, mac Lir had the ability to call upon the mists. He would wrap them around himself and his armies until no one could see them. I've seen such magic out in the middle of the ocean. One moment you can see, and the next? The mist is so dense you can't even see your own hands.

"He would wrap these mists around him like a great shroud." Manus lifted his hands, gesturing as if he wrapped a cloak over his shoulders. "Once, invaders almost saw the isle—perhaps similar to this one—that he lived on. Mac Lir called upon the mists and the isle disappeared."

The dog gave him a disbelieving look.

"I'm just telling you about your namesake, boy. At least enjoy the story, would you?"

If anything, the cù sìth enjoyed it less. The Fae beast turned its head away from him and heaved a great sigh.

"Come now! You don't want to hear anymore? It's said mac Lir is the greatest of all sea gods and that even the merrows love him."

"That's not true." The voice was the quiet drip of water against stone, the echo of ice gurgling. It was beautiful and haunting at the same time.

He held his breath and glanced over his shoulder at the most beautiful creature he had ever beheld.

She stood outlined by moonlight. The sheer white dress she wore plastered to her skin as if she had swum to the isle. Long, dark hair stuck to the fabric, covering her breasts, and brushing the tops of her thighs.

And her face was surely made by the heavens. Her dark eyes were like a storm brewing in the west. Her lips were stained wine dark, her skin the color of starlight. But it was her voice that captivated him. It carried the promise of fulfilled boyhood dreams.

"Is it not?" he asked. "I think I'm the one telling this tale."

"If you're going to tell a story, then you should tell the right one."

He could see she was uncomfortable. She rocked back and forth on her heels, her fingers toying with the ends of her long hair.

"What is the right one then, beauty?"

Her brows furrowed. "I don't like it when you call me that."

"Why not?"

"It feels as if that is all you see."

"That's a strange thing to say," he muttered and turned to face her. "What would you like me to call you?"

"Well, I'm not sure."

"Why not?"

"No one has ever asked me that before."

She was a strange woman, far stranger than he had expected. Manus rose from his crouch and crossed his arms. "You must tell me what you want me to call you."

"Saoirse," she blurted it out so quickly he raised a brow.

"That's a name."

"It is mine."

"But I want to call you by a nickname."

She cocked her head to the side. "Why?"

"They're a form of endearment."

"Surely you don't consider me dear to you?"

Again, he asked, "Why not?"

"Because you hardly know me."

"I don't know you at all."

Saoirse grinned, the smile so brilliant it nearly knocked him off his feet. "There, you see? You've admitted it as well."

"Just because I don't know you, doesn't mean I can't find you compelling, intriguing, or someone I'd wish to keep at my side for a while."

"Then you're judging entirely upon my appearance."

He knew the look on her face. A frown mixed with furrowed brows that suggested she was about to throw the largest fit known to womankind. At least now he knew she was just the same as any other woman he'd ever known. Manus was good with women.

"Now who's judging who?" he asked. "Seems like you appeared out of nowhere, soaking wet right to the skin as if you swam all the way out to this isle. If I'm an intelligent man, and I like to think I am, you're also the one who's been bringing me food and water. I've got a right to call you whatever I want."

"Why?" She sucked in a deep breath, her hands fisted at

her side. "Why does taking care of you give you any right to treat me as you wish?"

"Oh, I never said that. I'll treat you how you wish, Saoirse, and I intend to do that by starting with an endearment, so you know when I use it I'm focused on you. And only you."

Manus had seen plenty of beautiful women in his life. He liked to track down the prettiest whore and pay a hefty price for her. But even the most renowned prostitutes in all of Uí Néill couldn't hold a candle to the mysterious woman who stood in front of him.

Saoirse.

Her name rolled off his tongue like sweet honey and burned his throat like the finest of whiskey. She had kept him safe all this time, saved him from the ship, and why?

Manus watched her fists unclench and waited for the soft sigh he knew she would heave.

"All right," she murmured. "So be it. If you must find something to call me other than my given name, then I request it be something from the sea."

"The sea?"

She looked up, catching his gaze with those dark eyes, and stole his soul from him. "The ocean is my mother. Her waves rock me to sleep at night and her will keeps me alive. I would honor her gifts in the way you honored Manannán mac Lir."

A woman who appreciated the ocean as much as he? Manus thought perhaps mac Lir himself was looking down on him, saw his strife, and sent him a bride that would wipe all others from his memory.

Cheeks red, he cleared his throat. "Ah, well then. That's much harder to think up."

"Is that so?"

"The sea is my life. I spent every penny I had getting out here in the first place, but I was one with the ocean the moment my mother first dipped my toes into saltwater. Such endearments have stronger meanings."

"Precisely why I requested one."

She had him there. The girl had spunk, something he couldn't remember any woman other than his mother having.

He was used to simpering smiles and hidden knowledge beneath lids that coyly cloaked true emotion. He was used to women who knew the game between the sexes and played it well.

This woman didn't seem to know there was such a thing. The ends of her hair shifted in the breeze, already drying from the trip she had made. Manus realized with startling clarity he wanted to know more about her. *Everything* about her. And he couldn't remember the last time that had happened.

He cleared his throat and rubbed the back of his neck. The cord of his mother's necklace tangled in his fingers, the tiny white stone bouncing against his chest. "Pearl."

"What?"

"Pearl, that's what I'll call you."

"Why?"

The vehement way she asked suggested his answer was important. That this was a turning point he could never return from if he got this answer wrong.

"Pearls take a long time to make. Even longer to find."

She waited to respond, her eyes suggested she thought he might continue.

He didn't.

"What does that have to do with me?"

"Someday I'll explain it to you, my pearl. But that is not today. What have you brought me for dinner?"

The swift change of subject confused her. She backed away a few steps as he strode forward, stuttering and tripping over her words. "I-I-It's just a bit of a fish and a few oysters I found—"

"You already know my favorites," he interrupted. He lifted the food off the gilded plate and inspected the fine craftsmanship. "I've never seen anything like this before."

"It's just something to put the food on."

"Oh, I know that. What I don't understand is how you found it all the way out here. This should be in a nobleman's house." He glanced up at her. "You aren't a noble, are you?"

"Royalty? Me?" Her jaw snapped shut so fast she didn't seem able to open it. Instead, she shook her head.

"You've got a royal look about you."

"What?"

"Perfect skin, perfect teeth, not a single callous or blemish on you. The only people who can afford to look like that are royals."

"I live a different life," she replied. "I don't think it's fair to judge someone because they don't look like you."

"Ain't that the truth. Come here," he said and patted the sand beside him. "Share dinner with me."

"Why?"

"I haven't spoken to anyone but myself in five days. I'd like a little company tonight, if only to save my sanity."

She hesitated.

Manus wanted to warn her. It wasn't safe for a woman so painfully beautiful to be alone with a man like him. She should run. That's what he would have said if he were her father. But he wasn't, so he smiled like the wolf he was and waited for her to sit.

Saoirse sat just out of arm's reach, her whole body tense as if he might spring at her. He might. He was strung tighter than a drum and he didn't have a clue why.

She was just a woman. The same as any other. Yet his body wanted her like a dying man wanted water.

He cleared his throat. "What brings you here?"

She did not respond.

"How did you get here? I couldn't find any land nearby, at least not that my eyes could see. And I don't see a boat. Did you swim?"

Again, she did not provide him any response.

He plucked at the oyster, pulling at the shell with his fingers even though he knew he would need a knife to eat it. Padding footsteps slapped against the sand and Mac Lir raced towards them. He settled onto the sand and stared at the oyster with such intensity it almost made Manus laugh.

"You want some?" he asked the dog.

"They don't eat oysters," Saoirse replied. "It's not good for them."

"How do you know that?"

Again, she remained silent. He noted her curled fingers, the way she held tight to the thin fabric of her dress and breathed out a sigh.

"You don't want to answer any questions about yourself, do you?"

She shook her head.

"I didn't think so. Smart, that. You don't know me from the next strange sailor on a ship, and it would be a sad shame for a woman like you to trust too easily." He grunted, straining to rip open the oyster.

"Here," she said, holding her hand out for the oyster.

Now what did she think she was going to do with it? If Manus couldn't get it to open, a slip of a girl wouldn't be able to.

Curious, he handed it over.

Saoirse ran her fingers along the seams. She didn't pull, didn't rip, did nothing other than hum under her breath and stroke the outer shell. It opened a small bit, and she gave a quick yank.

Just like that, he had an oyster to eat.

"Neat trick."

"Not a trick," she replied, and handed the sweet meat back to him. "The ocean provides, one need only to ask."

How many times had he said the exact same thing? Manus tilted his head back and let the salty oyster slide down his throat. It was his favorite delicacy although most sailors never got the opportunity to eat them.

Yet another reason he thought it likely she wasn't who she said she was. Oysters? Raw fish? A gold plate?

"You saved me from the wreck, didn't you?"

She averted her eyes.

"You can say it. I know it was you, I remember."

"Memories can be strange things. Perhaps you only dreamt of me."

"No, I wouldn't forget eyes like those. You pulled me out

of the abyss, dragged me to this isle, and then brought me food. Who are you?"

Again, she did not provide him any answers. She stared at the waves lapping her toes and remained silent.

"Arturo would love you," he muttered. "He'd tell me I'm finally getting what I deserve."

"Who?"

"A friend." Pain twisted his chest, an ache he knew all too well. Loss never got easier to bear, he just became a harder man. He rubbed his chest. "Gone now, I suppose. He was on the ship with me. A shame, too. He had a wife back home and a new babe."

"A baby?" she whispered. "That's so sad."

"Such is the life of a sailor. We all know the risks that come with our line of work."

"Your life is so fragile."

"Everyone's is. A man can die from a cut on his hand, a cough, a sting of a bee. Why not live a life of adventure? There's no guarantee life won't be cut short without it."

"I'm not sure I understand what you mean," she replied. Her toes curled in the sand. "If you're always sailing from one adventure to the next without fear of pain or hardship, how are you safe? How do you care for the life you're living?"

"I care. I care about the experiences, the adventure, the things I've seen that no one else has seen."

"And have you?"

"I've seen things that would make your heart race. Strange beasts that shouldn't exist. Lands so far away the people look entirely different. I've brought back furs of animals that are taller than me with claws the size of my hand."

Her lips parted, eyes locked upon him. "What is it like?"

"Sailing?"

"No. Going wherever you want, whenever you want."

"Now, that's a sad thing to hear you ask, my pearl." He handed another oyster over, silently asking her to open it. "There are men out there who don't think women should travel. They want to keep them under their thumb, so to speak, and prevent them from experiencing the world. I know it, and I think you know it too."

She petted the oyster and chewed her lip. "Why do they do that?"

"I think for some, it keeps them powerful. In their minds if they limit the knowledge of their women then they always have the upper hand. But they forget an important thing."

"What's that?"

"Women always have the upper hand. You have something we want, and we'll do anything to get it."

Saoirse froze, the oyster peeking out to gently touch her finger. Her eyes slanted towards him. "What is it men want?"

"Oh, that's a loaded question and not one I should be answering."

"Why not?"

"We're alone on an isle in the middle of the ocean, and as much as I like to think I'm a good man, I'm not."

"You seem like a good man."

"There's a difference between a good man and a patient one."

He could see her pulse fluttering in her neck. It called out to him like the song of a siren. She was just as affected as he was.

"I have to go," she blurted, scrambling to her feet in a flurry of sand and water.

"Where are you going?"

"Away!"

He lunged to his feet, holding out his hands because he didn't trust himself to touch her. "Will you come back?"

Saoirse froze, her back to him. "I don't think I could stay away if I wanted to."

They were exactly the words he wanted to hear. Grinning, he clenched his hands into fists and forced himself to back away from her. "All right then. Go on with you."

She raced down the sand and disappeared from sight, likely towards some unknown home at the interior of the isle.

Manus licked his lips.

"Patient," he muttered. "I am so full of shit."

"Saoirse! Where is your mind today?"

Her sisters gathered all around Saoirse, plucking at the floating strands of her hair. Her family had been a terrible bother lately. It wasn't unusual for their sister to disappear. She did so regularly, choosing to be alone rather than with them. Why did they think it strange now?

She groaned and jerked her head to the side. "It is here with you."

"No, it isn't. We've been talking to you for minutes and you've been staring at the stone!"

"Perhaps the current topic is one I share no interest in."

"You've always liked the whales, what changed?"

"*Nothing.*" Saoirse lurched up, propelling herself through the small cave they shared. "Why are you so bothersome today?"

"Why are you so testy?" Her eldest sister giggled. "Is it because father has decided you shall marry?"

Another sister pretended to swoon. "Has our youngest sister already chosen her groom?"

"How could I?" Saoirse shook her head at their antics. "There is not one merrow man in the entire ocean who could capture my attention."

"That's a shame, considering you are also a merrow."

"Can you willingly say there is one you like?"

"Craig has an interesting look."

"Craig?" Saoirse swallowed. "He has a heavy hand. One that likes to find its way towards innocent creatures."

"Oh, that's just a rumor."

It wasn't. Saoirse had seen it herself when she was coming home from gathering crabs for dinner. He had backed a woman into a crevice, speaking in low tones and lifting his fist. The look of terror on the merrow's face would stay with her for the rest of her life.

She shivered. "I would rather not tempt fate."

"I think she's found a man," one of her sisters giggled. "That's where she's been sneaking off to!"

Perhaps it was easier to let them think so. They could question it all they liked, but Saoirse was planning her escape. There were only a few more weeks until the full moon. Her father was already pressing her to give an answer, but she persisted that he had given her a fair amount of time.

If her plan worked, she would be long gone before then.

"Please," she clasped her hands, "don't tell Athair. I don't want him to know. It would be best if it were a surprise."

"Go on then, sister. But when you return, promise you'll tell us who it is?"

She shook her head and launched herself out of the cave mouth. They would never know who it was. And they would remain the only thing she regretted about this entire foolish plan.

Her sisters were as much a part of her as her gills. They might be foolish creatures, vain and sometimes silly, but they had hearts the size of the seven seas. She didn't want to see anything evil change that.

She shook her head and flexed her tail. Now was not the time to be thinking such morose thoughts. She still had to figure out how to get the human off the isle.

Jellyfish slid past, trailing their long tendrils against her skin. The faint electric sting made her muscles twitch. The larger ones posed a threat even to merrows. She grinned and batted one away. The small ones were kinder than their brethren.

Her smile faded. She supposed she could say the same about merrows and their kin. The guardians weren't likely to let her human leave any time soon. Even with her on a ship, they would want to tear it apart for trespassing.

Could she stop them? Was it even possible to reason with a guardian?

She had never tried. As far as Saoirse knew, no one had ever tried. They let the giants do as they pleased and were glad their homes were safe.

Could they even talk? No one had whispered rumors of conversations between any sea creature and a guardian.

Saoirse would need to know all these things before she let her plan unfold. The human needed to understand the danger he was in. He would need to trust her, to understand she had his best interests in her heart.

She shook her head ruefully and sped through the waters. He wouldn't trust her easily. He didn't seem like a foolish man.

"A patient man," she whispered, bubbles floating from her lips.

What had he meant by that?

There were too many questions in her head, and she needed them answered before *she* could trust *him*. It wasn't as if she had any choice. He was the only escape she could see.

Otherwise, she would end up in the arms of a merrow man for all eternity. Gooseflesh raised on her arms at the mere thought. Whether it was Craig or any other, she couldn't see herself marrying a frog.

The human? That was an entirely different story.

His matted locks were strangely appealing. The frown perpetually furrowing his brows made her want to smooth the anger away. Even his body was intriguing, so unlike her own even when she didn't have her tail.

Saoirse bit her lip. Did he think the same of her? She liked to think he did. The heat in his gaze suggested he was interested. But was that enough for him to take her far away from here? So far that the sea would never touch her again?

Her heart hurt at the mere thought.

The isle stretched its roots in the distance. The earth rose to meet her, lovingly sculpted by the hands of old gods. Coral glowed far beneath her, fish and sea life appearing as if by magic.

Poking her head above the waves, she eyed the beach. He didn't appear to be on this side of the isle at all. Worry ate at her. This was where she usually found him. Why wasn't he here?

She circled the land twice but didn't see him at all. The isle wouldn't let him go into the heart, would it? Those were faerie lands. Magic lands humans weren't allowed to see.

But apparently, it had.

Only those with faerie blood could pass through the sentinel plants which had a taste for blood. She'd watched him beat at them for hours before, when she couldn't keep herself away from the sight of him.

What had changed?

She dove beneath the waves. A small tunnel at the base of the isle was the only way for sea creatures to get to the heart. She peered into the darkness and swallowed hard.

She hated tight spaces.

Wiggling herself in, she used her hands to pull forward. Scales scraped against stone, loosening until she felt the telltale sting she had lost some.

Her father would notice that. He noticed everything that might mar her beauty even though her looks were considered "strange" compared to the other merrow women. Saoirse grunted and yanked herself forward.

Now, she would have to come up with some kind of story. He'd already noted her lost scales from the last time she swam with Manus. She couldn't make the same mistake again.

Maybe she'd been daydreaming and ran into something? He might believe that. His youngest daughter was often called the foolish one. The story would need to be as tight as a clam shell.

Light filtered through the water ahead. The tunnel ended in a fresh water pool so clear it was like looking through air. Green plants carpeted the bottom and brightly colored fish darted through the waving fronds.

She hesitated, not wanting to appear if he were looking straight into the water. What would she say?

Saoirse knew she would have to tell him what she was. Merrows weren't a bad faerie. Humans used to like them quite a bit until the rumors started that they sang men into rocks. They weren't trying to kill men back then. They were trying to *warn* them.

Humans were foolish. They thought the beautiful women were beckoning them closer and dashed their ships against the ragged stones.

Hooking her fingers over the edge, she pulled herself forward just enough to stare up at the surface.

A foot nearly touched her head.

Clapping a hand over her mouth so no bubbles rose, Saoirse ducked back into the tunnel. He was *in* the water? Why was he in the water?

She twisted her body so she could lay against the stones and stare up at him. He wore nothing but his skin and treaded water as naturally as she did.

Human males were not as she expected. Their parts were so different! Long legs, not at all frog-like, although dusted with hair. That made her uncomfortable. What were these hairy creatures? Were humans part beast after all?

He swam away from her, to the edge of the pool where his toes flexed, and he stood with practiced balance. Fish nibbled at his feet, the larger ones brushed against his thighs, but he didn't react.

She tried to see his face, but the water warped it. One moment, she thought he smiled. The next, she thought it might be a frown.

It didn't matter all that much, she still found him rather handsome. Never before had heat blossomed deep in her belly when looking at a male.

Humans were so lucky. There would always be a male out there they found handsome, beautiful, strong. Merrows were stuck with frogs and shark-like men who were always drunk and cared little for their female counterparts.

"How am I going to tell you what I am?" she whispered as she stared up at him. "Will you despise me? Will you think I am an animal to lock away? Or worse, a fish you might eat?"

Something grabbed onto the delicate membrane of her fin so hard she yelped, flexed the appendage, and shot out of the tunnel.

Her fear was so great she couldn't stop her momentum. Saoirse propelled herself through the pool and smacked her back against his.

The man.

She froze. He froze. They remained with their spines against each other's.

He was so warm. The heat from his body sank into hers,

even through the scales. The ocean was a cold place to live. Her skin was used to the frigid waters of the deepest abyss. Touching him felt the same as lying in sand with the sun dancing across her skin.

"Pearl, is it?" he murmured. "I'm afraid you caught me in a compromising position."

"I could say the same."

Saoirse tried to keep her tail away from him. The long, eel like appendage must make him uncomfortable. But she couldn't keep herself above the surface without moving it. She winced as her scales rasped against his knee.

"Ah," he said. "So that's the way of it."

Her tongue tied in a knot. What was he going to say? Did she catch a hint of disgust in his words? She had never felt so self-conscious about being a merrow.

He waited for her to speak. His ribs expanded with each measured breath, calming her jarring gasps.

When she didn't respond, he continued. "I knew you weren't human. No average woman could pull me out of a shipwreck in the middle of the sea, swim with me to an isle, and then disappear into thin air. I just didn't know what you were."

"You do now."

"I do."

She gritted her teeth and waited.

"Merrows are rare where I come from," he finally said. "We call them good luck. Sometimes they help sailors when they're in a bad way."

"I've heard of such things."

"Is that what you were doing for me? A bit of charity?"

"No," she shook her head. "No, I couldn't let you die."

"Do you usually?"

"I've watched men drown and dragged their bodies into the depths with my sisters, yes."

"Why didn't you let me?"

"I don't know." Saoirse's voice elevated, rising to a high pitch that voiced her panic. "I saw you there in the water and I couldn't bring you down with the others. I couldn't watch the crabs feast on your body until there was nothing left but bone."

"*Why?*" he pushed.

"I wish I knew the answer."

They both remained silent, breathing together. She had never felt so close to a man, and so far away at the same time. She could touch him. Feel his heartbeat against her spine. Yet she did not know what he was thinking.

"I'm going to turn around now, Saoirse."

"I'd rather you didn't."

"That's not an option."

"Can't it be? Just for a few moments longer."

"'Fraid not."

She kept her back turned to him even as the warmth of his skin disappeared. She didn't want to see his expression when he saw what she really was.

It wasn't as if she knew him. Saoirse shouldn't be as attached as she was. He could think whatever he wanted of her. It shouldn't matter.

But it did. Her heartbeat thumped hard against her chest at the mere thought he might dislike her.

His hand touched her shoulder. Fingers sliding across the

sensitive tendons, pulling her hair away from her skin to reveal the glistening sparkle of her skin.

"Are you going to turn around?"

"No."

"I can already see you."

"I'm certain you can, that doesn't mean I will turn."

He didn't seem disgusted. His voice was as warm as the rest of him, not frightened or tight with dislike. Perhaps he didn't mind after all.

"Saoirse," he chuckled. "No woman as beautiful as you should hide her face."

"I thought you said you didn't care about beauty."

"I never said that. Any man cares about beauty, but some of us see it inside a woman just as much as outside."

She melted. It didn't matter he might be lying to her, or that perhaps he was good with words. He had said the right thing to ease her nerves.

Her tail fluttered in the water, fine membranes glistening from the small of her back and tapering down to her wide fin. She flicked the end and turned towards him.

He stared down at her with an expression of awe. His eyes devoured every detail, starting at the top of her head and meandering down below the water. She couldn't imagine that he didn't feel at least a little apprehensive about her existence, but he didn't seem surprised at all.

"May I?" he asked.

Saoirse didn't have the faintest idea what he meant. Captivated, she nodded in response.

He reached down, lifted her hand, and tilted it into the sun. He pressed his thumb against the sensitive bones, forcing her fingers to spread wide and reveal the thin webbing. Rainbows danced over the membrane, making her hand appear to be made entirely of magic.

"You know," he murmured. "I never told you my name."

"It isn't customary for humans to tell faeries their name."

"I thought that goes both ways."

She blushed. "I am a foolish merrow. I speak with my heart before I think with my mind."

"I'm glad of it."

"Why?"

He ran a gentle finger across her webbing. "I would rather know your name than my own."

"You're very charming."

"It's working then?"

She lifted a brow and met his gaze with silent questions.

He chuckled. "I'm trying to charm you."

"You're doing very well."

"Any suggestions?"

"For what?" Saoirse shook her head, uncertain what he was asking.

"Improvement."

She blinked. "Not at the moment."

"You'll have to tell me if you think of anything."

"Why are you trying to charm me?"

"I've never met a merrow before."

"What does that have to do with anything?" Saoirse frowned. "Are you trying to avoid the question?"

"My name is Manus."

The words echoed in her mind, over and over again. She tasted the sweet whiskey of his true name that exhaled like a lover's sigh. A knot loosened in her soul, one she hadn't realized was there but had been since the moment she met him.

So, this was what it felt like to be the keeper of a human name. It was a heady feeling. Her fingers flexed against his, whispered possibilities overtaking her. She could order him to do anything. She could force him to help her leave.

Would she ever forgive herself? Saoirse wasn't sure. He deserved to make his own decisions, no matter how desperate she was.

"Manus," she repeated.

He visibly shivered, her words dancing across his skin and her control sinking deep into the vessel of his soul. He met her wide stare with an expression so heated she felt it burn. "That's a strange feeling."

"It doesn't always happen."

"What is it?"

"A bond. A tie between faerie and human."

"What does it mean?"

"We are linked forever, you and me. Like the ocean knows each creature that lives within it, we shall always know how to find each other."

He cleared his throat. "And if we don't want to be found?"

"I don't know. I've never met another faerie who made a bond with a human."

"Why not?"

"We don't like to be far from those with whom we are linked."

His eyes slanted away from hers and his hand tightened on hers. "I didn't ask for that."

"Neither did I. I might have prevented such a bond if I had an idea it might happen, but as I said, it is unusual for such a thing to occur."

"Why are you here, Saoirse?"

Not Pearl. He did not call her by the endearment she had come to enjoy. Strange. What had upset him? The bond? It wasn't anything she could change. The moment they heard each other's true names, the knot had loosened in her. Perhaps it had tightened in him.

She pulled at his hold. "I hadn't intended on seeing you."

"Ah, yes. The isle didn't want me in the interior. Is it because this is your home?"

"I do not live here."

"That's not an answer."

She hissed. "It is my only answer."

"Then why did the plants allow me here for the first time, and then you showed up?"

"I don't know."

"You say that a lot, and I think you're lying."

"Faeries cannot lie."

Her kind were truth tellers, no matter how much they wished they could lie. Faerie words could be twisted. Even Saoirse was adept at saying one thing and meaning another.

Surely, he knew? She wracked her brain, trying to find an answer to his question. She didn't want him to be mad at her. Frantic, she blurted out the first thing she could think of.

"Only faeries may come into this oasis. It is why it wouldn't let you in before."

"I'm still not a faerie." He hesitated before he said the

words, just enough for her to notice.

"Why did you pause?"

"I didn't."

"You did. I heard your hesitation. I may not be able to lie, but I can tell one when I hear it."

He licked his lips and let her hand drop from his grasp. "My grandmother was rumored to have faerie blood."

"A changeling?"

"Not so much as that. Just a few drops of faerie blood that made her more likely to garner their favor."

Saoirse giggled at the thought. "Faeries don't care if humans share some of their blood. Those that we give our favors to are simply good people."

"Are you so certain of that?"

"The Unseelie Court may be different, but the Seelie Fae live with honor. They do not provide their aid to those who do not deserve it. If they deem their descendants unworthy, then they do not help them."

"Then the isle finds me worthy?" He snorted. "It wouldn't be the first to be wrong."

She stared up at his strong features, wondering what he looked like without the strong beard and tangled nest of dreadlocks. Were his features just as strong as she imagined? With such dark skin, she thought he looked much like the tree in her grotto.

"You say that so often. Are you trying to convince yourself it's true?"

"What?" He looked at her with raised eyebrows.

"It's just…" She looked down, afraid he might think her foolish. "Of all the men I've met, you are the last person I would say was unworthy."

"Have you met many?"

"Just merrow men." Were her teeth chattering? The thought of her own kind caused such a visceral reaction, and she couldn't control it. "They are not kind."

"All of them? I find that hard to believe."

"All of them."

He couldn't understand. It wasn't her species that was the issue. It was their life. Merrow men were stuck at the bottom of the ocean. They were so slow compared to merrows, incapable of protecting themselves against sharks or squid. Merrows were fast, darting through the ocean without a care.

Alone, forced to remain in the dark depths, merrow men turned to alcohol to ease their troubled minds. It made them ugly, angry, and they were even worse when they drank.

He watched every thought reflected on her face. She felt his gaze as if he touched her.

He hummed deep in his throat. The tones sounded like that of the great whales that passed by at night. Their haunting songs sometimes crept into her dreams, reminding her that the world was large, and she was nothing more than a small merrow.

"If that's the way of it, then I am glad you are here," he said. "It is a long and difficult road to walk when those around you are not willing to be kind."

"You know this life?"

"Most children do when they grow up on the streets."

Her heart bloomed again, opening like a flower to bask in the acceptance of his tones and the understanding she heard within his words. "Then you understand why I am here."

"Perhaps too much, my pearl."

She stared up at him as if he hung the stars in the sky. He understood her? He understood the things she had fought over again and again.

Manus cleared his throat, a blush spreading from his chest up his neck. "Are you staying then?"

"I would like to."

"Good."

CHAPTER 4

Journey to the Depths

Manus lay on his back in the sand, wondering when and how he got so lucky. A merrow? They were creatures of good fortune, at least for sailors who worried the ocean would swallow them up at any minute.

Mac Lir must have looked kindly upon him. Little Saoirse would be a talisman for him. A confirmation he would never die on the sea.

He grinned up at the clouds that spun like churning waves above him. Just how far would this luck go? Would she bring him fortune? The legends said merrows cast their favors upon men easily enough. They liked a quiet-spoken husband who took care of them.

Her story hadn't surprised him. Anyone who knew of the Fae knew merrow men were poor excuses for faeries. They all liked their drink and disliked any man who stepped in their way.

The voice of his mother whispered through his memories. She had loved to tell stories of creatures under the sea.

"Never fall in love with a merrow," she whispered in his

ear. "They are kindly and beautiful creatures, but their husbands will hunt you down and kill you without a thought."

He must be a foolish man because he was willing to take the risk.

How could he not? She was more beautiful than any woman he had ever seen, and she had saved his life. Manus had never met a woman who could do that although Arturo was likely to laugh at him.

"That's the point of a wife, boy," the spirit of his friend crowed. "They would die for you. They take the chance with every child they bring into this world and yet they do it again and again for the men they love."

Foolish thoughts, all of them. He hadn't ever desired a wife, and it made little sense he would want one now.

Manus lifted a hand and rubbed at his chest. The sting of magic still lingered there, deep underneath his ribs and wrapped around his heart like a thorny vine. She murmured his name with a tongue dripping honey and eyes so large they held the entire night sky in their depths.

She owned a part of him now even though he didn't like it one bit. He hadn't given it willingly. She snatched up the bright light inside his heart and swallowed it whole.

Merrows were dangerous, he agreed with his mother. This one could bring him to his knees with a smile.

A soft clinking sound echoed from waves lapping the sand, and he smiled. She had returned, as promised, although he worried what it might cost her.

"Not your business," he grunted, reminding himself that she wasn't part of his life. Not yet.

If he had it his way, he would take her all the way back to

Uí Néill and sit her in a quiet little cabin all to themselves. She would look good by a fire with a cat curled at her feet.

He rose up on his elbows, staring down the length of his body at the merrow lying in the waves. She had her head on her fists and her tail curled out of the water, flipping back and forth.

"Hello," she said.

"Welcome back. Safe trip?"

"As safe as most."

"I'm glad to hear it." The sun reflected off the small pile of objects in front of her. Raising a brow, he sat all the way up and pointed. "What did you bring?"

"Things I thought you might find interesting."

"Well bring them here then."

"I'd rather you come get them."

He thought for a moment she was flirting. It surprised him. She had proven to be an innocent little thing, and far too curious for her own good, but he quickly realized no flirtatious tones heightened the trill of her voice.

Her hands clenched into tiny fists. Her tail stopped flipping, instead, it lay still underneath the water. Even the shimmer of her scales dulled as her eyes dropped from his. She was uncomfortable, he realized, or perhaps even embarrassed.

That was something he could fix. Manus was a charming man when he wanted to be, and women were easy for him to understand. He read their bodies like a well-loved book.

He shot towards her, kneeling in the sand and tucking his finger underneath her chin. She was chilly but not cold and shivering as any other woman would have been. Her eyes met his, albeit slowly, and a muscle in her jaw bounced against his thumb.

"What is it?" he asked. "What chases the light from your eyes?"

"Merrows change outside of water. You've seen me without the tail but the transformation…" she hesitated. "It is not a pleasant sight."

"Why?"

"The body of a merrow is like slime when it is no longer attached to me."

"Like a jellyfish?"

"If we must draw comparisons, yes, similar to that."

"It will not startle me," he murmured.

She didn't seem convinced. Chuckling, Manus stroked the soft skin of her jaw and told himself not to marvel at the silken flesh. She was a woman, not a goddess, and he refused to put her on a pedestal.

"Truly," he continued, "I will not be disgusted or startled by anything you do, my pearl. I want to know you, every part of you."

"I don't know how you could."

Neither did he. A woman melting into a jellyfish turned his stomach, but if this was what the merrow needed from him, then he would school his thoughts and ensure that was what she got.

He glanced down at the pile of glinting gold and his jaw dropped. "What did you bring me?"

"Oh!" Happiness sparked in her gaze again and she looked down at the treasure. "Just a few things I found at the bottom of the ocean. Do you like them?"

Like them? These were priceless treasures! Golden crowns, heavy jeweled necklaces, even a goblet fit for a king. He could make so much coin from these if he found the right person to peddle them.

"These are stunning, Saoirse. Are there more?"

"More?" She shrugged. "There's more of them I suppose. We throw them out, so there is likely plenty along the bottom of the ocean. I could find others if you don't like these."

She moved to scrape the treasures back into sea. With a great shout, Manus leapt forward and pulled it all back towards him.

"No! No, I need no more than this. I was just curious. For humans, this is a considerable amount of wealth."

"Really?" She stared at him in shock. "But it's *trash*. What use could you possibly have for such things? Food or water I could understand, but these are just metal."

He watched her clink them together, smashing precious gold against delicate jewel. Perhaps she was right. They were useless objects in the long run, but he wasn't about to let go of a small fortune. If he ever got off this isle, he would make himself a wealthy man.

"Humans rarely make sense," he said. "But if we ever leave, we could live like kings and queens with that treasure."

"Leave?"

So that was what she wanted. He eyed the merrow with new found interest. She was using *him,* not the other way around.

Manus couldn't let her know he had discovered her plan. Let her play him while he wooed her. He intended to take the little merrow all the way home with him. If she cooperated and thought it was her idea, then it would only make his plan easier.

He would need to convince her of his interest though.

Swooping down, he lifted her tail and all into his arms. "Come on, out of the water with you."

She squealed, in happiness and delight he was certain. "Manus!"

The name zinged down his spine. "Saoirse."

"What are you doing?" she asked with a shiver.

"Bringing you to the sand, little merrow."

"I thought you wanted more treasure?"

"I do, but first I want you to be certain that nothing you do will ever disgust me."

"Oh," she whispered.

"Now, let's see how long you take to change back to the long-legged lass who captured my attentions long before she became magic."

Saoirse collected more "treasures" in the small bag she had made from Manus's shirt. He seemed to like them, and she enjoyed making him happy. The creases at the corner of his eyes made something in her belly quiver. His hearty laugh echoed through her soul until she dreamed about the sound.

Manus was slowly becoming a part of her. She held the knowledge of him in the deepest parts of her heart, hiding him from other merrows.

Her sisters commented that she seemed so much happier than she ever had before. Her smile was brighter, her laughter lighter, even the way she swam was much more graceful than they remembered.

They couldn't understand it. They didn't understand the concept of love at all.

Saoirse was certain this feeling was the elusive gift that only humans understood. she loved him. Nothing else could explain the lightness of her being whenever she looked at him.

Treasures stuffed his shirt so much that she feared it would rip. Perhaps that was all she would need. He couldn't ask for much more, how else would he carry it away?

He talked about leaving all the time now. She spent most nights at his side, watching the stars and listening to his stories. The land was a wondrous place full of people she would soon see.

He said he would take her with him. Saoirse was certain he wouldn't lie about such an important thing. He must love her though he hadn't said it. Manus looked at her with such gentle eyes, touched her with loving strokes, but never inappropriately.

She wrapped her arms around her waist and twirled. Her hair funneled above her in a coiling mass of dark green.

"Love," she whispered. "What a strange emotion it is."

It made her sick and happy at the same time. She sometimes couldn't feel the tips of her fingers because of it.

A shadow passed overhead cast by a massive dark form blotting out the sun.

She flinched. "Hello, guardian."

The beast did not respond, but when did they ever? Instead, the large female paused and stared down at Saoirse with a massive eye.

"Do you need me for something?"

Silence echoed in the water, but Saoirse could almost feel

the creature's thoughts. Guardians never spoke, yet Saoirse was certain their emotions were strong.

Disappointment radiated in great blasts that stirred the waters to churning. The guardian didn't like Saoirse disappearing so often, and it knew where she went.

"He loves me," she whispered, toying with the frayed strings of the shirt. "He wants to take me away from this place."

The deep hum echoing around her suggested the guardian did not agree with her.

"He wouldn't lie to me." Saoirse called out. "He couldn't. It's not within him to be so cruel."

But they were all cruel, the guardian sang in her mind. All humans had the ability to be cruel and were regularly. It was human nature, and they could not swim from that. Saoirse needed to be careful before she left the ocean for good.

Twitching her tail, Saoirse floated up and touched the guardian's large cheek. "I will be careful," she said. "I promise. I will not give my heart to someone unworthy of it."

Her heart stuck in her throat as the song changed. Be careful, the guardian reminded her. Be careful and be wise as so many merrows are not.

Saoirse pressed a kiss to the guardian's cheek. "Don't worry. Even if I go to land, I will always return home to visit you."

She hoped. She twisted away and flowed through the water as quickly as she could. What if she couldn't return to the ocean? What if in leaving, she was also saying goodbye forever?

Saoirse was young. The idea of an adventure and a new love was tantalizing. She hadn't considered that she might never see her family again. The taste of salt on her lips, the songs of whales so far away she couldn't see them. Would those all disappear from her life forever?

She wasn't sure what she would do if that were the case. Saoirse frowned and skimmed the bottom of the ocean. She was close to the isle, close to where she would need to decide what to do about Manus.

She reached out and touched her fingers to the sand. It plumed in great scattered clouds, obscuring her vision. She was used to the weightless quality of the ocean. She'd discovered life on land was harder. Her body easily tired, weary from days fighting against the pull of the earth. She struggled to walk, to run, to move.

In the ocean, she was graceful. Her body moved like that of the dancers she heard of in stories. She could do anything she wanted under the water. Speed through the waves, leap into the air above them, or dive into the dark depths.

Would she be able to continue that?

No, she knew she wouldn't. The land would suffocate her. It was what the land did. It took everything from the creatures who lived there and devoured them whole. The land even ate them after they died, worms and bugs feasting upon the bodies until they were little more than bone. Somehow, it felt different when those creatures were fish that then provided for merrows.

The sight of their own grisly deaths terrified humans. Saoirse remembered well a sailor who had seen a skeleton upon rocks. The horror in his gaze haunted her dreams for many years.

She clutched the bundle of treasures to her chest.

"It won't be like that," she told herself. "You won't be alone. Manus will be with you, and he is part of you now. He is part of your soul. You are part of his. Together, there will be no fear, no hunger, no ache."

She had to believe it. Otherwise, what good was life?

Saoirse flexed the strong muscles of her tail and pushed herself towards the surface. Maybe seeing him would make her feel better. He would understand her thoughts; he must experience very similar ones himself. She would talk with him, let him pet her hair as he so loved to do, and calm both their minds.

She poked her head above the surface and searched the beach for him.

There. Where he always was. Lying in the sand like a great sea lion, the sun playing across his features and darkening his skin to a deep chocolate.

Butterflies took flight in her belly. They fluttered up her throat until she swallowed, hoping to still their beating wings for fear they would erupt from her lips and reveal everything she felt. That she was mad about him. That he invaded her dreams and even in those he smiled with those crinkled eyes and said the same words over and over again.

"I want to know everything about you, and I will find nothing disgusting."

He hadn't. Even the slime from her tail dissolving hadn't resulted in anything more than a simple shrug.

"It's part of you, Saoirse. If I am uncomfortable, it will only be for a few moments. I am pleased that you exist, my pearl. Do not fret."

And she hadn't. For an entire week she hadn't thought a single angry word at all. Until today. He had to know their time was limited. That she only had three more sunsets before she had to choose a husband, and unfortunately a human was not in the running. If they were going to flee, they had to do it soon.

She swam to shore and tossed her findings next to him. He sat straight up with his fists raised, the loud clanking sounds startling him.

Saoirse pressed her fingers against her lips, giggling through the crevices. "I'm sorry, I thought you knew I was coming."

"You're a silent swimmer, my pearl."

"I splashed!"

"The ocean splashes regularly, that doesn't mean it's you." But he wasn't angry at her. His eyes crinkled at the edges and he bit his lip as he looked her up and down. "Are you coming out of the ocean today?"

"No."

"No?" He raised an eyebrow. "Why ever not?"

"I thought you would like to come into the ocean with me."

"I'm not as strong a swimmer as a merrow."

"No one is. But there is much I would like to show you. The world under the waves is a beautiful place, and it would be selfish of me to keep it to myself."

He pondered her words, tapped a finger against his chin, and eyed her carefully. "Where are we going?"

"The place where I found most of our treasures."

His eyes slashed towards her, gold shimmering in the depths of his dark eyes. "There's more?"

"There's always more."

"You've captured my attention, my pearl. How far beneath the ocean is this trove?"

"Not far. There are pockets of air within, I believe you will make it to the shipwreck if you are a strong swimmer."

"Didn't I tell you the ocean is in my blood?" he asked with a snort. "A wreck you said?"

"An old ship."

"Any markers?"

She hadn't ever looked. Human markers meant little to her. They put something on everything, little details that claimed ownership over yet more material objects.

She shrugged. "Not really. It's filled with these though," she gestured at the golden coins. "And it was dangerous to swim through the first few years. There was too much fabric."

"Silk?"

"I don't know what that is."

Saoirse didn't understand why he was so interested in the cloth. It was annoying at best even though she had yanked a dress out of a sunken ship just a few nights ago. He was distracted by her nudity, at least that's what he told her.

Maybe he was excited for the adventure. She plastered a bright smile on her face and shook off the ominous feeling. "Are you ready?"

"You want to go now?"

"The sun is up, the water is warm, and the wreck is waiting for us."

She held her breath as he looked her up and down. "How strong of a swimmer are you, my pearl?"

The question was strange, but one she was proud to answer. Flexing the muscles of her spine, she lifted her fluke and let it slap down on top of the water. "Very strong."

His grin was the sun, the moon, and the stars. It split across his features and warmed the usually hard expression that always made her wonder whether he was angry. Creases formed at the edges of his eyes, his shoulders shaking with some unknown mirth.

"Good," he said with a nod. "So am I."

Without hesitation he stood, stretching his arms over his head. The movement was graceful as if he was already diving underneath the waves.

Saoirse sighed and planted her chin on her fist. His beauty still stunned her. Merrows were used to their own feminine beauty, but never that of masculine perfection. And how could she not admire him? The ridges of his strong body were made by years of hard labor. Each scar told a story, each bump a tale of hardship and endurance.

A shiver danced down her spine. He was a fine specimen of a man, and it was a shame her sisters couldn't admire him.

That would open a can of worms. They didn't need to know the possibilities the rest of the world held. It would only make their own life that much harder.

The waves stroked his feet, his strong calves, and then delicately to his thighs. Manus flexed his muscles, rubbing his shoulders to prepare for cold water and Saoirse lost her breath again. His sun darkened skin poured over the muscles of his body like liquid bronze.

Could it be possible he wasn't a man at all? A prince? Or perhaps he was a god of the ocean, like his stories, come to steal her away.

She shook her head and pushed herself away from the shore. Dwelling on such fantasies was a child's game. She shouldn't put him up on such a high pedestal, she would only find herself disappointed.

Peering up through the waves, she saw the flash of his grin before he dove beneath the surface to join her.

His hair floated up, the knotted tendrils reminding her of the dark kelp which grew in the depths. He hovered in the crystal-clear water, sand billowing in great puffs from his kicks, with a smile revealing blinding white teeth. The golden hoops in his ears flashed, and the beads in his beard echoed with a clack.

Could he hear things the way she did?

Saoirse clutched sand in her fists, staring up at him with her heart in her throat. His eyes were the deepest of oceans. Dangerous, but exciting at the same time.

He kicked with his powerful legs and shot towards the surface. It broke the spell he held upon her. The membranes along her spine flattened as embarrassment turned her fingers cold. She was acting like a lovesick child.

Twisting, she rose to meet him. Her dark hair slicked back from her face and water dripped down her cheeks. She licked the droplets, enjoying the taste of salt on her tongue.

Saoirse hadn't thought it possible, but his gaze heated even further. His eyes traced a burning line from her lips to her eyes.

"Which way?"

"Follow me."

She dove deep into the waiting cold of the water. It was a chilling splash, one that reminded her above all else she was just a merrow. He was a human man. He wouldn't live as long as her; they never did.

Manus swam above her, his shadow merging with hers until she could pretend he had a tail as well.

"Foolish," she muttered, bubbles floating from between

her lips. "If he were a merrow, then he'd be just as ugly as the others."

She couldn't survive his beauty being stripped away from him. Disturbed by her own thoughts, Saoirse flicked her tail and sped through the water.

White sand blasted in her wake, leaving a trail of sparkling light she could see over her shoulder. A brightly colored fish swam in front of her and she marveled at its scales glimmering like the most precious of gems. At the sound of her bubbling laugh, a starfish lifted an arm and waved.

Manus kept up with her. He hadn't lied when he said he was a strong swimmer. His body cut through the waves easily, and his shadow never left hers. Not even for a second.

As they rounded the isle, Saoirse reached out her hand and traced the outline of his. He had reached one hand forward in his strokes, leaving it jutting out.

Curious, she flipped over and stared straight up at the surface.

He was watching her. Dark eyes locked upon her form and powerful legs did most of the work. The raised arm shifted, moving until his shadow traced along her cheekbone. Saoirse held her breath as the faint outline of his hand moved down her throat, between the valley of her breasts, and down to the curve of her hip.

She didn't know how to respond. Was this what men and women did on land? Was every interaction so visceral they couldn't breathe?

The fluke of her tail flicked involuntarily, sending her shooting away from the temptation he presented. He didn't need to touch her at all, she was already captivated.

His smile flashed again. Bright, like the side of a tuna when sunlight strikes its scales, and so blinding it seared into her mind forever. He lifted his head to the air and the spell shattered.

Her heart thundered against her ribs, pounding so hard she could hear it. She pressed her hands to her chest. They trembled so violently she feared she might have harmed herself.

Had she? Saoirse thought long and hard, trailing her thoughts down her body but could identify nothing physically wrong. Yet, the trembling would not cease.

The shipwreck loomed before them. Jagged edges of wood lashed out at the ocean, their points like swords ready to catch any that ventured too close. A once great mast had long ago snapped in half, tilting over the edge of the ship and pointing down into the abyss. Barnacles covered the hull, and eels stuck their heads out of their holes, watching the newcomers with black eyes.

Saoirse might have once been afraid of the dark place and the shadows that lingered in the belly of the ship. Now, she only saw the beauty hidden within.

Propelling herself to the surface, she silently revealed herself next to Manus. "Found it."

He let out a loud curse and spun around.

She giggled. "I'm sorry, I thought you were watching me."

"I was, but I lost track of you. I was staring at the monstrosity below us."

"Isn't it beautiful?"

He glanced through the water towards the ship. "I don't know if I'd call it beautiful. Ancient comes to mind."

"Old things are beautiful too," she replied. "Didn't you

want to see all the treasure?"

"Of course I do, but are you sure there are air pockets? There doesn't seem to be much left of the ship."

She nodded, albeit a little slowly. It had been some time since she explored the area of the ship where the air pockets had been. It was difficult for her to climb to those sections, and she hadn't wanted to.

In any case, it wasn't that far down. A child could swim to the bottom and back in record time, surely he could do the same.

"We'll be careful," she replied. "If there aren't air pockets, we'll come back up."

If he was worried, Manus didn't reveal it. He rolled his shoulders, nodded, and breathed deep through his lungs.

Saoirse panicked for a moment. He was breathing so quickly and so deeply that something had to be wrong. At her panicked noise, he gave her a wink, and a flashed grin, then dove.

Shocked, she ducked her head and watched him cut through the water like a spear. His powerful body dove deeper and deeper with no hesitation at all.

He hadn't lied. Only a creature who came from the sea could swim that well.

With a grin on her own face, she followed him into the depths with a bright flick of her tail. It was easily five lengths of a man to the ship, then they needed to find an entrance. She should have scouted ahead for air, but he rushed head first into the ocean with little fear.

She liked that.

Excitement bubbled in her chest, foaming and frothing

until it popped in her heart as the brightest of glee. She spiraled around him, her tail glimmering in the light and her hair a riot of dark color that tangled over his shoulders.

He grinned, powerfully pulling himself through the weight of the water with his strong arms. No wonder ropey muscles crisscrossed his body. It was so much more work for humans underneath the waves!

She admired his determination. It was a long way down, and not once did he hesitate.

Saoirse reached the ship first, catching the edge in her hand and peering into the nearest hole. No air, just a sea slug and a few clams that opened their mouths at her arrival.

Frowning, she pushed herself down the side, searching for a small bit of air where he could catch his breath. Otherwise, he wouldn't be able to see all the wonders of the ship! And she desperately wanted to prove to him that her world was just as beautiful as the surface.

He knew it. Saoirse had seen the longing in his eyes when she told him stories of swimming beside whales and their hunts for deep sea squid. He deserved to experience it first-hand.

Determined, she pulled at a rotting piece of wood and ripped it from the side. A few bubbles escaped. They weren't much, just a few, but that had to mean there was air.

She turned, but Manus was already swimming towards her. He closed strong hands on the side of the ship and disappeared into the opening she'd made.

"So brave," she observed, shocked by his lack of fear as she slipped in after him.

It was dark, and it took a while for her eyes to adjust to the dim light. Blinking, she glanced up where Manus had pressed himself against the ceiling. The faintest line of air created a space barely the width of her finger.

Saoirse's heart stopped beating for a fraction of a second. It wasn't enough air to keep him alive, it might not even be enough to get him to the surface.

He ducked back into the water, his gaze meeting hers with a surety that felt too final for her liking. He knew he wouldn't make it back to the surface, couldn't without a lungful of air.

That wouldn't do.

Saoirse's brows lowered in determination and she launched towards him. Spearing through the water with a flick of her powerful tail, she struck him like a stone plummeting towards the bottom of the sea. Her momentum pushed him backwards, but the wall would stop them.

Grasping his cheeks, she turned his head and closed her mouth around his. She inhaled deeply through her gills, fronds spreading open wide in her gasp, filtering the water into crystal clear air. They snapped shut as her body switched the air into her lungs, which she then poured between his lips.

He grew slack in her grasp. Was he dying? Had she done something wrong?

Saoirse's gills flared again, and she took another deep breath. Bubbles created a curtain between them as she tried to get him to take more air, but it billowed out of his mouth. She was frightened he'd passed out and didn't feel him move until his hands found her hips and drew her closer.

Even in the water, his touch burned like fire. This incredible man tugged her into his arms and wrapped her in his embrace. She exhaled again, and he drew air from her lips as if he were sipping the finest of wines.

He stroked his fingers down the indent of her spine. They lingered at the small of her back, dipping in the curve and stroking the scales that met the sensitive area. Feather light and gentle, he cupped the back of her head with his other hand and angled it up.

His lips softened against hers. She couldn't begin to fathom what he was trying to do, but it wasn't unpleasant.

Saoirse let her own mouth relax, allowing him to explore, and discovering him in return. Her chest bumped his and his legs tangled around her tail. She didn't know where he began and she ended.

Her eyes drifted shut and she let him take the lead. Manus pressed tiny kisses against the corners of her lips, drifting in the faint current as if they didn't have a care in the world. When he needed air, he brushed his fingers over the slits of her gills. They flared at his touch and she fed him air from her own lungs.

Every inch of him was warm. The firm plane of his chest held her comfortably while his hands calmed her every movement. It was as if he was in her head, like he could read her mind.

Eventually, he drew back with lungs full of air and a grin on his face. He lifted a brow at her stare.

Of course, they were supposed to be finding treasure.

Her shoulders shook with a shiver, but she gestured for him to follow her. Saoirse grasped the ragged edge of a doorway and pulled herself deeper into the ship.

The light filtered through holes in the sides, revealing the treasures she cared about. Eels slithered through the shadows. Silver fish darted through the window, their formation breaking around Saoirse. Their smooth sides brushed against her and sent her hair swirling in a coil.

Grinning, she beckoned Manus forward into the dark room.

He didn't hesitate, following her into the darkness and catching her by the neck. Surprised, she didn't stop him when he pressed his lips against her again and sipped air from her lips.

Bubbles floated from her mouth, the tip of his tongue stroking the outline of her bottom lip. Startled, she pulled back and swam towards the treasure.

But the taste of him remained. Salty, like the ocean, like the oysters she had shucked for him. And sweet, like the finest of jellyfish, rare and only tasted on special occasions.

It was a taste she could become addicted to, and she couldn't understand why.

Merrows did not press their lips together. Saoirse had seen humans do it, even men on ships found their way towards each other. It never made sense to her. Mouths were for eating.

At first, she thought they were animals. The pressing of lips must be some kind of attack, a threat, a way to warn off other creatures. But they continued to do it. Repeatedly, and they always smiled afterwards. As if they enjoyed it.

She pressed her fingertips against her mouth and tucked her newfound secret deep in her soul. If it were a kiss he gave her, not just the exchange of air, then he had given her a gift. No other merrow that Saoirse knew could say they understood this human pleasure.

A smile spread across her face. She lifted her hand again, gesturing for him to follow her. There was another secret to this ship although she wasn't supposed to show it.

Every now and then, merrows found themselves captivated by gold. She never understood the desire. The ocean provided far more than any human could ever make. But those who enjoyed the secrets of humanity, carefully hid them away.

She hadn't planned to show him, there were other treasures he could see. Yet, the kiss lingered on her lips and clouded her mind.

The tunnel extended through the bottom of the ship. Deep into the earth it bored, twisting and turning until it emerged in a cave system. She remembered air and a great pile of gold.

How did she express he needed to trust her? It would be a frightening journey for a creature who couldn't see well in the darkness, and who couldn't breathe unless she helped him. And yet, she was willing to take the risk to see the look in his eyes.

Saoirse reached out and grasped his hands, pulling him into her arms so she could stare into his eyes.

"Trust me," she said, not knowing whether he could hear or understand her. "I promise, I will keep you safe."

If he understood, he made no movements.

Hesitantly, she leaned forward and pressed her lips against his again. The kiss was meant to be calming, to ease any worry he might have. He changed it, forcing more of his heat into her body until even the surrounding waters warmed.

Saoirse pulled him even closer, wrapping her arms around him and tucking his head underneath her chin. He stiffened but allowed her to control his body. She ran a hand down his back and curled his arms around her. With her tail, she nudged his legs closer, curved her spine, and dove backwards into the dark tunnel.

He immediately clenched his body around hers. Bubbles echoed, his question lost in the water as they passed by. She caught only one word.

"What—"

Perhaps it was cruel, but her teeth flashed in the darkness. She pulled him up her body and pressed her lips against his. She flexed her tail, propelling them through the tunnel with ease.

His heart thundered against her chest, and she needed to give him air three times before she saw the faint light.

"Just a bit more," she told him, although he couldn't possibly understand her. "It will be worth all the fear."

One last powerful undulation and they burst free from the tunnel, into the air.

Manus spluttered, coughing and flailing his arms. She held him up while dodging his kicks.

"Manus!" she shouted. "Manus, we're here!"

"Here? Where is here? You couldn't have warned me?"

"I didn't think I'd take you here."

"You know humans can't breathe underwater, don't you?"

"I do," Saoirse chuckled. He finally stilled in her arms, hair hanging in limp strands across his forehead. "I kept you alive, didn't I?"

"Barely! What if you hadn't known I needed air?"

"You were taking care of that," she murmured. Her eyes strayed to his lips, the thin slashing lines turned down in displeasure. "Or perhaps you were entertaining yourself in other ways."

"Ah," he shook his head. "I shouldn't have taken such liberties."

"I hope you will continue to take them."

"You deserve someone better than me."

"I know you claim you aren't a good man," she said. Saoirse met his gaze with a heated stare. "Has it occurred to you I am not searching for a good man, but one who will break all the rules to have me?"

He groaned. "You shouldn't say such things, Saoirse."

Her name strummed through her veins like pure magic. It bubbled, foamed, popped in her heart until all she could think of was him.

"Did you kiss me?" she asked. "Or were you using me for air?"

"Both," he admitted in guttural tones. "Each time."

Her skin heated with the admission. He had kissed her. *Her*. A simple merrow, from a simple family, with nothing to her name but a family who desired her to marry.

This man surprised her around every corner, and she refused to hide her feelings any further.

Saoirse slid her hands along his shoulders, up his neck, to the back of his head where his hair tangled in her fingers. Coarse and thick, the kelp-like dreadlocks reminded her of the deepest oceans that lingered in his eyes.

"Kiss me again," she whispered, "when there is no danger of life or death. Just a man and a woman, with nothing else between them."

Her words snapped whatever control he held upon himself. Manus kissed her as if he were a drowning man and she his salvation. With teeth, lips, and tongue he devoured her.

She hardly remembered to keep them afloat, wanting to drift back into the embrace of the ocean where she knew they would both be loved. They were two halves of the same shell. Creatures born outside of their true element, linked by their love of the sea.

He drew back enough to breathe, his breath fanning across her face like a sea breeze. "Was that enough?"

"Never."

"Didn't you have something to show me?"

It didn't matter anymore. She didn't care about the golden treasure anyway; couldn't they continue to kiss? This newfound desire was difficult to force from her mind.

But his eyes were curious, and his fingers drummed a beat against her throat.

"Yes," she replied. "Turn around."

The cave was lit by a rare species of worm which grew from the ceiling. Their spit was bioluminescent and cast a blue light around the cave.

Saoirse helped him turn by holding onto his ribs. His back rested against her bare chest and she wrapped her arms around his shoulders.

"The gold is here," she said. "Do you see it? It's a merrow hoard, a rare one in these parts as most of us live in the abyss."

And what a hoard it was. The few merrows with the addiction carried handfuls whenever they could. Coins, crowns, goblets, all mashed together in a mountain of wealth that spilled into the water.

He pulled away from her, swimming to the edge and clambering up onto the mountain. His eyes were large with awe as he stumbled and fell onto his knees.

Saoirse watched him grab fistfuls of the coins. They trickled through his fingers and clinked, cascading down into the water and glinting as the blue light reflected off their shiny surfaces. Mouth agape, he turned back to her.

"How did all of this get here?"

"There are many shipwrecks in these waters, and some among us gather up the pieces."

"You?"

Saoirse shook her head. "No. I have only added one thing to this cave."

"What is it?"

She blushed. Would he think it was foolish? A child's desire to add something to the hoard but not seeing the meaning behind it all?

Yet, he had asked, and she was loath to deny him anything. Saoirse pointed behind him and up, towards a small rocky ledge that jutted out from the cave way. "There."

He stood and made his way over the mountain towards her one contribution. It was a golden statue, small enough to easily hold and barely larger than her hand.

Perhaps it was some country's prince, a ruler known throughout the human world. She thought the smooth lines of his face were too intricately made to let him wallow in the depths. The crown on his head was sharply pointed, and the sword on his hip made her dream about the wars he had fought.

And won.

She dreamt about that prince throughout most of her childhood, and even into her adult years. He was handsome, kind, a king that would make all other kings appear foolish. His intelligence was known throughout the lands and all the royal women wanted to be his bride.

The stories she made up in her mind fueled her happiness.

Now, Saoirse found she was afraid what Manus would say. Was he a made-up figure? Just a man an artist sculpted on a whim with no real roots?

Manus turned it over in his hands and nodded. "Cú Chulainn. One of the greatest kings in all the legends, son of Lugh and a mortal woman. It is a good omen to keep such a talisman. He'll keep you safe."

"He was a protector then?"

"Of everyone he loved and one of the most unfortunate men in history."

She swam closer, placing her elbows on the mountain of gold and staring up at him. "Tell me?"

"A story?" he asked, his voicing lifting in surprise. "Now?"

"Please."

"Won't the other merrows return and be angry we've invaded their treasure?"

"It's unlikely." She shifted, sending more gold tumbling into the saltwater. "I dearly love stories, and you tell them so well."

"Are you staying in the water?"

Saoirse looked at the piles of gold dubiously. "Yes."

He glanced at the wealth around him one last time and sighed. "All right then."

Manus settled onto the pile. He wiggled until his body created an indent in the coins, placed his hands behind his head, and cleared his throat.

This was her favorite time with him. He'd told stories at night when the moon was full and held its breath along with Saoirse. She liked to pretend she was in his stories, living the moments with the people who adventured, battled, and loved.

"Cú Chulainn is known throughout the lands as one of the most powerful men who ever lived. He's the son of Lugh and took after his father in battle. It is said when the ríastrad overtook him, the battle frenzy turned him into a completely different man. A beast. And he was handsome, so handsome that all the other lords worried that he would steal their wives and daughters away from them."

Saoirse sighed and laid her head on her forearms. "Did he take a wife? Was she as beautiful as he?"

"No," Manus shook his head and grinned. "He was too wild for that. He never took a wife, and the others resented him for that. In an attempt to get him away from their women, and to give their own sons a chance at marriage, the Forgall Monach suggested that Cú Chulainn was not as legendary a warrior as he claimed. Any warrior worth his mettle would train with the Scáthach of Alba, a woman more powerful and more deadly than any man alive. She lived in Dún Scáith, the Fortress of Shadows, far away in the Isle of Skye."

At the name, Saoirse sat back up. She leaned forward gleefully. "I have heard of Scáthach! Her daughters traveled here once, long ago."

"Her daughters?"

"They were as fearsome as she. Wondrous creatures wearing the armor of men and the helms of animals. The guardian threatened them, but they screamed battle cries so loud that we heard them in the deepest parts of the ocean. They earned the right to pass through our waters."

His cheeks paled. "I wonder what kind of creature would frighten a guardian."

"Frighten? No. They didn't frighten the beast, they were a

kindred spirit." She pressed her hand against her chest. "The guardian knows the pain of a woman wronged. They are born from the souls of the drowned and exist only to help prevent any from experiencing such heartache again."

Her soul ached to be held in the careful grasp of a guardian. They were kind, and although capable of much destruction, they harmed nothing without reason. Saoirse loved them so much that it hurt.

Could he ever understand that? Did he know the tearing feeling in a woman's heart at the chance a man might not love them in return?

He couldn't, she surmised, but she would not think less of him for it.

Saoirse lifted a hand and gestured for him to continue. "Cú Chulainn, what became of him when he went to the isle?"

"He trained long and hard with Scáthach and her daughters. He learned all the techniques which were known only to the women of the isle. But as a handsome, virile man, he could not keep his eyes from the women themselves. They were strong, brutal creatures who sometimes appeared more man than woman.

"Cú Chulainn found himself captivated by one, whose rival, Aife, became bitter and jealous. In a fit of rage, she challenged Cú Chulainn to a duel."

Saoirse gasped. "She did?"

Solemnly, Manus nodded. "She did. They fought for days on end, with blade and fist. The sun rose, and the moon sank over and over until the battle was finally won. Cú Chulainn pressed his sword against her throat, a victor as he had always been. In return, he requested to lay with her and got her with child."

Tears filled Saoirse's eyes immediately. She swallowed and lifted a hand to make him pause. "I thought you said he was a good man. A hero?"

"So the story goes."

"But he forced a woman to lie with him? The battle was already won, and yet he waged another with her body?"

Manus took a deep breath, his brows wrinkled. "I hadn't ever thought of it like that, but I believe you might be right."

"I don't believe he's a hero. Not anymore."

"And perhaps you are right. Even the old legends remind us that these stories are tales of men, not gods. Men make mistakes."

"Tell the rest of the tale, Manus. I would like to know what became of this Cú Chulainn." Fires burned in her chest, rage so pure and angry she didn't know what to do with it.

He shifted and rolled onto his side, so he could watch her expressions. "After learning all the skills he could, he left the Isle of Skye and returned home. He stormed a fortress of a man who wronged him, took his castle, his men, and his lands, and became a lord of his own right.

"The prophecies of Cú Chulainn always said he was a man whose fate was to be known in name, but to die young. With such knowledge riding on his shoulders, it's little surprise that the day an intruder arrived at his doors, he was nervous.

"Cú Chulainn called out to the man, 'Who goes there?' and there was no response. Again and again he asked until he issued a warning. 'If you do not respond, I shall fight you, and I shall kill you.'

"The intruder did not respond. They began a duel that was

brief, brutal, and bloody. The unknown man lay dying on the ground, and Cú Chulainn's curiosity got the better of him. He knelt beside the body and pulled the helm off the intruder's head.

"His own face stared back at him, young with vivid green eyes like his mother's. As his son lay dying in his arms, he whispered to his father, 'I came to carry the flag of Ulster to the gates of Rome and beyond with you.'"

The ending words of the story echoed in the cave. Saoirse reached up and wiped a tear from her cheek. "Then he did not have a happy story after all."

"No," Manus said, though he sounded confused. "I always thought he was made of legends, but now…no. I do not believe he had a kind or happy story."

"How did he die?"

"In a battle with Queen Medb, Cú Chulainn grew arrogant, and broke many geasa, taboos. Each was another nail in his coffin. Her champion, Lugaid, made three magical spears, designed and spelled to kill kings. First, he killed Cú Chulainn's charioteer, the king of all chariot drivers. Then, he killed Cú Chulainn's horse, Liath Macha, king of all horses. And last, he threw the spear straight through Cú Chulainn.

"The hero tied himself to a standing stone in the middle of the battlefield so he could die on his feet. A crow landed on his shoulder, the Morrighan come to guide his soul to the afterlife. Lugaid cut off his head, and in one final movement Cú Chulainn's sword fell and chopped off Lugaid's hand."

"And so Cú Chulainn got his revenge, yet again."

"He did many great things as well."

"Your heroes are men of great and terrible deeds."

He held out the figurine for her to take. The metal was cold on her fingers.

"That is the way of men, little pearl. We are cold and callous creatures. We come screaming into this world already dying. It is little wonder we are such selfish beasts."

Saoirse turned the prince over, staring down into the face which had graced her dreams for such a long time. She traced a finger over the prominent brow, the kind eyes, the hawk like nose, and stubborn chin. He had been good to her in her dreams.

Dreams were nothing more than the fancies of children. Real people were flawed, and it was the most painful lesson she had ever learned.

She let the figurine fall from her hands and sink to the bottom of the cave. It teetered on the edge of the tunnel that delved deep into the abyss and then fell into the darkness.

"I don't know if I like your world," she whispered. "It is angry and frightening."

"It is. But it is also beautiful and free."

"What is freedom? Is it something we dream about at night? Something our hearts dream up even though our minds know it's not real?"

"Ah, if you give up dreaming then all the possibilities of the world disappear. Whether or not they exist."

She swished her tail through the water, waving it back and forth as she thought about his words. Dreaming was important. It had kept her alive and happy for so long, removing it from her life would be difficult. Would she be the same person without her dreams?

Unlikely.

Saoirse chewed on her lip and nodded. "You are a wise man and a good man, Manus."

"Don't give me any compliments, little pearl. You don't know me all that well."

"I know you. I know your soul, your kindness, your trust. There is a good man beneath whatever walls you have built around yourself."

She looked up, her heart in her eyes and her stomach rolling like the sea in a storm. After baring her soul, she hoped he would return the sentiments. Instead, his gaze was focused on the water behind her.

Manus stilled. Even his breathing stopped for a few moments as he stared through the dimly lit water.

"Saoirse," he growled. "Get out of the water."

Her spine stiffened, and her fingers grasped the coins. "Why? What is behind me?"

She felt the soft brush of a large body against her fins. Smooth and silky, she recognized the texture.

Shark. Likely a bull shark considering the size of it, and one of the most aggressive species.

It could only mean one thing. The merrow men had somehow heard she was here, or worse, that she had brought a human. Sharks always worked with the nasty drunkards under the sea.

"We have to go," she gasped. Saoirse reached for Manus, holding her arms high and gesturing for him. "Come!"

"Saoirse, get out of the water!"

"Get *into* the water we have little time!"

He gaped at her. "Get into the water with the shark? No! I won't let you risk your life!"

"The merrow men are coming, we don't have much time!"

He let out a snarl that shook her bones but eased into the water beside her. The bull shark circled them, slow and calculated, its movements deliberate but not threatening. It made her nervous.

What were the merrow men up to? Did they know she had hidden a human man from them? Or were they threatening her only to force Saoirse to return and make her decision?

She grabbed Manus's arm and looped it over her neck. "Hold on."

Saoirse held him tight to her breast, the dark tendrils of their hair linking to create a barrier between the shark and them. It eyed her tail, hunger flashing in its dark eyes.

Teeth flashed in a grin. There were secrets in the water, tainting it like blood and bringing the monsters to feast. She clutched Manus tighter and launched into the dark tunnel.

The echoing crack of the shark's jaws clamping just beyond her fin rang in her ears. She raced forward, scraping her shoulders and tail on the jagged stone walls of the tunnel. Their flight was not graceful. Fear spiked through her body in a wave of heat and nausea.

Sharks didn't attack like that unless they were told to. And though it had not hurt her, it had forced her into the tunnel.

Was it herding her?

She rounded the loop, forcing Manus's mouth to hers and exhaling air. He spluttered, bubbles frothing all around them, but she didn't have time for such foolish behavior. He needed air, and she needed to rush.

Saoirse dug her fingers into his cheeks, forcing him to breathe.

They burst into the dim light of the shipwreck so quickly that she almost didn't catch them before they burst through the side. Saoirse caught her breath and stared around the wreckage, hoping she wouldn't see a merrow man through the cracks.

She was not so lucky.

Their bulbous eyes stared at her through each torn board. Red noses leaked mucus into the water while they swiped at their faces and overly large eyes. Webbed hands ending in claws shook, preparing for a hunt as never before.

Frog-like legs stroked to keep them afloat, although she could see some merrow men in the distance walking on the bottom of the sea floor. Hundreds of shadowy figures marching up from the abyss. All to kill the man she held in her arms.

Manus touched the side of her neck, tilting her face towards him and taking in her horrified expression. Brows furrowed, he nodded and touched his lips to hers.

It was as much a kiss, the newfound thing which made her soul take flight, as it was a sharing of air. He stroked the soft curve of her cheeks with fingers light as the softest of breezes. He sipped from her tongue and gently gifted the quietest part of himself. A subtle touch, a breath of life, and a promise of adventure.

She felt like the name he had given her. The small pearl who hadn't realized she was more than a plain grain of sand until he plucked her from her shell.

Manus pulled back with a soft smile, placed his hands on her shoulders, and shoved.

The push sent her careening backwards until the wall stopped her. It was a far enough distance that he could grasp a splintered piece of wood and pull himself out the nearest window.

She lost all sense of reason. He put himself directly into harm's way, and for what? They wouldn't hurt her! They would hurt him.

Hands shaking, heart already bleeding, she shot out of the shipwreck and into the open water. She frantically searched for him, for anything that wasn't a teeming mass of green skin covered in warts and lesions.

Where was he?

"Manus!" she shouted. Her wailing call echoed like the shriek of a guardian, like the song of a whale. It flowed over the merrow men who flinched back from the sheer agony in its tones.

A form shot up from the ocean floor. Strong, powerful, and oh so handsome, he fled the merrow men with blood streaking behind him like a red banner. His makeshift weapon was gone, and she fiercely hoped it was buried in a merrow man's chest.

Determined to save him, she streaked through the water like a falling star. She reached her arms out for him, scooped him up, and spun around.

Never before had she swum so fast. The long muscles in her tail burned, her heart thumped hard against her ribs, and her gills worked overtime to get him to the surface. He'd be safe there, she was certain of it. They couldn't catch him once he swam, Manus was too fast.

A clawed hand closed on her tail fin, sinking through the thin membrane and yanking. She cried out as pain sent icy nails up her spine.

In one last attempt to save Manus, she shoved him towards the surface.

The merrow man dragged her back down to the ocean floor where the others waited. Manus broke through the surface, his legs kicking wildly as he kept himself afloat.

Just before she sank too far down, he ducked under the waves to stare down at her. If she had been on land, tears would have streaked down her cheeks. Instead, the entire ocean became a symbol of her sorrow.

She reached her hand out for him even as the merrow men pulled her into the abyss.

CHAPTER 5

A Ship on the Horizon

Manus crawled onto the white sand shore, coughing up mouthful after mouthful of water. The sea had tried to take him again, and this time he hadn't thought he'd evade her. However, once again, his mistress sent him back to the land.

He curled his fingers in the earth.

"Where did they come from?" he coughed. "And where did they take—"

He spun, sat hard on his hip, and looked out to sea. The waves were calmer than he remembered, lapping gently at the land. It was such an innocent scene although he now knew the face of the danger the ocean hid.

Guardians. Merrow men. What other horrors lurked just out of reach?

A wave splashed foam onto his foot. Skin crawling, he backed up until he was far away from the tide. Manus wasn't certain he would ever look at the sea the same way again.

Saoirse hadn't exaggerated when she called the merrow men ugly. They were monstrous creatures. Their wide gaping mouths, eyes popping out of their heads, leathery skin, and claws that scratched at his arms.

Absently, he rubbed a hand down his bicep and flicked away the watery blood. He would heal unless their claws were tipped with poison, which he doubted. Though the creatures were frightening, they appeared more brutish than evolved.

He shivered again and drew his legs to his chest.

Saoirse's face flashed in his mind. She reached for him as they dragged her down, and she was so afraid. Manus had tried to protect her, but they were many and he was only one.

He'd failed her. They took her back to wherever horrid creatures like that came from. What could he do?

If he were a better man, he would swear to go find her. He would trawl the oceans with a net searching for the next merrow man he could find. He'd track down a guardian and force it to take him down to her kingdom so he could fight her father with a sword.

But Manus was none of those men. He valued his own life far too much to risk it for a merrow.

Even one who had saved his life.

A quiet snort echoed in his ear and a warm weight settled against his side. Manus lifted his arm and draped it over the eerie green and white shoulders of the cù sìth.

"Hello, Mac Lir. I wondered where you had gone off to."

The fae snorted again and stared out to sea.

"Yeah, me too." Manus glanced in the same direction, but nothing disturbed the strangely still seas. "We'll keep watch for her. Maybe she'll escape from them."

She didn't.

Manus waited for three more weeks with the faerie dog at his side. They would each leave in intervals, gathering food and water from whatever they could find. Without the merrow providing for them, it was far more difficult to stay alive.

The isle allowed Manus to pass through to the interior. He found little food, less fresh water, and nothing useful for escape. Every now and then, he would hear a strange chirping sound, but he couldn't find the owner of the sound.

The Fae were toying with him. He knew this isle must be overrun with their kind, invisible and impossible to catch even if he tried.

At the last moment when his strength was about to break, he stumbled from the brush to find the cù sìth standing with its hackles raised. Its lips rose in a snarl, bright teeth shining in the sunlight.

Manus shaded his eyes and nearly fell in shock. Outlined far in the distance was the clear shape of a ship. He would know the tall masts anywhere.

Something in his being heated. Though the sea was dangerous and its creatures wild, his blood called for adventure. For freedom. For something other than this gods-forsaken isle, and a lost merrow who haunted his dreams.

"Mac Lir, enough!"

The faerie stilled, growling deep in its throat.

"Go get 'em boy. Bring them to me."

The faerie charged forward and dove beneath the waves. Manus didn't know if it were possible for a cù sìth to communicate with any man. He hoped it was.

Exhaustion weakened his knees. He fell onto his hands and reminded himself to inhale. His lungs would work if he forced them. His stomach would quiet if he bade it, and the shaking muscles would build back up if he found salvation.

A ship. There was a ship.

He only needed to stay alive for a little while longer.

Heartbeats passed, and still Manus stared into the sand. His arms shook, but he refused to fall onto his face. He would wait on hands and knees for the men from the ship. He would not sink any farther than that.

He didn't know how long he waited, but eventually his ears pricked at sounds. Oars dipped into the water nearby, sprinkling droplets as they hit the surface. The hull of the boat scraped against sand in a harsh grinding sound. Boots hit the water, followed by the grunt of a man as he pulled the small boat ashore.

Manus listened to the crunching sounds of a man walking towards him. Heavy, sure, strong.

All the things he would have been if he hadn't starved for three weeks.

He heaved himself onto his haunches with the last of his energy, listing backwards as his head lolled. His hands settled on his thighs and he watched the large man approach.

Strange, he hadn't thought to see a man with such coloring. The sailor was tall and broad, blonde-haired and blue-eyed. The mane of gold shook around his head like that of the lion Manus had seen once in his life.

The stranger crouched, looked Manus up and down, and said, "Are you dead yet?"

"No."

"Can you make it to the ship?"

"I can."

"And you'll work?"

"I've done so my entire life."

The behemoth of a man nodded. “Then you’re lucky a cù sìth is willing to help you. The mutt stays here.”

“That’s the one thing I will not allow,” Manus croaked through cracked lips. “Mac Lir stays with me.”

The other man arched a brow. “The god of the sea?”

“I named him myself.”

“An accurate name if the beast approached you in the same way.” He stared at the faerie and shrugged. “He’s your responsibility if you take him on this journey. We sail for Uí Néill, and you’ll be dropped off there.”

“That’s good,” Manus said with a tired nod. “That’s home.”

“You’re a lucky man.”

He knew it. Manus had always been blessed with luck, from the first beating at the hands of another boy who tripped on his own feet and fell off the docks. He might be broken and starved, but Manus always came out on top.

Manus groaned as the blonde man wedged a shoulder underneath his arm and yanked him to standing. The ocean grabbed at his feet, stroking gentle waves along his calves.

He imagined it was apologizing.

I’m sorry for hurting you.

I’m sorry for killing your friends.

I’m sorry for taking her away from you.

If he were a stronger man, he would tell the sea they were over. Done. He couldn’t remain loyal to such a woman who would take everything he loved. Repeatedly, the sea took and took. Yet, here he was.

The blonde grunted, shoved the boat from the shore, and leapt into the it. “There’s a blanket at your feet. If you’re a smart man, you'll grab it."

Manus did not move.

"Either stubborn or dumb then, which are you?"

"Why did you come?"

"Dog didn't give us much of a choice."

"Why?" Manus repeated.

He looked up and met the icy gaze of the Nord. Viking, by his guess. Now that his mind was clearing with fresh salt air, he could see the twisted braids and beads in the man's beard. It was too far south for such a ship. And yet, here they were.

The Viking nodded. "In my land, a creature such as that is wild. I wanted to meet the man who tamed the faerie."

"It's not tame."

"It comes at your beck and call."

"I asked; it agreed to help."

"That's a dangerous game to play with the Fae," the Viking chuckled. He picked the oars up in massive hands and rowed. "You know they like to hold favors over our heads?"

"I know the old legends well."

"You should not have made a deal with the cù sìth."

"It's my business, Viking."

"It's your head," he corrected. "I don't know you, you don't know me. But if you're going to be on my ship, you keep that dog away from my men. I'll have no faeries bringing bad luck onto my journey."

Manus nodded. He didn't want to share he too carried faerie blood. Was that why he was still alive?

Arturo's voice whispered in his mind, *"They'll spare you boy, you're a faerie. Like them. Just tell my wife and child I love them, and your debts will be paid."*

He had a feeling that the debts on his soul could never be repaid.

The ocean swelled and guided the boat towards the Viking ship. His vision blurred, and for a moment he thought he saw her in the water. Dark hair like seaweed and a smile on her face that would break any man's heart.

"How did you get past the guardian?"

"The water beast?" The Viking grinned, and his teeth appeared pointed for a moment. "They know better than to attack a Viking ship. We do not pass through often, but we have tasted their hide too many times for them to attack us."

"They fear you?"

"I like to call it mutual respect."

Manus wasn't so sure about that. The Vikings didn't seem the respectful type, even as they hauled him onto the ship. They grasped his clothes with hands that were too strong. They were too tall, too large; they had more mass to them than any man he'd seen before.

For a few moments, he feared he wasn't aboard a ship with Vikings at all. He worried they were Tuatha dé Danann, faeries who were here to steal him away.

Then they clapped each other on the back, swore, pissed off the side of the ship and he knew they were men. And men he knew how to deal with.

Manus sank onto a pile of drying nets. Mac Lir leapt out of the small boat and into the waters. The Vikings shouted, pointing at the Fae beast swimming in the middle of the sea.

But Manus saw something else entirely. He watched the beast's eyes change color, become more human and infinitely old.

"Thank you, Manannán mac Lir," he murmured.

The dog sank beneath the waves and he wondered whether or not it was a beast at all. Faeries were shape shifters at heart. Was it possible Manannán mac Lir himself had guided Manus towards Saoirse?

He sank his fingers into the thick netting and tried not to stare into the ocean again.

Monsters lie in wait there. Monsters with no form, eyes, face, nor mouth. The worst monster lurking in those depths was that of his own guilt.

"What have you done?"

"Athair, please."

"Do not speak! It was a question I did not want answered."

Her father slashed his hand through the water. The current pushed her back into her brother's chest.

Saoirse flinched forward so she wouldn't feel the rough skin against her back. The warts, the lesions, the hated scales that weren't human at all. She'd had a taste of beauty and wanted nothing to do with their tainted forms.

"You were with a human," her father growled. "You know our laws."

She twisted her fingers in front of her. Silent, as he wished her to be.

"You've pushed me too far, Saoirse. I would have given you the choice of any merrow man you desired. But this? I will have no more of this foolish behavior."

"I have no desire for any merrow man."

"What did you say?"

His face turned mottled green.

Saoirse heard the gasps of her sisters, some covered their faces in fear of the resulting outburst from their father. Yet, she couldn't stop now.

"I will not marry a merrow man. I love someone else."

"Love? Love is a figment of human imaginations to make marriage more palatable."

"I know love is real. I felt it when I was with him, and I will not survive without it."

"You will survive just fine," he spat. "No daughter of mine is so weak that she cannot survive marriage. Take her away. Lock her up so she cannot run before her marriage to Craig."

"Craig?" she gasped as her brother's arm locked across her shoulders. "I will not marry him. I will not marry anyone!"

"You will do as I say."

"Athair! You cannot do this to me! Please!"

She expected him to yell, to argue, perhaps even to hit her. But he did none of the things she expected.

Her father turned his face from his youngest child and held up his hand so he could not see her beg. "Take her away."

"Wait." she whispered. "Athair, you must look at me."

Warts scraped across the delicate skin of her chest. She struggled against her brother's grip, her tail wildly writhing.

"Athair! You will look at me if you condemn me to a life of unhappiness! Athair!"

Her father turned his back, straightened his spine, and remained silent.

Saoirse struggled the entire trip out of the cave. She bit at her brother's arms, drawing blood and spitting green ooze into the water like an animal. Drool hung in strands around her shoulders, leaking from his oversized lips. Milky white and mucus thick, they reminded her where she was.

Underwater. In the depths of the ocean where no one could hear her scream.

Her sisters trailed along behind them. They wept into their hands but watched her with heated gazes. They wanted to know the story of her love. What it felt like, how it had happened, what manner of beast had infected her with such an emotion.

Love wasn't real. Any merrow knew that. Love was something that merrows liked to dream of. It was a fairytale, something that perhaps the High Fae experienced but Lesser Fae knew was impractical.

It led down paths that were dangerous. People did foolish things while drunk on love, bitter spats, fights, arguments, and eventual death because the longing that came with it was equally horrible.

Her sisters likely thought she would die. And perhaps she would.

Saoirse could feel the burning pain of loss deep within her chest. It seared through her flesh and bone until she was certain everyone could see the embers glowing. She hated them. She hated every creature that stood between herself and Manus.

A sob rocked through her until she curled up in a tiny ball with a limp tail trailing like a banner of defeat. Her brother didn't care. He thought she was reckless, just like her father.

And perhaps she was. If she hadn't saved the human, then she might be happy with the idea of a merrow man like Craig.

He would provide for her. He would take care of her in his own way.

She would never need to worry about food. She wouldn't miss her family because he brought her to land.

But she would never experience adventures or the world above the waves.

"It's not that bad," her brother grumbled. "You'll be like the rest of the merrows. Married with children and lots to do. You'll forget all about your human as soon as you're busy with your own family."

"I don't want to forget. I want to remember him for the rest of my life."

He snorted. "No, you don't. You'll hold onto the memories for a while, but then they'll fester. Old wounds either bleed until you run dry, or you heal them up and only pick at them when you want to feel the pain."

"Speaking from experience?"

Saoirse said the words with poison laced in their tone. She meant to hurt him. To make him bleed as she was bleeding.

She never expected the answering hum that twisted in her gut and echoed through her spine.

"You aren't the only one who has experienced loss, little sister. Now grow up and bear it like the rest of us."

Individual currents wrapped themselves around her. They hugged her with a gentleness that brought tears to her eyes. Even the ocean wanted to apologize for taking part in her loss.

What kind of life did she live? Her people were suffering from hatred, and she could do nothing about it. They continued to feast upon hatred, anger, loss, and there was no stopping the addiction. It spread from parent to child, generation after generation.

She was only one among many who would feel the pain of the merrows spread through her veins.

Bars made of stone loomed in front of them. They only used the cage for the worst of their kind. For merrows who stole, who harmed, who killed.

Thankfully, no one else was inside. She remembered a hard time in their existence, when she was just a little minnow, when there had been no space at all between the bars. Flesh, fins, and knobby arms had stuck between the bars, searching for the smallest amount of space possible.

That wouldn't be her fate.

Saoirse sighed and allowed her brother to push her into the cage. The quiet thunk of the lock turning in place made her flinch.

"Just stop getting into trouble, Saoirse," he grumbled. "You're making it worse for all of us."

He turned and drifted away until she could no longer see him.

Shivering, she gripped her arms and sank down onto the sea floor. Coral bit between her scales, but she didn't care. Her life was about to change forever, and she had no say at all in it.

What was she to do? She couldn't escape from the cage. She couldn't change her father's mind. Her future turned dark and gray.

She wasn't certain life was worth living like this, not when she'd had a taste of what it could be.

Nails clinked against the bars, tapping incessantly until she looked up.

A cluster of her sisters floated nearby. They waited for her eyes to meet theirs and then their faces split into bright, sunny smiles. But then again, they wouldn't know they were sunny. Many of them would never see the sun in their lifetime.

"Sister, what is it like?"

"We want to know!"

"Love? Is it real?"

"It couldn't possibly be real! Look at her, all curled up like that, there's not a chance in the ocean that love is real."

"But what if it is? I want to know what it feels like!"

Saoirse held up a hand. "Stop."

"You must tell us!"

"Stop it, please. I don't wish to speak of it."

"Saoirse. You're being so selfish! We want to know what the human affliction feels like!"

"It's not an affliction," she murmured, drawing tighter into herself. "It feels like the first time an oyster opens its mouth. Fearful, shy, it takes its time to reach out into the saltwater and taste the sea on its tongue. And then it realizes the world is wide and great, but not so fearsome after all. It lets the dirt get sucked between its shells willingly and it works them round and round to create a pearl all for itself."

Her sisters remained quiet through her speech. The eldest drifted forward and pressed herself against the bars. "But Saoirse, we eat oysters."

"You wouldn't understand. It's not like food, or water, or even the delicacies of the sea. It's unlike anything I've ever felt before."

"Then why do you look like you're in pain?"

"Because I am," she whimpered. "I am so far away from him, and I know I shall never return to his side. The knowledge is killing me."

They flinched back from the cell, grasping each other's shoulders and creating a ball of shuddering merrows. "Are you ill? Is it truly a sickness then?"

Some cruel part of Saoirse opened wide. Its dagger-filled mouth gaped open like the bottomless pit of the sea. They would never understand her pain. They would never understand what they had watched happen and did not even try to stop.

She glanced up at them with cruelty in her heart. "Yes. Yes, it is an illness that spreads like an infection you have never seen before. It rots from the inside out until your beauty is gone, and all that is left is a ragged shell of a creature. Love makes you ugly when you lose it."

Their shrieks were music to her ears. Great blasts of water pushed her against the back of the cell as they fled from her words. She couldn't bring herself to care. Let them think love was a dangerous, barbed thing. Perhaps it would save them the brutality of what she was experiencing.

Curling back into a ball, Saoirse breathed in the saltwater and tried desperately not to think of the next morning.

Craig.

Strong, wart covered hands stroking her skin.

A merrow man with complete and utter control over everything she did.

She shuddered.

At the very least, she would always have her memories. She could feel the press of his lips against her shoulder, against her lips. The sound of his laughter unhindered by the weight of the ocean. The sparkle of appreciation in his eyes every time she left the waves and raced into his arms.

Saoirse sighed and pressed her fingertips against her lips. Sleep would come late on this night, but she would drift into dreams filled with his image. As she would for the rest of her life.

"Saoirse, wake up child."

The voice broke through her dreams of a man who sang songs of the sea but left footprints in the sand. She stirred, uncoiled her tail which lay across her face, and lifted herself onto an elbow.

"Máthair?"

"Child, it's time to go."

"Go? Is it already time for the wedding?"

"No, my dear. You will not get married today."

The words were an electric shock down her spine. "Athair changed his mind?"

"No, I did."

These were the last words she expected to come out of her mother's mouth. Saoirse twisted her body, grasped the stone bars of the cage, and pressed her face close to the openings.

"Máthair?"

"When your father and I first met, I, too wished for a different life. Merrows are born to suffer, child. That is our place in this world." She reached through the cage and brushed her fingers across Saoirse's cheek. "If you have a chance to break free, then I will do everything in my power to help."

"Won't Athair be mad at you?"

"Likely, but I'm willing to take the risk."

Her mother held up the key to the cell. Life burned in her eyes, so bright it lit an answering spark deep within Saoirse. If even her mother, the perfect example of what a merrow *should* be, could break the rules... surely that meant it was acceptable for Saoirse to do the same.

The key crunched in the coral filled lock. She flinched, holding herself still as if that would make the sound quieter. No one could know she was escaping. No one could know it was her own mother who had set her free.

She rushed from the cage and launched herself into Máthair's waiting arms. Saoirse pressed her face into the crook of her mother's neck, breathing in saltwater and the scent of warmer waters. Her mother had not been born in the depths of the ocean but had come here with her father long ago.

"Where will I go?" Saoirse whispered. "I know nowhere that is safe."

"You will go to my sister, if need be. But I have another idea."

Máthair pulled back and held up a small seashell. It was strangely shaped, like a corkscrew with fine filaments at the end.

"Few merrows know the guardians can speak."

"I've always thought they spoke with me."

"This is different," her mother corrected. "The guardians can *speak,* Saoirse. We just can't hear them. With this in your ear, you can hear their tones and converse with them. Not a one-sided conversation reading body language, but true conversation."

"Oh." Saoirse reached out and reverently held the small shell between her fingers. "I just—"

"Place it in your ear and give it a twist, yes like that. Good job. It doesn't hurt, does it?"

"No, Máthair."

"Good. Find the nearest guardian, ask her to give you passage from our waters and to follow the human ship."

"Ship?" she asked, confused. "Why do I need to find a ship?"

"Your human has gone to safety, chased away by the merrow men. Find the guardian. She'll know which one, they've been watching you for a very long time."

"Why?" Manus had left her? Why would he do that? And why would the guardians care about a merrow girl who was one of hundreds? Saoirse wasn't anything special, other than her dark hair.

"Your soul doesn't belong here with us. They knew it the first moment I brought you to meet them from your egg." Máthair brushed a strand of hair away from Saoirse's face, letting it float behind her head with gentle grace. "They predicted you would leave us at a young age."

"I am not young."

"For a merrow, you most certainly are."

Her mother drew Saoirse into her arms, and it felt very much like the kind of goodbye which lasted forever.

Saoirse drew in a deep breath and squeezed hard. She wanted to remember every instant of this moment when her quiet, withdrawn mother saved her child from suffering the same fate. Saoirse was not alone in her desire for freedom, and that was all that mattered.

"Go," her mother rasped. "Go now, before they have a chance to stop you."

She didn't hesitate. As soon as her mother's arms released, Saoirse shot through the ocean as she had never swum before. Her tail muscles burned, her stomach ached, her hair pulled back so tight her skull screamed as she blasted through the dark waters.

The discomfort was little more than a passing inconvenience. She fled towards freedom, and that was worth a little pain.

Up and up she swam until she saw the beckoning light of the sun. Sunny rays created stunning spears of gold that reached for her with open arms. Just a bit further, and she could turn her face to the open air and the screeching sound of seagulls.

Every instant felt as though someone might grab her tail. That she would hear the enraged shout of her father and a call for a hunt that terrified her to the marrow of her bones. She couldn't afford to lose this chance. Not now.

Saoirse crested the surface and inhaled through her nose. Though water stuck in her throat and her gills gasped, it suddenly felt more natural than breathing underwater.

Shrieks of sea birds and the shushing sound of waves accosted her senses. She'd never been happier in this moment knowing she had made it.

She was free.

A great wave swelled next to her, riding the back of a guardian who had apparently followed her. Its grey skin was marked with scars from countless battles with whaling ships, sharks, and even the occasional faerie. Her great eye tilted up, peering through the water into Saoirse's face.

She had dealt with them enough to know what that expression meant. Sighing, Saoirse sank back underneath the water and faced the guardian's disappointed expression.

"I'm going," she said firmly. "I refuse to linger here when the man I love is out there. It isn't fair I should taste such exquisite ambrosia and not follow it wherever it goes. You cannot stop me."

The shell in her ear quivered, quaked, and rattled with such vigor she worried it would fall out of her ear canal. But then she heard it. The deep, reverberating tones of the guardian.

"I will not try to stop you, child."

"You won't?"

"Saoirse, you were not made for the sea." The guardian swam closer and reached out a finger. It tapped Saoirse above the heart, so gentle for an appendage that was the same width as her body. "You have a piece of it here, in your heart. But the rest of you has always longed for the sun."

"Then you'll help me?"

"I will, but I need you first to know merrows always suffer. It is your purpose in life. If you go to the land, I cannot protect you. No one can."

"I am strong on my own."

The guardian smiled. "You are, I know that. But the land differs greatly from the sea, and I worry you do not understand what it takes to be a human."

"Do you?" Saoirse asked, wrapping her arms around the offered finger. "Can you tell me what it's really like?"

"I have never been to land."

"Have you seen it?"

"I've seen the teeming masses of people. The strange animals when they sink beneath the waves. Humans are cruel and unkind, they do not care for each other as we do under the sea."

"It will be a great adventure." And that was all Saoirse wanted. To see what Manus saw, to understand the world as he did.

"Just be careful, Saoirse. Merrows are young, you in particular have yet to see what the world can do to a person. You love with your whole heart, and I do not want to see you lose it."

"If I let him go, I've already lost it, guardian."

"I know. And that is why I am allowing you to leave. The ship followed the cold current north. Follow it as far as you can until you find the other ships. Uí Néill is where they travel. Hold on to the sides of ships if you must, to listen for their destination. But let no one see your true form."

"I understand." She squeezed the guardian's finger in a hug and pressed a kiss against her knuckle. "I will miss you."

"And I you, child."

With a flick of her tail, she fled from the waters of her home towards the unknown. Saoirse's heart beat rapidly, but in anticipation rather than fear.

She traveled for days on end. Dolphins kept her company for a time. They chattered stories in her ears, making her giggle and laugh even though she was tired. When they needed to leave, a few orcas took their place. They differed from their cousins, more dangerous and solemn. Their stories came from colder waters where blocks of ice floated in the ocean.

Saoirse was rarely alone, even while she slept. Otters

tucked their furry bodies under her arms, cuddled along her sides, and helped her float while she rested. A few even let her hold their favorite stones, which they carried with them for their entire lives.

The first week of travel lacked any ship sightings. The second, a few appeared on the horizon.

Saoirse grasped the sides, slick with water and rot, and desperately listened for words that sounded familiar. They were not traveling towards Manus, so she had to let go. Even though her arms and tail shook, they journeyed away from her future.

It was by chance she found the quaint boat carrying only four men. There was one sail, no bottom deck, and one net to its name, but it was plenty for her to hold onto as long as they didn't look behind them too closely.

Thankfully, they all seemed to be in a hurry to get home.

"Did you hear?" one of the men asked. "The Silver Harpoon has a new ale tonight."

"They say that every year, and there's never been a new ale. It's the same old watered-down drink they give us every time we go in."

"No sir! I've heard from very reputable sources that it's the truth this time."

"Do you mean that McDonall fellow you're always going on about? He wouldn't know the truth if it bit him in the ass."

"He's the most truthful man in all of Uí Néill."

Saoirse's fingers clenched on the sodden wood. "Uí Néill," she repeated.

This was the ship which would guide her. Ducking underneath the waves, she trailed it all the way to land. The water grew foggy, and the fish fled, but she continued on.

The guardian hadn't exaggerated. Saoirse peered up towards the docks and held onto the fronds of tall seaweed. There were so many people up there.

She couldn't count the throngs of men and women who shouted and screamed so loudly she could hear them underneath the waves. They waved cloth at each other and wore so much on their bodies she thought they must be tired all the time. And they came in so many different colors.

She searched for him but didn't see the strong jaw and accentuated features she admired. Frowning, she traveled up and down the shore until the light disappeared. Only a sliver of the moon guided her.

"I cannot give up," she whispered. But there was little more she could do.

Saoirse lingered on a single dock far from the city. Her fins drooped, and her arms weighed heavy as she anchored herself on the end of the wood. Laying her head on her folded arms, she watched a small cabin nearby.

It wasn't much, just a tiny shack near the sea. The wood was rotting in places, stuffed with rags to keep the room warm.

The orange light of a flame flared bright, covered briefly by a hand, and touching a candle. She had only heard of such things in stories. The flickering light was enchanting. Like an angler fish, but with far more life.

Who lived in such a place? A small family, with a single child and a mother who loved them dearly? Or perhaps two children, a boy and a girl with a wonderful future filled with faeries and magic?

Saoirse loved to think up stories that would fill the pages

of her mind. Someday, she would tell them to others. Perhaps even to Manus, should she ever find him.

A body crossed in front of the candle, throwing a shadow on the wall. Tall and broad, it was a strong outline of a man. His shoulders could hold the world. His aquiline nose was a jagged point, like a hawk or an eagle.

She lost her breath. She knew that profile as well as the small statue of the forgotten king.

"Manus!" Saoirse clapped a hand against her mouth.

What if he didn't want her here? She hadn't thought to question during her entire journey whether he'd left because he had to. What if he'd willingly left her behind?

Could everything have been a lie?

Saoirse wasn't certain what she would do if that were the case. Her heart would splinter into a thousand pieces and her body would disintegrate into sea foam. She would float away on the ocean's current and forget about the cruelty of man.

His shadow turned and disappeared. She clutched the dock with a grip that made the wood creak. The delicate membranes between her fingers ached with the pressure.

The door to the cabin opened, and he held a light above his head. "Hello? Who goes there?"

Her nails scraped the wood. It was him. It was really him. After all she had gone through, all the distance she had traveled, and here he was.

"You there! On the dock!"

"No," she gasped and ducked down into the water.

She couldn't be ready for this, not now! What would she say? She journeyed across the sea to find him? Who did that?

Saoirse wasn't ready to declare her love, and that surely

was what he would think when he saw her.

She wasn't even certain she knew what love was. And yet, it sprouted in her breast like the great tree in the grotto under the ocean. It wanted to spread its roots throughout her heart.

And she wasn't inclined to stop it.

Pressing her fingers against her lips, she listened. The padding sounds of bare feet on wood echoed the staccato of her heart.

He was here. He was really *here.*

She reached into her ear and slid the spiral shell out. Tangling it in the strands of her hair, she resolved herself to a life above the waves. He would take care of her. He had to.

CHAPTER 6

By Moonlight I Will Love Thee

Manus lit the candle and watched the flame dance on the wick. It was one of his last matches. He'd have to go to market for more but wasn't certain he'd have the coin.

That was always the hardest part of returning after a long trip. His cabin wasn't secure. No locks barred his doors to prevent scavengers from stealing his belongings, no boards protected his windows. They had been kind this time. He still had blankets on his bed and a table, although they had taken his chairs.

They found his stash of coins and took the lot. That was an issue. He had a few other stashes, but none so big as the missing one. He shouldn't have left the treasure on the isle, although the Vikings might have stolen it anyways.

"Blasted idiots," he grumbled.

Money was the one thing he knew he needed. Manus had to go back out onto the sea. He had to answer the call deep in his chest that already ached, no matter how close to the ocean he lived.

And then there was the added complication of a dark-haired woman with skin like moonlight. She haunted his dreams and now bled into his waking life.

The morning last, he woke and was certain she was at his bedside. Manus could feel the silken strands of her hair wrapped through his fingers. She smiled down at him in that crooked way which was the only flaw to her perfection. And then she disappeared from sight, faded like the mirage she was.

He sighed and blew out the match which burned dangerously close to his fingertips. There was an ocean between them, and it was unlikely he'd ever be able to find her again.

"Let it go," he reminded himself. "She isn't here, you fool. And she never will be."

"Manus!"

The sound was so quiet, he almost didn't hear it. The voice was like that of a song.

"Saoirse?" he whispered, turning towards the door. "No. You're dreaming, man. Let the memories go or you'll drive yourself mad."

He sat down on the end of the bed and tugged his boots off, so he wouldn't chase the siren calling his name. His movements were so harsh that his toes cracked. Each heavy crack of boots striking the floor reminded him he was here. In a cabin by the sea. Not on an isle where the most beautiful of women lay in pure white sand…

"Stop it," he growled.

His leg bounced and finally he gave in. Berating himself the whole way, he lit the candle in his lantern, opened the door, and lifted it high.

"Hello? Who goes there!"

For a second, he thought he imagined it all. There was no

one near his door, not close enough to make a sound.

Then he saw the shadow at the end of the dock. It moved so quickly he might have imagined it, but Manus heard the answering splash. Someone was on the end of his dock. Hiding.

"You there! On the dock!"

He would not abide a child lingering in the shadows, or any thief who thought to sneak in and grab the rest of his money. Barefoot and furious, he stomped down the thick, muddy shore and stepped onto the dock.

"I know you're here. I saw you. It's no use hiding."

They would be at the end, likely holding onto the thick posts for dear life. Swimming at night was a dangerous thing!

Manus set the lantern on the end of the dock, leaned over the edge, and stared down into the empty space. No one was there.

"What the bloody hell…"

Something scraped underneath the dock. Quiet and subtle, he might not have noticed the sound if he hadn't been listening so intently. He furrowed his brow, leaned over the dock further, and stared into the water.

His heart stopped. Saoirse's face appeared, lit by moonlight that stroked the planes of her cheeks. She lay on the bottom with tendrils of her dark hair spread out around her in an inky cloud. Her black eyes were wide with shock, and, he hoped, a little with pleasure at seeing him again.

Slowly, he reached out a hand towards the waves.

Saoirse shifted, and her hair slicked back as she floated to the surface. Rivulets of water trailed down her face, tiny pearl drops that traced the beloved features he longed to touch.

She reached out a hand and met his fingers with her own.

"It's you," he whispered. "How is this possible?"

"I came a long way."

"How did you get away from them?"

"It's a long story," she said and licked her lips. "You weren't easy to find."

"We're very far away from your homeland."

"It's a strange place. I am not used to such rocky shores, and everything is very loud."

"Are you staying?"

"If you wish it."

He recognized the hopeful expression on her face, and it nearly crippled him. She thought so highly of him, of the street rat who bought his way onto ships because no one would even hire him as a sailor. And she looked at him as though he hung the moon in the sky, just for her.

It unnerved him.

"You can stay as long as you wish," he blurted.

Because, no matter how much she thought he was a good man, he wasn't. He would put her in his cabin which was falling apart at the seams just so he could have her. He wasn't worthy of her attentions, but he would be damned if he gave her up.

"Do you want me to stay?" she asked again. "I have traveled across the sea to find you, but I will not linger if you do not wish it."

"How could I wish for anything else? I have dreamt of you every night, my pearl. I'm not convinced this isn't still a dream."

Her cheeks turned a pretty shade of red. "Then help me out of the water, Manus. My family has likely realized where I have gone by now, and I would like to be safe."

"And dry."

"For now."

Manus pressed his chest against the dock and held out his arms. She pulled herself part of the way while he heaved her up and into his waiting arms. There were easier ways of doing it, but none that would keep her clean of mud nor safe from the scrape of rock.

He palmed the back of her head with a happy sigh and pressed her against the crook of his neck. She was wet and cold, with her hair plastered against her back all the way to her knees, and he couldn't have been a happier man.

It felt as though he had waited a lifetime to have her in his arms again.

"Absence makes the heart grow fonder," he murmured against her head. "It's what one of my dear friends used to say. He'd go off sailing and miss his wife something fierce after just a few days. Said when he saw her again, it was like the first day they met."

"I believe your friend is right."

She shivered violently, her entire body shaking in his arms. He rubbed her arms briskly.

"Come inside. I'll set you by the fire and give you something to wear."

"To wear?" She pulled back and looked up at him. "Will you put me in the clothing of your women here? It looks terribly uncomfortable."

"What, a corset?" Manus chuckled. "I'm afraid I don't have many of those lying around."

"Why not?"

"I don't live with women."

"I suppose that makes sense."

He tucked her underneath his arm and guided her towards his home. Would she be disappointed? He had no idea what kind of home she lived in before.

"What are merrow homes like?" he asked.

"Not like this," she said, staring at his cabin with wide eyes. "We live mostly in caves. Merrows try to decorate them as much as possible. My mother has strands of pearls strung up across the entryway to her home, seashells affixed to the walls, jellyfish casting light in the dark shadows. But this is so much more than that."

He tried to see the cabin through her eyes but failed. It was a shack. Broken walls, no windows, nothing but ruin covered in mud from the sea.

"More?" he asked. "I'm afraid I don't see what you do, my pearl."

"How could you not? Look at the way the light dances off the wood! And it's not water logged and soft, but strong and whole. Pieces of the trees that grow here so abundantly it makes tears raise in my eyes." She swiped at her cheeks. "Tears, Manus. I couldn't cry where I come from, and here I can. I hope you don't mind tears; they may be rather frequent."

"I only mind if they are tears of sadness." He squeezed her against his side. "Tears of happiness I could get used to."

A woman at his side. When had his life changed so drastically? Arturo must be rolling in his deep sea grave, laughing at his dearest friend who had so recently said he would never take a wife.

A wife.

The words danced through Manus's head until he could

think of nothing else. He wanted a wife.

Saoirse wasn't going anywhere, that much he knew for certain. He had lost her once, and he'd be damned if he would do it again. No one could know she was a merrow and therein lay a problem. A woman living with a man without the bonds of marriage was sacrilege.

They would have to get married.

He stared down at her with equal horror and awe. Her bare feet squelched in the mud, leaving tiny footprints next to his large ones. So tiny. So perfect.

The moonlight danced over her bare shoulders and trailed down the smooth skin of her arms. Strands of hair covered most of her nakedness but left little to the imagination. He had seen her like this before but now it felt somehow *more.*

He opened the creaking door and let her step through into the dimly lit shack.

"Oh Manus," she breathed. "It's lovely."

The face he made wasn't gentlemanly, but he'd never pretended to be one. She had a strange way of thinking. Saoirse deserved so much more than a ramshackle cabin by the ocean. She deserved a castle, a stately manor overlooking the sea where she could still be close to the place they both loved.

But he was wandering off into dreams which could never come true.

"Is that so," he said.

"Well, just look at it! You must live like a king."

"A what?"

She pressed her hands to her chest and stepped towards the fireplace. "What is this?"

"A fireplace."

"What do you use it for?"

"To heat the place."

"With what?"

The sheer pleasure on her face made him pause. He had forgotten she spent her entire life underneath the ocean. Everything must be new to her. From fireplaces, to beds, to… his world spun. She'd have to be taught everything.

"Look at me gathering wool," he grunted. "Step aside, my pearl. You'll shiver out of your skin if I don't warm you up sooner rather than later."

"I'm used to the sea, Manus. I'm quite all right."

"There's a shirt on the bed over there. Cover yourself."

"Bed?"

He gestured. "That. The white fabric, pull it over your head."

"All right."

Manus stuffed the fireplace with what little dry wood he had gathered in the few weeks he'd been home. Tinder on the bottom mixed with peat would fill the cabin with a sweet scent he always missed on the sea.

He much preferred peat to heat the home, but it was expensive. It burned far longer than wood and that made it a commodity in this area.

The last match struck, flared bright, and burst the small pile he'd made into flames. Manus held out his hands so the warmth could dance on his palms.

"I think I'm finished!" Happiness bubbled in her voice.

He glanced over his shoulder, a wide grin spreading over his face even before he saw the muddled mess she'd made of his shirt. The sleeves somehow locked her arms against her sides, the fabric was inside out and backwards. But she looked so damned proud of herself.

"Well, you've certainly tried." His knees creaked as he stood and made his way over to her. "But I'm afraid this is all wrong."

"You didn't tell me there was a right way to do it."

"You should be able to use your arms, Saoirse." He tugged on the sleeves, pulling them away from her torso and twisting the fabric. "I don't know how you've done this. It has to come off, Saoirse. We'll start again."

"It can't be that horrendous."

"My dear, I have never seen someone make such a mess of something like a shirt."

He fisted the ends of the shirt and tugged it up over her head.

He lost all the breath in his lungs. This was far different from seeing her on the isle, or even rising out of the ocean like some kind of sea goddess. This was a real woman, standing in the middle of his shack, with nothing but the drying strands of her hair covering a body he intensely longed for.

The peaks of his cheeks heated bright red. He told himself to calm his thoughts. She was little more than a child in this world, didn't even know how to put a shirt on the right way, let alone understand the workings of the world.

And hadn't he realized that on the isle? Saoirse sat too close to him, asked him questions he couldn't answer, cared little for the propriety of things.

"Manus?" Her quiet murmur caught his attention.

"Yes?"

"Well it's just.... I worry things might be different. I

understand that you may not have wished for me to come. You left rather quickly, and I know my people can be frightening. But I had hoped you might have missed me."

"You're rather forward."

"I travelled across the seas to find you, Manus. I think I'm afforded that."

"What did you think would happen, my pearl? I cannot read your mind."

She tilted her head back and a dark green lock of hair slid over her shoulder like a dancer in some fancy ballet. "I thought at the very least I might get a kiss."

"A kiss?"

"Is that also forward?"

It was too much. Far more than any woman would ever say in the company of men.

He thanked the heavens that no mortal had ever tempted him, for god had gifted him a woman from the sea who cared little for propriety. She cared for *him,* although he couldn't understand why, and she let nothing stand in the way of that. Not her family. Not the ocean. Not the world itself, for she had travelled across it.

Manus didn't know what god he needed to thank, but he would never forget their kindness.

In a great surge of movement, he yanked her against him and pressed his mouth against hers. She tasted like the sweetest treasures of the sea. Her lips were the softest touch of the tide, and her arms were the gentle grasp of the one being he'd loved his entire life.

A flush of heat spread from the top of his head to the base of his spine. She took all his sense and threw it to the wind, scattering his mind until he was little more than a mess of sensations.

She was so soft, every inch of her body like fine velvet. He flexed his hands on her back and tried to remind himself not to grab her too forcefully. The tiny waist beneath his fingers might bruise, the fragile ribs might break, and he would not leave marks upon her flesh.

His fingers flexed again, and he marveled at the hold she had on him. Somehow, someway, she had completely destroyed his reason.

Manus drew back when they were both breathless and pressed his forehead against hers.

"Marry me," he declared. "Tomorrow, tonight, whenever we might wake a vicar."

"What?"

"Marry me. Please, Saoirse. My life was not the same with you gone, and I wish to never be parted from you again."

"Do you mean it? Now?"

"You have the power to make me the happiest man in the world. My wife straight from the sea."

"How could I say no?"

A surge of elation nearly lifted him off his feet. "Do you mean it?"

"Only if you will kiss me again and again, for the rest of our lives."

"I can promise much more than that," he said, grunting as he lifted her up into his arms so she was eye to eye with him. "A bride of the sea. How did I ever catch you, my pearl?"

"I didn't see a net when I came here. Not one that was yours."

"Your point?"

"You didn't catch me, Manus." She traced a line from his eyebrow to his lips. "I threw myself onto the shore so you might find me."

"And I did, my pearl. I did."

"Saoirse, it's time to wake up."

She snuggled deeper into the warmth that surrounded her. She felt weightless, as if she still floated in the ocean, but it was so warm. The ocean was cold, chilly, sometimes unforgiving in the way it would bite at her skin. This was like sleeping on a cloud.

The most pleasant scent filled her nostrils. Caramel and something raw and earthy, like tobacco, although she'd only smelled it once in her life. Saoirse never wanted to leave this heaven on earth.

"Saoirse, get up. Or have you changed your mind on marrying me?"

"What?" she murmured. "No, I could never change my mind about that."

"I found a vicar. It's very early in the morning, but he was inspired by our romantic tale, so get *up*."

"What is a vicar?"

"The man who'll marry us."

"Aren't we already married? Faeries are not so picky. We've said we want to marry each other, and that is enough."

"That's what I'm trying to do," Manus said with a chuckle.

"I even found you a wedding dress."

"A dress?" Saoirse sat straight up, nearly cracking her head on his chin. "What do you mean you got me a dress?"

He pointed towards the foot of the bed, and Saoirse let out a startled gasp so loud she had to cover her mouth. The thing placed at her feet was not like the others she'd seen at the bottom of the sea. The fabric was entirely intact, so delicate it looked as though it were made of sea foam. Lace fell in waves from the neckline and no sleeves would hide her arms.

"Oh, Manus." Tears pricked her eyes. "It's beautiful."

"You seem to think everything is beautiful. It's only half finished, so I got it at a good price. But I figured you wouldn't mind."

"Half finished? What glorious things must this artist create?" She reached out and stroked it with a tentative hand. "It looks like it's made of magic."

"Have you never seen faerie dresses before? I imagine they're much more glorious than this."

"Merrows don't leave the ocean and my father would never let us visit the Seelie Fae. This is the first real dress I've ever seen."

"I'm glad you like it then."

Like it? She would wear the sea; how could she not be instantly in love with the dress he had gotten for her?

She dragged the fabric across the bed and pressed it to her chest. The lace itched her bare skin where the shirt he loaned her dipped below her shoulder. Still, she refused to let it make her think ill of the beautiful thing. Perhaps it would feel better on.

"Is it the same as the shirt?"

"Yes," he said with a chuckle. "You're actually holding this one correctly. That's the front."

"Good."

She scrambled from the bed. Blankets fell onto the floor, and she did not stop them. Grasping the hem of her shirt, she whipped it over her head.

Manus made a strange hissing sound behind her.

She would never understand humans. They acted as though nudity was only acceptable in certain situations. Others, like now, had an effect on him she couldn't understand. Saoirse intended to find out as soon as possible.

The dress slid over her skin like the finest water, trailing over her and molding to her form. She smoothed her hand down her stomach. The inside of the dress was much more pleasant feeling than the outside. Tiny pearls were sewn into the lace, dotting the dress with sea treasures so fine, she was certain they must have contacted the Fae.

"Manus?" Saoirse turned, her smile so wide it made her cheeks ache. "What do you think?"

He sat on the bed and leaned back on his hands, taking his time looking at her from head to toe. Her entire body tingled at his perusal. She desperately wanted to press her hands against the heated burn of her cheeks but held herself still so he might look upon her dress.

"It's incredible, although I think you might give the vicar a heart attack looking like that."

"Why?"

"Any sane man will salivate the moment he sets eyes on you."

Saoirse wasn't certain what he meant, but she knew it was

good. He couldn't take his eyes off her.

"Are we going now then?"

Manus blinked, slowly taking his time to lift his gaze to hers. "That was the plan."

"Is it still?"

"I'm trying to be an honest man, my pearl. The things I want to do to you require marriage first."

"I'm not human, Manus. The things you want to do may be perfectly normal in my world."

"I promise you, they aren't." He stood and held out his hand for her to take. "Are you ready?"

She had waited her entire life for this moment. Captivated, she slid her fingers into his. Callouses bit at the delicate skin of her palm, but she had never felt anything as decadent.

Manus led her from the quaint little space and guided her into the night. Moonlight bathed his form in a glow that was almost godlike. He glanced over his shoulder, still holding her hand, and smiled.

They clambered over large driftwood, and up wooden planks hammered together. Stairs, she reminded herself. He called them that, and she would need to remember that if this were to be her life.

Saoirse wanted to stop and stare at everything. The cobblestone path was meticulously laid. Stones fit together almost perfectly, and she wondered who had done the work. Was it possible that humans could also utilize magic? Mortals could never complete such intricate designs on their own.

Buildings rose out of the darkness like great monoliths. Starlight glimmered on the glass windows, blinking at Saoirse as she passed. There were no lights within the great structures.

Unable to contain her curiosity, she tugged on Manus's hand to slow him. "Do people live in these?"

"Yeah."

"How many?" She stared up and up at the four-story building before them. "Are they princes?"

"No, these are communal houses. Falling apart at the seams, but slightly better than my shack."

"Falling apart?"

"You can't see the thatch roof is rotting? Some windows are missing panes, and it looks like the lock was broken off the front door. That's not a safe place to stay unless you know how to protect yourself."

"Oh," she whispered, seeing the home in a new light.

She still thought it impressive. Merrows didn't build things under the ocean. They tended to be more interested in discovering than creating.

And yet, her brother once had strung together a strand of pearls to give their mother. It wasn't anything compared to the building, but it was the start of an intelligent society realizing their hands could do something.

Their father had ripped the necklace apart and her brother never tried again.

Frowning, she let Manus tug her deeper into the port city. The buildings grew, each structure built closer and closer until there was no room at all between them. Her feet became dirty, grit and mud sticking between her toes. She was uncomfortable but didn't dare ask him to stop.

They were going to get married. She wouldn't make him pause for anything other than the world ending. Dirty feet certainly weren't that.

"There," Manus said. He pointed far ahead of them at a gray shape which was just taking form. "That's the church."

"Church?"

"Where many worship God."

She nodded. "It is good to honor the Tuatha dé Danann. They appreciate it when humans remember all the Fae have done."

When he didn't respond, she glanced over at his sharp profile. His brows were furrowed, and he licked his lips before responding.

"They don't honor the Tuatha dé Danann."

"Then who?"

"The Christian God."

"Who is he?"

"I'll explain it to you later."

She tugged again, forcing him to pause. "I want to know what kind of God will be there, Manus. I don't like thinking someone other than my people will sanction this marriage."

"It's my God, Saoirse." He tugged her against his broad, strong chest and tucked a finger under her chin. Carefully, he tilted her head up to look at him. "We're already married in the eyes of your people, aren't we?"

"Yes."

"Then let us marry in the eyes of *my* people."

She couldn't argue with that even though she didn't like the idea of marrying in front of a god she'd never met. What if she didn't like him? Or worse, what if he didn't like her? There were too many questions to answer. She knew what the wrath of a god looked like, and it wasn't pretty.

Shivering, she let him pull her towards the gray shape

which grew impossibly taller with each step they took.

The church was terrifying. The high spires jabbed at the air, while solemn looking men stared down at her, wings gracing their backs. She stared at one until it seemed to move. Flinching, she tucked herself again Manus's back.

Fae blood ran in her veins. She should not fear mortal made creations, and yet she did. The things humans created were both wondrous and horrifying.

"Here we are," he murmured. He pushed open a small door near the side of the church which blended into the stone surface. "In you go."

She hesitated for a moment before plunging into the darkness. The stone structure swallowed her whole, and the belly of the beast was even more terrifying than the outside. Meager light filtered through colored glass windows while stone statues glared down at her from great heights.

Was this human god already displeased with her presence?

Saoirse met the gaze of a severe stone man who glowered down at her. He wore a strange hat on his head and held a staff that looked far too easy to clobber people with. He leaned forward just enough that she worried he might take a step onto the floor in the next instant.

The Unseelie Fae used stone statues as warriors. She'd listened to the stories in her youth and swam back to her bed with nightmares already at the edges of her vision. Saoirse never thought she'd see such magic in her life.

She gulped and stepped backwards. Her spine hit what felt like a wall until the flat surface inhaled.

Manus's arm crept around her middle and tucked her back against him. "What is it?"

"The statues."

"What about them?"

"They look as if they are alive."

He pressed a kiss to her temple. "They aren't, my pearl. No magic has stepped foot in this building for a very long time."

"Until me."

"Blessed with the grace of the sea." He pressed another lingering kiss to her hair and then slid his hand down to hers. Warm fingers laced through hers. "Come with me, Saoirse. I'll keep you safe from the statues, and if they step from their pedestals, I shall crush them to dust."

"Promise?"

His brilliant grin was enough of an answer.

Saoirse's shivers disappeared. His eyes crinkled in the corners whenever he smiled, a sure sign he had lived a life where smiles weren't a rare occurrence. The honey gold flecks in his eyes glowed when he was pleased, like the sun dancing across the surface of a black sea.

How could she not be captivated by him? The humans claimed merrow women sang sailors into rocks, but he was the one leading her to trouble. Every sway of his body, every twitch of his lips, every squeeze of his fingers around hers were a siren song she could not resist.

"Father?" Manus called out.

"Father?" she repeated. "This man is your father?"

"No, no. Not mine. It's what we call them."

"Why? That's terribly confusing." Saoirse wrinkled her brows.

"It's just…" Manus sighed and shrugged. "I don't know the answer to that, my pearl. It's how it's always been."

They walked down a long hall with strange, long seats bracketing each side. She wanted to pull on him again and ask what they were for, but he rushed her past the interesting new seats. There were so many strange things here! How would she ever learn them all?

"Manus, you've returned." The voice was quiet and humble. It was a voice she could listen to for hours on end, like the crashing of waves against a sandy beach.

She whipped around, yearning to see who owned such a voice.

The new man stood at the top of a few stairs. There was a table behind him covered with many objects, including a golden man who looked similar to her own. The Father wore white robes, with a black sash around his neck. And though he was not young, he certainly wasn't old. Wrinkles had just begun to form on his kind face, and his eyes sparkled with life.

This was a man she wanted to know, Saoirse realized. He radiated a certain energy she hadn't encountered in any human before. Kindness pulsed in golden light, so vivid she could almost touch it.

"Ah, father, there you are. I've returned with the woman we spoke about."

"This is the lass who has caught your attention? I didn't think it possible to tame your wild soul. Come closer child, I'd like to see the miracle worker."

Saoirse didn't realize he was talking to her until Manus planted a hand against her spine and nudged her forward.

Why did she have to talk to this man who called himself father, but did not have a son? She tucked her trembling hands into the lacy folds of her skirt and stepped forward into the candlelight.

"Ah, you are very lovely, aren't you? No wonder Manus wants to snatch you up. Any man would be honored to have such a woman grace his arm."

"Thank you," she whispered.

All this attention made her uncomfortable. What did this man see when he looked at her? Fidgeting, she tucked her hair behind her ears.

The vicar flinched back immediately. "What is this?"

"Now, father, keep an open mind," Manus interjected.

"An open mind? You've brought a faerie into a holy place!"

"There's nothing wrong with faeries."

The vicar's face grew red. Saoirse couldn't tell if it was in anger or fear. "Faeries have no place in the house of God. I will not perform this marriage, nor will any other sane man."

"You already said you would, father."

"And you *lied*."

"I did no such thing."

"You omitted the truth, which is just as bad." The vicar pointed at Manus, jabbing the air as if his hand were a sword. "I may follow the word of God, but I was raised here, boy. I know the stories of the Fae, and I know what they are capable of. You play with fire! I want nothing of it in my church. Begone."

Their shouts rose into the rafters and echoed back down until she was struck with them over and over again.

Manus flushed with anger, his hands fisting at his sides. "You have no right."

"You raise a hand to a priest and you'll be in more trouble than just a few nights in the gaol."

Saoirse gulped and whispered, "Stop it."

They didn't. She backed a few steps away from them, wrapping her arms around her waist. Did they not understand they were frightening her? She didn't want to be in this terrifying building anymore with its stone guards and angry priest.

They continued on and she pressed her hands to her ears. Their words struck her hands and wiggled between her fingers.

"You think a few nights behind bars frightens me, father? You more than anyone knows where I came from, and I suggest you not be foolish enough to tempt me."

"Temptation is a sin, one I know you over indulge in."

"Don't preach to me of sin as if you are pristine and ready to go to the holy lands! I knew you before you donned the robes—"

"Stop it!" Her shout echoed louder than theirs, fierce and bright as freshly fallen snow.

The two men froze and turned as one to stare at the little merrow. Saoirse watched their lips, waiting for them to move, but they did not. Slowly, she dropped her hands and straightened her spine.

"I don't know what I did wrong," she said. "I'm sorry if I insulted your home by entering it without permission."

The angry lines around the vicar's mouth softened. "Child, that is not why I am angry."

"Then why?"

He stepped towards her, hesitating only when she mirrored his actions in the opposite direction. "What are you?"

"I am one of the merrows."

"My mother used to tell me stories about your kind. How

beautiful the women were, but caged underneath the waves by their husbands, or caging others. Is it freedom you seek?"

She nodded.

"Are you certain it is freedom with a sailor you desire?" His eyes turned kind again. "Manus is not one for loyalty. You could have anyone you wanted from the land. A prince, if need be. Your life with him will not be an easy one."

Manus's fists lifted. "You have no right, father."

"I have every right. I will not marry a woman to a man she does not know or understand. She is innocent to this world." He rolled his eyes. "Manus, stop looking at me like that. I may be a priest but I'm an Irishman first and foremost. I was raised with stories of the Fae just as you were."

"She can make her own decisions."

"Can she? Have you told her what you can offer her?" The priest pointed at him again. "The threat of starvation always looming around the corner? No money to buy new clothing, stealing from whoever has loose pockets, wondering if you have enough money to buy peat for the winter? There are better ways for her to live, and you know it. You'll throw her out to the cold as soon as the sea calls you."

"Why you pompous—"

Saoirse could stand this arguing no further. She stepped between the men, her shivers creating ripples down the dress until the lace looked as frothy as sea foam.

"*Enough*. I will not say it again." Their wide eyes met hers at the harsh crack of her words. "I am a grown woman, and I appreciate your concern, but I will not have yet another man making decisions for me. We are already married in the eyes of the Fae. I don't care if you or your god deems us wed."

"You do not know who you are pledging yourself to," the priest sighed. "You are choosing a life of hardship with a man who will always consider you second best to the sea."

Anger flared bright in her chest. "I'm afraid we must not see the same man. It is not that I am blind to his weaknesses, father, I see them clear as day. But I also see a man who acknowledges his faults. There is no such thing as a person without flaws, and I choose to be with a man who knows what he is."

"That's a pretty way of saying it, but it doesn't show you understand what your life will be."

"My life will be what I choose. No more, and no less."

The priest searched her gaze, his eyes delving into the darkness of hers until he found what he wanted. He gave a curt nod, then turned to the altar.

"So be it. If I cannot convince you of your own folly, you will have to learn it yourself."

She didn't think he was right, and she certainly didn't think he would ever prove her wrong. Saoirse reached for Manus's hand and tucked it into hers.

He gazed down at her with pure joy in his eyes. "Are you sure about this?"

"I've never been more sure of anything in my life. I've already pledged myself to you Manus, a thousand times over in my mind and if I must, I will scream it to the sky. I crossed the seas to find you. I would do it again in a heartbeat."

"What did I do for such a creature to find me?" he asked quietly. "I have never been looked upon kindly by any god. Why you?"

Saoirse reached up and pressed her palm to his cheek. "I

see the man you keep hidden from the world, and I like him very much. I think, perhaps, you do not. At least not yet."

"See him? Or like him?"

That was a question she couldn't answer for him. Instead, she smiled a secret smile and tugged him towards the priest who patiently waited at the altar.

She knelt beside him and copied his movements. It was a rather easy ceremony. Repeat the words, copy the actions, allow the priest to bind their hands together and proclaim them man and wife. It was more than a faerie wedding, but less than she might have expected from such creatures.

"Do you take this woman as your wife?" the priest asked.

"I do." Manus's voice lifted to the rafters, strong and confident enough to weaken her knees if she had been standing.

"Do you take this man as your husband?"

She looked Manus in the eyes, in those dark earthy eyes with threads of gold and copper.

"I do."

"Then by the power vested in me, I pronounce you man and wife."

Manus lurched to his feet, drawing her with him and tugging her into his arms. He bent low and growled in her ear, "I will not disgrace you before a priest, but you and I are going home right now."

"My lady," the priest called out. "Be careful."

She wouldn't dignify the words with a response. Saoirse might not have been raised a princess, but she felt very much like one as she walked down the steps. Manus waited for her at the bottom with his hand outstretched.

It didn't matter that there was dirt underneath his nails. It didn't matter that he came from nothing, that he lived by the sea instead of with other people, that he had no money or material wealth to his name. He looked at her with the abyss in his eyes and in them she saw home.

He was a prince made of bark and earth, come to life by her wishes and dreams.

Manus rushed them through the streets, not pausing to answer her questions. He didn't seem to even hear her as they raced down cobblestone back to the sea.

The hushed sound of their breath splintered through the air. It mixed with the slaps of their feet as they ran across the mud flats. Manus wrenched his door open, planted a hand against the small of her back, and pushed her over the threshold.

Giggling, she stumbled into the small home, filling her eyes with the golden light of the sunrise. It gilded the edges of every small furniture piece and the edges of his bed.

"Manus, it's morning already."

"I woke you too early," he said. He closed the door with a harsh crack, then wedged a chair against it for good measure.

"What are you doing?"

"Making certain no one can interrupt us."

She lifted a brow. "Interrupt us? What are we doing?"

Manus did not reply. Instead, he picked up a blanket from the bed and tossed it over the window. The room fell into darkness other than a few spears of light from holes in the fabric.

Curious, she peered through one as he struck another match and lit a few candles. The warm light spilled through the shack, turning his skin to burnished bronze.

"Manus?" she asked again. "What are we doing?"

One moment he was on the other side of the room, and the next, she was pressed against the wall with the full length of his body pressed against hers. He leaned down, his lips tracing a line from shoulder to ear.

"Did you mean it?" His voice was hoarse and ragged. "Every word you said to the priest?"

"I did. Faeries cannot lie."

"Ah, yes. I had forgotten." He caught her ear between his teeth, gently worrying the sensitive skin until sparks showered through her body from the pointed tip to her toes. "No one has ever said those words about me."

"Then they are all wrong."

Manus pulled back, and she lost herself in his eyes again. She saw mountains with trees so green they burned her eyes. Waterfalls tumbled from great heights, billowing in clouds of frosted white. Ancient beasts who lifted their many antlered heads with flowers blooming along their spines. She saw the world of the Fae in his gaze, and so much more than that.

"Kiss me," she whispered. "I am yours, Manus of Uí Néill. And I will have no other."

Manus wanted to give her a wedding night that would shift the foundation of her world. He wanted to tantalize her senses, whisper promises in her ear, pretend to be the gentleman he wasn't. She deserved every bit of his control and leashed passions.

But then she said the words that marked her as his forever. A wedding vow meant little when the woman's gaze wandered. This strange woman willingly gifted herself, her life, her soul, everything she was with a promise that stole his heart.

The tethers of his control snapped with a nearly audible crack. He surged forward, pressing his body against her and devouring her lips with an aggression that surprised him. She tasted of the sea.

She stung his soul like saltwater on a sunburn and then soothed his aches with a gentle touch.

Manus lifted his hands and framed her face, tilting her head to plunder her mouth even further. His hands were shaking. He pressed his fingers harder against her cheeks and realized with fear that it wasn't aggression or passion burning in his veins. It was a need so raw and violent that he wanted to brand himself with her touch, with her essence, with her soul.

He would frighten her, and she would be smart to run from him when he was like this. There would be no tender touches, no murmured praise, nothing but a scorching hot flame that would devour her whole.

And yet, he could not stop himself.

He dragged his lips from her mouth, trailing across her high cheekbones and down the graceful column of her throat. Her breath caught, her legs quivered.

"I do not know how to be the man you deserve," he whispered against her skin. "I cannot be a gentle man. I cannot be a good man."

"You are," she whispered, and fisted her hands in the dreads of his hair. "Love me as a man loves a woman, Manus. Do not treat me as if I were made of glass. I am Fae, and I am more than any woman you've had before."

Her words arced through his mind like a lightning bolt. They traveled down his spine and nearly blew out his knees for want of her.

"I want you fiercely," he ground out. "More than any creature I've ever seen before."

His fingers shook as he loosened the tie on the front of her dress. He tugged at the white bow until it released and fell into a silken puddle on the floor.

The lace parted, fabric held together by little more than a prayer. He nudged it to the side so he might see the smooth skin of her shoulders. She didn't have a blemish on her. No scars, no pockmarks, not even a raised ridge where she might have harmed herself once in her childhood. Saoirse was all milk white skin that turned silver in the moonlight.

He pulled the lace down with a single finger hooked in a delicate swirl. It slithered down, caught at her waist, and she looked as though she were walking out of the sea into his arms.

Manus had seen her pristine skin before. He'd seen her without a shirt or a stitch of clothing to her name, but this was different. It was one thing to see a faerie in her natural habitat. It was an entirely different thing to see her standing in his home as vulnerable as a newborn babe.

"Your hands are shaking," she whispered.

He watched with rapt attention as Saoirse reached forward, grasped his hand, and pressed it to her lips.

"You have no idea what is about to happen," he panted, reminding himself she was fragile.

"You're thinking too much." Her lips turned up in a half smile. "I thought we weren't supposed to think?"

If all were going well, then she wouldn't have a thought in her head other than the taste of him. Manus couldn't breathe. He was staring at perfection and every time he touched her, he worried he would leave a mark.

His dirty fingers didn't deserve to touch a creature such as this, no matter that he had stolen her away. Merrows were myths and legends. She was a goddess, and he was nothing more than a street rat.

She stepped forward on feet that made no sound in the quiet shack. "I don't know what I'm doing, but you'll tell me if I do something wrong. Won't you?"

A shuddering breath escaped him. "Why?"

"Why what?"

"Why would you ever allow me to touch you?"

She smiled and pressed her palm against his cheek. "Why would you ever think a woman wouldn't want you to?"

"I'm only good for whores."

"Who told you that? You're a handsome, honorable man. I do not recognize this part of you, this piece that is self-conscious and can't understand my feelings towards you. It's unlike you."

She was right. Manus was a confident man, one who wooed whores to his bed with little issue. He'd never hesitated with them. They squealed in delight when he came anywhere near their shop.

Maybe that was the reason. He never knew if the ladies of the night were interested in him or his money. Likely the latter, but that meant he didn't have to please them if he didn't wish it. Manus enjoyed paying particular attention to their needs, but after a long day of work, they still got paid. If they were disappointed, he didn't worry.

What if he disappointed her?

Her gaze searched his, and a spark of recognition flared so bright his cheeks burned red. She knew, or at least had guessed some of it.

He bit his lip as she stepped back. Her fingertips caught on the edges of the lace dress, and she pushed it down her hips. It slid to the floor with the soft sigh of a calm sea, and she stood before him as she was meant to be.

Long dark hair framed her arms and made her skin seem even paler than he thought possible. It swayed at her rounded hips, high above slender legs that ended in delicately arched feet.

His gaze lingered upon moon touched skin and the shadows that played over the valley between her hips.

"I don't want to temper you," she consoled. "You are not a blade I wish to dull. I will take you in whatever way I can, Manus. If that is as an animal, then I must ask you to remember that I am part fish."

He chuckled and ran a hand over his knotted locks. "It's not that easy, my pearl."

"Tell me what you desire, my husband, and I will give it to you a thousand times over."

Her husband.

Her husband.

The words rattled through his mind and shattered what little reservation he had left. Manus cursed, stepped forward, and scooped her into his arms. She held onto his neck and let loose a bright bubble of laughter that splintered on the ceiling and showered down upon them in a chorus of bliss.

He laid her down on his bed, whispering that he wished he

could give her more. She deserved gold, diamonds, precious gems sprinkled around her body in goddess-like adornment.

Her spine arched into him, and he palmed the silken flesh of her breasts. A groan vibrated his throat in sheer bliss. It was everything he had wished for, everything he had dreamed she would feel like. Soft as satin, warm as a fire in winter, and pliant as the softest of clay.

He leaned down and drew a pebbled peak between his lips. Stroking his tongue back and forth, he waited until her breathing hitched and her fingers curled in the sheets before he moved to the other.

Saoirse was a surprisingly responsive lover. Every swirl of his tongue made her back arch further, every gentle bite of his teeth made her gasp in pleasure. It was music to his ears, and he was all too pleased to oblige the way her body begged for his touch.

The muscles of her stomach contracted as his fingers danced down her soft belly.

"Trust me," he whispered against her heart.

"Always."

He stroked the inside of her thighs, encouraging her to let them fall open. There was no hesitation, only complete and utter trust as she bared herself completely.

She was warm, wet, and all too welcoming for a man's sanity. Manus groaned and pressed his forehead against her collarbone.

"My pearl, I don't know if I can be gentle, and you deserve that."

She pressed harder against his fingers until the heel of his palm was flush against her burning heat.

"I don't want gentle, Manus, I want you."

Saoirse pressed herself into his touch, heat covering her body as never before. He turned her into a creature of the earth. Her blood was molten lava, her body made of rough trees, and her breath the icy north wind.

He rose over her, the long tails of his hair stroking across her sensitive skin. "Do you?"

"Now."

He reached between them, notching himself where his fingers had played. "There will be a little pain—"

She pressed her fingers against his mouth to silence him. "Enough, Manus. We have waited long enough."

The overwhelming sensation of tightness filled her. It was too much, too full, too evocative, and yet she didn't want him to stop.

He was tender and sweet although he said he couldn't be gentle. Each inch that he slid forward caused massive exhalations to dance across her neck and chest. Manus pressed his lips to her throat, obviously holding himself in check until she relaxed around him.

Saoirse hadn't thought it would be like this. She'd seen such acts before. Whales and sea creatures mated with an animalistic fervor she'd never understood until now.

She tangled her fingers in his hair, pressed her lips to his, and waited until he had seated himself fully.

"Enough," she muttered against his lips. "You have been gentle, now give me everything."

The rocking movements of his body increased, each thrust like a tidal wave crashing through her body. He was the ocean and turned her into the many currents that surrounded him, swallowed him, devoured every bit of what he might give her.

Unexpectedly, she shattered. Saoirse tossed her head back against the pillows and stared up at the ceiling, but all she saw were stars. The thousands of glowing lights that decorated the sky. Or perhaps they were the glowing beacons of the underwater cities, bioluminescent and secretive.

She was unmade. Pieces of herself flung into the air by the great release that rode her body, rocking back and forth as he plunged deeper and deeper into her depths.

Manus tossed his head back, the cords of his throat flexing, casting shadows across his form as he let out a guttural groan.

The weight of his body fell onto hers, surrounding her with warmth and safety. Saoirse tucked her arms underneath his and encircled his ribs.

He was not soft, like her, but rugged. Ridges of scars laced across his body, a hard life laid out in a map across his skin. She bumped her fingers over his ribs and traced the laced pattern of scars that crisscrossed all over his skin.

Breath puffed against her neck, and he pressed his lips where the air had chilled her skin.

"Are you all right?"

"Better," she replied with a smile. "Far better than I might have expected."

"I'm glad I didn't disappoint."

"How could you? I'll take any bit of you that I can."

She whispered the words even though she wanted to scream them to the rafters. He was hers, and she was his. They were bound by faerie and human law. No one could take her from him, and she was never returning to her home under the sea.

For the first time in her life, she was completely safe.

It was an overwhelming feeling. Saoirse wasn't certain how to deal with it. She didn't need to look over her shoulder, worried that her father or brother would be there in the shadows. She didn't need to wonder what man she might marry, or what direction her life would take.

Saoirse was her own person although perhaps she was slightly Manus's as well. But that didn't matter much. He was a good man to his core. He just didn't know it yet.

He stirred, pressing his face in the hollow where her neck met shoulder, and sighed.

"It is the beginning of the day. We should get up, and I should try to find work."

"Stay a little longer," she begged.

Saoirse wrapped her arms around him tighter. She snuggled into his chest, inhaling the earthy scent of sweat and man.

"Maybe for a little while longer," he agreed.

He rolled them to the side with his arms wrapped tight around her spine. She let him arrange her as he wanted, draping her leg over his hip and letting him place his chin atop her head.

It was quiet, peaceful, and heady to know that she was cared for. At least a little. They hadn't said the words, but she was certain he felt the same way. He had to.

A rumble of a chuckle spread through his chest.

She smiled, "Yes?"

"What?"

"What's so funny?"

He shook his head, rubbing his chin on her head. "I've never fallen asleep with a woman before."

"Never?" Saoirse leaned back slightly to see him. "Even the priest mentioned that you were well known in these parts."

"I don't stay with them. I enjoy them, they enjoy me, and then I leave."

"Why?"

She furrowed her brow as he hesitated. It made little sense that he wouldn't want to stay. This was wonderful. The feeling of his arms around her made her heart sing a song she'd never heard before but found beautiful.

"I never wanted to," he finally admitted. "Until now."

"Oh. That is acceptable then."

"Is it?"

"Yes." She snuggled back down into his arms and breathed a quiet sigh. "That is perfectly acceptable."

Saoirse did not let herself rest until she heard the peaceful sound of his deep breathing. He fell asleep with her in his arms, and she was pleased to be the first.

CHAPTER 7

Bliss and Agony

Saoirse pressed a flower to her nose, inhaling the sweet scent that spun her senses like a top. She hadn't thought it would smell like this. Lavender wasn't found in the lands that surrounded her underwater home, so this was a rare treat.

"Do you like it?" Manus asked.

He stood on the other side of the stall, his eyes following her every move. She knew how strange she must look. Saoirse rushed from vendor to vendor, grabbing everything she could get her hands on and exclaiming how miraculous it was. They gave her strange looks and tolerated her odd behavior with quick smiles.

"It smells like… like…." Saoirse struggled for the words. "Like far off lands and adventures."

He rounded the stall and plucked the sprigs from her fingers. "That's because it smells like here, and I dare say this is as far as you've ever been."

"I've never been so far in my life!"

"Precisely." He tossed a coin to the woman smiling at them and handed the plant back to her. "It's said to have a calming effect."

"What is? This?"

"The lavender. People place it inside their pillows when they cannot sleep."

"Really?" She looked at the purple flowers, intrigued by the possibilities. "How fascinating."

"Is it?"

He'd asked the same question throughout the day. Was it actually that interesting? Perhaps not to him. But everything was new for Saoirse, foreign and strange, but delightful to every sense.

Glinting colored lights caught her eye. It sparkled like the sun through water. Her heart stopped, and she rushed across the busy street without thought. Manus called after her, but she couldn't stop. Not now that she had seen the newest, captivating find.

She ducked underneath a brightly colored sheet flapping in the wind and then skidded to a halt.

Tiny pieces of colored glass hung on strings, tangled with feathers that shifted in the slight breeze. Clinking glass mixed with the quiet hush of wings. The sun hit the softened edges, sending colors dancing across the wooden stall and spilling onto the ground.

She lifted the hem of her new dress and poked her bare toes into the light. Blue danced over her skin, familiar and yet not. It was like seeing the ocean through new eyes.

One mobile in particular caught her attention. Seashells hung next to shards, the wind singing through them and calling out to her like the ocean waves.

The man behind the counter had a kind smile that reached

up into his eyes and twinkled. He wiped his hands with a white rag and stepped forward.

"Can I help you, m'lady?"

"Oh," she murmured and clasped her hands to her chest. "I don't know where to start. These are beautiful."

"They hardly hold a candle to you."

She blushed bright red at his words. The men were charming here, far more than merrow men could ever hope it be. She didn't know how to respond to their teasing, their compliments, or their flirtatious advances.

Manus usually scared them off. But he wasn't here now as the carriages blocked him from her.

Glancing over her shoulder, she spied him searching for her on the other side of the street.

Protection was appreciated, but unnecessary. Saoirse might be a merrow, but she could take care of herself.

She tucked a strand of ink dark hair behind her ear. "How do you make them?"

"Glass is a rare find in these parts. Do you know how we get it?"

"No."

He gestured for her to come behind the stall. "Come around then, I'll show you."

"Won't that keep you away from your other customers?"

"There doesn't appear to be any right now, and it's probably the wrong market to sell my wares. Haven't gotten a single person all day who was a serious buyer. Let me show a pretty lady what I'm capable of. It's a small consolation for such a wasted day."

She took the arm he offered. Muscles flexed beneath the

white linen shirt, a promise that this artist was a working man.

Saoirse couldn't imagine how he could create such beautiful objects. Surely it was magic. The hairs on her arms raised at the thought.

She'd only seen a few people capable of magic in her short life. They were marvelous creatures, capable of spinning dreams into reality and worries into fantasy. Her father hadn't wanted her anywhere near them. He said it gave girls fancies.

Saoirse already had more fancies than she could keep ahold of.

"Do you know anything about glass?" the man asked.

"No."

"Some people think it's magic, you know. That it's a gift from the Tuatha dé Danann themselves."

She lifted her gaze sharply, squeezing her fingers on his forearm. "Is it?"

"No." He patted her hand, both in comfort and as a request for her to relax her grip. "It's a magic from the earth, certainly, but not how you might think. Sit here, and I'll show you."

Saoirse tucked her hands in her lap and reminded herself not to swing to her legs. Manus had tried telling her this morning that she would need to learn how to be human. Swinging legs while seated was not lady like.

The man lifted a wooden crate and set it at her feet. "This is where glass comes from."

With a flourish, he pushed the lid off the crate and her heart skipped a beat. Would it be amazing? Would it be some magical creature she'd never seen before?

She leaned over, stared down into the crate, and blinked. Sand filled it to the brim. White and nearly undisturbed, it might have been sand from her home.

"Sand?" she asked.

"Sand m'lady." He chuckled at the face she made. "Come now, don't look so disappointed! Why don't you stick your hand in there? See what you might find."

Stick her hands in the sand? She'd done it a thousand times. Saoirse almost told him that she'd grown up deep within the ocean, rolling across sand dunes as a child and throwing it in the faces of her sisters. She quickly shut her mouth, knowing that would reveal too much.

The sand was cool against her palms. It slipped and slid through her fingers in a way so familiar it nearly brought tears to her eyes. She had only been gone for a few weeks, and already she missed the sand more than she could admit.

Her fingers bumped against something hard with jagged edges that bit at her skin. Gasping, she yanked her hands from the sand and stared with wide eyes at the man.

"What's in there?"

Glee made his eyes sparkle. "Oh, I don't know miss. Why don't you pick it up?"

"Will it bite me?"

"No, just be careful. I would feel awful if you cut yourself."

Somehow, she wasn't certain he was telling the truth. His eyes were sparkling too much, and he didn't warn her the first time she plunged her hands into the crate.

Saoirse narrowed her gaze and refused to be cowed. He might expect her to flinch away from the discovery, but she had battled sharks. This human man had no idea what he was dealing with.

Again, she sank her hands into the sand and swirled the

grains. The sharp object had been in the very corner, farther away so she had to lean nearly into the crate to get it.

Cold shards touched her fingers. It was larger than she expected, and not nearly as sharp as she thought. Tiny spikes dug into her palms but didn't threaten to pierce flesh. The cold surface was smooth, solid, and yet surprisingly delicate.

The artisan must have seen the wonder on her face. He chuckled and gestured with his hands, "Go on then. Pick it up and have a look."

Her biceps flexed as she lifted the surprisingly heavy find. Sand slid off its surface and she gaped at the giant piece of glass between her hands.

It looked like spilled wax, slightly foggy, but stunningly beautiful with its spires of twisted tendrils and thick base.

"Oh," she exclaimed in awe. "Is this what it looks like before you change it? How is it made? Magic? Must you use magic to temper it? How do you turn this into those beautiful prisms?"

He burst into laughter and held up his hands. "One question at a time lady. Although, I can likely answer them all if you'd like to come see how I work."

She nodded, holding the raw glass close to her chest so she wouldn't drop it. This was the most precious substance she'd seen on land so far, and she'd seen lace so delicate it looked like sea foam. What other wonders had these beings created?

The artisan carefully took the glass out of her hands and placed it back in the box. "Come with me."

The hand he offered was covered with callouses. Saoirse realized she had only seen humans with work roughened hands.

Glancing down at her own, she hesitated a brief second before placing her velvet soft hand in his. His eyes widened in surprise for a moment. He'd noticed, she was certain he would, and didn't know how to explain the reasoning behind her untouched hands.

It wasn't that she hadn't worked, she had. She wasn't a royal, nor was she rich. The water had different ways of handling such things. Merrows didn't feel the effects as humans did, and her palms would likely roughen the longer she was here.

Still, it felt almost shameful and embarrassing to have him notice such a thing. She ducked her head and let him lead her behind the row of stalls to where the artisans kept their carts full of wares.

"Lady," he mumbled, "if you are some noble miss masquerading through the market, you should not be alone with the likes of me."

"You aren't the first person to tell me such a thing, and I cannot understand the reasoning behind it." She looked up and met his blue gaze. "Should I not be able to meet and speak with whoever I wish?"

"It isn't proper."

"Says who? Why wouldn't it be proper for someone to meet those who create their wares, their art, the things we use every day? I should know the man talented enough to decorate my home if I was a noble lady."

Relief spread across his face. "Then you aren't?"

"What?"

"You aren't a noble lady?"

"No." She shook her head ruefully. "I don't think I would

be any different if I were."

"You're a rare one, aren't you?"

Saoirse wasn't certain the look he gave her was good. It was a thoughtful expression, his brows drawn down and his lips pursed. An expression that made her worry he was wondering who, or what, she was.

"Where are we?" she blurted out, hoping to steer his thoughts away from his curiosity.

Mud squelched between her toes, but she didn't mind too much. Deep tracks were furrowed in the ground from carts traveling over them each day. She saw some vendors rushing back from their small stalls, carrying armloads of new wares back where customers might wish to buy something. White sheets covered most of the carts and protected the goods from the sun.

But not the cart in front of her. This one looked more like a fireplace on wheels. Round as a barrel, with a flame churning within, the strange cart caught her attention immediately.

"Is this yours?" she asked.

"You are astute; it is. Come, I'll show you."

The closer she got, the louder the inferno churned. Saoirse held her hands up to her ears and stared at the artisan. Her fingers shook with fear.

"Is it dangerous?"

"It is if you get too close. Come now, my lady, I won't let you be harmed. Look inside."

Inside? She inched forward. What was he keeping inside that monstrous creation?

"Don't worry," he said with a chuckle, placing a warm hand against her spine. "It won't bite you. Have you never seen a kiln before?"

"A what?"

She peered into the roaring flames and waited for her eyes to adjust. Molten glass pooled in the depths of the fire. It glimmered like starlight, holding its breath for the moment when the artisan would turn it into something new, something beautiful.

At her gasp of surprise, the man chuckled and reached for a metal tool.

"Now step back," he warned, "I don't want you to get burned. Let me show you what else I can do."

The metal tweezers seemed to vibrate in his hand. Perhaps they too realized that something wondrous was about to happen.

Saoirse held her breath as he reached into the kiln and drew out a long strand of glass. It stuck to the metal, dripping like thick honey. He quickly laid it on a small metal table next to the kiln, rolling and twisting it with dual tongs until the glass gave way to a shape.

She could see what he was doing, but still had no idea what he was creating. This was magic, she decided. Not the magic she was used to with glittering lights and powers of unearthly qualities. It was the kind of magic buried so deep within humanity they didn't know they had it.

The artisan grunted, breathed out a sound of relief, and held up the glass piece to the light.

"Come look at it, my lady. Quickly now, I've got to put it in a blanket to cool. I think you'll like this one."

She rushed forward, excitement heating her veins until she felt she might burst.

Within his hand, he held the tiniest merrow she had ever seen. The tail was fine, so delicate, that she could see the bumps of rigid scales down the thick length. Her hair floated around her head, with her arms raised to stroke the tiny fish that darted through the long length.

There was no color, but it didn't need the embellishment. The merrow was perfect in all her clear glory. An homage to the magic which brought them to life, and the beauty underneath the sea. Water would reflect through its surface and give it life with coral reefs, schools of fish, and the echoes of whales.

"How did you—" She glanced up and realized he didn't know what she was. His gaze was on the merrow, not her. Eyes wide with reverence, he stared at his newest creation as if wishing it could come to life.

"It's beautiful," she whispered. "You have a rare gift."

"Thank you. I rarely receive such compliments."

"Do you sell them?" She desperately wanted the tiny merrow for herself, but also knew it would fetch a considerable amount of money. The man deserved to be paid for his efforts, and she had little.

"Few people are interested in such things here. My art isn't practical. It's breakable, and it's difficult for the folks in these areas to buy something they know they can never use, only look at."

"I would fill my home with them if I could."

Her adamant declaration was so forceful that it made him rock back a step. The shock in his gaze warmed to a heat she had only seen from Manus.

This artisan wasn't a terrible looking man. His eyes were blue as the sky behind him, his facial hair carefully combed.

Though he wasn't nearly as dark as Manus, he was still intriguing in his own way. His hands had been graceful as they twirled the molten glass and created life with his fingertips.

If she hadn't already been in love, she might have liked this man quite a bit.

Her gaze softened, and he reached forward to tuck a strand of hair behind her ear. "You're a rare beauty, my lady."

"Why do you keep calling me that?"

"Certainly, you are a royal disguised as a peasant. If you are not, then you are one of the Fae masquerading through our streets, and as such deserve all the respect I could possibly give."

"I'm not tall enough to be Tuatha dé Danann," she said with a blush. "If only I were one of the royal Fae."

His fingers tightened on the strand of hair in his grasp. "What—"

"Saoirse!" Manus's voice barked. "There you are."

She hadn't heard such a tone in his voice before. It rang with darkness, rage, and an underlying hurt. He didn't know merrows could hear emotion in voices, it was why their own voices were so beautiful.

Heart pounding, she glanced over her shoulder. "Hello, husband."

Manus stalked towards her, all lethal power and barely controlled aggression. "Hello, wife."

"Wife?" The artisan dropped his hand. "My apologies, sir."

Saoirse thought perhaps Manus's bared teeth would be considered a grin in some cultures, but it made her shiver in fear.

He ground out, "Not your fault. We haven't bought a ring

for her yet, how would you have known?"

His hand dropped onto her shoulder and tightened. Had she done something wrong? Was she supposed to announce herself to the world as his wife?

She couldn't. Perhaps he didn't understand the way of the Fae, but ownership over another creature was as good as a name. His name could control her, just as much as her own now that they were married.

Wincing, she patted his hand on her shoulder. "This kind sir was showing me the glass. Isn't it magical?"

"It's just melted sand."

She latched onto his hand and forced him to stay when he moved to leave. "Manus, look at it!"

A muscle on his jaw ticked. She watched the rapid grinding of his teeth until he finally turned. "I've heard there was an artisan here who spins glass like silk. I assume that is you?"

The other man cleared his throat. "I'm not quite so talented, my lord, but I appreciate it."

"I'm no lord."

"I thought—" Again the artisan cleared his throat. "No matter. Have a look before I lay it to rest."

Manus took the offered metal tong and turned the merrow in a slow circle. The winged crinkles at the edges of his eyes deepened for a moment. "She's beautiful. Almost as stunning as the real thing."

"The real thing?" The artisan's eyes darted between them. "Are you... Could you be saying... Sir?"

"Don't think about it too much, you'll hurt yourself."

Manus handed the art piece back to the other man, planted his palm against Saoirse's back, and hustled her back through the stall and onto the street.

"Wait!" she cried out. "I wanted to see if we might take something home!"

"We're not buying anything of his."

"Why not? The glass was beautiful, Manus, and there was the most stunning piece with seashells and all the colors of the sea—"

"Saoirse enough!" Manus's voice was low, but it felt as though he slapped her.

She blinked up at him, willing the tears to remain in her eyes. She hadn't done anything *wrong*, and yet he was yelling at her with all these people looking. All she wanted was something pretty that might remind her of home. She'd given up her home to be with him, to make a new home with him. Did he not see that?

Manus made a pained sound, sighed and stepped away from her. He ran a hand over his hair while his eyes flicked from the tears in her eyes to the ground.

"Did you not see how much danger you were in?" he growled.

"I wasn't in any danger, he is a kind man."

"This one might have been kind, but the next man who pulls you into an alley won't be. Good god, woman! You nearly gave me a heart attack!"

"I didn't mean to."

"Saoirse." He grabbed her arm and swung her around. Cupping her face in his hands, he pressed his forehead to hers. "Humans are not kind creatures. Everyone here is like your merrow men, looking for the next person to take advantage of. You cannot leave my side."

"You shouldn't be so quick to judge others," she replied. "Some of them might surprise you."

He released her with a muttered curse. "I need a drink."

"Manus, your hands are shaking."

She watched his fingers curl into fists that clenched so hard his knuckles turned white.

"Come with me," he grumbled.

They passed by the cobblestoned streets, deeper into the city where gravel and dirt dug into the soft skin of her bare feet. The people were less clean here. Their faces were streaked with sweat, and grime embedded underneath their nails and covered their clothing.

These people made fear dance across her skin with stings similar to that of jellyfish tentacles. Their eyes were hungry, black like a shark and bottomless like the deepest abyss. They weren't on the main street for a reason. She didn't think they had enough money to feed themselves, let alone buy all the wondrous things the vendors had showcased.

A man walked towards them and his eyes traveled from her toes to her head. He let out a slow hiss of breath, a high-pitched whine of a sound that made her flinch. Manus lashed out a hand. He caught the man by the throat and tossed him into the wall.

For a moment, she wondered if they would claw at each other as merrow men might have. But something in Manus's gaze made the other swear and stumble past them.

"Manus?" she called out. "I don't like it here."

"Yeah? No one does, my pearl. Get used to it." He ducked through a door and left her standing on the street.

Saoirse rubbed her arms and swallowed hard. Why was it

suddenly cold here? The streets had been warm, full of sunshine and bright smiles. Now, a chilled wind brushed down her arms. It coiled in her palms and whispered dangerous secrets in her ears.

Manus opened the door again and held out his hand. "It wasn't a request, Saoirse. Follow me at all times."

She bristled at his tone but followed him. The street was a dangerous place, and the shadows moved in the corners of her eyes. She didn't want to know what kind of Unseelie lurked in this desolation.

The room beyond was only half full of men and women in various states of disarray. Some women bared their shoulders, something Manus had told her never to do, and others were more sensibly dressed. The men were all covered in dirt and sweat, much like those on the street.

Manus pointed towards an empty table near the large hearth merrily crackling. "Sit there."

She would have to tell him later how little she appreciated his tone. The worn boards were smooth and soft, trailing warm grains against her soles as she made her way towards the rickety seating. Sliding onto the bench, she set her back to the crowd and stared into the fire.

Some things were different here. Far more different than she ever could have imagined. Some humans were wealthy, some were talented, and some were so painfully poor it made her heart ache. Why would they let their own people waste away? Or worse, continue to live a perpetual existence of hardship and strife?

Saoirse shook her head and let it drop into her palms. Maybe someday she would understand them, but for now, it just made her head pound.

The bench across from her creaked.

"Manus, I don't want to be here," she murmured. "I want to go home."

"That'll depend on which home you mean, lassie." The voice sang out, dancing through the air like the trickle of gold coins with the heat of lava pouring from deep sea vents.

Her spine stiffened. Something deep inside of her recognized that kind of voice and answered its call with the burbling of water, the roar of rushing rivers, and the thrum of hidden sea caves.

"Who are you?" She looked up, anger burning in the back of her skull.

The man seated in front of her was surprising. His sheer size was not what she expected although everything was different here in this land. A white shirt strained across his broad shoulders, tapering to a trim waist that spoke of hard labor. A light dusting of freckles spread across his sharply angled face, meeting the hairline of his shockingly red hair.

He wasn't dressed like the others here. His clothing was finer, his hair neatly trimmed, and no hair graced his jaw or chin.

But she wasn't all that surprised that he stood out like a sore thumb. All Fae did.

"I think you know I'm not going to tell you my name," he said with a wry grin. "I won't expect yours either."

"What are you doing here?"

"I could ask the same of you, little merrow."

Her hands clenched on the table. "How do you know what I am?"

"It's not hard to tell. That hair shines green even in this golden light, and you'll forgive me for saying, but a faerie is far easier on the eyes than a human." He leaned forward, interest coiling like a snake within the depths of his dark green eyes. "Now, why are you here?"

"I followed my heart."

"Your heart?" He pointed towards Manus, whose back was still to them. "That one?"

"Yes."

"Oh, little merrow, that was a foolish decision. Humans are entertaining for a time, but they're always disappointing." He leaned back, anchored a shoulder against the wall, and hooked his heels on the table. "Speaking from experience."

"My decisions are my own, and I would prefer it if you kept your opinions to yourself."

"Ah, where's the fun in that lass?" His booted feet shifted side to side. "Do you have any guesses yet?"

"On what?"

"What do you think I am?"

She scoffed. "That's hardly a challenge, leprechaun."

"It is for some. My size is rather confusing, wouldn't you agree?"

"Not at all. Tuatha dé Danann are large, Lesser Fae are not. It's why you and I are both similar sizes to humans, although," she paused and looked him up and down, "you are larger than most men."

"The largest of my entire family. It's a personal accomplishment I'm rather proud of."

"I don't think you can give yourself credit for your size."

He lifted a finger to his lips. "Come now, lass. Don't break a man's heart."

"I don't have time to quarrel with a leprechaun about the size of his flesh. Begone with you."

He wiggled, presumably to make himself more comfortable on the bench. "Not interested in that option. I think I'll stay right here and meet the paragon who caught the attention of a merrow."

"I'd rather you didn't."

Saoirse desperately wanted him to leave. After the way Manus had reacted to the artisan, she couldn't imagine what he might do if he saw this behemoth of a man sitting in his seat.

The leprechaun gracefully gestured, his fingers dancing in the air until suddenly a golden coin appeared between his fingers. It sparkled in the light and forced all her attention onto the single piece.

"Oh," she whispered. "Where did you get that?"

"Just a trick of the light, lass. Now, would you mind answering a few questions for me?"

She couldn't stop staring at the gold coin as he rolled it over and through his fingers. Strange, she didn't feel like herself but didn't mind in the slightest. The coin was too interesting to care that her mind was wandering.

"Good," he continued. "Why are you really here?"

"I followed him across the seas."

"Where did you meet him?"

"He was shipwrecked off my home. I saw him floating in the water and thought he drowned. My heart hurt at the thought, so I saved him."

"Did you heal him?"

"I don't think so." She frowned. That was something

important she should remember, but she didn't.

"Try again, little merrow."

"I might have. I didn't want him to die, but he wasn't dead when I grabbed him."

"But you healed him when you brought him back to the isle."

"Perhaps a little? Just with merrow tears, and they aren't supposed to do that much."

He cursed, but it didn't matter. The coin spun over his fingers that flicked so quickly it looked as though they were their own wave.

"Those heal more than you know, merrow. What would you do if I tried to take you from him?"

"I would fight tooth and claw. And if you succeeded, then my heart would rip in two and my blood would meet the waves." She reached out a hand hesitantly, waiting for the moment when the coin would stop. "May I have it now?"

It stopped, hovering just between his middle finger and thumb. "Are you sure you want it?"

"Yes."

He arched a brow. "Just how young are you?"

"I'm close to my first century. May I have it *now*?" Even she heard the petulance in her voice.

"Oh, lass, you are a young wee thing aren't ya?" He spun the coin until it laid flat across his knuckles. "Take it, and I'll give you my name."

"I don't want your name."

"A leprechaun coin is a promise, little one. I'll watch over you as best I can, whenever I can, but you take this coin and I'm as much a part of you as that man hovering by the bar looking like the world is falling down around his ears."

Saoirse hesitated. "I don't want to belong to anyone else."

"You won't. You have my word."

She nibbled her lip, but the golden light was far too compelling. Saoirse lunged across the table and snatched it from his fist.

The coin was warm and heavy, the metal almost soft beneath her fingertips. Its beauty was almost painful so close to her eyes. Etched on the surface, a small merrow swam through golden waves.

Saoirse let out a soft, pleased sigh. "Thank you."

He nodded. "My name is Declan."

"It's a pleasure to meet you, Declan. My name is—"

"Saoirse."

She blinked, looking up at him in surprise. "Yes. How did you know?"

"It tells me a lot more than you'd think." Declan nodded towards the coin in her hand. "You'll have to keep it on you at all times. Leprechaun gold is bad luck if you lose it."

"Oh," she breathed. Saoirse pressed the coin to her chest and held it tight as if her own fingers would let it slip away without permission. "Does it want to be lost?"

"Not as you might think." He leaned forward, the ever-present grin on his face. Saoirse noticed that his teeth were slightly pointed. A little of the real leprechaun was leaking through the glamour he held in place.

"Then I shall be careful with it."

"You sure this is the path you want to walk, little merrow?"

She nodded firmly.

"All right then," he said with a disappointed glower. "I'm

not going to say I like it. So, you keep that coin with you at all times. If something bad happens, I'll know."

"Who are you?" she asked. "You don't speak like the others, and you wouldn't be here unless you were banished and yet…."

"Yes?"

The roguish grin on his face sent a shiver running down her spine. "You don't seem like you were banished."

"Let's just say I'm on a little adventure from my home. It's important to get perspective on the world, wouldn't you agree?"

"But *who* are you?"

She searched his gaze for an answer, and her own memories for anything the merrows knew about the leprechauns.

They were traditionally a very secretive lot. The dwarves enjoyed their riches, but leprechauns were a completely different race of Fae. They bled riches. Gold ran through their veins like blood, and gemstones dropped from their eyes like tears. Everything about them was a mountain of wealth and glory.

Leprechauns kept to themselves. She knew there were a few lines of royalty although they were not recognized by the Unseelie court. Saoirse remembered rumors that stretched under the waves.

A prince of the leprechauns, incapable of being controlled by his parents, so wild and free that even the beasts wanted nothing to do with him. They sent him to the human world to learn humility, and to appreciate their origins.

She had heard nothing since, and it would be hard to tell if this was the prince himself. After all, every leprechaun had red hair, freckles, and were built like gods.

Unless....

At her raised brow, his grin widened just enough to reveal a solid gold back tooth.

"It's you," she whispered. "You're the leprechaun prince?"

He winced. "Not my favorite name to go by, but if you must."

"I've never met a prince before." Saoirse leaned forward, keeping her voice hushed so no one could overhear them. "Am I supposed to curtsy?"

"Please don't."

"But I'm supposed to?"

Declan glanced away, and that was all the answer she needed.

"My goodness!" Saoirse lost her breath. "What other things have I done that would get me killed in the Unseelie court?"

"There are several things, little merrow, but you'll find we're far more lenient than our Seelie brethren."

"I've heard they're much more invested in rules."

"Aren't you part of the Seelie court?"

"In a way. My merrow tribe lived on the edges of both kingdoms, but so far away that the customs didn't carry with us."

He breathed out a low whistle. "You're one of the rare wandering Fae? A creature not dedicated to either court?"

"I suppose you could say that. I didn't know we had a name."

"You're more dangerous than I thought."

Two jars slammed down on the table between them.

Saoirse recognized Manus's hands, strong and scarred, wrapped around the glasses so firmly she worried they might break.

"Dangerous, is she?" he growled. "I think I could say the same for you, mate."

To his credit, Declan did nothing other than shrug. "It's not every day you meet someone like her, now is it?"

"And why's that?" The dangerous edge to Manus's voice stole the breath from Saoirse's lungs.

"Oh, I think you know why considering you stole her from the ocean and dragged her to this hell on earth. Shall I call you her husband or her captor?"

A snarl twisted Manus's lips. "I'll ask you leave, *friend*."

"But your little lady friend here has made such a good impression. I'll give you one warning because I like her." A coin appeared between Declan's fingers. "You don't know what you're dealing with."

"I think I know perfectly well. A pretty boy like you walks into a bar like this, and he usually gets his teeth readjusted."

Declan nodded with a feral grin that bared teeth sharpening by the second. "So be it. Heads? Or tails?"

He tossed the coin into the air and Saoirse watched it wildly spin between the men. Something important was happening. Something she couldn't understand but knew she should.

It was there, bubbling just underneath the surface of her mind. If she could just reach it, then she could stop whatever was going to happen. But she couldn't *remember*, something to do with a guardian, and with the longing for waves that crashed through her mind until she couldn't think of anything at all except—

Saoirse lunged forward and snatched the coin from midair.

Time slowed. The other people in the bar leaned forward in anticipation but their eyes didn't dance the way they had. Declan slowly turned his head towards her, and that pointed grin spread impossibly wide.

"You're smarter than you look," he mouthed. "Good luck. And if you have need of me, remember the coin."

She blinked, and time started up again. Manus lunged forward. His hands closed around empty space where the leprechaun had sat only moments ago. The coin in Saoirse's fingers disappeared. Vanished, just like its owner.

"Bloody hell," Manus grumbled, running a hand over his head. "What was that thing?"

"A leprechaun."

"What?" His eyes grew wide. Slowly, he sank onto the bench in front of her. His hands were shaking again. "Tell me you jest."

"What's wrong with leprechauns?"

"They're cursed creatures! And you—" he paused, lunged forward, and turned her hands over. "You touched the coin. It's not still on you is it?"

"No."

He must have heard the hesitation in her voice. His gaze snapped towards her, narrowing at her innocent expression. "What aren't you telling me?"

"The coin is gone, Manus. I touched it, but it disappeared with him."

He searched her eyes for a lie that he would never find. Faeries couldn't lie. With a sigh, he slumped back and let her hands drop to the table.

Saoirse sipped at her own tankard of ale. She lamented the frailty of humans and their foolishness. Manus knew faeries, he understood their ways, and even he did not consider she might twist the truth.

The merrow coin heated against her sternum, a reminder that the leprechaun had left his mark, whether Manus wanted him to. There would always be a bond, an undeniable connection.

She didn't want to wonder why she took the offer. Manus could protect her, he had been all day. But there was still an unease that settled deep within her stomach. This wasn't her homeland, and she knew nothing of their ways.

It would be good to have her own kind looking after her.

"We should just go home," Manus grumbled. He tossed the tankard back and let it slam down on the table. "Let's go."

Manus stared at the rotting roof and wondered why it had taken him so long to get here.

He'd made a promise, and he prided himself on being a man of his word. So why hadn't he shown up on this doorstep weeks ago?

Because he was also a coward, he admitted to himself. The thought of telling Arturo's wife he wasn't returning tore at Manus's soul. It wasn't fair. Of all the men to survive that wreckage, Arturo should have been that man.

Instead, his body lay at the bottom of the sea. His bones

were likely picked clean by fish and those merrow men who still haunted his nightmares. It wasn't a fitting end for such an honorable, good man.

What was he going to say?

"Your husband was the best man I've ever had the pleasure of sailing with," he tried. "No, that's not right. I wasn't in love with the man."

What else could he tell her? Arturo was like a brother and it was a damn shame he wasn't here anymore.

A cry drifted through the window into the night air. Manus winced. The baby would grow up without a father, and that was even more of a damn shame. He knew the pain first hand. The child deserved someone who loved it.

He straightened his jacket, stepped up the small stairs leading into Arturo's home, and knocked.

It took a few seconds for his wife to open the door, and Manus realized he'd never asked her name.

She was a pretty little thing with a splash of freckles across her cheeks and hair the color of gold. In her hand she held a broom, dust covering her simple gown.

"Can I help you?" she asked.

His tongue refused to work. In her eyes, he saw his own future. A pretty little wife, a babe, a small cottage by the sea. A wife who lived alone because her husband disappeared every chance he could get.

A wife who would inevitably find herself alone and starving.

"Och, you're looking a wee bit pale there," she muttered. "Come in with you."

"I really shouldn't—"

"In." Her stern tone reminded him of his mother.

Manus let himself be pulled into her humble home and almost closed his eyes as a pang of pain struck him in the chest. This was the place Arturo spoke of so often.

It was a quaint little house, as his friend had claimed. Pretty and filled with a woman's touch. Small tapestries hung from the walls, a hand stitched quilt over the small bed. Even the cups were painted with flowers.

The baby cried again, and Arturo's wife raced towards the crib. "Sorry, it's her feeding time and I can't miss it, or she gets grouchy."

He watched her life the tiny bundle into her arms and coo. In his mind, he filled in her image with that of Saoirse. His merrow would look wonderful with a few children, a life.

"It's all right," he murmured as she turned away from him. "Take your time."

"I apologize, I'm usually better with guests. Are you a friend of Arturo's?"

He tripped over his words, "I-Well-Yes. Yes, I was."

Her spine stiffened. "He's not coming back I take it."

This was the moment. His moment to stay true to his word and be a better man. The words stuck on his tongue, his throat closing in anxiety.

"He talked about you all the time," he said. "You were never far from his mind, even in the end."

"Was it quick?"

The baby reached around her mother and took a handful of cloth in her chubby fist. He fixated on the movement and realized he couldn't lie. "No, ma'am it was not."

She sighed. "How did it happen?"

"The ship sank. And I know it sounds crazy, but we sailed into faerie waters. I was the only one who survived, and only because a faerie saw fit to save my life."

Arturo's wife draped a blanket over her shoulder and chest, then turned to look him in the eye. "Why you?"

"I don't know."

"You say a faerie saved you, but the same faerie didn't save my husband?"

"*She* doesn't understand why she saved me. I've asked her a hundred times and every time it's the same answer. She doesn't know."

Silence stung his ears as Arturo's wife looked him up and down. The baby shifted under the blanket, drawing his eyes to the daughter his friend would never see.

Manus cleared his throat. "He said to tell you how much he loved you, and trust me he did. He never stopped talking about you, the child, the life you were going to build together."

"And yet he always went back to the sea," she replied. "He always took his life in his own hands, and I told him it would be the end of him. Of us."

Tears shimmered in her eyes, tearing at his heart until he felt as though he was laid bare before her.

"I'm sorry," he croaked. "For everything."

"It wasn't your fault that he heard sirens calling his name. But I thank you for bringing his message."

He turned on his heel, incapable of walking fast enough. Manus wanted to leave this house filled to the brim with emotions and dark memories.

"Oh, sailor?"

He paused at her doorstep.

"Take care of that lass who has you all tied up in knots. Don't be like my Arturo. Be there for her when the storms come a'calling."

The haunting words rang in his ears as he fled her doorstep and raced towards home.

Saoirse stood at the end of the rickety dock, white nightgown whipping around her legs and lashing behind her like the great tail of a guardian. She hugged her arms firmly around her waist. The waves crashed upon the shore in great slaps, bringing with them the silver light of the moon.

Her dark eyes scanned the horizon, searching for something she couldn't name. It wasn't her family. Though she appreciated their memories, she could not condone their lives. The elixir of freedom still flowed through her veins. That life was no longer hers.

So, what was it? What was she looking for? Something deep within her soul yearned for more, but she didn't know what the *more* was.

She dug her fingers into her sides.

A hole ripped open deep inside the fiber of her being. She didn't know what the ache was, couldn't name it or point to the place where it hurt. Yet, there it was. The aching burn of the unknown.

Bare feet padded down the worn planks. Each heavy thump of heel against wood reminded her that she was not alone. That her life was no longer only hers.

Not anymore.

Manus heaved a sigh behind her and wrapped his arms around her waist. His heat sank into her back, easing the tense muscles of her spine instantly. His chin settled on her shoulder as he snuggled her tighter in his arms.

"What is it, my pearl?"

"Hm?" Saoirse hummed the quiet sound. "What do you mean?"

"You're brooding."

"Brooding? I wouldn't even know how to do that." She felt his chest expand in a great sigh that tickled the side of her neck.

"Do you miss them?"

Saoirse hesitated a moment. "I miss aspects of them. Some of them were kind even if their thoughts were backwards."

"Would you go back?"

"Never." She shook her head. "I couldn't go back under the waves after seeing all that I have. This place, with all its dirt and secrets, is still beautiful."

He reached forward and tucked a strand of hair behind her ear, tugging lightly on her lobe. "Your ability to always see the good in things is the first thing I adored about you. Did you know that?"

"Other people can see goodness in the world."

"Not like you do." He squeezed her waist and blew out another breath against her neck. "I should apologize for my behavior today."

"I understand why you yelled."

And she did. Saoirse understood that she was a rare creature in this place. He worried she would disappear with the merest puff of wind. She didn't agree with him but understood why he was nervous.

He had shaken with the mere thought of losing her. That alone told her all she needed to know about his feelings even if he could never verbalize them.

"No," he muttered. "It's not enough. I acted like a cad, and I had no right to do it."

"You were worried about me."

"And there are better ways to handle it. I've never had a... lady."

She turned in his arms and hooked them around his neck. His words vibrated with sadness, fear, and something else she could not name. It tasted like salt water on her tongue and the bitter remains of seashells.

"I don't know what you're trying to say Manus."

"It's just that... Well, fine. I'll just say it and you take it as you will. I've never considered myself a man who might marry. I spent my time with ladies I paid, and none of them were mine. I didn't have to worry about losing them because I never had them in the first place. You understand?"

"I think I'm following," she said, trying her best to keep amusement from her voice.

"When I saw you with that artisan I wanted to spin his head around. He was *touching* you and although I still have no right to say what you can or cannot do, but I wanted to toss you over my shoulder and lock you away from any other man's eyes. I'm not *used* to that, Saoirse."

She watched him struggle to formulate the words. They moved so fast through his lips that she could barely understand them, but it didn't matter. She could feel the words as they brushed through her mind and tingled in the base of her spine.

He cared. He cared so much it turned him into a different person, and he couldn't understand it.

That was okay. She could deal with that.

Saoirse stood on tiptoes and pressed her lips against his. The kiss was chaste and soft, sweet like all the things she did.

"It's okay," she whispered against him. "All is forgiven."

"It is?"

"I could never stay mad at you for too long, Manus. I crossed the seas for you, and nothing will ever change that."

His hands slid down her spine, holding onto her ribs with a touch so gentle it nearly brought tears to her eyes. "What did I ever do to deserve you?"

"You pleased a god."

"Indeed, I must have. For you have a heart large enough to heal the wounded edges of mine." He leaned down and kissed her until her toes curled.

She loved this man. Loved him painfully, achingly, and so thoroughly that it made her worry for her soul.

CHAPTER 8

THE PRICE OF GOLD

Saoirse blearily blinked her eyes open. She stared up at the ceiling, her mind racing to catch up.

They had lived in the shack for a while, but she was hungry now. Last night, Manus had shaken his head when she asked for a bit of bread. Instead, he'd given her water and tucked her under the covers.

"The water will fill your belly," he'd murmured. "I'll try to figure something out while you're asleep."

But it wasn't better. Her stomach gnawed at itself as if it could eat her body instead of food. It hurt so much that she worried it might kill her.

What had awoken her?

Saoirse restlessly moved her legs, touching a solid warm weight at her feet.

"Manus," she said. "Are you back?"

"I'd hoped to keep you innocent of this," he replied. "I'd hoped to keep you safe."

She tilted her head. He sat with his head in his hands, barely perched on the bed. His spine was a soft curve, coiled in on himself in shame and defeat. She could sense the emotions heavy in the air, so thick it clogged her senses.

"You didn't find food."

"There are no jobs for a man who was born to be a sailor. They all know me. I can't farm, I can't be a shop keep, I don't have any skills."

She reached down and rubbed her hand down his spine. "Then we will find another way."

"There's only one other way, and I am loath to beg you to put yourself in danger."

"Danger? What would put me in danger?"

He turned, gathered her hands in his, and cleared his throat. "On the isle, you used to bring me gold and gems. You'd find all those beautiful coins and treat them as if they weren't important. But they are here. It's how we pay for food, for drink, for everything we have."

"I understand the concept of money, Manus."

"I don't have money." His cheeks reddened. "I think I'm past the point of poor, and closer to just waiting for death. I spent everything I had, and I can't find any way to replace it."

Saoirse blinked, lights flickering to life in her mind. "You want me to find more gold."

"Is it even possible? There cannot be many shipwrecks around here."

"There are always shipwrecks. But Manus, going into the water isn't just dangerous. It's deadly for me. If any of your people see me— "

"They won't. I won't let them see you. We'll take a small boat, row offshore, no one will know what you're doing until we return. And even then, we'll say it's your inheritance."

"My what?" She cocked her head to the side in confusion.

"It's customary for women to have some kind of dowry when they get married. For most in this area it's livestock, but everyone already thinks you're some kind of noble. It wouldn't be a surprise for you to have a treasury to your name."

His eyes were strangely heated as though a fever ran through his veins. She'd never seen him like this before. Not even on the isle when she had brought him fistfuls of sparkling necklaces and priceless jewels.

That her family might find her was a very real danger. It was, however, unlikely they would come this far north. At the least, she might be spotted by a few sharks who would tattle. It wasn't the end of the world.

"It can only be one time," she said. "Once my family catches wind of where I am, then I can't go back in the water."

"Would they already know?"

"I don't think so." She hoped not. Her legs already itched, desperately wanting to free themselves from the confines of humanity. Saoirse wanted to feel the water gliding along her skin again. "We would have seen them by now."

The shack was too close to the water. Merrow men could walk to it, and their strength was still massive on land. Considering they hadn't been raided yet, Saoirse thought it safe to say her father didn't know where she had run off to.

Manus squeezed her hands. "You'd be saving us. I understand it's a lot to ask from you, but Saoirse, we'd be set for life."

"How much do you want me to get?"

"It's just once? You're certain?"

She nodded.

"Then whatever we can find. All of it. I have a few mates from back in the day who have an extra dingy, and we can pay them to keep their silence."

"Manus." She licked her lips. "Where are we going to put it? There's nowhere safe here."

"You let me worry about that. I've got friends in high places, though they won't admit to knowing me yet. Once we have money, people will flock to help us. We just need to get it." He lifted a hand and slid his fingers along her jaw, into her hair. "So, you'll do this?"

"If this is what you want."

"I want to take care of you. I want to give you a life you deserve, but I can't do it alone, my pearl." He tugged the back of her neck and pressed their foreheads against each other. "You are a blessing, Saoirse."

She didn't feel like a blessing. Her entire body ached from hunger, and she knew he was in no better state. Manus's cheeks were gaunt, his ribcage visible, and he moved slower than he used to. They needed something to change.

Apparently, it was her turn to save them.

Swinging her legs over the edge of the bed, she held onto his shoulder to balance herself. "I'll need to be far away from any ships, and even then, you have to make sure no one sees me."

"I can get the boat. Get yourself ready."

They helped each other stand, and Manus rushed out of the door.

Saoirse didn't need to prepare herself. There was nothing here which would assist her in the ocean. The sharp knives in the corner were good for human food, but they wouldn't stand a chance against a shark or an orca.

She bit her lip and twisted her fingers together. Was this a good idea?

So much could go wrong. So much could happen under the surface where Manus couldn't see her. If her family found her again…

No. She wouldn't let herself think like that. Athair would have sent every merrow man he could to retrieve her. Not because she was special or rare, but because she had betrayed him in every sense. If he knew where she was, he wouldn't rest until she was back in the depths, locked away for life.

A shiver danced down her spine. No matter what, she would never allow that to happen. The waters here were cold, the current strong. Merrow men wouldn't be able to find her.

"I can do this," she whispered.

The pounding of approaching feet echoed, and the door opened to reveal Manus's lanky form. "Are you ready?"

She nodded.

"You don't need to change?"

Saoirse looked down at herself, taking stock of the plain blue linen dress, and shrugged. "It's coming off anyways."

His mouth gaped open for a moment before he shook himself. "That's right. Strange how quickly I can forget that you aren't human. For a second I worried you would grow cold."

"The water is my home, Manus. It will never feel cold."

She let him take her hand and guide her from the small shack. An ancient boat was tied to the dock with a frayed rope. It hardly looked safe although she didn't worry for herself. Saoirse could always survive, but he was a little more sensitive to the dangers of the ocean.

"Is it safe?" she asked as she padded down the dock. "It looks as though it should have been put to rest long ago."

"I wouldn't take it out into open waters, but it'll carry us away from the shore safe enough. Give me your hand."

Saoirse took the offered assistance and let him lower her into the belly of the boat. She tucked her legs underneath her, smoothed her skirt, and watched as he clambered in with her.

The oars lifted and settled into the water soundlessly. Each rise sent droplets skittering across the calm waters of the bay. The water streaked pink as the sun lifted its head and kissed the sky.

She thought the waves were calm in slumber, then realized she was wrong. It was holding its breath, waiting for the moment when she would dip her toes in once again. The merrow was returning to the grasp of her great mother. The ocean knew what she was doing, and it watched her with a solemn gaze.

Manus steered their boat through ships with limp sails, past seals which popped their heads out of the water and peered at them. Glassy eyes met hers and Saoirse felt her soul take flight.

She had missed this. The world under the waves was one so rare, so beautiful, that it tore at a person's soul to leave it.

The guardian had been right. Every moment she was away from the ocean felt as though she was inhaling shallow breaths. Her life was dull and colorless.

"Saoirse," his deep voice broke through her reveries. "Here's good enough."

She turned her gaze towards him, and the world bloomed into color. Perhaps she would never understand what it was about him that called to her, but his very existence was a siren call she could not resist. He was color, life, and magic all wrapped in one being who made little sense.

Now, she would dive into the water and risk her life to keep him alive. Nodding, she reached for the hem of her dress, only to pause when he grabbed onto her wrist.

"Just—" he hesitated. "Be careful."

"I'll do my best. The ocean is not a very safe place."

He bit his lip, white teeth worrying at the full flesh. "Come back to me."

Did he think she was going to leave for good? Saoirse could never leave his side, no matter how much she wanted to return to her home. Life wasn't worth living without the other half of her soul.

She reached out and pressed her palm to his cheek. "I will always come back to you, mo ghaol. Never fear that."

My love.

She shouldn't have said it. Her heart was already on the line when it came to Manus. He owned so much of her that Saoirse worried she would completely disappear. And yet, it was the truth.

Love for him shone so brightly within her chest that he must have seen it. Judging by the stunned expression on his face, she doubted he'd even guessed.

"I should have said it sooner," she murmured. "Perhaps in a hundred different ways as well. I don't mean it as a goodbye, I hope you know that."

He said nothing. Instead, he kept staring at her with that dumbfounded expression that set her teeth on edge.

Saoirse took a deep breath and yanked her dress over her

head. The light blue linen drifted through the air and landed in Manus's lap as light as a feather. She didn't hesitate. Saoirse dove into the water in a curving arc and created no ripple when she disappeared underneath the waves.

Happiness, so vivid it was almost painful, splashed through her body. It tingled on her skull where her hair lifted up. It effervesced down her spine and lashed her legs together, yet it did not hurt. All she felt was euphoria as scales rippled down into a billowing fluke.

Her tail was powerful and strong. It flexed at the merest whim of her mind and propelled her through the icy ocean. Down and down she went, stretching her arms out so the ocean could stroke more of her body. This was where she belonged. This was where she had been born, and she'd missed it so desperately. She hadn't realized it was the cause of her unhappiness.

Bright bubbles of laughter exploded from her lips. *Home.* She was finally home.

At the bottom of the ocean, she paused and looked back up at the surface where a single small boat bobbed in the middle of a vast nothingness.

It was difficult to be a creature of two souls, she mused. They both longed for the freedom of the ocean and the whip of salty air. And they were both bound by chains. His of desire for wealth and comfort, hers for safety and love.

Her thoughts turned dark, her expression wistful. If only there was a way to save them both. As it was, the only thing she could do was bring back fistfuls of gold.

A pit in the bottom of her stomach suggested this wouldn't help at all. That in the end, all it was going to do was create more trouble.

Money was a dangerous thing for humans. She'd seen them spend it wastefully at the market, haggle over prices, buying things they didn't need for people who couldn't care less. Yet, they always bought the thing that meant very little.

Her gills flared in a deep inhale. This was the only way, she reminded herself.

She turned and let the current take her where it wanted to go. Sunken ships always found themselves in the same area. The ocean moved the puzzle pieces beneath the waves wherever it wanted them to go.

Jagged stone jutted out of the ocean floor, bracketed by long strands of kelp that nearly reached the surface. There wasn't as much ocean life here as her home. A few fish wiggled past and brushed against her sides, but there weren't many whales or dolphins.

A jellyfish touched her head with its long tendrils. The zap of electricity made her giggle and bat the strands away.

"Go on," she chuckled. "Off with you, I'm not your newest meal!"

If a jellyfish could look put out, this one did. It sullenly floated away.

Saoirse flexed her muscles and sped through the water. She curved her arms in front of her, spinning as she swam. Barrel rolls were always her favorite trick, and the dolphins loved to watch her spin.

There were no dolphins here; not yet. She could hear their joyous laughter echoing from some far-off space. They were followed by the melancholy cry of a whale and then sudden silence.

A ship loomed in the distance. Its shape was little more than broken masts and dark shadows, but she remembered it from her first trip here. A great beast lurking in the depths.

Saoirse couldn't guess how long ago it was laid to rest. Chunks of the sides were missing, stolen by the ocean and sea creatures. A crack ran down the center of the ship, two halves of a whole spilling out the guts of gold and gems.

She had never felt uncomfortable near a wreck before. The ships were dead—a memory rather than a real thing.

This one sang a song she did not like. It wailed through the currents with forgotten screams and anguished cries. The souls of the dying stayed with this creature of wood.

Floating upright, she hesitated in the foggy water. Was there movement in the depths? She couldn't make out what kind of creature it was but was certain she saw a fin. It didn't look like any sea creature she had ever seen before.

Chests full of gold waited just outside the ship. They must have tumbled from within when the deck cracked in half. She could swim and grab whatever she could hold.

As much as she was enjoying being herself again, Saoirse didn't want to linger in this place. It was terrifying and far too dangerous for her liking.

She pressed her hands against her belly and started forward. Slowly, so as not to frighten whatever lingered within the depths.

Nearby, the ancient sails were flapping in the currents. She could use them as some kind of bag to carry all the gold. It would be a long and arduous journey with so much weight, but it would only need to be one trip. Gritting her teeth, she tugged the fabric free from the confines of dirt and muck. Though it was only a small piece, it would do.

Saoirse hesitated. Fear made her stomach clench, nearly doubling her over with pain.

She rushed forward and thrust handfuls of coins to the center of the sail. She would tie it later, but for now, she needed to rush. A sense of urgency pressed down upon her shoulder, digging into the base of her skull.

"A little one has come to visit?" The voice drifted out of the ragged remains of the ship. "A merrow, perhaps?"

Saoirse froze with her hands on the wealth spilling to the sea floor. Her eyes locked on the shadows moving in the ship. Could it be coiled tentacles? There wasn't a creature with a shape like that, not one that she knew of. Was this some beast even the faeries had forgotten long ago?

Glowing yellow eyes blinked open, then another set, until a horde of yellow eyes stared at her through the writhing darkness. Thick, ropey bodies twisted in a mass. The eels were knotted around each other, clustered so tightly together Saoirse couldn't tell where one started, and where one began.

"Will you not respond?" The voice asked. "I so love a pretty little merrow's voice."

She shivered. "I only speak to those I can see. Who are you?"

"*What am I,* is your real question. Is it not?"

"Few creatures could exist at such depths. I am curious as to what you might be, but I mean no disrespect."

"Move, my lovelies."

The eels undulated in agitation, shifting and snapping their jaws until they parted in the middle like a curtain. Saoirse still couldn't see through the shadows, but she knew something lurked there. Something stared at her through the black mire.

A pale white hand emerged. It clasped the back of a thick eel and flexed. Sharp bones pushed at the thin skin, standing out in stark relief. The creature pulled itself from its home within the nest of eels, revealing long white hair and an emaciated body which was vaguely human although far too thin to boast of such beginnings.

It crawled over the thick eel bodies, grunting as it slid to the sea floor and pushed up onto its arms.

Saoirse had heard of such creatures, although only in legend. The bean sídhes stayed on land. They wailed a warning to all hunted by death. Their haunting cries could be heard in the early light of morning, or the sudden darkness and despair of night.

They were not meant to drown. They couldn't die, not really, but they could rot at the bottom of the ocean for all eternity if they were banished there.

Whatever this woman had done must have been a terrible and grievous crime for such a punishment. And surely it was a woman, for her form might be emaciated but Saoirse could see the sagging skin where curves may once have been.

Clawed hands sank into the muck that squished through the skeletal fingers. "Why have you come here?"

"I wish only to share in your wealth, honored maiden." Saoirse bent at the waist in a bow few merrows could hold.

"My wealth? What use does a merrow have for such a thing?" The bean sídhe pushed herself up onto hands and knees, then stood. She was tall and lithe, perhaps a beauty when she was on land.

"I have a lover, a human who desires to live in comfort."

"Humans are a waste of space. They drove us from our lands, turned us into little more than animals who feast upon their scraps."

"He is not like the others," Saoirse said, twisting her fingers together.

"They're all the same, child." The bean sídhe leveled her with a chastising look. "Don't blind yourself to their flaws."

"I love him," Saoirse blurted. "With all that I am."

"Love? Love is a figment of our imaginations, you know faeries cannot love."

"I think we can. I think we've been told for so long that such a blessing is only for the humans, and we've forgotten it's possible. It's so strong, I feel it in my fingers." She held out her hands as if they might glow from the powerful emotion bursting at her seams. "He is everything."

The bean sídhe tsked. The sound floated in a bubble from her mouth and burst in an echoing call. "I've seen faeries like you before. The stories never end well."

Curiosity dug into the base of Saoirse's skull. She hesitated, her fingers curling in the gold, and finally murmured, "What happened to them?"

A smile curled across the bean sídhe's face. It was raw, ragged, and filled with so much hunger that Saoirse flinched back.

"They died," the faerie replied. "They tied themselves to a human whose life would end someday. You know they only live fifty or so years? A hundred if you're lucky, but those are rare cases. Humans are fragile creatures. One moment they're with you, and then?" The bean sídhe snapped her fingers. "Gone, like a candle snuffed by a careless hand."

"The faeries died?" Saoirse asked. "How is that possible? Surely, they could have returned to their homes, back to where they came from. Did their families shun them?"

"Oh, you're so sweet." An eel untangled itself from the others and draped itself across the bean sídhe's shoulders. "They died of a broken heart, my dear. Faeries love with their entire being, and you said it yourself. He's part of you now, a light that drives you forward. What did you think would happen when he dies?"

She hadn't thought about it. Manus always vibrated with life why would death come for him? But it would, someday.

Saoirse felt like a fool. She should have realized he would die, and the repercussions of that. By falling in love with a human, she had cut her own life short.

The bean sídhe let out a shrieking laugh. "You didn't know? Or you hadn't thought what that truly entailed? Little merrow, you must be the most foolish of creatures to bind yourself to one with limited time."

"No," Saoirse said and shook her head. "I will not regret my decision. I love him, and life without love is meaningless. I would take a short life with him than a long life alone."

The other faerie spun so her back was turned towards Saoirse. Her spine was straight, long white hair floating around her and crackling with electricity. An eel slid around her arm and stared back at Saoirse with a cold gaze.

"I—" Saoirse cleared her throat. "I didn't mean to offend, maiden."

"You did."

"I am frequently careless with my words. I should learn to think before I speak."

"You should." The bean sídhe held up a hand, her shoulders oddly stiff and her body unmoving. "Take what you want and go."

Saoirse tied up the sail and stuffed it to the brim. She hefted the bag over her shoulder, grunting at the weight but not wanting to give the bean sídhe time to change her mind.

"Thank you," she quietly said.

"You are a cursed faerie," the bean sídhe replied. "Your human has a soul, you know. I've seen them. White, ephemeral things that drift through our world for all eternity. But you?"

Saoirse found herself caught in a gaze as black as the deepest abyss. The bean sídhe glowed, her hair emitting a light that illuminated the ship and all its shadows. Thousands of eels twisted and turned, their sharp teeth gnashing and tails whipping.

The bean sídhe bared her own teeth as pointed as the eels. "You have no soul because you are one of the Fae. When you die, you will turn into sea foam in a final death no one can save you from. Remember that when you return to your warm bed."

Emotions she couldn't name rushing through her, Saoirse fled from the cursed shipwreck. The bean sídhe was a cruel creature, lonely and tired after so many years of banishment. Her words were meant to bite and harm.

Unfortunately, they succeeded.

Saoirse felt niggling worms of doubt sinking into her flesh and through her resolve. They punctured holes in the future she had seen for herself until it unraveled like a threadbare sheet.

Death? She'd never even considered it. Fae didn't worry about dying. They were as good as immortal although they could be killed in war. Merrows had very few natural predators and could live thousands of years. She'd known some that seemed as old as the ocean.

She shuddered. Manus would age, it was what humans did. They grew weaker and tired as death slowly sucked away what little life they had.

In bonding with him, she'd given herself the same fate. She would age, she would grow tired, and she would feel hunger so painful it made her entire body hurt.

The physical toll of carrying the heavy bag of gold sent electric pangs skittering from her abdomen to the top of her skull. Unthinking, she grabbed the nearest fish and tore the soft flesh from its side with her teeth. It stopped struggling immediately, part trauma and part weak thrum of death.

She couldn't stop eating it, tearing away until the fish was little more than bones. Only then did the reality set it. She'd killed it and lie bled out from between her fingers.

Someday, she would meet another creature who could kill her. Be that a bean sídhe wailing in the night, the Morrighan herself, or a careless human. No matter what it was, someday she would fade.

"No soul?" she whispered into the murk of the ocean.

Did she really not have a soul? She felt very similar to humans, always had, so certainly there was something? She was a faerie capable of love. That had to count for the god the humans prayed to.

Her meal fueled her muscles and helped propel her to the surface. The sail dug into her shoulder, leaving red welts that might take days to heal. Saoirse gritted her teeth and found Manus's small boat.

It was vaguely where she'd left it, having shifted with the

waves and drifted on the currents. The outline was as dark as the shadows in the depths, but somehow filled with a life she could see through the wood.

He leaned over the edge, strong hands grasping the rim of the boat as he tried to peer through the water to find her.

All at once, everything was all right. Her fears abated in the wake of love so powerful it burned her lungs and made her gills flare wide.

It was worth it, losing immortality and the inevitable fear of what might come. It was entirely worth it to know he existed and to feel this tingling emotion of love so vibrant and pure.

Air kissed her cheeks as she surfaced, and sunlight danced across her forehead. Saoirse blew out air to seal the gills flat to her neck. She grunted, lifted an arm, and hooked it over the edge of the boat.

"Manus," she called out. "Come and take this, please."

"Saoirse?"

His beloved face leaned over the side, staring down at her with an expression she couldn't name.

"It's heavy." She lifted a shoulder to show the makeshift pack. "Take it, I think I got more than enough."

He hefted the weight up and off her, shoving it into the center of the ship before leaning down for her.

"Come here," he murmured. "I've got you."

Manus slid his hands underneath her arms and effortlessly pulled her into the boat. His biceps flexed, sunlight bouncing off his caramel colored skin. But it was the warmth she saw in his eyes that made her sigh in happiness.

"Wait," she said. "Hold me on the edge please."

"Why?"

"My tail, it needs to slide off and if we're in the boat, I'm not sure we'll get it out." The mucus wasn't pleasant on the best of days. She couldn't imagine trying to pick it out of the boards.

"Ah," he mumbled.

His arms slide underneath hers and he nudged her backward so she could lean against his chest. He rested his chin against her shoulder while they watched the sun rise.

"Manus?" she asked.

"What is it, my pearl?"

"I'm glad I'm here."

He hadn't asked her if there was danger under the waves. He must have felt her trembling, seen the raw fear in her gaze, understood she didn't wish to give the terrors a voice. Instead, he held her safe and quiet against his heart.

"I'm glad too."

"And someday…" She inhaled a deep salty breath. "Someday, when we're both old and tired, I will look back on this moment and know that above all else, I made the right decision to choose you."

He squeezed her waist, a man of few words and even fewer emotions. But he understood her. She was certain of it.

"Good," his baritone vibrated in her ear. "Because I'm going to treat you like a queen."

"Where are we again?" Saoirse asked.

She stared up the tall building and tried not to be afraid of the gargoyles standing at attention. The stone steps felt strange against her bare feet. Manus had argued she needed shoes, but no one could see her feet anyways. The dress he poured over her head this morning was so long it brushed the ground. Would someone be lifting her gown to check?

He grumbled but allowed her the freedom to walk barefoot as she desired.

"This is the O'Sullivan manor. They're an old family in these parts, have been in the area for centuries."

"And what are we asking them to do?"

"He manages a bank. They'll be able to help us keep all these riches safe."

"Will he?" Saoirse looked up at Manus. She felt his nerves running through her like the rising tide. "You don't seem as confident as I thought you might be."

"O'Sullivan does not particularly like me."

"Why?"

A red blush stained Manus's cheeks. "I slept with his wife."

"I don't see why sleeping would be an issue." At his pointed expression, she nodded. "Ah. Not that kind of sleeping."

"Most men do not appreciate meeting others who know their wife as intimately as they do."

"Would you like it if another man knew me in such a way?"

He froze with his hand lifted to the door. His brows drew down, his spine straightened, and a ripple of tension spread up his spine into his shoulders. Saoirse watched in fascination as his raised hand curled into a fist and the knuckles turned white.

"I'd kill any man who touched you like that."

"Do you think he feels the same?" She radiated innocence, blinking up at him with large dark eyes.

Saoirse knew what she was doing. Manus thought poorly of people immediately upon meeting them. He could be cruel at times, unthinking in his endless judgment. She softened him with a mere word or comparison.

Manus shook his head. "I don't think O'Sullivan has ever been the killing type. It would get his hands dirty, and he's far too delicate for that."

He pounded on the door three times and took a few steps back.

Saoirse wasn't certain why Manus was so nervous. His fingers tapped against his pant legs and he looked uncomfortable in the tight black suit that hardly fit his broad frame. Her own yellow dress was too tight at the waist and made breathing difficult. Yet, for some strange reason she couldn't understand, he insisted they dress this way.

It made little sense. Why would they willingly wear clothes they didn't like? Why couldn't they be comfortable, like everyone else?

But this was the way of humans, and yet another thing she would need to learn.

The door cracked open and a pinched face appeared. The man stared at them for a few seconds before slowly closing the door.

Manus leaped forward and stuck his foot in the way. "I'm here to see O'Sullivan."

"The master isn't taking any visitors."

"He'll want to speak with me."

"I don't think so, sir. Do you have an appointment?"

Growling, Manus set his shoulder against the sturdy door and shoved hard. Saoirse could hear the man stumble back, strike a solid object, and curse.

"You have no right to force your way into this house—"

"I do when it's O'Sullivan. Tell him I'm here."

"Manus," she chastised, although it was likely too late. The man had already stiffened his spine, sniffed disdainfully, and disappeared around the corner. "Perhaps we might have been a little kinder in our treatment of the poor man?"

"He works for O'Sullivan, he gets worse than that on a daily basis."

"Are you certain? He appeared quite frightened, and I have no wish to harm anyone."

Manus stroked her jaw with a finger. "Let me deal with this, my pearl. These are my people, not yours, and I know how they work. Come with me."

"Where?"

He did not answer. Instead, Manus took her hand and laid it on his forearm. Together, they walked down the narrow hall into a wide room with seating arranged around it. Saoirse stared all around her at the bright splashes of color, the ornately carved chairs, and a large contraption in the back with what looked like wings held down by cords.

A thick carpet cushioned her feet. The pattern was one she did not recognize. Orange, red, yellow, it was a garishly colored piece but one that made the room slightly more welcoming.

"What is that?" She asked, pointing to the strange beast in the corner.

"It's a harp. We play music on it."

"I've seen them before, at the bottom of the sea. The ties were always broken though."

"Strings."

"Hmm?" Saoirse looked up at him with a question in her gaze.

"They're not called ties, they're called strings. You may touch it if you'd like."

"I couldn't. It's not mine." But she desperately wanted to. Her fingers already tingled at the thought. What would it sound like? Deep and sad like whale song? Or high pitched and chattering like that of a dolphin's laughter?

"We're guests here. Besides, we have enough money to replace it if you break it."

She wanted to shake her head, to proclaim she was mature enough to wait until the master of the house gave her permission, but the strings gleamed in the light and the gold curved spine called her like the whisper of a siren. Her fingers tingled until she finally relented.

Saoirse glided across the floor and rounded the harp. She reached out a tentative finger and plucked a string.

The most wholesome tone echoed from the instrument, filling the room with a sound like the beating of butterfly wings. Saoirse's eyes widened, and her soul took flight along with the stunning sound. It made her chest hurt and expand all at the same time.

"You like it?" Manus asked.

She looked up and caught the reverent expression on his face. He stared at her as if she were made of magic. Perhaps she was because she reached out to make the sound again and felt like a goddess.

Settling onto the stool behind her, she scooted as close to the harp as she could. Experimenting with music like this was a rare treat, and one she would consider a gift. Saoirse intended to use every moment to her benefit.

Her fingers danced across the strings, plucking each to create different songs, both tremulous and grand. Once she understood the sounds this strange beast made, she knew how to replicate the music in her mind. She played a merrow lullaby, a whale song, a wail of a sobbing mother, and the sigh of a new bride. The strings hummed against her fingers, urging her to continue.

Finally, she paused. There was still music left inside her, but it didn't want to be released. Not yet. It waited to learn from still silence before creating something anew.

A robust voice broke through the calm. "Bravo! Magnificent, my dear girl."

Her head snapped up so quickly she felt her neck crack. A man stood in the doorway, so large he filled the entire space. His belly stuck out far in front of him and strained the buttons keeping his shirt closed. Strange curled hair graced his upper lip, nearly touching the prominent brows that wisped towards his forehead.

He stepped into the room and Saoirse stared at his oddly thin legs. They weren't proportionate to his body, she mused. Perhaps he was a faerie as well, for he shouldn't be able to remain upright with all his weight in his shoulders and belly.

Saoirse stood, holding herself steady on the harp and swallowing hard. She wanted to apologize but couldn't make the words cross her lips. The music had been so lovely, possibly the most incredible thing she'd experienced thus far on land. She couldn't apologize for finding it.

O'Sullivan flapped a surprisingly small hand in her

direction. "Please, my dear, sit back down. Such talent should be rewarded. Manus, I was prepared to throw you out until I discovered this marvelous creature you brought me."

She swallowed and glanced over at Manus, who was clearly having difficulty holding himself together.

"I doubt you could throw me out if you tried, O'Sullivan."

"Is that so? It's been a long time since we rubbed elbows, Manus, but I'm not a poor man anymore. Have you arrived for my wife?" O'Sullivan stared at Saoirse with an angry look in his eyes that made her shiver. "The trade may be agreeable."

"Don't look at her."

"Why not? You couldn't possibly have a claim on such a beauty. She'd have to be mad to waste her time with the likes of you."

Saoirse didn't like the direction of this conversation. Clearing her throat, she made her way around the harp and stood beside Manus.

"Lord O'Sullivan, is it?" she asked.

"You're a sweet thing. I'm no Lord, my dear, but I appreciate the compliment."

Saoirse dipped into a curtsy, as Manus had taught her, and held her breath. He had explained women rarely spoke unless they were spoken to. It was a concept she was familiar with.

Merrow men were like this man with the strange facial hair. They blew up as soon as another male got near them. They wanted to be the biggest, the strongest, the most fearsome male in the ocean no matter what the other looked like.

She could deal with this. This was someone she finally understood and recognized.

"Thank you for excusing our rude entrance to your home,"

she said in tones dripping honey. "The splendor of this manor is surely enough to grant you the title of Lord."

O'Sullivan chuckled. "Where did you find this little actress, Manus? She's impressively astute. Rise, my dear. Your ploy has reminded me to be a gentleman, for which I thank you."

She rose from her curtsy and focused a bright smile upon the man. "Thank you. And if it pleases you, I should greatly like to address you as my husband does."

The wispy eyebrows lifted to his hairline. "Husband? Good God, what have you done?"

Manus grunted. "Is it so hard to imagine?"

"Frankly, yes. I never thought you'd subject a woman to your company for the rest of her life, let alone one so exquisite. What have you done to the poor girl?"

"Nothing!"

"Are you so certain? No woman in her right mind would agree to live with you—"

Saoirse leapt forward and placed her hand on O'Sullivan's forearm. "Please, pardon my forwardness; I would thoroughly enjoy a tour of your home, O'Sullivan. I have heard many tales of its splendorous attention to detail and would very much like to see it for myself. Was it you who designed such a lovely home?"

He sputtered, mouth gaping open as he tried to respond to her. "I-Well- No my dear, we hired a team of artisans to come and build the entire structure."

"Certainly, you had some say. I can see a man of your intelligence in every piece of this building!"

"Can you?" His mustache twitched.

"Absolutely. And I would love to meet the woman who has

captured your heart. Shall we walk and meet her? You can tell me about all the intricacies of this building on the way."

"Manus?" O'Sullivan glanced over her head. "Either she's an incredible actress, or you've caught yourself an angel. Regardless, I find I'm rather unsettled."

"She does that to people."

"Come on, my dear," he said and patted her hand on his arm. "I'll take you through the house and we can meet my wife. I'm uncertain she'll like to see your husband again, but it appears there are topics the men must discuss."

She smiled. "Thank you, O'Sullivan."

"Don't thank me yet. I haven't agreed to whatever request your fool of a husband is about to make."

O'Sullivan guided them through his home, stopping here and there to declare he had assisted in some architecture, he'd designed the parlor, and whatever else he could take credit for. She knew he was trying to impress her, and frankly he did.

She laughed all the way to the small seating room. It was easy to pretend to be this person, the one that cooed at men and calmed their worries. She hated every moment of it.

The banker's wife was a quiet woman, unassuming, with a smile on her face that looked like it might shatter any second. She sat on the couch with a teacup in her hand and trembling hands that clacked the cup against the saucer.

"Husband?"

O'Sullivan waved a hand in the air. "Yes, dear, I am fully aware Manus is here."

"Who is on your arm?"

"His wife." He brought Saoirse forward and gestured for

her to take a seat next to his wife. "This is Deirdre, my beloved wife."

"It's lovely to meet you, mistress."

"Decidedly forward, isn't she?" Deirdre glanced at her husband for a moment, and then her eyes turned towards Manus.

Saoirse didn't like the way the other woman's eyes widened in appreciation. Jealousy burned in her chest. This woman had known Manus intimately. In the ways he would kill another man for knowing her.

Why hadn't he thought she might want to kill the woman seated beside her?

Manus followed O'Sullivan to the other side of the room and took the offered glass of amber liquid. Deirdre did not take her eyes off the men.

Saoirse cleared her throat. "I understand you are married to O'Sullivan?"

"The correct way to refer to him is Mister O'Sullivan."

"Ah."

Deidre turned to her with a fiery gaze. "Why are you here?"

"We needed to speak to your husband about a business venture." She repeated what Manus had told her although she didn't understand what it meant. "We believe Mister O'Sullivan might assist us with an investment."

"Manus has no claim to fortune, it was one of his better attributes."

"He does now."

An exclamation from the other side of the room interrupted them. O'Sullivan set his drink on a warm wooden desk and shouted, "What? You have how much?"

"Keep your voice down, man. There are ladies in the room."

"Where did you get that? I'm not helping you on some get rich scheme where you robbed some poor man blind. Or heaven's forbid, did you *kill* someone for that money?"

"I killed no one, O'Sullivan."

"Then where? You didn't get it riding a ship into the horizon, I'll tell you that. No ships have returned with a cargo that large."

A muscle bounced on his jaw as Manus silently pointed towards Saoirse.

All eyes turned to her. Her cheeks heated in embarrassment, but there wasn't anything she could add. This was the plan. She was the heiress to an immense fortune, one whose father had long ago died and needed a man to marry regardless of his station. She'd added that they'd fallen in love with each other, and Manus agreed.

O'Sullivan cleared his throat. "You? You're the one with the money."

"She's an heiress," Manus explained. "It's old family money, and we obviously can't bury it behind the shack. I must put it somewhere safe, and I'd like to buy a house befitting someone of our station."

"Your station?" O'Sullivan scratched the back of his neck. "You'll have to forgive me, but I cannot reconcile the foolish young want-to-be sailor with a man of wealth and stature."

"Get used to it, old man."

Saoirse stood. "Manus, please. These people have let us

into their house and have been perfectly hospitable."

"He's insulting both of us."

"Then let him insult. His words cannot harm us, and I'd much rather he help." She clasped her hands to her chest. "Mister O'Sullivan, any assistance would be greatly appreciated by both of us, no matter what my husband says."

"You want a house and a safe place for your riches," O'Sullivan grunted. "I never thought the day would come."

"Then you'll help us?" Manus asked.

"I'm not pleased about it, but there are a few properties for sale in the area. We could speak to the curators. I'll have to vouch for you."

"And will you?"

Saoirse held her breath, terrified that this man and his wife would turn them down. There were other options, but Manus said O'Sullivan was the most trustworthy. He was a good man at his core.

She heard Deirdre huff out a quiet, sullen breath.

Hands curling into fists, Saoirse reminded herself that she was not human. Merrows did not stoop to the level of human women. She had endured storms, shark attacks, the pawing of merrow men. She could endure the disdain of a woman who had once touched Manus.

Still, every fiber of her being wanted to slash at Deirdre with gnashing teeth and nails.

O'Sullivan nodded. "All right. I'll help you. I want to see where this story goes between the two of you. That's my condition. You stay in touch, Manus."

"Understood."

They clasped forearms, and Saoirse felt a knot unravel in her chest. This was what he wanted, what they both wanted. A normal human life.

Together.

Manus gestured all around, a smile on his face like she'd never seen before. "Well? What do you think? Is it everything you ever dreamed of?"

Saoirse glanced at the gold and white interior. She hadn't ever dreamed of a home, let alone one that made her eyes water. It was too bright. The surfaces were too reflective. Everything about the house was just too much.

But how could she ruin his happiness? Manus loved this home, so much that he already invited people to a dinner party. She didn't even know what a dinner party was.

"It's quite beautiful."

"Beautiful? There are better words that than Saoirse! Magnificent! A feast for the eyes!" He flung his arms out and laughed. "And it's ours. You made this happen, my pearl. I cannot thank you enough."

She made nothing happen. She had stolen from a bean sídhe who didn't need the money any more than they did. Guilt ate at her belly, taking large chunks with each inhale.

"Manus, I think I'd like to go lie down."

"Wait, hold on." He grabbed her arms and held her at arm's length. "I didn't tell you we've hired staff."

"Staff?" Saoirse wrinkled her brows. "What do you mean?"

"People who will work for us. They'll clean the house, manage the gardens, the grounds, everything we need. They'll do it all."

He sounded so excited.

She sighed. "Why do we need people to do all that? We can manage on our own. We have thus far."

"It's not how things are done. I know this is confusing for you, and likely overwhelming. You'll get used to it. I promise." He kissed her forehead, lingering for a few moments. "Now, go on. There's a maid waiting in your room. She'll help you get dressed."

"I want to get *undressed*."

"That's something *I* can help you with." A wolfish grin spread across his face.

"Manus."

"You're right, I have too much to do for such distractions. Go upstairs, I'll see you later tonight."

He spun on his heel and walked out the front door, whistling a jaunty tune.

Saoirse wished she was as happy. The large house felt so empty. The rooms echoed with her steps, so much that she stayed barefoot just for the silence. Statues lined the halls, staring at her with disappointed expressions and vacant eyes.

Now there were more people here? More strangers to wonder where she came from, to pry into her past. She couldn't keep twisting her words and smiling while Manus explained where she came from. Eventually someone would catch her alone, and she wouldn't be able to lie.

Troubled, she made her way up the grand staircase and down the long hallway towards her rooms. She had insisted she only needed one room. Apparently, that was also not done.

Even the doors were different here. Hers had tiny bluebells carved all around it, hand painted and laid with gold leaves.

She paused in front of it and shook her head. It was all too much.

The door opened to reveal another person standing behind it. Saoirse shrieked in surprise, and the other woman let out a gasp, dropping all the clothes in her arms.

"My lady!"

"Who are you?"

The woman ran a hand over her blonde hair and smoothed down her pale dress. "I'm your lady's maid. I thought the master might have told you?"

"Master?"

Saoirse shook her head. Everything was changing, and she didn't know how to feel about it.

The maid blushed. "I'm sorry, did he not inform you I would be here?"

"No, he informed me. I'm just not used to having a lady's maid."

"I can't imagine why not? If the tales are true, you're some far off princess. It's an honor to be waiting on you, my lady."

Princess? Was that what he was telling people now? How was she even meant to respond to that?

Saoirse shook her head and made her way towards the bed. "I would like to rest."

"Of course. Here, allow me to turn down the covers for you. It's rather chilly outside, I can run the coals through the sheets to warm them."

"Please don't. I'll be fine on my own."

"That's what I was hired to do, my lady. Here, let me help with your dress—"

Saoirse couldn't handle this. She couldn't allow another woman to wait on her hand and foot, not while she still had perfectly good hands. "Please. That's enough."

The maid bobbed into a quick curtsy and turned to leave. She hesitated and said, "I appreciate you and Manus hiring me out of the whorehouse. There are some places where the women are treated well, but that was not one of them. This gives me a fresh start."

She disappeared out the door, running as if the Wild Hunt chased her.

Saoirse sank onto the bed. Her bones ached, her heart squeezed, and she felt as though she were ancient. This wasn't the life she had expected. And although there were moments of blooming happiness, there was also a constant river of anguish.

Falling onto her back, she sighed.

This was what her life was supposed to be like, or at least, what her human life should be. She had money, she had a home, she had a doting husband. What more could she want?

All she could think of was a tiny isle with white sand.

CHAPTER 9

Pretending to be Human

Saoirse hovered in the back of the room, clutching a wine glass close to her chest. There were so *many* people in their home.

Teems of men and women had shown up at the announcement new money had arrived. Already she'd been told their cliff side home was the beloved summer house of a renowned Baron. When his wife had died, he sold the entire plot when his grief grew too powerful for him to survive.

They were saddened by the passing of the Baron and thought it likely his son would wish to buy this land back. Would they be interested in selling?

She'd never met so many rude, noisy people in her life. They flooded into her home, told her how she should look, act, dress, and then swanned off as if they hadn't been insulting.

Finally, Saoirse gave up. She tucked herself into a corner with a glass of port and silently nodded at anyone who tried to speak with her. Let them think she was an uncouth princess, they wouldn't dare start any rumors.

They still thought she was royalty. And apparently that

meant more than the quality of her character.

Manus was on the other side of the room talking to a tall man with billowing white hair. They gestured wildly, laughing and swinging their drinks in all directions. It was going well, so it seemed, although Saoirse had no idea who the man was.

She didn't know any of these people, yet she was expected to admit them into her life without complaint.

The port swirled on her tongue, coating her mouth with a heady flavor that calmed her nerves.

"I thought I might find you here." The voice was warm, too forward for any of these strange people who had walked into her life.

She swallowed and glanced up at the tall, red headed man standing beside her. "I didn't think to find *you* here."

"Is it so surprising?" He grinned. "I am, after all, a prince."

He had more of a calling to the title than she did. Declan was dressed as a man of his stature should dress. Tight fitting waistcloth, pale doeskin breeches, a black jacket that barely contained the broad span of his shoulders. Even in the clothes of a noble, he looked more wild animal than most.

"So," she began, "you masquerade as a noble here on earth? Isn't that beside the point?"

"What point?"

"I assume you were sent here to learn a small bit of humility. How are you supposed to learn that if you are still spoiled?"

"I observe them. Humans are a fascinating lot and are so easy to read."

She stared into the crowd filled with swirling colors, wondering just what he saw. Too many of these peoples wore masks instead of faces. They said one thing, but clearly meant another. They whispered behind their fans, pointedly staring at her but refused to explain what captured their attentions.

"I don't know if I agree with you," Saoirse replied. "They seem to hide their true selves, even from those they love. Humans are difficult to understand."

"It gets easier the longer you're among them."

"Does it? I can't imagine understanding them. I prefer our ways."

The feral grin spreading across his face sent a shiver down her spine. Warning bells rang loud and clear. He wasn't one to be trusted, no matter that his glamour was a handsome man. Leprechauns were Unseelie.

She reminded herself not to tempt him. This was the perfect place for an Unseelie to go wild and Manus would be so angry with her.

Declan lifted a hand for her to take. "You have to learn their cues. Human emotions are easily read by the way they use their body, unlike the Fae who are still waters."

"Are you going to teach me?"

"I thought you'd never ask."

She set her glass on a table next to them. "How?"

"We're going to dance."

Dance? She didn't see how that was going to help anything. But she wanted to understand them all, not just Manus. She reached out and placed her gloved hand in his.

Immediately, Declan turned hers over and plucked at the white fabric, pulling it slowly off her hand finger by finger.

"What are you doing?" she gasped. "Manus said it is not appropriate for a woman to be bare handed."

"Precisely. We see their true colors when we challenge their ideals of what is appropriate. Look around us, Saoirse. No, not like that. Don't gape at people as if you don't know what I'm doing, someone will interrupt us. Under your lashes, so no one knows you're even looking at them. Good. Now, how are people reacting?"

She let out a slow breath. "The ladies nearest to us are bright red and holding their fans up so they can talk behind them."

"Are they wildly beating the fans or are they holding them still?"

"Still."

"Good," he said, and finished up removing the first glove. He tucked it into the breast pocket of his jacket and held out his hand for the other. "What of the men?"

"They're watching you rather intently but are not moving."

"And Manus?"

She had to lift her head to find him. Her stomach clenched. "He's still talking to the white-haired man. He hasn't noticed."

Declan pulled off her other glove with a flourish and tucked it away. "Let me summarize for you then. The women wish they were you right now. Their fans are still because they're whispering how scandalous it is that an unmarried man would dare to touch a married woman like this. The men are remaining still because they too are jealous. They have watched you the entire night and thought of doing the same."

"Are you sure?" Saoirse shook her head. "I don't think they care I exist other than as something new to watch."

"That's where you're wrong. And I can prove it to you."

"You can?" She met his heated gaze. "How?"

Declan did not respond. Instead, he peeled off his own gloves with a flourish and held out a bare hand for her to take.

"I couldn't. It's not right."

"You and I are creatures from another world, Saoirse. They can't understand this, nor could they ever understand our connection. We can bend to their ways, or we can show them how faeries dance."

She could already see the imagined anger on Manus's face. Dancing with another man was likely forbidden as well. But Declan sang a siren song she desperately wanted to follow.

Perhaps that was why she felt so out of place. Saoirse was not human. Faeries wouldn't have lied, whispered, and giggled behind fans. They would have had sharpened blades at the ready, perhaps, but at least she would have known their true opinions.

Saoirse reached out and placed her hand atop his.

Warm skin, as smooth as her own, heated her flesh. Declan pulled her onto the dance floor with their hands raised high.

The fans began to flutter, and the men set down their drinks. No one moved yet, but it was painfully obvious the entire crowd held their breath in anticipation. The music played on, the other dancers took their places, and Declan's grin remained in place.

"You knew this would make them unhappy," she muttered.

"Of course I did. Parties like this can only be improved through a little uncomfortable social interaction."

"I have no wish to create waves. Especially not when this night and these people mean something to Manus."

"Manus?" Declan stepped forward as the music started,

raising his hand for her to take. "You mean your husband?"

"I don't think there's another Manus in the room."

"Ah, my apologies. I had forgotten he was here."

The words stung. She didn't need to be reminded that her husband had yet to even notice his wife was in the arms of another man. Every turn about the room provided glimpses proving he wasn't looking at her.

"Don't let it bother you too much, love," Declan said. "Human males are so easily distracted."

"And faerie men aren't?"

"I can't say we're perfect, but we certainly know when to pay attention to our mates."

She sighed. "I wish I could agree with you. Merrow men are not fantastic at anything related to their mates."

"Merrow men are barely Fae."

"I think they would disagree with you."

They rounded the line of people, breaking away from each other to new partners for a brief moment. She lifted her hand for a tall, thin man to take, who immediately froze. Bare handed and waiting, she realized he didn't know what to do.

"It's all right," she said, and moved past him into Declan's arms.

"Do you think they know we're different?" He mused. "There has to be a part of their tiny brains that recognizes a predator amongst them."

"Predator? That's a strange way to think of yourself."

"You disagree?"

"I think they would be frightened of anything different. You flatter yourself to think it is because of our species. They don't understand us. If we were human, they would have the same reaction."

"Interesting." His brows furrowed in confusion. "I've never considered that possibility."

"And yet, you proclaim to be talented in reading them."

"Reading them and knowing them are different things, little merrow. Although I'm certain you'll find that out soon enough."

The music stopped, and the partners stepped away from each other. While all others politely clapped, Declan kept ahold of her hand. He forced her to remain close to his side.

"We're done here," she said. "I have nothing else to say to you. Thank you for the distraction, but I don't intend to cause any further scenes."

"You'd rather waste away here pretending to be something you are not?"

"I'm not pretending at all, Declan. This is who I am and always will be. Where I live does not change that."

A gentleman stepped forward, holding his hand against his chest. "My lady, are you quite well?"

"Yes, thank you."

Declan released her hand and took a step back. "Have a lovely evening, my lady."

He strode away without a care in the world. Saoirse wished she felt the same. So many people were staring at her now. She could almost hear their whispered thoughts.

Holding her head high, she moved through the crowd to Manus's side. People parted like a wave before her. None of them said a word, no one tried to catch her attention. They all wondered who she was, this strange creature who was far too beautiful to be likeable. Saoirse was someone they could never understand.

Perhaps Declan was right, in a way. She was trying to fit in, but they weren't likely to ever accept her. They would always sense the faerie in her blood.

She stood beside Manus who did not stop speaking.

"You see, it'll be a good investment for the both of us. The ship will be magnificent, far more profitable than either of us could ever dream. I know the seas—"

"Manus."

"They listen to me. They always have, and if I were captaining your ship, I would take that into consideration. Too many ships are lost because their captain doesn't respect the ocean's power."

"Manus."

The white-haired man nodded at her. "My lady, I'm afraid we have not yet met."

"No."

Manus looked down at her, surprise in his gaze. "Saoirse! I apologize, my pearl, I had forgotten you do not know many people here. May I introduce you to Captain Ramsey?"

She was tired of meeting new people. They were all the same, mistrustful and too curious. Still, she squared her shoulders and forced a smile. "Ramsey is not a name I recognize. I take it you are not from here?"

"My family is from here, but I was raised in the Caribbean."

A warm flood of emotions crashed over her head. Excitedly, she leaned forward and said, "I miss the Caribbean very much. It is a stunning place, and the waters are crystal clear."

The captain lifted his eyebrows. "You've been? I would

have taken you as a princess from a much closer province, considering your complexion."

She had said something wrong. He stared at her with suspicious eyes, and Manus rocked back and forth on his feet. But what had she said wrong?

Saoirse glanced up at her husband for clues. When he didn't look down at her, she cleared her throat. "I have traveled all over the world. Although it was not my father's preference that I do so, I believe it important to understand other cultures and beliefs."

It was bending the truth almost to the point of pain. Her tongue pricked with the hints of lies, pain reminding her how fine a line she walked.

Thankfully, the captain seemed pleased with her response.

"Here, here! I see you have married an enlightened woman, Manus. Rare in these parts."

Saoirse heard his quiet sigh of relief. "Yes, indeed. I am a lucky man to have found such a gem."

The captain made his excuses and left to find his wife. The moment he turned his back, Manus spun towards Saoirse. He crowded her through a side window onto a balcony shaded by curtains and the waning moon.

"That was close," he murmured as he backed her against the railing. "A little too close."

"I told you we'd have to worry about that."

"I don't listen well."

Saoirse rolled her eyes. "I can tell."

"Where did you learn to do that?" He touched her cheek with a hand still calloused and rough.

"What?"

"Rolling your eyes. It's not something you've ever done before, and I assume a rather human trait."

"Faeries are able to emote disgust or disapproval. We roll our eyes as well."

He cupped her face and stroked her cheek with his thumb. "I learn something new every day about you and your kind."

"Why were you talking to that captain about a ship, Manus?"

"Why were you dancing with that tall bloke we met in the bar?"

He had her there. Saoirse gaped up at him. "I didn't think you were looking?"

Gently, Manus tugged her against his chest. His hands spanned her waist and stroked the long line of her spine. "I'm always watching you, I can't help it. You looked like a real princess dancing with him. The two of you were almost otherworldly."

She couldn't lie to him. No matter how angry she was, or how much she knew he was trying to distract her, Saoirse thought he deserved to know the whole truth of her life.

"He's not human either," she corrected. "He may masquerade as one of your nobility, but I can assure you, he is not like any of you. Faerie dancing differs greatly from humans."

"I can see that." Manus brushed a strand of hair behind her ear and lowered his head. He pressed their foreheads together, sighing. "Do you regret it? Do you wish you had chosen a faerie lover and run off to the Otherworld?"

"That's a cruel thing to ask."

"Because it's true?"

"Those are two very different futures, incomparable to each other. If I had chosen a faerie, I would have married a merrow man. Even if, by some strange luck, another had fallen in love with me, it's unlikely my life would have been happy. Faeries are cold, hungry, and always desperate for more power."

His fingers stroked the back of her neck. "Then why do you still look disappointed?"

"Humans aren't what I expected. I thought your kind would be more honest, perhaps a little more adventurous. But your nobility is eerily similar to ours. The people in there wear masks instead of faces. They frighten me."

"How could they frighten you? You're a princess from another land, an heiress to a massive fortune, and *my* wife."

Manus spread his hands wide on her back, spreading warmth through her entire body. He slanted his mouth over hers and poured love into her. She tasted whiskey—vivid and stinging — on his tongue.

He pulled back for a deep breath. "Don't dance with too many men, my pearl. I don't think my heart could take it."

"Your heart?" She reached up and traced the swirls of his ears. "Or your pride?"

"Both. You are everything to me, the reason I am here, my wealth, my happiness, my glory. I don't know what I would do if I lost you, Saoirse."

It wasn't a lot, but it was enough for now. She tucked herself under his chin and breathed out a sigh of relief. He cared, she knew it, and somehow she would endure this strange life of servants, secrets hidden behind fans, and houses that moaned in the night.

"I love you." She pressed the words above his heart, willing them to sink into his form and fill his body with magic. His chest expanded, his spine straightened, and she felt a small bit of herself fill the cavity of his body.

Merrow magic was rare and weak compared to all other Fae. She could only give him confidence, health, and impress happiness into his skin like a shield against all that would tear him down.

Even if it cost her life, Saoirse would protect him from the perils of the human world.

Seagulls screamed above the dock, circling the fisheries for any scrap that might fall. The thumping crack of knives against wood tangled with the quiet slap of raw fish striking the ground. Children raced through the crowd, reaching up with quick fingers to pickpocket anyone they could find.

"Stay close to me," Manus said, threading her arm through his. "I'd rather not have to chase a small boy today."

"Are they always boys?" She watched one race through the crowd, a growling man chasing him while loudly swearing.

"The girls usually stand on street corners and beg, they're far cuter for pitying women like yourself. Or—" he hesitated before clearing his throat. "There are other opportunities for poor women, and they aren't ones we should particularly talk about."

"You always say that." Saoirse chuckled. "It's almost as if you were raised a lord, rather than a poor boy running around like this."

"That's because I was."

She froze.

Manus stumbled as she held his arm still, then glanced back. "Saoirse?"

"You never told me that you weren't always a street rat. You've joked so many times about being born on the streets that I always thought…" She shrugged. "I don't know what I thought."

"I wasn't rich or noble-born if that's what you're thinking."

He tried to continue walking, but she tugged on his arm again. "Manus, tell me! I want to know."

"We've got a ship to look over, my pearl."

"This is important. It's part of who you are, and I want to know."

A muscle in his jaw jumped, but he relented. "My mother was a kitchen maid. She wasn't well known, but one of the footmen found her pretty and then I came about. They let her stay in the house while I was a child, but when I started talking they kicked us both out. That's all."

"That's all?" Her mind raced, remembering suddenly how sure footed he was. Manus had bought their house without walking through it. He'd pointed out rooms by name, but she had assumed it was something all humans knew. She shook her head. "You grew up in the house we live in, didn't you?"

Manus licked his lips, obviously uncomfortable with the conversation. "I did."

"Is that why you wanted to buy it?"

"There's a certain amount of justice in my return. I now own the house of the man who threw my mother out onto the streets. If I could, I would have buried him in the backyard to dance upon his grave every night."

She didn't like this side of Manus. The dark edge of his tone was a blade that burned her heart. She had known their house didn't feel safe or loved. They were living in a tomb of bad memories and a past he couldn't let go.

Manus sighed. "Come on, don't put more into it. We have a lovely home, we are both happy. Let the past stay in the past, Saoirse."

"Can you?"

He said no more and dragged her down the docks towards a large ship with clean, white sails hanging limp from three masts. It was an impressive ship, a kind she had only seen once in her life. A royal ship.

Manus opened his arms wide, tossed his head back, and laughed. "Isn't she a beauty? My pearl, Ramsey didn't lie to us. This the most magnificent creation I have ever seen."

"It's beautiful and will weather many storms."

"Storms? I think it could weather a faerie sea itself!"

"I doubt that, my love. It's too small to survive a guardian's wrath." She stood beside him and smiled. "But I think it shall carry us a good distance from shore safely enough."

"Would you like to explore it?"

"I can't think of anything else I'd rather do."

She placed her hand on Manus's arm, and together they stepped onto the ship.

They spent the better part of the afternoon wandering through every nook and cranny. Manus knew ships like he knew his own hand. He pointed out small cracks which would need to be filled with sap, the fine craftsmanship of the carvings, the comfort of the captain's quarters.

This was clearly the love of his life. Saoirse watched him become more confident with every moment he was on the ship. His strides lengthened, his spine remained stiff, his eyes narrowed to catch every detail he might not have seen. He was a sight to behold.

He wrapped his arm around her shoulders at the prow of the ship. "Do you see it?"

"The ocean? It is lovely today. The waves rock us gently, for they know you wish to begin new adventures soon."

"No, not that, my pearl."

She followed the line of his raised arm to the masthead. Ships always had some kind of carved being watching over them. Saoirse had marveled at the carved whales, fish, and warriors. But this one was particularly meaningful.

A merrow lifted her arms into her hair and watched the ocean. Her tail lashed at the waves, warning the ocean to be careful with the men on board.

"Manus," Saoirse breathed. "She's beautiful."

"I asked for her," he replied. He squeezed her tighter. "If I'm going to have a ship, then I'm going to make certain that my faerie looks after me no matter where I am."

"I love it. She's beautiful."

"As are you."

Manus lifted her arm above her head, spun her in a circle, and caught her against his chest as she laughed. "I'm going to name her the *Saorsa*."

"Freedom?"

"That is what she will gift to me, to my men, to all who stand board. And all will know that the ship with the merrow woman is one who shows compassion and ensures all aboard have an equal say in their lives."

"When will they know this?"

"As soon as I hire them."

Laughter bubbled from her chest. He lifted her off her feet and swung her in circles until her head spun. Only when she shrieked did he let her touch the ground again, pulling her close and pressing his lips against her forehead.

"Thank you," he said. "You have made this possible for me, you perfect creature. There is nothing in this world gold could buy which would be a worthy reward for all you have done."

"I need nothing other than your love."

He hugged her tighter, and together they stared out to sea.

Thunder rolled in the distance, a great storm which would crash upon the shore and crackle with lightning. It rushed across the sea chased by churning waves white with foam.

The rumble vibrated through Saoirse's chest, and she smiled. Storms were rare where she came from. She could hardly hear the sounds so deep underwater, but sometimes she swam to the surface so she could listen to the powerful call. It was lovely and impossible all at the same time.

Lightning flashed and illuminated her room, causing her smile to fall. Her room, private and alone, although it was right across from Manus's. She didn't like being so far away from him, but his response was always the same. It wasn't proper for a man and woman of their station to be together in the same bedroom.

"It simply isn't done, Saoirse," he had said. "If we're going to live like this, we have to fit in."

Humans had strange customs. It made little sense they would insist upon something so ironclad as marriage, but then also require the couples to remain separate.

Her toes twitched as they often did when she was frustrated. A remnant from when her tail would flick side to side in the water, something her brother enjoyed pointing out. Saoirse was easy to read, even for humans it seemed.

She sat up in bed, her hair a wild dark tangle. It was only allowed freedom in her own bedroom. Her maids wouldn't let her outside the room without a tight braid that yanked her face back.

"The lady of the house," she grumbled as she swung her legs over the side of the bed. "Not a single one of them believes I am the lady of this house."

They thought her quaint. Otherworldly. Endearing. Not a woman who ran the household.

In truth, she would likely do a poor job of it. Gardening, cleaning, rearranging furniture, it was all far beyond her knowledge or her interests.

How did human women not die of boredom?

Restless, she padded from her bed to the doors of her balcony. Lightning struck the ocean far out to sea, but from her cliff side home she could see it as if she were standing beside it. The vivid blue light burned her eyes.

The storm was a widow maker. Black rolling clouds threatened any ship which stood in its way. Thankfully, she saw no small dark shadows, bobbing at the mercy of mother nature.

Her nightgown lashed around her legs, twisting through the twin pillars and snapping behind her. Any moment, a maid would yell at her to put her wrap on. A woman would get chilled outside, and what would the master do if his lady fell ill?

Sometimes, she wished she could tell them she was Fae. That a simple cold wasn't something she needed to worry about. Illnesses for the Fae were far different than those humans suffered.

Saoirse wrapped her arms around her waist. She hadn't felt so alone in a while. Manus was easy to be around, and he doted on her when she was near him. But lately, he was always at the ship. He wanted everything to be perfect before they went on their maiden voyage.

She understood the desire. It was the first ship he would captain, and he had coveted the title since he was a child. The sea called to him. The longer he was away from the waves, the more frantic he became.

Waves crashed against the cliff far below her, echoing out their groan. The sound slid up her spine and exploded in the base of her skull. She couldn't wait to go out on a ship even if she could only feel the water moving its solid base.

Warm hands curved over her shoulders, sliding down her arms and pulling her back against a firm chest. Goosebumps rose as his callouses scraped her sensitive skin. He wrapped them both in a blanket and rested his chin against her shoulder.

"You're still awake."

"I couldn't sleep."

He hummed in her ear. "Ah. Does the storm frighten you? I imagine you didn't get to experience many that far in the ocean."

"No, I like storms. They're beautiful in the way they release their emotions in abandon. I've met nothing like them before."

Lightning struck in the distance. Saoirse held her breath, waiting for the moment thunder would boom. The clouds lit brightly from deep inside the dark masses. It crackled and built until suddenly it released in a line that zagged all the way to the ocean.

"Of all women, I should have known you'd like the storms best." Manus held her closer, rubbing his hands up and down her arms. "Are you not cold?"

"Why does everyone ask if I'm cold?"

"Because they're cold, and we see you standing outside with barely anything on and wonder how you could stand it."

"I'm hardier than humans, so it seems. I grew up in the frigid deep. A little cold air is nothing compared to what I'm used to."

He chuckled. "I look forward to hearing your thoughts about our winters. Even the depths can't compare to snow."

A few fat drops of rain splattered on the stone balcony. Saoirse let him draw her inside though she wished to allow the water to play over her skin. She missed it.

She missed it so much her soul hurt.

Manus slid his finger under her chin, tilting her head up so she was forced to stare at him. "Stop thinking about it. You are *here*, with me, and no one will ever take you from me."

"It's hard not to think about my home."

"I am your home, now. I keep you safe and warm. I heal all your wounds and I dry your tears if they are shed." He lifted her hand and pressed her palm to his heart. "You can feel it, can't you? This is where you belong."

Saoirse spread her fingers wide, feeling the steady beat match her own. "You're still worried I might leave."

"How could I not be when you stare at the ocean as if I stole you from it?"

"This was my choice, Manus."

"And I won't ever let you forget it," he fiercely growled.

Somehow, she had frightened him. Saoirse allowed him to lift her up into his arms and carry her back to bed.

The soft down feathers cushioned her back, so soft it felt as if she were drifting atop the waves. Manus followed her down. He nudged her thighs open, settling against her with a groan that vibrated through her entire being.

"I'm not leaving you," she whispered. Lightning crackled and lit up the bedroom. It gilded the edges of his form in blue and silver while leaving his face in dark shadows.

He was a god among men, looming above her with clear intent. Saoirse couldn't have told him no even if she wanted to. He was everything she had dreamed of and more.

The golden statue of a prince was perfection personified. He was a childish dream of a future filled with fantasy and magic. Manus was real, flesh and blood, bone and marrow. His skin was warm and bent to her will no matter what she demanded of him.

He traced the line of her throat with a feather light touch. "Have I not given you enough to keep you occupied, my pearl? I bought the largest house I could find, hired maids, gardeners, horses, and still you hide in your room."

"I don't like so many people staring at me, wondering who I am and asking questions I cannot answer."

Manus dipped his head and touched his lips to the hollow behind her ear. "I forget you are so innocent. My perfect little pearl, incapable of telling even the smallest lie."

She arched into his kiss. Warmth bloomed from wherever he touched, heating her chilled skin. When had she become so cold? Did it matter? He was a furnace filled with burning passions that would set her ablaze.

His hand trailed down her throat, danced along her collarbone, and settled between her breasts where he could feel her wild heartbeat.

"You are mine," he growled in her ear. "Mine and no other's."

"I am yours."

All at once, he was everywhere and nowhere. His hands slid along her side, his teeth pulled at her ear, his hips pressed into hers. She writhed beneath him.

"Manus," she moaned.

"Say it again. Over and over until it's burned into your memory, my pearl."

"I am yours."

Lightning struck, and thunder rolled at the same time. The storm crashed through the windows, banging the glass panes against the wall. Silver light illuminated Manus in small flickers of life.

She watched each flashing moment as if she wasn't within her body as he pulled her nightgown over her head.

Manus's neck gracefully arched as he pulled a rosy bud between his teeth. The muscles of his back flexed, creating hills of smooth skin like swells of great waves. His fingers dug into the aching muscles of her spine. She bent at his request, allowing him further access to play across the dips of her body.

She pulled at his heat, at the passions so vivid she could almost see them hovering in the air. With each breath, she bound herself to him ever more tightly. The threads of their lives were so entangled they had created a labyrinth from which they would never break free.

Lightning sizzled. She tasted electricity in the air and gasped as Manus delved between her legs. The tangled strands of his hair scraped her inner thighs, but she couldn't focus on anything other than the sensations he created.

Thunder shook the house with a great boom. They could have all been on fire, and she wouldn't have noticed. Electricity flowed through her veins. It buzzed through her mind until all she could hear was the rush of waves crashing against the shore.

Manus trailed his lips up her body, pressing a warm kiss against her lips. "You are mine."

"Yours," she gasped.

He plunged into her like a man possessed. She caught the strained expression on his face in a bright flash of light. He was marking her, claiming her, forcing her to recognize that she was entirely his no matter where she was in the world.

A rumble of thunder trailed up her spine, and she cried out as lightning struck the balcony outside. The room flared bright. Her wicked pirate arched back, driving himself so deep inside Saoirse couldn't tell where one of them ended and the other began.

They cried out together, melding as only two people in love could do. Together they quaked and shuddered, battled the raging sky and shouted their release. They were creatures of passion. Even mother nature agreed tonight and mirrored the weather to the raging inferno inside their souls.

Manus branded his touch onto every inch of her body, worshiping her like a goddess and punishing her like a slave. In return, she allowed her own passions to fly free. Saoirse begged for his touch, murmured encouragement, and sighed happily when he listened.

Throughout the entire night, she wondered whether he was apologizing, convincing her to stay, or saying goodbye.

He dropped to his side and pulled her tight against him. "I want you to be happy here. You know that, don't you?"

"Of course I do." Saoirse pressed a kiss to his slick chest. "I know you want me to be happy."

His body fell lax as sleep overtook him, and she let him rest.

Saoirse didn't have the heart to tell him that no matter how much he *wanted* her to be happy, she couldn't be. Not fully. Not while the sea was out there, waiting for her, and she had made her life on land.

She tucked her head under his chin and pressed her palm against his steady heart. The beat lulled her to sleep, filled her dreams with a quiet drumbeat, and eased the ache in her chest.

Warm lips pressed against Saoirse's bare shoulder. She smiled, her half-awake mind already certain who touched her with such familiarity.

"Manus," she murmured. "Is it time to get up?"

"It's far past that time, my pearl."

She slowly rolled onto her back and opened her eyes. He was seated on the edge of her bed, dressed in soft breeches and a white linen shirt unbuttoned at the throat. He had pulled his dreadlocks back with a leather thong. Beads at the end clacked together as he shifted.

Saoirse stretched her arms over her head. "Where are we going?"

"It's a surprise."

"A surprise?" She yawned. "Manus, I don't like surprises."

He pressed a finger against her lips, eyes twinkling. "Shh, my pearl. You're going to love it. Get out of bed, your maids are waiting to dress you."

"I can get dressed by myself."

"But isn't it so much more fun to have someone else do it?" He winked at her and stood, leaving the door ajar on his way out.

Saoirse covered her face with her hands, groaning at the mere thought of getting up. She was having such lovely dreams. Waves rocking over her body, fish tangled in her hair, a powerful tail propelling her through the water…

"M'lady?"

Saoirse dropped her hands. "Good morning."

The maids bustled into the room, one to stoke the fire and the other to dress Saoirse in whatever clothing the maid picked out. It was as if Saoirse was some kind of elaborate toy. They dressed her, did her hair, powdered her face with makeup, and then set her in a corner to rot while they went on with their lives.

"The master says up, so you must get up." The bedframe shook. "You cannot stay abed all day, m'lady. Unless you are not feeling well?"

"I feel fine." She whispered, although she was exceedingly tired and wasn't certain why. She'd slept well through the night.

"I think you'd look stunning in this lovely sea green. Wouldn't you agree?"

The maid held up the dress which spilled over her arm onto the floor. It was a stunning creation, beautiful in all aspects of the word. It would make her waist look trim, keep her warm with the fur around the shoulders, and yet feminine with the stunning embroidery.

Saoirse couldn't care less.

She sighed and sat up. "Yes, that will do."

The maid tucked her hand underneath Saoirse's elbow and helped her stand. Together, they walked to her small dressing table where they began the arduous journey of placing layer after layer of fabric together.

Saoirse obediently stood still. They could do whatever they wanted with her, not because they had power over her, but because they knew more than she did. Both of the maids had to work on her hair. The long length would be hours to finish if only one person were braiding it.

They had suggested cutting it once. "Just a trim," they had said.

Saoirse's reaction had not been a kind one. They had not brought a knife to her room again.

"How do you get your hair to look like this?" One of the maid's asked. "It's so dark, but it shines almost green in the sunlight. Like whale oil."

"This is my natural hair."

"Surely not! It's not possible to have hair this color."

"I can assure you, it is."

They babbled on, chattering about things Saoirse did not care for. The maids always had something to comment on. The looks of the new gardener, the taste of dinner last night, how the butler thought he was better than everyone else.

They hadn't said a word in the beginning, but quickly realized their mistress didn't care if they spoke. As soon as they realized this, the floodgates opened. They rarely stopped to take a breath between sentences, now.

Saoirse liked it, in a strange way. Their words floated about her and burst in bright bubbles of sound. She didn't care what they said. The words meant little. It was the rhythmic sound she appreciated so much. The same sound that could lull her to sleep and ease her nerves.

"My lady?"

"Yes?"

"I think we're finished. What do you think?"

Saoirse opened her eyes and stared at the creature in the mirror. She looked anything but human. Her eyes were too slanted, her hair oddly colored, her skin milky white perfection. Still, she looked beautiful and the maids would be disappointed if she said anything else.

"You've outdone yourselves, ladies. I don't deserve your talents."

"You shouldn't be saying that to maids, but we appreciate it."

With a soft smile, Saoirse stood. "You deserve all the compliments I have and more."

She ignored the uncomfortable expressions on the maids' faces. They were strange women. Try as she might, Saoirse would never understand them.

They both dipped into curtsies. "The master said he would wait for you in the stables."

"The stables?" Saoirse sighed. "He knows I don't like to ride."

"I don't believe he was intending to ride milady. A man delivered a carriage today."

"A carriage? Don't those require a driver?"

They giggled behind their hands and slipped out the door in a rush. Likely because they didn't want to answer any more of Saoirse's strange questions.

She smoothed a hand down the bodice of her sea foam gown. It wasn't practical for whatever Manus had planned, but it was something like armor. She was presentable at the very least. As long as she didn't speak, she would remain a paragon of womanly duties.

Now was not the time to dwell on her newly found life. Saoirse straightened her spine, swept down the halls of her home, and out towards the stables. She didn't like horses. They were strange beasts who always watched her and pawed at the ground when she came too close.

They didn't want her anywhere near them either. She was more suited to a kelpie mount who would crash through the waves with a fearsome shriek. Not these imitations of faerie beasts.

"Are you ready, my pearl?" Manus called out. "There are many surprises today!"

He stood next to a glistening black carriage. The wheels were taller than her, and gold curtains covered the windows, barring the interior from her sight. It might have been impressive for a human, but it looked like everything else to Saoirse. Frightening, foreign, and yet another strange thing to endure.

But he wanted her to be pleased. His smiles were rare, and he was grinning from ear to ear today. She wouldn't ruin that.

Saoirse plastered a smile on her face. "What have you acquired, husband? Will this turn into a beetle at sunset or is this truly a carriage made by human hands?"

"Entirely human made. Did you think we were incapable of it?" He pulled black gloves onto his hands with an audible snap. "Are you ready?"

She nodded and marveled at the oddities of her husband. He was a wild beast packed into a suit and tie. His dreads were tied back with a loose leather thong, the heathen hair something he refused to get rid of. Tan breeches hugged his legs so tightly she was certain women would faint when they saw him. A black waistcoat covered the white linen shirt, but she knew it was still unbuttoned.

They were a strange pair. Both wild and tame at the same time.

A crow croaked above them, its eyes staring down with clear intent. Manus mock shivered and gestured for her to come closer.

"The Morrighan watches us my darling, perhaps you should come here. For safety."

"Well, she *is* a faerie. She knows a good story when she sees one."

"A faerie like you or a Fae beast?"

"We're all faeries," she replied. Giggles escaped through her lips in effervescent sounds of joy. "There's no such thing as a Fae beast."

"There's not? Then what are the creatures?"

"Some of us are better at shape shifting than others."

She enjoyed his shocked expression far more than she should have. Saoirse held out her hand for him to take.

"Are we leaving, Manus?"

His jaw snapped shut. "You did that on purpose, didn't you?"

"Did what?"

Lightning fast, his arms lashed out and wrapped around her waist. Saoirse pressed her palms against his chest with a gasp.

"You are a wicked creature, I should have listened to the priest." He nibbled at her ear as he growled out the words.

"I believe the priest claimed *I* should run from *you*."

"Oh, that's not how I heard it, my pearl. You were always the vixen luring me away with her song and her pretty smile."

"I've never sung to you!"

"You never had to," he murmured against her throat. "Your body sings a song only I can hear."

How could she ever tell him how much that meant to her? That he expressed his love in a thousand and one different ways? She could read him easier than any other human alive.

Saoirse pulled back and ran her finger down the bridge of his nose. "Then I shall hope it continues the song for many lifetimes to come."

He kissed the tip of her finger. "Shall we?"

She thought he would help her into the carriage as she had seen many wealthy women do. They would arrange their skirts just so, nod to their footman, and the door would seal them inside the strange compartment. Saoirse dreaded the mere thought of being entombed.

Perhaps he knew her better than she thought. Manus helped her to the front where the coachman would sit. The board was slightly uncomfortable but cushioned by the thick weight of her skirts.

"Manus? Is this appropriate?"

He sat next to her, the entire carriage rocking with his weight. "Probably not. But this is our day together, and I know you care little for propriety."

"I like this gift already."

Manus reached beneath the seat and drew out a long whip. "Besides, the horses would miss you if I tucked you away."

The nearest horse flicked its tail, glancing back at them with a dubious expression.

"I doubt that," Saoirse said with a laugh. "But I would much rather be here where I can feel the wind in my hair."

He cracked the whip, and they left the haven of their small cliff side home. Saoirse craned her neck to watch the estate disappear behind a line of trees. It was a beautiful home. Though it was a shame bad memories haunted its halls, she hoped someday they might fill it with happy memories of their own.

Rolling green hills filled her vision with emerald. Wind tickled the long blades of grass, sending fields flickering to life like the green fronds beneath the ocean. She was most comfortable here. Strands of her hair broke free from her tight crown braid, tickling her cheeks.

Knee high stone walls bracketed off sections of land. Each

square marked where one farmer's land began, and another's ended. Dots of sheep scattered across the emerald hills.

She liked sheep. They were a strange beast, with odd eyes and fuzzy bodies, but they were kind. She could feel their love and devotion even though they kept their distance.

A few horses wandered although they were usually kept in pens, so their owners could find them. Saoirse smiled and waved at a farmer who paused in his work, leaning on a hoe and watching them pass by with a curious expression. He'd probably never seen anyone so rich riding atop a carriage.

He waved back at her hesitantly and returned her bright grin. There was much good she could do here, with all those who needed help. So few wanted to get their hands dirty.

"Manus?"

"Yes, my pearl?"

"Could we perhaps give back to the community?" She pointed towards the farmer's home. "Some roofs look a little worn. We could donate whatever we could to get them ready for winter."

"I like that idea." Manus reached out and grabbed her hand. He pressed a kiss to the back of her fingers. "You'd give up some of our fortune to help others?"

"It's not our fortune anyways. It's a bean sídhe's who didn't mind sharing her wealth with a fellow faerie."

She didn't have the heart to tell him faerie coin was usually cursed. Using the money at all made her uncomfortable, even though she knew it came from humans first. Had it been with the faerie long enough to become cursed?

The carriage rocked to the side, wheels caught in a deep rut. The horses snorted and pulled hard, tossing Saoirse against

Manus who held her snug against him.

They rolled into town and she thought they might stop. It was market day. Crowds of people teemed around stalls overflowing with flowers, fabric, food, and more. She loved the colors of market day even though some people were a little pushy.

A few ladies made eyes at Manus, some even waggling their fingers for his attention. Saoirse ignored them as best she could and let out a relieved sigh when they passed through the town onto a small dirt road that led towards the sea.

"Will you tell me what we're doing now?" she asked.

"We're almost there, my pearl. Have a little patience."

She didn't want to have patience. There was no possibility he was taking her for a swim; Manus wouldn't risk her safety to give her what she desperately wanted. But she didn't know what else he might surprise her with.

They travelled over the rise and down towards the white sandy beach. Far at the bottom, a tiny cottage nestled in the yellow seagrass. Smoke curled from the red brick chimney. It was a quaint little cottage, one that radiated the warmth and comfort of home.

Manus drove the carriage up to the front, hopped from his seat, and tied the horses to the neat little fence surrounding the home. Ivy grew up the stone walls, unfurling bright green leaves nearly as large as her hands. Whoever lived here clearly cared for the grounds.

The front door opened, and a man stepped through, wiping his hands on a white cloth. Even with his back turned as he closed the door, Saoirse recognized him.

Eyes wide, she met Manus's pleased gaze.

He grinned. "It's haunted me for a while, my pearl. Now, you shall see everything he has created, and we will commission a piece for our home."

The artisan turned on his heel and froze. "My lord, you're early."

"We made better time than I expected." Manus helped Saoirse down from the carriage and set her down in a flourish of skirts and furs. "Might I present my wife? I believe you have met before."

Saoirse met his gaze with awe. "I had never thought to see you again, artisan. Your talents have remained in my thoughts."

"Oh." He cleared his throat and blushed. "You both look a fair bit different from I remember."

"I imagine we do. I apologize if we deceived you in any way."

"I always thought you were a royal, even with that ragged gown and dirt smudged on your cheek." He tucked the cloth into his breast pocket. "Welcome to my home."

She stepped forward, Manus close on her heels. The gate gave away beneath her hand without even the slightest of squeaks.

The artisan opened the door again, cheeks still red. "I was heading out to check the sands, but I'll find them later. There was quite a storm a few nights ago. Did it reach you up in the big house?"

"Yes, it did," she murmured as she crossed the threshold into his home. "Do you think there will be more glass?"

"There always is, my lady."

It was far warmer inside the house. She hadn't noticed the

chill in the air until stepping inside. Without thinking, she toed off her shoes and wandered.

A small stove sat in the corner next to a table, ivy carved onto its legs. Herbs hung from the ceiling, drying for winter and filling the air with a sweet scent. Saoirse filled her lungs and trailed her fingers over the hanging lavender to release more of its perfume.

Trinkets sat on the fireplace. Small glass animals, tiny bottles filled with flowers, and sand dollars from the beach. She touched the mantelpiece with a soft smile.

The men hesitated behind her, the artisan finally breaking the silence. "Does she always make herself at home like this?"

"Not always," Manus replied. She could hear the smile in his voice. "Only the places she likes most."

She glanced over her shoulder to find them both staring at her shoes.

"I remember this," the artisan mused. "She wasn't wearing shoes the day I met her either."

"She tends not to."

"That's strange for a lady of her stature."

"I wouldn't say anything about the lady is normal."

She made a face at Manus. "I'm perfectly normal, perhaps it is all of you who are strange to me."

The artisan cleared his throat. "Considering you were raised a princess in another land, I am quite certain we must all be strange to you my lady."

That silly rumor once again. Saoirse curled her hands into fists, frustrated that she would be trapped in the lie again. Instead of confirming or denying, she gestured to the room.

"Why are we here? I appreciate seeing you, artisan, but I am curious about the intent of the visit."

Manus walked to her side and plucked a glass horse from the mantle. "I thought you'd like to see his workroom before we request a commission."

"Is that where you work?" she asked the artisan.

He nodded.

"I would very much like to see that. I haven't seen glasswork like yours before, not even among the richest of houses." Saoirse paused, thoughts whirling in her mind. "Why is that?"

The artisan rubbed the back of his neck. "Well, I'm like your husband, my lady."

"Like my husband?" she repeated the answer. "What do you mean?"

"When I was a boy, my mother set me out in a field because I was ill. A little too old to tempt the faeries in most cases, but even when I was young I had a talent for art. They took me in, healed me, taught me everything I know about glassworks." He sat down at the table and pulled his shirt to the side. Next to his throat was a symbol she knew very well.

Her heart caught in her throat. It was a small flower, barely noticeable and some might think it a scar. The Seelie Fae marked their human slaves. She didn't know whose symbol this was, but she knew what it meant all the same.

"I'm sorry," she breathed. "They should never have taken you."

"It wasn't as bad as you might think. They were kind enough, fed me well, taught me to use my hands in ways I could never have dreamt." He held his hands palm up for her to look at. "Although, they aren't really mine anymore."

Her stomach fell in a pit of dread. She stepped forward and caught his hands in hers. Faint silver lines circled his wrists. She hadn't noticed before, but they were even slightly different colors than the rest of his body.

"I've seen nothing like this before," she murmured. "What did they do to you?"

"It wasn't painful, my lady."

"They shouldn't have done this." The violent tones rocked her body forward.

The artisan widened his eyes, and she knew he had pieced everything together. Quietly, so Manus wouldn't overhear them, he said, "It wasn't you who did this to me."

"I am sorry all the same."

She folded his fingers flat, lifted his hands, and kissed the center of his palms. Merrow magic flowed from her lips to his skin. She pressed compassion, understanding, and healing energies into his body.

He breathed out a shocked tone. "My lady, you don't have to—"

It was too late to stop. The faerie gift glowed along the edges of his stitched hands, and his fingers twitched.

The artisan stared down with wide eyes. "They feel... they feel..."

"Better?"

"*Yes.*" The word vibrated with his shock. "Like they know they're my hands."

"Faerie gifts sometimes come with a price. These hands have always known they belonged to another, and they did not want to accept you." She curled his fingers into his palms and squeezed. "Now they do."

"Will it affect my art?"

"I think your craft will only become even better. They'll work with you now, not against you."

"Thank you, my lady. Thank you so much."

She smiled. "It's the least I could do. You've gifted me with so many dreams of wonderful glass figures."

The artisan stood abruptly, energy zinging through his body and crackling in the air. "Then let me bring your dreams to life. You've seen how I work, now come with me. Let me show you what I am capable of creating but could never sell."

She took his offered hand and danced her fingers along the seam. Manus hovered in the shadows, a ball of nervous energy who held himself back. He wouldn't like another man touching her.

Thankfully, he did not step in.

They walked towards the back door. She could see barely glowing runes etched onto the surface. Some she recognized, words of lasting power and hidden secrets. Others she did not. Their fine lines had been painted by a careful hand.

"Magic?" she asked. "Who placed these in your home?"

"A faerie friend. When I returned, all my friends and family were dead. Two hundred years had passed in this world." The artisan gestured at the door. "This was my final parting gift from those who had taught me so much."

She squinted at the top rune, knowing there was something familiar about it. Saoirse gasped in shock. "That's a door to the Otherworld."

"Indeed, it is."

"They gave you a door to Faerie?" She stared up at the artisan with a new appreciation for his skill. "They loved you."

"In a way. The Seelie court was never a friend to me, but they loved what I could do. Come, we will not be bothered."

In any other circumstance, Saoirse would have forced Manus to remain behind. The Otherworld was a dangerous place for even the most astute person. However, she could see sunlight leaking beneath the door and knew the runes of protection.

Whoever had created this door had wanted to keep the artisan safe.

Saoirse stepped forward and pressed her hand to the worn wood. It pulsed with love, desperation, and a longing so pure it made her palm sting.

"She loved you," Saoirse observed. "Quite a bit for a faerie."

"She thought I was special."

"But you couldn't be together."

The artisan shuffled. "No, faerie nobility cannot be with humans. Not in the way we wanted, and nothing else would have sufficed."

"That's where you get all your inspiration. Not from the Otherworld." She turned with her hand still pressed to the enchanted door. "Your inspiration comes from her."

"In everything I create."

Her heart filled with a love so bright it seared her insides. No wonder faeries avoided this emotion like the plague. It hurt even when it was someone else's.

Manus met her gaze. His features softened, his eyes tender

as he stared into her dark eyes. He felt it too. She was certain of it.

"Shall we?" she asked.

"After you."

Saoirse pushed open the door and walked into a garden filled with the most spectacular sight she'd ever seen.

Plants of all shapes and sizes bloomed larger than her head. Giant blue hydrangeas surrounded glass sculptures of life-sized people. Women frozen mid dance. Men bowing and offering roses to their beloved. Faeries of all shapes and sizes twirling, singing, playing music. An entire frozen court, each lovingly created out of the finest glass.

Sunlight played off the figures, reflecting rainbows all around the faerie grotto. A soft wind blew tiny seed pods in dancing lines. Faerie lights joined them and bounced around Saoirse. They settled in her hair and trilled high pitched notes.

She pressed her hands to her mouth.

Home. She was home, or as near to it as she could get.

"It's—" Her tongue laced in a knot. She couldn't think, could barely breathe.

Manus stopped beside her and tugged her into his arms. "It's beautiful."

The artisan walked through his garden with his hands clasped behind his back. "It's taken me years to create so many, although not as long as you might think. The hands do a lot of the work for me."

"How many have you made?" she asked.

"Hundreds. Now and then a faerie will come and take one, they always leave something as a gift." He paused beside a small pool. "I know you had intended to request a commission, however, I have a piece I think you will want."

Captivated, Saoirse followed him down a winding path made of seashells and bits of sea softened glass. Each step sang a song in her ears and nipped at her feet with sharp jabs.

The pool was crystal clear. It sank into dark depths so blue they challenged the sky. Salt water stung her nose and filled her with memories. A ring of velvety stones circled the entrance to the sea.

She ached to slide into the water. Her merrow family couldn't be here, not in the Otherworld. They lived on the edge and too far away from the faerie kingdoms for them to know where she was.

Manus's hand clenched on her arm.

He always knew when her mind wandered beneath the waves. She shook herself and politely asked, "Where is it, artisan?"

He pointed towards a shadowed corner where a small stream trickled into the pool.

A glass merrow woman sat on a stone, brushing her hair with an ornate shell. She stared into the distance with a sorrowful expression. The tail was made out of bright green glass, matching the vibrant color of her hair.

She was the most stunning creation Saoirse had ever seen in her life. It was even more lifelike than the others, almost as if she would turn her head to stare at them.

And for some strange reason, it made Saoirse unbearably sad. Tears blurred the edges of her vision and her breath caught in her throat.

"Manus," she whispered. "That's the one I want."

"Are you certain? We could request anything at all to be made. He will happily make anything we desire."

She couldn't be more certain if he had put a blade to her throat. This was the glass creation she needed to have in her home. They would need to hide it from any human viewing as it was clearly faerie made. Even if the statue needed to be kept in a secret cave, she must have it.

Unable to speak, Saoirse nodded vigorously.

Manus frowned at her. He knew something was wrong, he'd always been able to feel that even when she tried to hide it from him.

"Artisan," he said. "We'll take that one home with us."

"I am happy to create any additional commission you would like."

"I have a few I'd like to order, if you don't mind?"

The artisan gestured towards a table surrounded by frozen servants. "Have a seat. We'll sketch out a few ideas and I should have them ready in a few months."

They left Saoirse to stand staring at the merrow.

She couldn't understand the violent emotions flooding through her veins. Happiness, sadness, disappointment, all melding together into one ball that sat in the pit of her stomach. She hated it. She wanted it to disappear altogether and leave her be.

This was a good life. It was a peaceful life where she lived in a land of plenty with a husband who clearly loved her. No matter that she missed the sea, that part of her life was over.

A lance of sadness pierced her heart and sent poisonous tendrils throughout her body.

The glass merrow seemed to turn her head and meet her gaze with sorrow mirrored in her eyes. They were two kindred spirits, this lost creature and the stranded merrow. Without the sea, Saoirse was drowning in her own pitiful sadness.

This was what she had given up. This was the choice she had made.

She turned and made her way towards the table where the men sat. With each step, she heard a faint wailing of a forgotten merrow and a melancholy sea.

CHAPTER 10

Golden Light, Rolling Seas

Manus lifted his head from his desk, grumbling as he ran a hand over his face to wipe away the lingering effects of sleep. How long had he been down here?

His eyes caught on the candle spluttering at the base. Apparently a while. The candle had been new when he snuck down here to add the final touches to the document Captain Ramsey had given him. The man was relentless and determined to have a paper trail should Manus turn around and no longer want the ship.

There weren't enough devils in hell to convince Manus not to sail. The crew he'd hired were reliable; he interviewed them all himself and was convinced they'd work hard. He was ready to be lulled to sleep by the rocking waves. The stillness of the ground unnerved him.

He reached forward and pinched the flame. Darkness fell over him like a warm blanket.

Saoirse needed to know. She was too sweet, too innocent, and she'd never understand why he had to go alone.

He couldn't bring her. Merrow men lurked beneath the

waves. Their webbed fingers and stretched faces haunted his dreams still. He saw them pulling her out of his arms again and again. That damned hand reaching for him even when they both knew he couldn't save her.

Manus's hands curled into fists. He couldn't do a lot of things but keeping her safe was more important than breathing. If that meant not seeing her for months on end, then he would damned well do that.

Tingles raced up his fingers. He wanted to touch her, brand the softness of her skin to his palms so that he would remember her when he was stuck on a ship full of men for god knows how long.

Would he forget her? *Never*.

Would she forget him?

The thought was unsettling. He liked to think he wasn't an unforgettable man, but he'd caught her staring at the water too often for comfort. She heard the siren call just as he did.

"Selfish," he muttered.

And he was. He kept her here when she wanted to go home, but home wasn't safe, and the world was against them. Two sides of a coin which could never face each other.

He stood from the desk and placed a hand firmly against the small of his back. She'd make a joke that he was getting old, and Manus hoped he was. It was only another marker that they'd made it long enough to grow old. That she hadn't left him, as all merrow wives were wont to do.

Making certain all his paperwork was still stacked in a corner, he slipped from the small study and made his way towards the stairs. A few more signatures could wait. For now, he had more important business to attend to.

The house was eerily silent as he made his way to the grand stairwell. Saoirse stayed in her room, just across the hall, and he stayed in his own. It was a strange custom, but the last thing he wanted was for the servants to start talking.

His palm glided over the soft wood of the banister, soothing his troubled thoughts. Arturo's wife haunted his memories.

"Be there for her when the storms come a'calling."

And the storms would come. Because all sailors heard the call of the sea and all of them died. If he couldn't shake the curse on his soul, then he would make sure she lived in the lap of luxury for the rest of her life.

He wouldn't leave her a broken woman with a child and nothing to her name. He'd do everything he could to keep her safe.

"Master?" a quiet voice whispered from the shadows. "A word?"

"Etain?" Manus turned. "Is something wrong?"

The pretty little maid stepped from the shadows, her fingers twisting in the fabric of her skirt. "No, everything is well. It is a beautiful home."

"I trust it's to your liking."

"My sister and I like it very well, thank you. It is... better."

It didn't escape his notice how she hesitated. He glanced up the stairs towards his own little heaven, sighed, and walked back down towards the maid.

"You seem troubled."

"It just doesn't seem right that we're here, that's all."

"How so?"

"These people," she gestured behind her, "they're not like

my sister and I. They were born into positions like this. They've spent their entire lives working in houses like this and I'm just afraid to touch anything. What if I break a vase?"

He tucked his hands into his pockets. "Then I'll buy a new vase."

"Money runs out, Manus, you know that as well as I."

His name slipped from her lips too easily. But then again, they'd grown up together on the streets. He'd stolen bits of bread for her and her sister, even when they both found employment in the whorehouses. They'd kept him safe when his mother died until he could get his feet under them.

She sniffed. "It just don't seem right. We'd like to leave, if it's all right with you. It's just that… Well maybe people like us aren't meant to rise above our station. Right? Maybe there's just people who shouldn't live like this. Maybe we deserved what life handed to us."

"Etain, shut up." He pulled his hands from his pockets and opened his arms. "Come here."

She rushed towards him and let him wrap her in a warm embrace. Her shoulders shook under his hands, her hair tangling in the scruff of his chin.

"Look at what I've done, right? You think I'm staring at all these people thinking I don't belong among them?"

"Of course you are."

He chuckled. "Well, maybe a little. But I've got myself a pretty little piece who worships the ground I walk on. I've got a house that makes even lords envy me, and a ship ready to sail at my command. We *aren't* stuck in the lives that were handed to us. And no one is ever going to make me believe that."

"She loves you," Etain whispered against his shoulder.

"Loves you more than any woman has a right to love. Love like that is dangerous, Manus."

"Only if I leave her."

"I've seen it before. Seen someone love another so hard that their soul leaks a little bit every time they see that other person. It drains them, turns them into dust."

He leaned back enough to stare into her eyes. "What are you trying to say?"

"You gotta love her back, or she's going to turn into dust too."

"I love her more than anything."

"More than the sea?"

The question burned. It made his heart hurt and his head spin. "I can't answer that, Etain."

"Someday you're going to have to."

He would, and it wasn't a conversation he relished having. That kind of love terrified him, because Etain was right. The love they shared was powerful, dangerous, dark, and it consumed him.

Manus wasn't the same person he used to be. He saw her and something in him melted. He wanted to touch her hair, stroke her cheek, drag her into his arms and never let her go. But that meant putting her in danger, because he couldn't let go of the sea either.

Had he forgotten how to breathe? He sucked in air, but he couldn't seem to fill his lungs.

Etain stepped back from his arms. "She went for a walk, if you're looking for her."

"She went – what?" He shook his head. "She can't go for a walk, it's nighttime."

"We all go for walks in the nighttime."

He swore. "Not her. She doesn't go outside without me or one of the footmen."

"Why not? You can't turn her into a captive, if she wants go outside, she should be able to."

"Because outside is dangerous." He spun on his heel and stomped towards the front door. "If she gets hurt, it's on your head."

"Why are you so protective over this girl, Manus?"

He whirled, jabbing a finger through the air and pointing at her. "Do you remember the first time you saw a girl? Not the ones we grew up with, but the ones who walked the streets with bows in their hair and smiles on their faces? The innocent ones, the ones who never saw the things we saw. You remember those girls?"

"Of course I do."

"She's one of them. She doesn't know the kind of things we've had to do to stay alive. She's never seen the gutters, never felt a man pawing at her without permission, never saw her mother trying to drink herself into oblivion. She hasn't watched someone die because food was scarce or simply because they didn't want to live this life anymore." He wiped a shaking hand over his mouth. "She's pure, lily white, and glowing like the goddamned northern star. She's all I have, and I won't see her sullied."

He raced out the door, the chilly air penetrating through his linen shirt. He didn't stop for a jacket. Fear sent him sprinting from the manor and frantically searching for her.

Where would she have gone? The sea?

His heart stopped. She wouldn't have gone to the ocean,

would she? Even Saoirse wasn't foolish enough to tempt her own safety. She knew the merrow men could crawl out of the ocean and steal her away. She shouldn't even be close to the water.

Manus couldn't think straight. He didn't know where to begin searching for her until he looked up the hill and saw her. Far away but standing on the edge of the cliff with her skirts whipping around her ankles.

She looked like an angel standing up there. So far away from him, yet he knew every detail of her face without being able to see her. He knew the soft curve of her waist, the tiny curl near her ear which always curled in the opposite direction from the others, the dimple on her cheek which only appeared late at night when she was tired.

Gods how she made his chest ache.

It would take him a few minutes to get to her, but Saoirse wasn't moving. She held her arms wrapped around herself and stared off into the distance. He frowned.

She was staring at the sea.

"Damned woman," he muttered. She was always staring at the water and he knew what that meant. He'd heard the stories of sailors with merrow wives who disappeared one night, never to return. He couldn't lose her. He didn't know what he'd do if she left his life forever.

He glanced up at her form again and paused when he saw the male figure walking towards her. At first, he thought it was that damned leprechaun. The faerie was always showing up at the wrong time.

But then he realized the man was obviously trying to be quiet as he approached.

Manus had never felt such fear as when the man raced forward and grabbed Saoirse by the shoulders, whirled her around, and shook her hard enough to rattle her.

He didn't shout for the man to stop, he didn't need to. Manus sprinted towards them. A silent, dark shadow that streaked through the night as though the faeries had given him wings.

His fist flew out, catching the man in the jaw and knocking him to the ground. The thief spat out a wad of blood. He bounced up to his feet a little too quickly and threw a punch of his own.

Manus's breath whooshed out, the man's meaty fist catching him firmly in the stomach. But it gave him the opportunity he needed. Air wasn't required to charge forward, wrap his arm around the man's waist and wrestle him onto the ground.

He straddled the man, slamming his fist into whatever flesh he could find. Face, shoulders, neck, anything.

This thief had dared to touch his wife.

His wife.

"Manus!" Saoirse's voice broke through the red haze of his vision. "Manus enough, let him go!"

His hands were aching, swelling already around bruised bones and blood streaked knuckles. The slight moment of hesitation was all the other man needed to drag himself away and run.

Manus leaned back on his heels, breathing hard and watching the man's quick retreat. This was why he hadn't wanted her alone. This place was dangerous, even in the richest parts.

"Manus?"

Her voice splintered something inside him. A ragged breath tore through him and he snatched her arm. He probably tugged on her too hard, she fell against his chest with a gasp.

"Are you all right?" He traced her body with his hands, over and over again. "Did he hurt you? Did he touch you anywhere other than your shoulders?"

"Manus, please—"

"Saoirse just answer me, for gods sakes."

"I'm *fine*."

Breath sawed from his lungs and he gathered her closer against his heart. "You scared the life out of me."

"I'm fine." She stroked her hands over his back.

"You're shaking," he muttered. "You are not fine."

"You're here now. I know everything will be okay now."

He thought she was shaking but, as he cupped the back of her head, he realized it was him. He was the one shaking at the mere thought that he might not have found her in time. That she might have been out here alone when that man took her away.

Manus pressed a kiss against her temple and closed his eyes. "You are everything to me, my pearl. Tell me you know that."

"I know."

"Say it again. Please."

"Manus, you're scaring me."

He probably was. He was scaring himself with the intensity of his feelings and the knowledge that he was going to leave her. That she was going to look up at him with tears in her eyes when he said the sea was calling.

A coward, that's what he was. A coward and a fool for ever thinking he could hold onto such a glorious light and not tarnish her with his touch.

He pressed against kiss to her temple and held her close against his heart. A star shot across the sky, falling like the weight attached to his soul, dragging him down into the abyss of self-loathing and fear.

He wished to be a better man. He wished to stay close by her side, to raise a family as he'd always wanted to when he saw those little girls prancing down the street with bows in their hair.

But above all else, Manus wished that she would stay with him just for a few moments longer.

Even if he didn't deserve her.

Saoirse rolled over and stretched her arms over her head. Sunlight filtered through her balcony window while wind brushed the gauzy curtains into rippling movements. The air was chilled now, autumn was in full swing and some said winter may come early this year.

She was excited for winter. Snow was an entirely new and exciting weather for her to see. Some of the kinder servants had told her stories after everyone else had gone to bed.

The faeries danced upon icy winds and scattered thousands of perfectly carved snowflakes upon the ground. They spent the entire year carving each one to be unique in design and creation.

The mere thought of it made her giggle. It didn't seem likely. Faeries would spend that much time and detail into creating something for humans to enjoy, but she hadn't travelled through the Otherworld. It was possible, and she wanted to meet the creatures who dedicated their lives to such a feat.

She rolled onto her side and stretched out her hand, hoping to find Manus on the other side. Cold sheets met her fingertips.

Another night when he slipped away. Propriety be damned, she didn't want him to go back to his room. She didn't like waking to a cold side of the bed while having to wonder where he'd gone off to.

Frowning, she sat up. As she rolled, her hand fell on a small parchment left on Manus's pillow.

Excitement lifted the hairs on her arms. Were they to go on another trip? Had he yet another surprise for her?

She unfurled the scroll and tried to make sense of the scratched marks. It wasn't in any language she'd ever read before. The human writing wasn't easy to learn. They had so many letters, markings, and strange ways of expressing emotion. Manus had given up on teaching her and she grew too frustrated.

A soft knock on the door heralded the return of her maids. They entered quietly as if they did not want to wake her.

"I'm already up," she called out. "Good morning, ladies! How are you?"

They flinched at her voice. One tentatively replied, "We are well, my lady. How are you feeling?"

"Wonderful. It's a beautiful day outside, is it not?"

Saoirse hopped down from the large bed and made her

way towards the mirror. They could make her as pretty a doll as they wanted today. Manus had another surprise for her. And though she didn't know what it was, she was certain it would be life changing.

The maids did not reply.

She met their startled gazes in their reflection and furrowed her brows. Something was wrong, but it couldn't be. The sun was shining, the birds were singing, how could anything be amiss?

Hesitantly, she released her grip on the letter and held it up for one of them to take. "Could you read this to me please?"

"Can you not?"

She shook her head.

The maids looked at each other. One blushed bright red, reached out, and plucked the letter from her fingers. "A patron taught me how to read, mistress."

"Start on my hair," Saoirse ordered. She turned towards the mirror and focused on keeping her expression as still as a tranquil pool.

"My pearl, you looked so beautiful sleeping this morning that I could not wake you. Every morning you look the same, and I take all the blame for not telling you sooner. I leave today for—" the maid paused and held the letter out to Saoirse. "My lady I should not be reading this."

"Read it."

"This is personal, perhaps I should get the butler—"

"Read it." Saoirse's tone did not allow for any argument.

The maid winced but returned her gaze to the contents of the letter. "I leave today for the West Indies. Captain Ramsey has agreed to charter the voyage, so our wealth remains in your capable hands. I apologize I could not tell you this in person, my pearl. I trust you understand why I could not bear to see the disappointment in your gaze. The ocean is not a safe place for you. Be well and know that you will be in my thoughts. Signed, Manus."

Saoirse swallowed, but kept her gaze on the mirror. Her face would not move. She would not show her reaction to these women.

Inside, her heart was breaking. Manus had known this entire time he would never take her on that ship. He hung freedom in front of her, dangling it like a treat, and all the while knew she would never be given that gift.

"My lady," the maid brushing her hair murmured. "We thought you knew."

"What time did he leave?"

"Before the sun rose. He made every effort to make certain you were comfortable in his absence. Being the wife of a sea captain isn't an easy life. They're always gone."

"How long?" The words were strained and rushed. She cleared her throat. "How long are they usually gone?"

She saw the maids exchange a look in the mirror. "You don't know?"

"Manus did not see fit to speak to me about his travels. How long are they usually gone?"

"Months, my lady. The West Indies is a considerable journey that could take a year to complete."

A year? An entire year alone in this gods-forsaken place with only humans to keep her company?

Saoirse's mind spiraled. She lost control over her face which tightened in anger and humiliation. These women knew.

They had known the entire time where Manus was going.

She could sense their emotions. Sadness, pity, and the faintest hint of glee.

Words slammed through her lips, rushing forward to set fire to the rest of her life. "Who were you to him? Before he hired you on as my lady's maids?"

"I don't—"

"Tell me."

"We were his favorites," one of them ground out. Saoirse didn't care which one. "At the brothel, there were a few of us who were considered 'special'. Manus always chose one—or more—of us, when he returned from a long trip."

"How long?"

"What?"

"How long has it been since he chose you?"

The maid closest to the door shook her head. "It's not right to be discussing such things. We like our job, my lady. We don't mean to hurt you or the lord, it's just that you asked and—"

"Get out."

They froze, their eyes as big as sand dollars.

The one who had read the letter licked her lips. "My lady, he saved us. The life we led before was not an easy one, and certainly not a safe one. He didn't tell you because it's not important anymore. We can all tell how he feels about you—"

When they did not move, Saoirse whirled around, her fingers clawing into the wooden chair back. "Get out!"

They spun in a whirl of skirts and raced from the room. Pounding feet echoed down the hall, along with shouts of inquiry, then sudden silence. It was as if the entire house waited with bated breath for what their mistress would do next.

Responsibility pressed down on her shoulders. She was supposed to be some paragon for these people. A figurehead for their grounded ship.

How could she possibly be that when she was a creature meant to be wild and free?

She couldn't breathe. Saoirse pressed her hands to her throat and begged her human body to work. Her fingers touched the faint lines where her gills could open, and tears welled in her eyes.

The ocean would help. It would hide all her pain, tears, and frustration. No one could tell she was ripping open at the seams.

Saoirse lurched to her feet, stumbling from the room onto the balcony where she could grip the stone railing and tilt her face towards the sun.

This was what she had wanted. A human life with a human husband in a human house.

She took in a deep breath and held it until her lungs burned. How could she have known what this life would be like? No one had told her.

The stone railing creaked, her grip so strong it threatened to crack the white marble. She stared down at her inhuman hands and wondered how long it would take for them to realize what she really was. In the absence of their master, all attention would be cast upon her.

Would they like having a faerie in their midst? She'd heard tales of humans destroying kind souls who only wished to help. Or worse, elevating them to status of a god.

Someone entered her bedroom, knocking on the door and shuffling their feet.

"My lady?" the butler asked. "Are you well?"

"I wish to be alone."

"Understandable. I wanted you to know we're all here for you."

She turned, seeing his bright red cheeks and the way he wrung his hands together. "Pardon?"

"You must excuse my forwardness, ma'am. But the house staff didn't like the way the master ran off in the early morning. I feared he might not have told you and it didn't seem right."

"Liam, isn't it?"

"It is."

"Thank you for your concern. Please share with the rest of the house that although I am...not pleased, I am well and appreciate their thoughts."

"I will, my lady."

He bowed and closed the door behind him as he left.

Saoirse folded onto the floor of the balcony. Silent sobs wracked her frame while her fingers began to tremble. The desire to leap off the edge and fall into the sea was so fierce, so strong, that she almost flung herself over.

But she didn't. She was the lady of this house, and regardless of what she wanted, this was now her life.

Wind yanked her hair from the tight braid, sending strands lashing across her cheeks and back. The long length flew free and wild in the wake on the oncoming storm.

Saoirse stood with her arms wrapped around her waist,

staring at the raging sea. The cliff edge was a few meters from her. Temptation just out of reach. Black clouds boiled in the skies and the ocean churned. A mirror of her emotions and fear.

Winter would soon touch this land with frost and icy winds. The servants explained to her that was why Manus had left in a hurry. The ship would be forced to remain in the harbor until next year if they were caught in the cold.

It had been weeks of waiting. Weeks of trying her best to act human, to be the mistress of a grand house and learn their ways.

Weeks of failure and wasted time.

She had given up. No matter how much she tried to be a lady, there was always something wild in her that rebelled. The women here might hide behind fans, but their fangs were blunt compared to hers. She wanted to tear them apart, to curse them, to fling their pieces to the sharks.

A ragged voice broke through her thoughts. "I am growing weary of your tumultuous emotions, merrow."

"Then stop prying, leprechaun."

Declan crunched through the gravel to reach her. He paused just behind her, his great bulk a wave of heat carrying the metallic scent of gold. "What are you doing out here?"

She didn't respond, merely handed him the letter she held in her hand. The folds were deep, the edges ripped, but she had taken to carrying it, nonetheless. It was the last bit of him she had. And the only thing fueling her anger.

Declan read the words and swore. "That bastard."

"He did what he thought was right."

"You're still justifying his actions? He *left* you."

"And I am still standing." She squeezed her arms to hold

in the shiver that rocked through her body. "This was the life I chose, Declan. This and no other."

"You chose it, yes, but you can still change your path. One decision does not create a cage."

"It has for me," she murmured, staring out at the waves. "We are bonded, he and I. There can be no other."

Declan crossed his arms firmly over his chest. "You went through with that nonsense, did you?"

"I didn't think there was a way to stop it."

"Well, you could have just…not bonded with him."

She gave him a censuring look.

"Sorry, love. I know it's probably a sensitive subject." He held out the letter for her to take. "What are you going to do?"

"I don't know." She crumpled the letter and tucked her hands back underneath her arms. "The temptation will always be there. I'm coming to realize that no matter what I do, I will always miss the ocean. And no matter what I say, Manus will never let me near it for fear I will disappear forever."

Declan walked around her, blocking her view of the sea. He filled her gaze with a broad chest, strong arms, and golden rings flickering as he cracked his knuckles.

"Look at me, merrow."

She squared her shoulders and met his gaze.

"If you had a chance, if you were freed from all your ties, would you slip back into the ocean?"

She bit her lip. Would she?

Her shoulders curved forward and her expression fell. "Yes," she whispered. "I would."

"It's not a bad thing to admit it. You should never feel guilty for being as you truly are. Faeries weren't meant to remain in the human world."

"That's not true. This is, and always will be, our first choice."

A flash of anger sparked in his eyes. "They drove us out. We created something better in response."

"Did we? Funny, that's not how I remember the tale."

Declan gestured at the manor behind her. "Is this what you thought it would be? Is this what you wanted? Because I cannot believe that deep under the sea you knew everything this life would bring with it. Responsibility. Servants. Money. Noblemen and their wives staring at your every move and judging you harshly based on them."

"No!" Saoirse shouted. "Is that what you want to hear, Declan? All I wanted was *him*. I didn't care if we had four walls around us. I wanted his love, his attention, his laughter. I wanted to shape my life around him, have a family, grow old together."

"It doesn't look like that's what you're doing. It looks like you're standing on the edge of a cliff, wondering just how long it would take you to hit the water and disappear forever."

He saw right through her so easily it frightened her. Saoirse hadn't even felt herself inching towards the edge of the cliff, but that was what she had done. Step by step, closer and closer to the freedom of the waves.

And the bitter loneliness. The painful end as heartbreak slowly ate away at her sanity until she sank to the bottom of the sea.

A tear slid down her cheek. "Oh, Declan. This isn't the life I thought it would be."

He opened his arms to her. "Come here, merrow. Dry your

tears."

She rushed forward and let his warmth envelop her. It wasn't the same as Manus, but she supposed she shouldn't have expected that. No one would ever measure up to the man who filled her heart, no matter what mistakes he made.

Declan smoothed his hands up and down her spine. "It will be okay, Saoirse."

"How could you possibly know that?"

"There's only two options for you. To remain the wife of a human who disappears for months on end or return home."

"I have no home." She sniffled. "I cannot return to my family. They will either lock me up forever or chase me from their waters."

"They are not the only merrows in the ocean."

Saoirse pulled back. "What?"

"There are a few groups around here, they call themselves pods. They're kinder than their deep water cousins. If you ask, they'll take you in."

"My mother mentioned a cousin," she mused. "I didn't know what she meant but perhaps it has something to do with the merrows who live here."

"You'll likely never know. But you'd be with your own people. Safe and sound."

"Do you hate them?"

"Who?"

"Humans. You don't trust them at all."

"When you've seen what I've seen, you can't trust them anymore." He released her and stepped back. "They lie, cheat, and steal. Humans aren't the paragons we once thought them to be, and every single one of them has the capacity to be cruel."

"I can't believe that. I have seen so much good in them."

"Who? Your little artisan? He's more Fae than human now." Declan lifted his hands and wiggled his fingers. "Or did you think those were human hands they put on him?"

"Now you're just being cruel."

"It's in my nature."

She didn't want it to be in hers. Saoirse understood that many of the Fae were jaded. Most were power hungry, and the humans stole so much from them. But she had thought Declan would have seen the *good* here as well as the bad.

Although she had seen throngs of people with judgmental gazes, she had seen them help each other as well. A woman handing a piece of bread to a hungry child. A servant helping sweep after a long, hard day. Even elderly men and women passing down traditions and knowledge.

All these things made humans worthwhile. They were good people, and she wouldn't forget that.

Her ears burned with the desire to hear true silence once again. She wanted the ocean to press down on her chest. Maybe that would ease the anxiety that stole her breath away.

"My place is here," she croaked. "This is my choice. These are my people now."

"You're fooling yourself if you believe that." Declan shook his head. "I'll stick around for a while. It looks like you may need a man of the house."

"It wouldn't be appropriate."

"We aren't proper, Saoirse. You and I were creatures born of midnight and monsters. The Wild Hunt approaches. We'll need each other if we want to survive it."

He sauntered away, leaving Saoirse to gape at the open sea.

The Wild Hunt. She'd forgotten the Lord and his people who rode across the human lands and collected faeries who should not be there. Would he try to take her?

Would it matter?

She shivered and wrapped her arms back around herself. She should go inside, introduce Declan to the servants, answer the questions they would inevitably have.

Waves crashed against the cliff. Seagulls cried out overhead. And Saoirse remained frozen on the edge of the cliff, listening to the song of the sea.

Great bangs echoed through the halls of the manor. Plates and vases shattered on stone. A few murmurs raised in a sudden silence, questions that would not be answered as further bangs rocked the manor.

Saoirse had already shredded her own room. She had tossed the sheets off the balcony, shattered the mirror, ripped apart the bedding in her desperate search. She had stalked across the hall, shoved aside the butler, and started in on Manus's room.

Some might say she wasn't thinking straight. She could hear the servants whispering that she'd lost her mind. It was a shame the mistress was too delicate to live without the master in the home, and who should they contact? She had no family they knew of.

The poor dear needed help.

She snorted and tore through a pillow. Help. As if they

would have any idea how to begin to help her.

"My lady?" The butler said, clearing his throat. "You have a visitor."

"I don't have time for visitors."

Clunking footsteps marched into the room. She heard the butler argue as he was pushed from the room, and then the door slammed in his face.

"What in the devil are you doing, Saoirse?" Declan growled. "I'm supposed to be here to keep their attention off you not explaining your eccentricities!"

"I lost something," she murmured, searching the room for her next victim. "I don't know what it is, I can't remember. It's like my mind remembers something but won't tell me what."

"You're not making any sense."

"I know that!" she shouted. "I can feel I'm not making sense, but I also know I don't feel like *myself*. There's something missing. Something I should have."

Declan grabbed her hands. "Saoirse, sit down. Come on, no, you will not look anymore. Sit down."

She slowly sank onto the edge of Manus's ruined bed. Her heart raced, and her eyes flicked around the room, attempting to find yet another hiding place where he could have put... *something*.

"Saoirse, what have you lost? Focus."

She shook her head frantically. "I don't know. I can't remember, it's like everything I knew is filtering out of my head. My memories. My family. I can't... Declan, I can't."

Saoirse buried her face in her hands, sobbing. She was shaking and afraid of the changes she couldn't control. Her mind was supposed to be a temple.

Now, it felt like a prison.

He folded her hands in his, shifting them back and forth until a golden light appeared between their fingers. She watched the soothing movements with rapt attention. Her heart slowed, her head bobbed, and slowly her mind cleared.

Declan opened their hands. A gold coin sat in the center of her palm. The very coin he had given her long ago in the pub.

"Focus on the coin, Saoirse. Let your mind wander. You might not know what you lost, but you know where it is."

She followed the coin as he danced it across his fingertips. The coin wasn't what she desperately wanted, but perhaps he was right. If she relaxed, breathed, centered herself, then perhaps she might *feel* what she wanted.

Saoirse's mind calmed into a trance-like state. Declan skillfully rolled the coin over and over his knuckles.

It was from her home, whatever the item was. She remembered rolling waves, seagulls, but most of all the taste of salt on her tongue. Her family was far beneath her. Hundreds of children, all with tails like fish and hair like kelp. They gathered to sing, but they were horrible at it.

Her lips curved in a soft smile. Not a single one of her sisters could hold a tune. They said they would leave it to the sirens, but she knew it bothered them.

Songs were sacred to merrows, and they dearly loved to listen to music. Sometimes, they would swim towards the surface, hovering together and waiting for the whales to pass by.

Once, when she was very little, Saoirse had swum away from the sounds to explore. And in the darkest depths of the sea, she met a very young guardian who sang a song so pure that it rattled her soul.

"Oh," she whispered. "I remember."

"Where is it?"

"I had it with me when I arrived. But I don't remember where I put it."

"Think harder, Saoirse. Where could it possibly be?"

And then she remembered. Manus had shown her a small music box, his mother's favorite trinket. The song reminded her of the guardian's, so she'd placed it there for safe keeping.

Saoirse sighed. "A music box."

"This one?"

Her eyes snapped open, although she did not remember closing them, and saw Declan held the box in his hand. "How did you know?"

"There's only one music box in the house."

"But where was it?"

He winked. "It's gold, darling. Anything gold speaks to me."

"Open it."

The bright music twinkled from within as soon as he twisted the base. The lid lifted and revealed a tiny dancer spinning in a circle. At the end of the song, a drawer opened at the bottom.

Hidden within was a small spiral seashell.

"Now I remember," she breathed. "This was the gift my mother gave me before I left. How could I forget so easily?"

"The farther he is away from you, and the longer he is gone, the worse you will get." Declan reached out and ran a hand over her head. "Your bond will make you deteriorate even further."

Sudden panic made her push up from the bed and sprint

out the door. She careened into the shambles of her room. Sheets tangled in her feet, but she safely stumbled to the balcony.

Breathing in the salt air, she twisted the shell in her ear where it was meant to be.

Song filled the ocean and the sky above it. The guardians cried out for their lost child, mourning a merrow girl who had not returned to their waiting arms. They screamed in rage, sobbed in sadness, and then fell to sudden silence.

Saoirse waited the long heartbeats until they began wailing again.

Declan placed his hand on the balcony next to hers. "He will not return for at least another six months."

"Will I even last that long?" she asked.

"You have a choice. Do you wish to die here, waiting for your human to return? Or do you wish to die in the arms of your own kind?"

"I can't make that decision."

"You will have to soon enough."

"Captain?"

Manus turned, tearing his gaze from the waves for a mere moment to glance at his first mate. "What is it?"

"We've a stowaway."

His curiosity peaked, Manus tilted his head to the side and watched as a small boy was thrown to his hands and knees on the deck. Mangy and young, the boy was hardly of age to be on a ship.

But he remembered being that age and wanting nothing more than to be a sailor.

The boy whimpered as Manus thundered towards him. He'd have to get used to the commanding nature of a captain. Manus couldn't make himself any less intimidating, or the other men would rise against him. Mutiny was something a ship couldn't survive, no matter how new she was.

"How did you manage to hide yourself on my ship, boy?"

The child wiped his nose and glared up at him. "It wasn't all that hard."

"No?"

"I hid myself in a rum casket. Emptied the goods into the sea and your men loaded me on without even checking beneath the lid."

Manus arched a brow. "Really?"

He heard the scuffle of nervous feet. Whoever had loaded the rum onto the ship was likely running off to hide himself for a few days. They'd seen the wrath of their captain already, and he knew they agreed he was a terrifying man. Fair, but lethal.

"I ain't done nothing to you or your men."

"No, you haven't. But you are here without permission, and we are in the middle of the ocean. I meticulously planned to have enough rations for exactly the amount of men on this ship. You showing up means we no longer have the food and drink we require to survive. Do you understand?"

The boy's eyes were as large as dinner plates. "I hadn't thought about that."

"No, I expect you didn't."

"Are you going to throw me overboard?" The boy squared his shoulders and bared his teeth. "I'll fight you."

"I don't think you'd stand much of a chance. But no, I don't intend to throw a child to the sharks."

Manus nodded to his first mate, ignoring the eye roll the other man gave him. The crew would get used to the idea of having a boy around. The child's small fingers would prove useful in the coming months.

"Come with me," Manus ordered. "I have something to show you."

"You sure you aren't going to toss me?"

"We'll give you a trial run on the sea. If you prove to be a good sailor, then I'll allow you to remain. If you aren't, we'll revisit feeding the sharks."

"I'm a good sailor." The boy straightened his shirt. "You'll see."

"Surprisingly, I have no doubt of that."

He saw something of himself in the boy although he was loath to admit it. Manus noted the marks of hard work. Scratches on the child's hands, leathery elbows poking through a threadbare shirt, the slight wince as he stood and the way he pressed his arm against his side.

They walked to the bow of the ship. Manus kept his pace slow and leisurely, making certain to stop and speak with the crew. They needed reassurance just as much as the boy needed to breathe through what Manus suspected were broken ribs.

Once they traveled as far as they could, Manus pointed to the masthead. "Do you know what that is?"

"A merrow. Cursed faeries shouldn't be on boats."

"Who told you that?"

"My pa."

"He the one who punched you in the chest?" Manus chuckled at the boy's startled expression. "I remember the feeling of broken ribs, it's not hard to see it in another."

"What's it to you?" The boy wiped his nose on his sleeve. "Ain't nothing anyways. A bit of bruising is all."

"I'll have the doctor look at you."

"Doctor?"

"I believe every ship should have one, although most aren't willing to pay them. Now why do you say a merrow curses a ship?"

"Faeries are bad luck. Besides, merrows make deals with men and then drown them."

"I don't know about that," Manus replied. He leaned against the railing and looked the boy up and down. "Merrows have always been kind in my experience."

"You've met one?"

"Several. I was one of the unlucky men to meet their husbands too." He made a face. "They were the ugliest creatures known to mankind. So, if the merrows are dragging men to the bottom of the ocean, I suspect they wish to marry *them* instead of their own kind."

The boy stuck out a hand. "Alroy. That's my name."

"Manus." They shook hands as men did, firm and strong. Manus ignored the boy's wince and nodded to the merrow. "Faeries aren't good or bad. They're a little a bit of both. Merrows keep watch over the seas, to make certain no unsuspecting human stumbles into the Otherworld."

"What if we want to?"

"Why would you? The Otherworld is a dangerous place for humans. Faeries aren't particularly kind to us."

Alroy brandished his fists. "I could take 'em. They wouldn't know what hit 'em!"

He mimed punching, throwing out his arms in wild directions. The boy wouldn't stand a chance if a faerie decided he was worth their attentions. Manus suspected it was more likely they would ignore the boy entirely.

"Have you ever heard of the man who married a merrow?"

Alroy frowned. "No. Why would anyone do that?"

"Well, merrows can find gold wherever they are. Shipwrecks, lost jewels, even ancient tombs all buried underneath the ocean. They bring it up for their husbands and let them live a life of happiness."

"Gold ain't worth all that."

"No?"

"People should marry who they want. They shouldn't be forced into it because they want money." Alroy scuffed his bare feet on the deck. "Besides, who would want to be married to a fish anyways?"

"They aren't always fish," Manus said with a chuckle. "But I see your point. In the old stories, the man was always in love with the merrow. She promised to live on land with him as long as he was faithful, and in return, she would give him a son.

"He was good and true. There came a day when he had to travel to market. When he returned, his merrow wife was gone. The boy remained but there was no sign she ever existed."

"Why?" Alroy asked. "Why would she leave without letting him know why?"

"Legend has it the sea calls to them. They desire it so badly, they have to go." Manus stared out at the sea, a troubled worry settling in the pit of his stomach.

Would she leave? He doubted it. Saoirse loved him more than life itself, so it seemed. She wouldn't leave him because he had followed his dreams. Of anyone, she would understand the call of the sea.

Alroy tugged his sleeve. "What happened then?"

"Hm?"

"In the story, captain. What happened to the man and the merrow? Did she ever come back?"

"Oh." He squinted his eyes, trying to remember the story his mother had whispered to him at night. "Aye, they found each other. Ten years later, when their boy was all grown up, they rowed out towards their ship. The merrow woman appeared. She said she had come for her husband now that their son could take care of himself."

Alroy shivered. "What did she do?"

"Nothing. Her husband reached into the water and let her drag him down into the deep."

Alroy raced away. He shouted the story for others to hear, exclaiming that the merrows would certainly find them and drag them into the depths.

It was a fanciful tale. Manus hadn't believed it when he was a boy, and he wasn't about to believe it now.

Still… It had merit.

He reached into the breast pocket of his jacket and pulled out a tiny glass merrow. The likeness to his wife was uncanny. Light reflected on her smiling face, catching the sadness of her eyes. She clutched a seashell in her hands and stared at him as if he had placed her in a cage.

Carefully, Manus folded her in his grasp as he stared at the rolling waves.

Saoirse knelt on an embroidered pillow in the small grotto where they had hidden the glass merrow. Vines framed the cave wall and the quiet rush of the sea echoed throughout. Light reflected the waves on the ceiling, creating a pattern that eased her mind and terrified her at the same time.

She pressed her hands to her chest and breathed out a quiet sigh. "What am I to do?"

Memories faded every day. Important memories that made her who she was. Memories that created the woman Saoirse knew. As they faded, she became confused, complicit, quiet. No one knew what was happening to their mistress.

Declan remained to take care of her. He carried her to bed and pressed cold compresses to her forehead each night. He was tireless in his desire to keep her alive.

But they both knew each day Manus was gone, the more dire her situation grew.

Why hadn't she thought of this? She might have told him, explained to him all that could happen if he didn't bring her with him.

It hadn't felt right. She would have ruined all the good they had built between the two of them. And he would feel trapped. Saoirse could already see the disappointed expression on his face when she told him they could never go to sea again.

No, it was better this way. She would survive until he returned. Only a few more months.

She pressed a hand to the bulge of her belly. Even Declan didn't know this small secret growing inside her.

"We're going to be okay," she whispered. "You and I will survive this."

"Are you so certain of that?" Declan asked from behind her.

"You are supposed to be in the main house. The servants will gossip about where we are."

"They already think you're having an affair. You've heard their whispers just as I have." He settled next to her on the stone floor. "It's not the end of the world if they talk."

"It would be if Manus hears tell of it."

"In the Indies?" He snorted. "He isn't going to hear anything on the other side of the world."

"Don't be cruel."

"You're killing yourself staying here, Saoirse. You know if you return to the sea that you'll have a little more time."

"I can do this."

"For me." Declan reached forward and took her hands. "Do it for me, Saoirse. I'll stay behind, make your excuses, even let your husband know what happened. I cannot stay here and watch you die."

A tentative smile spread across her lips and a bubble of familiar mirth burst in her chest. "Why Declan, that almost sounds as if you like me."

"I'm fond of you. We're in the same situation, you and I, cursed to live on human lands." He squeezed her fingers. "But you can go home. You can live out the rest of your life with your own people, in your own skin, without hiding who you truly are."

"And what will I give up by doing that?" she whispered. "I want to see him one last time."

"He took that from you the moment he set sail from these shores. He won't be back in time, Saoirse. I want to see that babe grow into a beautiful young woman like yourself." He winked. "Maybe she'll be interested in a handsome leprechaun."

Saoirse snorted. "She'll be interested in whomever she wishes. Thousands of men will desire her hand, and she will pick whichever one she desires the most."

"I hope, for your sake, that you are correct."

She stared at the glass merrow and weighed her options.

Manus would return, eventually. There was no way for them to guess how long that might take. Ships traveled as fast as the wind and sea would let them. But it was unlikely he would return for at least another few months, or worse, a year if they were held up in the city where they would trade.

She would drift away until there was nothing left of her at all. Her mind would fracture, her body weaken, and eventually she would answer the pulsating call of the sea. It wanted her to return. It sang for her, the guardians calling for her day and night.

One way or another, she would go home.

Saoirse shook her head, a small sobbing breath puffing between her lips. "I want to be here for him. I want to stay until he returns."

Her eyes burned with the pressure of trying to keep tears from rolling down her cheeks. Declan's expression crumpled in pity.

"I know," he replied. "I know you want to stay here for him, but is there really any other choice?"

There wasn't. He knew that, just as Saoirse knew she was fighting a losing battle. It didn't make it any easier to admit defeat.

She dropped her head and slowly nodded. "What will you tell the servants?"

"That it looked like a rogue wave crashed through the grotto, taking you out to sea before I could grab you. It's close enough to the truth that it's not quite a lie. The waves took you out to sea before I could drag you back." He flashed a grin. "I'm not a faerie who likes to swim."

"Will they believe that?"

"I've enough magic left in me. They won't have a choice." A gold coin flashed between his thumb and forefinger. "It's a believable story. They've never seen you in water before, and with all those skirts it's unlikely even a strong swimmer would survive."

"And Manus?"

The coin disappeared under a clenched fist. "He'll know what happened."

"You'll tell him the truth?" When Declan didn't respond, she pressed with a firm tone, "Declan, you'll tell him the truth."

"He doesn't deserve the whole truth. It would be less painful for everyone if you let him believe the same story as everyone else."

"I won't go knowing he thinks I willingly left."

"You're making the choice."

"I *know*, Declan. I'm doing my best to keep myself together, but I will not allow him to think I don't still love him." She shook her head. "Please, Declan. Please don't take that away from us."

He growled, his glamour slipping to reveal golden skin that glittered in the dim light. Sharp teeth gnashed, but he gave in. "Understood. He'll know the truth. But you understand he'll come after you?"

"It's the only hope I have left. Manus wouldn't let me go without a fight. And if, by some chance, I'm still alive? Then I hope with all my heart he finds me."

She stood, her bones creaking and her head spinning with the effort. Even her physical form hurt now that he had been gone for so many months.

Was this what the bean sídhe had warned her about? That tying herself to a human would slowly eat away at her until there was nothing left?

Saoirse hoped she never had to find out.

Piece by piece, she unwove the layers of clothing her maids had placed on her this morning. Even living with humans this long had not made her self-conscious about her body. Nudity was a normal part of life for faeries. It was humans who were wrong in their shame.

Declan solemnly held each article of clothing until she stood bare as the day she was born. A small pool of water stood behind the glass merrow. It led to the sea through small caverns Manus said he'd played in as a boy. Dangerous pastimes for a human, but he'd had many stories to tell.

A shiver trailed down her spine. Another sign she was weakening by the moment. She had never felt cold in her life.

Until now.

Saoirse reached up and untangled her hair from the

winding braids. Pins dropped to the stone floor and echoed in tiny pricks of sound.

"Promise me. Promise me you'll tell him the truth."

"I vow it." Declan's words rang in her ears and bounced off the walls. It was a binding oath, one he would have to fulfil, or he would follow her to the grave.

Giving him one final nod, she stepped into the water and disappeared beneath the surface.

Declan waited until the final ripple subsided. Only then did he stand and return to the main house to give them ill news.

CHAPTER 11

THE RETURN

The sun rose over the horizon and illuminated the port town of Uí Néill. Manus held onto the mast of the ship, far above his crew. It did not befit a man of his station to be up in the sails, but he couldn't care less.

He was finally home.

Tilting his head back, he inhaled deeply. The wind brought with it the fresh scent of salt, the acrid sting of fish, and the burn of smoke rising from the chimneys. It was the scent of his people, and he had missed it.

"Captain!" A voice shouted from below.

"Set down the anchors, boys!" A cheer drowned out his next words. "We're home."

All he wanted to do was get off this ship and back into the arms of the woman he loved. Time away from Saoirse had put so many things in perspective. She could be safe on the waters with him. The waves never crested a height where he might have worried her brethren could be find her location. And if he dressed her like a man, not even the biggest gossips of the faerie world could tell it was her.

His plan wasn't ironclad, but it was enough for him to be comfortable bringing her with him on the ship. There were so many plans to be made. She would want to see the world, and he wanted to show it to her.

Manus had never dreamed of having a wife who would share his love of travel. He had thought it would be hours of arguing, angry fights, lashing words as he went off to sea. It was why he hadn't told her in the first place.

But now he was certain she could come with him. And she would, because Saoirse would do anything for him.

They settled the ship to her bed, laid to rest until the next journey. The men were happy with their share. Manus was generous with their cut. He already had a fortune and knew where to find more if need be. They could keep most of the spoils.

They laughed as they set the boats to the water and tightened the last ropes on the Freedom. Manus patted the railing one last time, in thanks for the safe travels and in hopes for many more journeys to come.

His first mate waited for him in the last of the boats. Together, they watched the line of sailors laughing as they made it to the docks.

"It was a successful maiden voyage," Manus mused.

"To many more."

"Aye."

They stepped into the boat. Manus held himself still. It wouldn't do to show how excited he was to return. Too many sailors believed in superstitions, and a captain who preferred land to sea was a bad omen.

But he very much wanted to see his wife.

"Do you have anyone waiting for you?" he asked the first mate.

"Not particularly, captain. A few ladies in a brothel nearby, and I haven't given much thought to settling down. Do you?"

"I have the prettiest wife in the lands. My personal good luck charm."

"Your fortunes are great then. Few captains have a happy wife waiting for them upon their return."

He chuckled. "I can't say she'll be happy. I slipped out without telling her."

"She might not even recognize you." His first mate pointed to his beard. "You look more beast than man."

Their laughter echoed over the open waters and neither stopped until they reached the docks. Manus stepped out last, taking his first mate's offered hand and leaping onto the worn wood.

"It was an incredible journey, captain. I look forward to many more with you."

"Rest assured, I'll want you by my side on the next adventure."

They parted ways, and Manus made his way through the streets of his childhood. Dirty children raced by, screaming fishwives shook their fists, the tang of fish blood filled the air, and it was all endearing in a strange way.

It had been far too long since he'd wandered these streets. Although a part of him wanted to continue wandering, he also knew someone had likely seen the ship on the horizon. He'd need to rent a horse and get back to the house as soon as possible.

"My lord?" A small voice asked.

He looked down to see a boy, no older than ten, holding out his hand for a coin. "My pa said someone would need a horse from that ship. Be you willing to take this one?"

It was an ancient animal, but it would do. Nodding, he dropped a few gold coins into the child's palm and savored the look of awe.

"I'll take the horse for good. Tell your pa to buy a much better one for his plow."

"Aye, my lord. That'll do."

The boy ran off, little legs pumping to bring the good news to his father. Or to spend the money. Either way, it wasn't Manus's duty to figure out what the child would do.

He mounted the horse and set off at a decent canter. The old nag wouldn't survive a full gallop towards the manor. He didn't mind though; the surrounding landscape was beautiful and the land solid beneath his feet. What more could a man ask for?

Manus thought of his wife and couldn't stop the smile drifting across his face. Saoirse would be so pleased to see him. Even though he had been gone for a long time, there was a part of him that never stopped thinking about her.

Surely she would have felt that? He laid awake at night, staring up at the stars, knowing she was out there looking at the sky as well. He could almost feel her love from leagues away.

The manor appeared ahead of him, the path worn by the feet of thousands who had ridden past it. As a child, he'd marveled at the people who lived within those four walls. Now, those people were Manus and Saoirse. He intended to fill the house with many more family members soon.

The thought spurred him on. Children, he wanted children.

Like the child on the ship, a boy who would ride the seas with him. A daughter, whose dark hair and eyes would solemnly watch the waves for faeries.

He rode into the courtyard like a bean sídhe on the wind. The horse foamed at the mouth but galloped upon the stone right to the front door. The butler rushed out and waved his hand.

"My lord! You've returned!"

"I have. And I'd like to see my wife."

"Master, *wait—*"

He didn't pause to listen to whatever the man wanted to prattle on about. Servants were always so focused on what was proper, and he didn't have time for proper. Propriety be damned; he'd waited a very long time to see Saoirse.

And if she was still abed, more the better.

He took the stairs two at a time. His boots cracked against the wood, a staccato beat that echoed the beating of his heart. He was nearly there.

Soon, he would see her again. As much as he hated to admit it, she'd become a part of him. Saoirse, his sweet Saoirse.

Never again would he insist they sleep in separate beds. Never again would he set her aside when there was work to be done. He'd be a better husband and focus less on being a better lord.

Who cared that they had money and station now? If the other nobles wanted to gossip, let them. No one could take away his wealth and they damn well weren't taking his wife.

He set his shoulder to her door and shoved hard. It slammed against the side wall, echoing as he strode in like he owned the place.

"Wife?" he called out. "I have returned."

No one responded to his call. Frowning, he glanced around the room which was oddly put together. She wasn't so tidy. Saoirse had a way of making messes everywhere she went. Her maids could hardly keep up with her, a fact they enjoyed telling him, but Manus liked being able to track her through the house.

"Saoirse?"

The silence was deafening.

Footsteps heralded the approach of an entire servant army. The maids reached him first, their hair in disarray and skirts held up around their ankles.

"My lord, we didn't expect you to return so soon."

"We're so glad you've arrived safe and sound. When we heard no news, we became worried."

His accountant arrived next, pulling off his hat and gloves. "Master, we kept careful watch over your fortune. We can easily continue on in such a manner for a long time. I assure you, we have not misused your wealth in your absence."

The head housekeeper was next, brushing aside the maids with an angry swipe. "It's good to have you home, my lord. There is much I must speak with you about. Plenty of work to be done, I'm afraid."

Manus didn't want to hear any of it. They chattered like hens in a yard until he snapped. "Silence!"

The entire crowd of people fell still. A hairpin might have dropped to the floor and he would have heard it.

"Where is my wife?"

Not a single servant dared to say a word.

"You there." He pointed at the butler who had tried to get his attention upon arrival. "Explain."

"My lord I-I-I'm uncertain that I'm the appropriate person to do so."

"Where is my wife?" Manus thundered.

One of the maids, the whore he'd appreciated most in the brothel, stepped forward and laid a hand on his arm. "Manus, I'm sorry. She's gone."

"Gone where? I'll go and get her. A wife should know to stay and wait for her husband's return."

Anger simmered in his blood. Not at Saoirse, but at the servants who tried to keep his attention away from that which was important. Who cared about the gardens, the money, or the house? He cared about his bride whom he had not had enough time to enjoy.

"No," the maid murmured and shook her head. "She's *gone*, Manus."

"What are you trying to say?"

"She went down by the sea, she often walks at the shore. We thought nothing of it, but her friend…the red headed lord? He came back and said she was swept out by a rogue wave. There was nothing he could do. We looked for her, Manus. We looked for days. I'm so sorry."

They believed it. Every one of his servants believed the most ridiculous tale he'd ever heard before. They thought she was dead.

Their faces fell in sadness. Tears welled in the eyes of the head housekeeper, a woman he knew to be emotionless and cold. They thought he would fly into a rage, blame them for her death, or worse fire them all.

What they didn't know, was that Saoirse could swim. She could swim better than any human and no rogue wave could tear her from his side.

But she could leave him.

His heart clenched, and his palms grew sweaty. She had left him. She had decided that her old life was better than this one.

Gods, he couldn't breathe.

"Leave me," he growled. "Leave me be."

He backed into her room and slammed the door in the faces of all those who remained. They loved him, or some strange semblance of love he couldn't understand. Did he even know what love was?

The only person who had ever loved him had left.

Hands shaking, blood boiling, breath rattling out of his lungs, he turned towards the room which was too put together and let out a rage filled roar. She'd left him? Why?

He swept his arms over her vanity, sending her bottles of perfumes to the floor. They shattered and filled the room with cloying scents, but he didn't care. He only wanted to tear into everything more.

He'd given her a good life. He'd bought her the most beautiful house in Uí Néill, loved her as no man had ever loved a woman before. And she repaid him by leaving?

For hours he raged in her room, shattering furniture, tossing sheets and pieces of her bed over the balcony out to sea. He hoped she was out there in the bay, watching his rage and feeling as though he would do the same to her should she ever return. She had no right to leave him!

Hours later, when his rage died down and the ache in his heart became too strong to ignore, Manus knelt amid the destruction he'd wrought and sobbed.

He'd lost her, and he knew why. It wasn't her fault his soiled hands had touched her perfect flesh. It wasn't her fault his pathetic attempts at winning her heart had failed.

It was entirely his.

Water rushed over Saoirse's shoulders and poured down the hollow of her spine. The ocean caressed her like a lover who'd not seen her in years. It tangled through her hair, sending it flying behind her in a billowing mass of black ink.

Tendrils of kelp brushed her arms and fish rushed past her. Bubbles of laughter erupted from her lips. She rolled over and over, spinning in euphoria like a top set free from its string. The farther she got from shore, the more she felt like herself.

Pieces of her mind fit themselves back into the holes of her psyche. She could breathe again after feeling for months like she was gasping for air.

She smoothed her hands up her sides, feeling the pin prick of scales and the flaps of her gills as she gasped in the sweet, salty water.

This was how she was supposed to live. This was where her life began and would end.

In the arms of the sea.

She needed to find the other merrows, the ones Declan had spoken of. They were likely her mother's cousins. She'd come from these parts, or at least waters that weren't warm with rocky shores. Merrow pods migrated, she had no way of knowing where they would be this time of year.

Saoirse dove deep into the bay, searching for the one person who might be able to guide her in the right direction.

The shipwreck loomed in the distance, dark and foreboding. She didn't want to see the bean sídhe again. The woman's nightmarish visage would haunt her dreams for the rest of her life.

An eel slithered from the darkness. It stretched its neck and hissed as she swam past.

"Just a little further," she murmured.

Tingles slid up her spine as hundreds of eyes blinked open and watched her approach. She settled a hand on the tiny bump of her belly, took a deep breath, and opened her mouth.

"Don't talk," the bean sídhe interrupted her from the mass of eels. "You have returned already. For money or for information, either request will be denied. Begone from this place, cursed merrow."

"I need your help," she blurted.

"And my help is not for sale."

"Please!" Saoirse lurched forward with her arms outstretched. Eels snapped at her fingertips, hissing and coiling in a mass of rage.

The bean sídhe shushed them with quiet hums. She petted their backs, long strokes that calmed their ire. All Saoirse could see was her pale white hands until a gap in the writhing bodies revealed her skeletal face.

"You are desperate," the bean sídhe mused. "Why I wonder? Has your human disappeared into the sea and you wish to find him? You know the ocean keeps her treasures."

"No, I need to find the merrow pod which lives in these waters. Do you know where they are?"

A pale, milky hand reached out to her. "Why are you searching for your own kind?"

"I need to find them."

"We faeries trade in knowledge, merrows. What has sent you back into the arms of the ocean when you know it's a dangerous place for one who has run from it?"

"I'm no longer running." In response, a current pushed against her back, whirling around her tail and trailing up her spine. "I need to find my people for the safety of myself and my child."

"Child?" The bean sídhe's eyes widened. "What have you done?"

Saoirse rubbed a hand against her belly. "Only that which can be born from true love."

"You have condemned an innocent soul to the same life you ran from." The bean sídhe shook her head in disgust. "I will tell you where the merrows are, but only because I know the harrowing journey ahead. That pod differs from the others, you'll see why, and you are not suited for the life they lead."

"But my child will be?"

"Your daughter won't have a choice."

"Daughter?" Saoirse gave the bean sídhe a shy smile. "Can you tell for certain?"

"Humans and merrows can only produce girls." She lifted a hand and pointed towards the darkness. "Follow the whale song. They travel with a pod of orcas who are more likely to bite you than bring you to their favorite merrows. Be careful when you see them and hold your distance."

"How will they know I'm there?"

"Oh, they'll know." An eel stretched out and nipped at the

tip of her tail. "Now, go."

She didn't have to be told twice. Saoirse launched herself away from the darkness, from the fearful tomb of undulating flesh.

Hours passed, but she didn't feel the ache or pain of movement. Her muscles longed for use, her tail whipping back and forth in wild abandon. She was free. For the first time in what felt like forever, she was free.

She let herself enjoy the moment. She'd earned a few moments of bliss before the hole inside her chest opened back up.

One thought of Manus, and the ocean swept away the tears leaking from her eyes. He might be home even now, finding the empty bedroom, home, and life he returned to. Would he miss her?

Saoirse knew deep in her heart he would. He would miss her but not a single soul would know.

Had Declan told him yet? She hoped he had been there when Manus arrived. The servants would have so much to say, rumors would start, and she hated to think of what they might come up with.

Hopefully, they all believed she was dead.

Saoirse stroked her belly and shook her head. When had her life degraded to this? It wasn't fair that anyone think she was dead, even less that Manus believe it. It was bad enough he would always question what he did wrong.

Guilt latched onto her heart with gnashing teeth. There was no other way. Declan was right, the ocean had washed away much of the pain his absence had caused. Already, she felt more like herself. The baby stretched inside her, pleased with its new home as much as its mother.

She sighed. If given the choice, she would make the same decision again. She had to choose which future would give her enough time to live for the baby to be born.

Manus had to understand that.

Clicking calls echoed through the surrounding water. She didn't know how long she'd traveled. Hours, days, it was all the same in the depths of the ocean. But these were different cries, not the dolphin song nor familiar whale song.

These sounds were aggressive. They attacked her sensitive ears and warned her to stay still, to freeze, to flee from the predators likely speeding towards her through the murk.

She hesitated, floating in the water and rotating as she tried to find the beasts. They weren't sharks who were easily encouraged to leave merrows alone.

Orcas were highly intelligent and deadly beasts. If they wanted her dead, they would chase her to the ends of the oceans. Their teeth shredded bodies in seconds, their powerful forms sliced through the water with impressive speed, and they liked to play with their prey.

Her gills flared wide. They would not take her. Not yet, not when she had come so far to find the only family she had left.

A black flash skirted past her, buffeting her body with a powerful current of water that shoved her towards another black and white spotted body. But Saoirse was prepared, and she was desperate. Baring her teeth, she flared her fins and lifted her hands into claws.

"You will not take me," she growled. "I am here to speak with your masters, and I will not die before I meet them."

The orcas slowed in their attack. They stared at her, the

depths of the ocean reflected in the dark pools of their eyes. She knew they understood her. Why were they not leaving?

Then she saw them. Bodies rising out the depths with spears in their hands. Strong women with muscular bodies and cords wrapped around their biceps with jingling shells hanging to their wrists. They were shadows in the water, warrior women each one.

"Welcome sister," one called out. She swam forward, and Saoirse saw the other merrow's face was tattooed with wave patterns. "You have come a long way to speak with my pod."

"I wish to join you."

The shadows doubled, tripled, then grew in a number so large Saoirse couldn't begin to count them. So many merrows, all together in safety and health. They would be a good family to join if they would have her.

"Why should we allow you to join us?" the merrow asked.

Saoirse thought it likely this was the leader. No other had the tattooed markings, that she could see, and they waited for this woman to speak.

"I have traveled from distant, warm waters. I came here to share my life with a human man." Rumbles whispered across the waves as the merrows drifted closer to each other, their disappointed comments stinging Saoirse's ears. "I love him. He is a good man, but the sea calls to him. I cannot compete with our mother."

"No, I imagine no creature on earth could do that."

Saoirse nodded in agreement. "He travels far from my side, and through our bond, I am fading. I ask not for myself, but for the babe growing within me. Give her the life she deserves."

"Should your child not be with its father?"

She pressed a hand against her stomach, fear dancing along her skin. Some might say the babe belonged with Manus. But she knew this was the right choice. Manus wouldn't know how to raise a merrow child, and the babe would bond to him and likely die while he was off on one of his adventures. He would never know why.

"No. I will not burden him with such a child. Faeries need to raise faeries."

It was the right thing to say. A few of the merrows nodded in agreement, some of them even swimming closer to see the newcomer. Light reflected in their eyes. Pools of glowing green stared at her from the darkness of the sea.

Saoirse swallowed and turned towards the leader. "I request sanctuary from all who would harm me. I do not require you or your family accept me as your own. My time is limited in this world. I ask only for protection from my blood kin until the child is born."

"What would you have us do about your deteriorating mind?"

"Nothing." She answered honestly. "Let me die."

"You do this for a *human*? Why?"

"I love him enough to risk my immortality. I want a good life for the child we have created, one I would approve of, one that is familiar to me."

"Does he know of the babe?"

"No."

The leader decided and gave a simple response. She sternly nodded, slid her spear into its holder, and opened her arms. "Welcome, daughter. You will my join my family for as long as you are with us."

Tears gathered in Saoirse's eyes, but the ocean wiped them away as she raced forward to be folded into the arms of her people once more.

Manus stared into the fires of the great hall, a bottle of rum loosely held in his hand. He didn't care if it dropped to the floor with the others, they'd already done their job. Drunk was an understatement for his current form.

He hadn't wanted to be merely drunk; he wanted to forget he even existed. Two bottles of rum down and already the room was a little hazy. Black dots pricked at his vision, something he likely should worry about, and the entire room listed to the left. But this was how he wanted to be. He couldn't remember anything when he was this drunk.

A sweet scent danced through the air. Salt, sea breeze, the brush of wind against his skin. And suddenly all he could think of was a candlelit night when dark strands of hair brushed across his chest and a voice whispered in his ear, "Manus, my love."

He swatted at the air over his head, trying with all his might to bat away her ghost. She had no reason to linger. She'd left.

And he still couldn't get her out of his thoughts.

Every time he blinked, he saw the way she tilted her head when she had a question. The graceful arch of her neck when she laughed, likely at something he said that embarrassed or pleased her. The dance of her fingers as she walked down the stairs, each fingertip alighting on the railing for brief moments before skipping over the wood.

Every movement was fluid grace, and every glance seared him to the bone.

Her dark eyes haunted him. They stared back from the shadows, swirling in the gloom and glowing with so much love and trust that his heart nearly burst.

The flames crackled and grew tall. He stared into their depths with as much concentration as his foggy mind could muster and swore he saw them coalesce into a single figure. A merrow who swam through the fire.

Snarling, he flung the remainders of the rum into the hearth. It exploded in a wave of heat and broken glass.

Manus stumbled backwards, his hazy mind remembering that fire could burn, but his feet forgetting how to move. He tripped over his boots and landed back in his chair with a loud thump.

"So, this is how the master of the manor spends his days."

He recognized the man walking into his great hall but couldn't pinpoint from where. The tall redhead took up too much room. His face was too handsome, too even, too…inhuman.

Manus bared his teeth. "I didn't give you permission to shadow my doorstep, Fae."

"I don't need permission." The leprechaun sidestepped a pile of bottles and leaned a shoulder against the fireplace. Crossing his arms, he looked Manus up and down. "You look terrible."

"You're smart enough to guess why." Manus reached for another bottle, his fingers hanging limp in the air when he realized he'd already drank it all. "Damn it."

The leprechaun watched as Manus fumbled. His eyes burned, but Manus refused to itch the back of his neck where the faerie's magic seemed to weigh the heaviest.

"Why are you here?" Manus grunted. "Haven't you done enough?"

"What have I done?"

"The servants talk." He waved a limp hand in the direction of the door. "And I'm not blind. I saw the way you looked at her, and I know you had a hand in what happened."

"Do you?" The leprechaun arched a red brow. "Enlighten me."

"I know your kind. I've seen you wandering the streets, complimenting the ladies while giving the men dirty looks. You're a rake, a ruffian, the kind of man who preys on the weak. And you saw my Saoirse as an easy target."

"Your Saoirse?"

"Yes *mine,*" Manus growled. "Unless you seem to think she's now yours?"

"I wouldn't claim ownership of another person."

A loud laugh erupted from Manus, cold and cruel. "And here I was thinking Fae couldn't lie."

The silence which followed his outburst stung his ears. The leprechaun stared at him with eyes that delved deep into his soul, and he didn't like it. The man saw too much.

The leprechaun cleared his throat. "You think Saoirse and I were…what? Lovers?"

"Like I said. People talk."

"Yes, she was always worried about that. I happen to enjoy poking fun at your ridiculous ideals, but she was more sensitive to human strife. She didn't want any of you to be unhappy."

The leprechaun was too friendly with his wife, Manus mused. He spoke as if they were friends, dear friends, and those words stung. Saoirse had never once voiced her worries to Manus. She was always bright and happy, no matter what she had seen.

He sighed and pinched the bridge of his nose. "If you make her happy, then I wish you both the best."

"Excuse me?"

"Just take care of her," he ground out. The words were a knife to his gut, twisting and turning with each syllable that fell from his lips. "She's important to me, no matter what you might think. I know she's not dead, and I know she wouldn't have returned to the nightmare of a life she had. That leaves you. So take care of her, or I'll track you down and gut you."

The leprechaun gave him an odd look. "You'd let me have her?"

Manus's hands were shaking. His fingers curled into his palms, fists wanting nothing more than to pound into something. But this wasn't about him. Even drunk and wavering, he wanted to make sure Saoirse was happy. If this man was who she had chosen, then he needed to warn him.

"She's a gentle woman with a heart of gold. Be careful with her, leprechaun."

"But you'd let me have her?" The faerie snapped his fingers. "Just like that?"

"Not *just* like that, she's a person." And she should be able to make her own decisions, but he had to have some control. She had left him. He got to decide whether she came back. "Just—don't let her forget she was loved by a fool who gave her all the wrongs things to make her happy."

The leprechaun shrugged. "Don't think I'll ever see her again, mate. I don't make it a habit to dive into the ocean and hold my breath. Never liked cold water."

"What?"

"She's off. Who knows where really, just off into the ocean where she belongs."

Manus shook his head, having trouble following what the faerie was saying. "What do you mean you don't know where she is?"

"I mean, I told her to go back to where she belonged but didn't tell her where. I know there's a pod of merrows around here somewhere, but I don't know how to find them."

His vision blurred. "You told her to go?"

"Well you certainly weren't going to." A feral grin spread across the leprechaun's face, full of hidden anger and rage. "Someone needed to have her best interests in mind."

"You're the reason she left me?" Manus lurched to his feet. "You sent her out into the water with no protection, no one she knows, not even a general direction where to look?"

"She's a faerie. She knows how to take care of herself."

"She is my wife!" Manus thundered.

The smile on the leprechaun's face changed. Glamour shivered and fell, revealing a terrifying faerie with golden skin and teeth like knives. He was tall, red headed, and glimmered like molten metal. "Not anymore."

Manus didn't care the faerie was looking for a fight. He didn't care that the faerie was impossibly strong and could use magic to bring him to his knees. This was a matter of pride.

His fist flew through the air and cracked against the other

man's cheekbone. Fire blossomed along the ridge of his knuckles. His hand shook, but he wasn't about to stop any time soon.

The leprechaun had said enough. In his drunken state, Manus didn't care that the other man was right. He didn't care that Saoirse deserved to live with her family if that was what she desired. He only cared that this man had admitted to being an instrument in the disappearance of his wife.

And he would hurt for it.

Another punch slammed into the leprechaun's jaw. Manus felt it crack under his fist and the rush of satisfaction as blood splattered on the mantelpiece.

He pummeled the leprechaun, smashing his fist into whatever piece of flesh he could find. It didn't matter if his knuckles split, or his bones cracked, the pain was nothing more than a fleeting memory which was both satisfying and enraging.

He wanted the leprechaun to feel pain. Every crack of flesh meeting bone vibrated through Manus's arm. It rolled around in his head, reassuring him that there was no way the other man couldn't understand his frustration, anger, and the pain violently rocketing through his body.

"I tried to be the bigger man," Manus growled when the leprechaun stepped back. "She deserves a man capable of that."

"Does she? Or have you put your own ideals on her?"

"Shut up." Manus drove his fist down, swift and true.

The leprechaun ducked in an impressive showcase of speed. One moment he was crouched on the floor, bleeding from multiple splits in his face, the next he was five feet away and leaning against the fireplace again.

Manus watched as he swiped at the blood dribbling from his lips and flashed sharp teeth in a mockery of a grin.

"Careful human," the leprechaun warned. "You won't like it if you push me too far."

"I gave you a chance to be the better man."

"Did you now? All I heard was you telling me how things are going to be."

"She deserves someone to look after her. Someone who will take care of her, give her everything she desires."

"Maybe she just wants someone. Period. Maybe she didn't want someone to take care of her. She wanted someone to *be here with her*."

The words flew like arrows and sank their serrated edges into Manus's chest. They dug through his skin, burrowing and tearing until he couldn't breathe. He stumbled back a step and grasped the mantel.

"Is that what she said?" he gasped.

"Not in so many words. She made me promise to tell you why she left even though I disagreed with her."

Manus braced his forearms and stared into the flames. "Then she went back to what she was comfortable with. Back to that place where they locked her in a cage, where they didn't appreciate her for what she was."

"I doubt the merrow pod around here is like that. She left because you two are bonded, and the longer you were gone, the more likely it was for her to die."

"What?" he gasped.

"The bond, you idiot. Do humans no longer speak of it? The further you are from each other, the more strain it puts on her. She exists because you exist." The leprechaun spat blood on his floor. "You've got a mean right hook for such a little man."

"She was dying?" He squeezed the stone mantle until his fingers ached. "Why didn't she tell me?"

"She didn't want you to feel trapped. The land isn't your home, and she'd rather take the pain than take away what you love."

"Until now."

"Until I showed her how stupid she was being. Since you disappeared, she should die in the arms of her family."

"Then she really is dead?" Something cracked in his chest. A chasm opened up with dark eyes staring back at him.

Manus could handle the heartache if she had left him. He'd been left before, and it wouldn't be the first time a woman found him lacking. But to know she was dead?

It destroyed him.

He fell to his knees, gasping through the pain in his chest. How did anyone survive the loss of a loved one? He was barely aware of himself at all. The world fell away, and all that existed was the aching hole in his chest.

Dead.

Her laughter sounded like bubbles breaking on the surface of the water. He had listened to her laugh for hours, trying to make her chuckle or giggle just to hear it again. Had he ever told her how much he loved it?

He would never again see the way she would sweep her hair over her shoulder and stare down at something new she found. It was usually something simple, cutlery, a hairbrush, a small decorative pot. But he had never looked at what she held. All he could focus on was the graceful arch of her neck and how badly he wanted to press a kiss to the curve.

Pain spread its clawing ache further, dancing down his arms and curling his hands into fists. He'd never acted on all the things he wanted to do, because it wasn't *right*. So many things he'd wanted to say, to do, to watch, and he hadn't done them because the world told him not to.

"You're not breathing," the leprechaun said. His words were tentative and curious as if he didn't know what Manus was going through. "You should probably do that."

"How am I supposed to breathe when she no longer does?" He glanced up, fierce and loyal until the bitter end. "What kind of monster are you? Why couldn't you let me continue to think she lived out a normal life? That she left of her own accord?"

"Even faeries have to follow through with unbreakable bonds."

The leprechaun knelt. He stared at Manus with keen eyes, the glamour dropped. If he had been in a better state of mind, Manus might have marveled at the strangeness of the faerie.

His skin wasn't made of metal although it looked as if it was dusted in it. His eyes were cold and hard, his sharp teeth poking through his lips. The leprechaun cocked his head to the side and stared directly into his soul.

"You want her back?"

"How could I not? She was everything."

"You didn't act like she was everything. You left without warning her what your plans were, leaving a note she couldn't read. Her maids read it out loud, did you know that? It embarrassed Saoirse."

The name finally registered in Manus's drunken mind. "You know her name."

"I know everyone's name, Manus of Uí Néill."

He gulped. "Do you know a way to get her back?"

"She might not be dead yet, although it's been months since she slipped back beneath the waves. If you are swift, you may catch her yet."

"Why would you help me?"

The leprechaun shrugged, blood dripping down his chin and hitting the floor with a quiet sound. "You obviously know how to fight, and you care about her. These were facts I did not previously know."

"Had you known, would you have encouraged her to stay?"

"No." The leprechaun shook his head. "The sea was the only way to slow the effects of your bond. If there was a way to save her, I would have taken it."

"You are fond of her."

"Yes."

"You—" Manus paused and licked his lips. "Love her?"

"As only her kind could. Don't worry human, I don't intend to steal her away from you. I have no need of a wife."

"Then, there is a possibility of finding her?" His heart lifted, pain easing for a brief second until he noticed the leprechaun hesitating. "Well?"

"There is a possibility, but I cannot say with any certainty you will be able to find her, or she will be alive and well."

"How? How do I find her?"

Again, the leprechaun hesitated, and Manus knew it would not be an answer he would like. It didn't matter. He would do anything he could to get her back, knowing she had left for her own safety.

He would prove his worth. If she wanted him to live in a

cage under the sea, he would do it. Whatever it took to bring her back into his arms.

The leprechaun rolled his lips between his teeth and grunted. "You'll need a swift ship, one that can turn at a moment's notice."

"I have that already."

"And you'll need the courage of a thousand men, because you might not come back from this alive."

"For her, I would do anything."

"Then you need to sail directly into faerie waters and pray she hears your screams."

Manus blinked. "Pardon?"

"Merrows travel alongside guardians. They have a strange relationship, no one can really explain it. However, there are faerie waters near here. A portal into the Otherworld, guarded by fierce merrows and their greatest weapon. If you sail into those waters, Saoirse is sure to hear you. If she loves you, then she might save you."

"That's suicide."

"Maybe. Or she might wait for you."

He'd need to find a crew of men willing to put their lives on the line. He wouldn't put anyone at risk without their knowledge. Were there men like that? Perhaps not in Uí Néill, but there were enough who owed him some kind of recompense for previous grievances.

Manus grimaced. "It's possible. But first, I must know how to fight the guardian in case it attacks."

"You don't fight a guardian." The leprechaun sauntered away, leaving the same way he had entered. "Good luck, human. You'll need it."

Manus raced through the house, not sleeping until he had a crew of men who agreed to travel with him. Days passed, but he did not see the rising or setting of the sun. He had a reason to focus now.

He didn't surface until he was standing on the deck of his ship, staring off into the horizon.

"Captain!" a man shouted. "All sailors aboard!"

Manus glanced at his first mate, lifting an eyebrow. "What say you?"

"It's the foolhardiest trip I've ever been on, captain. I'm not looking forward to seeing a guardian, as it sounds particularly frightening." He cleared his throat. "But none of us would be here if we didn't believe in the cause."

"Gold and treasures."

"And a woman who somehow captured the heart of a wandering man."

"I didn't know you were a romantic." He arched a brow, suddenly wondering if he should know this man. His first mate was a mystery, found on the streets and proving to be a capable man. He hadn't expected loyalty.

"Hardly. I see value in people and actions, captain. Shall we?"

"Give the orders."

His first mate spun on his heel, shouting, "Hoist the sails and bring up the anchors, boys!"

They shared a look of trepidation. "To faerie waters we go."

CHAPTER 12

Waters Running Red

The merrows gathered together in the never-ending blue of the ocean. Suspended as they were, they could watch for predators from every angle. Each carried a sharpened spear made of coral and lashed to carved stone. The females adjusted their grip, narrowed eyes watching for the slightest movement.

In the center of their protective circle, four women floated. Two supported the middle merrow's arms, keeping her suspended in the water while the other swam in slow circles around her.

"Focus on the pain, Saoirse. Focus on the movement and the feeling of your child."

"I can't!" she grunted as another pulse made her flick her tail wildly. "Please, help me."

"You are doing well. Soon your daughter will enter our world and you shall hold her in your arms. You must embrace the pain."

"I want to sleep," she whimpered. "I want this to stop."

Merrow live birth was difficult as they were not meant to pass a child through their fishlike tails. It was possible although usually excruciating for the mother. Still, like so many others, Saoirse was willing to take the risk.

She had been too late to lay the mermaid's purse where her child might have grown without risking both of their lives. Now, she must go through the gauntlet.

Alannah, the matriarch of the merrow pod, circled her and cast a critical gaze up and down her tail. "You will survive this. You promised me a child in return for your safety. Have I not looked after you? Have I not prolonged your sanity to bring the child into the world?"

Blue tattoos swirled down the merrow's face and disappeared into the long length of her hair. Saoirse knew the waves traveled all the way down to where her tail met her torso. It was a painful process to become matriarch, but well worth it.

She curled her tail up as another wave rocked through her, the fins at her hips fluttering. Her belly was too large for her to tail to move easily.

"I can't do it, Alannah!"

"You can, and you will! Push!"

Saoirse grunted and threw her muscles into the job at hand. She had to bring her daughter into the world. Not because Alannah wanted her, the matriarch was kinder than she pretended to be, but because she wanted to see her. Before she died, she wanted to see the child she and Manus had created.

Her spine arched in pain, her gills sealed shut, and her tail lashed wildly. The merrows holding her arms helped, allowing her to squeeze their hands when necessary.

For hours she writhed in the open blue of the ocean. For hours her blood stained the water in spurting clouds and then, nothing at all.

Exhausted, she fell limp in their hands. "I can't," she whispered. "I can't do this anymore."

Alannah surged forward, strong hands framing Saoirse's face. "Stopping now will only hurt you and the babe further. You have little time, Saoirse."

"I'm trying!" she wailed. "I have tried for hours and I'm in so much pain."

"Just a little more. Just give us a little more or we will intervene."

She knew what the hidden words meant. The worth of merrow lives were measured in years. Saoirse was older, and therefore less necessary than the child within her belly. If she could not bring her daughter into the water on her own, they would slice her open and pull the babe out themselves.

A part of her wanted to ask them to just get it over with. The end was near, and her torment would be over.

The other part remembered the worried expression Manus wore when she stubbed her toe or sliced her finger on the sharp edge of a letter opener. He wouldn't want her to give up so easily.

The waters echoed with a low grumble. Deep and reverberating, the sound was a song she remembered. Almost immediately, Saoirse's body fell limp in the arms of the merrows who parted like a wave for the being swimming towards them.

Her lips parted in a soft sigh as the guardian's hand reached for her. It scooped her from the grasp of the merrows and carried her close to its chest.

"Hello," Saoirse panted. She touched the shell in her ear to ensure it was still there.

The whale song of a guardian filled the waters, quiet and steady as the waves. "Welcome home, little merrow."

"I am in pain. My child does not want to greet the waves."

"Few do." The guardian shifted its fingers, gently rubbing its thumb over the swell of her belly. "Will you accept my assistance?"

How could a guardian help? Saoirse didn't know what it could do but nodded her head. She would accept anything at this point.

"This will hurt, little merrow. Know I am not doing it to cause you pain."

The giant thumb pressed down upon her belly. Pressure swiftly became blinding agony. Saoirse tilted her head back and let out a wail that echoed through the waves. The merrows flinched back, lifting their spears as they prepared to threaten the guardian.

Saoirse held out her hand, palm out and fingers spread. They needed to remain calm. The guardian didn't mean to harm her, it didn't want to, but it also wanted to help save her child.

It pressed harder, just enough that she felt something inside her give. A bloom of red burst, a cloud that preceded the weak cry of a baby.

She reached out her arms, unable to see the child but knowing it was there. Her soul blossomed, spreading petals like the roses she had seen on land. Her daughter.

Her daughter.

"Give her to me," she whispered. "Please, can I see her?"

The guardian's finger shifted, ever so gently, and a tiny body floated towards her on the current.

Saoirse grabbed her daughter and snuggled her close to her

chest. She was a tiny little thing, all tail and head with tiny fingers already grasping the strands of Saoirse's hair. Her eyes were open and so dark they looked like the dead of night.

The little one was already swishing her tail back and forth, ready for a hard life under the sea.

Cradled in the guardian's hand, Saoirse could curl around her daughter and hold onto her tiny fingers.

"Welcome to the world," she whispered. "I won't be here long with you, but I want you to know how much I love you."

"Many things change, Saoirse," the guardian sang.

"What do you mean, honored one?"

"There are whispers in the waves. A ship approaches."

Her fingers curled against the baby's back. "A ship? How soon?"

"The wind travels slowly, but they ride the waves with determination. The seagulls say the man who stands upon the bow shouts your name."

"Manus," she breathed. "He has come for me."

"Is coming, little merrow. You will need to hold on for a while longer."

Saoirse held her squirming daughter to her chest and vowed she would stay sane. There wasn't much time left, but she could do it. The knowledge that Manus was coming eased some pressure in her mind.

She wasn't herself, but she could remain alive for a little while longer.

The guardian removed its hands, letting her drift down into the waiting arms of the merrows below. Saoirse floated with her daughter held against her chest.

Coos greeted them.

"Oh, she's beautiful!"

"Look at her, what delicate features."

"Such tiny fingers!"

Alannah pushed through the crowd and reached out her arms. "Congratulations, Saoirse. Let me see my new daughter."

"She is my daughter." Her steely tones made the other merrows freeze. They released their hold on her arms and shoulders, letting her stay upright under her own power.

Alannah's brows drew down. "What?"

"I am not yet dead. This is my daughter until my body turns to foam."

"That was not part of our deal, merrow."

"It is now." Saoirse looked up. She couldn't see the surface, but she could feel he was closer to her now than ever. "My husband comes for me."

"He is not welcome in faerie waters."

"And still, he comes."

Manus would know the dangers of faerie waters. He'd lived it before. Knowing that he would brave such dangers for her warmed the cold corners of her heart, cracking through the ice she had built around herself to remain safe.

Danger awaited him at every corner, and she didn't know how to help. The merrows would attack the ship as would the guardian. Though the gentle giant likely wanted to help, it would do what it was made to do.

Destroy.

She shivered, then turned to meet Alannah's frigid gaze. "This is my family. I came to you for sanctuary, believing there was nothing I could do to mend my grief. I have a chance now to give my daughter a real life. With a father and mother who love her, to help her become a better woman than we can give her in the waters."

Something shifted in the tattooed woman's gaze. She sighed and relented. "You are right. Merrow life is not easy, and I would not wish it upon a child if there was another option. We have already informed your family of your predicament. They have agreed to disown you as you have married a human. If you believe this man is good and worthy of a merrow child, then I will concede she is your child."

"Will you grant him sanctuary in these waters as well?"

The steel returned to Alannah's spine. "If he comes into our territory, we will tear his ship to pieces. It is our way, Saoirse. You know this to be true."

She did. And though it made her shiver, it also set her resolve.

Now she could prepare for the storm barreling towards them. With a child, there was no chance she could meet him. A ship was large, and she was small.

Saoirse's best option was to wait for him to reach her. Then, with what little time she had, she would plan a way to save him.

Their daughter gurgled and tugged on Saoirse's hair. She grinned from ear to ear when Saoirse glanced down at her.

"Your father needs to name you," she whispered.

She was bound and determined that he would.

Manus held onto the railing of the ship, staring fiercely out to sea. Footsteps behind him cracked on the sodden wood.

"Captain? We're nearing faerie waters."

"I know."

"Do you?" His first mate stood next to him. "Ah. Yes, of course."

A wall of storm clouds marked the edge where it was safe for the ship to travel. Manus remembered this darkness all too well, the terrifying roar of thunder, the bright blasts of lightning.

But more than anything else, he remembered the deep grumble of the guardian, bodies floating beneath the waves, and the gentle caress of fingertips on his cheek.

"Captain?"

"What is it?"

Manus knew what the first mate wanted. He wanted a plan which would ease the minds of the crew. They wanted the reassurance their captain wasn't completely insane.

Sailing into faerie waters was only done by those who had a death wish. Everyone spoke of what happened, the horrifying fear of what might happen to those who tried to make their way into the Otherworld. Death awaited them.

Manus didn't want to disappoint his crew. He spun on his heel and strode across the deck.

"Men! Leave your duties for a moment and gather here with me."

They dropped their ropes, brushes, and brooms, rushing to cluster around the captain few of them knew.

Manus hadn't chosen these men for their talents. He didn't care if they knew a ship up and down, he half expected the ship wouldn't return with them. These sailors needed to be brave, to know about the Fae, and to risk their lives at a moment's notice.

"I cannot promise you a treasure," he said when they had gathered around them. "I cannot promise you glory. But I can promise that you are about to see something few men have seen before. What awaits us in those waters is dangerous, large, and wants nothing more than to kill us."

The men began to shift. Small movements caught Manus's eyes. The twitch of fingers, the bounce of a leg, the drawn down brows. They were afraid of what might happen, and what he might say next.

"Death awaits us, boys. Death and honor and glory. You are here for an adventure of a lifetime, and that I promise you shall see in mere moments. We sail to the edge, kill the sails, and set down the anchor."

"Captain," his first mate interrupted. "The sea is too deep here. The anchor will not halt our progress."

"It's not to stop the ship. It's to give the faeries something to climb."

With that said, Manus turned on his heel and returned to the bow of the ship. They would follow his commands, he'd paid them to do that, and it didn't matter his plan was insane. They weren't technically going into the faerie waters.

Killing a ship in the middle of the ocean wasn't the smartest move. He didn't know if the guardian would think they were too close and grow angry. It was always a possibility.

But there was also a chance he could speak with it. Saoirse spoke of the creature as if it were intelligent. Surely, if that were true, it could also be reasoned with.

The sails fluttered in the sudden wind as his crew turned the ship directly towards the storm. He trusted his first mate to guide them and stood with his arms crossed watching the waters.

Manus needed to be ready. He needed to make sure the crew had a chance at living. He wouldn't be like his previous captain who'd sailed them directly towards death. He knew better.

They slowed at the edge of the storm. The sails slapped as they were drawn down, the anchor chains rattled as men dropped them over the side. Manus savored the splashing sounds and prayed they would work the way he intended.

Everyone held their breath, waiting. The crew stilled; not even the slightest exhale could be heard. They stared towards uncharted territory and prayed their deaths would be swift.

Rain barely touched the deck. It was a wall of splashing movement close enough to touch and obscure their vision.

Manus knew the intention behind the storm. It wouldn't sink a ship, he'd been in enough widow makers to know that. The rain was a warning, the thunder a sign, and the lightning a screaming cry to turn back now.

They didn't have to worry about anything above the waves.

"Captain—"

Manus lifted a hand for silence. He narrowed his eyes and waited just a bit longer.

They didn't have to wait long. A smooth back crested the water in the distance, pale gray and effortlessly graceful. It might have been a whale, the arched spine was familiar, but Manus could see the long tendrils of dark hair flowing down the guardian's back.

A sailor let out a choked sound.

"Get below deck," Manus called out. "Man the port sides

and turn the cannons boys. If we have to fight, then we'll give them the fight of their lives."

The slapping feet rushing below deck was enough to set his heart racing. A fight with a guardian wouldn't last long. It was too big, too strong, and he wasn't convinced the guardian he had seen was the only one in the ocean.

A deep groan rocked through the ship. The wood beneath his feet vibrated with the sheer force of her call.

"Captain?" his first mate asked again. "What in the name of God is that thing?"

"That is a faerie."

"Faeries aren't that big."

"Some of them are. Some are terrifying and beautiful, others are just terrifying." Manus lifted a telescope and watched her approach. She raced towards them far faster than any mere whale could. "That is a guardian. She watches over the merrow pods and ensures no humans cross into territories where they shouldn't be."

"Like us?"

"Precisely."

Manus set his jaw and dropped the telescope. The guardian would be upon them in moments, and he needed the ship to remain intact. He had to force it to listen to him, even for a few moments, and perhaps leave his men alive.

He hopped up on the railing of the ship, holding onto the sail ropes to balance himself.

Tilting his head back, he shouted into the wind, "Guardian of the seas, we beseech you to hear our call!"

His shout rang loud and true. It carried through the wind and struck the water as if he had dived into the waves. The guardian did not slow.

Again, he tried, "You have a merrow amongst your charges who belongs to me! I have come to beg her forgiveness!"

Did the guardian slow? To his eyes, it appeared the guardian hesitated for a moment before returning to her charging pace.

"That merrow is my wife! I left her for adventures on the sea, and I was wrong. I wish only to confess my folly and beg her to return to me."

The guardian reached their ship and reared out of the water. She loomed above him, rivers of water pouring off her shoulders and splashing upon the deck.

Her skin was paler than he remembered. Gray, but also with no color. Shadows played across her pronounced musculature, and he shivered when he realized she put most men to shame. Her entire body was made of rip cord muscle.

Scars laced across her shoulders and chest. Small breasts suggested this one was also female although he had no way of knowing for certain. She stared at him with black eyes, no whites to make her appear human. They were so focused upon him he almost didn't notice the lack of nose and wide gill slits upon her neck.

Manus watched in horror as the gill slits slapped against the side of her neck, vibrating with the deep bass he now knew was the guardian trying to speak.

"I cannot understand you, great beast of the deep." He swallowed through the raspy fear in his voice. "I ask you look upon me with pity. My crew is below deck, we have no wish to fight you. But I will do everything in my power to find my bride again."

The guardian cocked her head to the side, throat working as she tried to convey something to him.

Manus wished he could understand her. He wished he knew how to speak to a creature this large, but he didn't. And the reality was if this creature didn't want to help him, then he would do whatever it took to die with honor.

"I will only ask you one more time," he warned. "Where is my wife?"

The guardian did not move. She seemed to be waiting for what he would do next.

He suspected she had never seen cannon fire before. Most ships wouldn't have had a chance to fire at her, they never would have seen her.

It was a shame to attack such a creature. She was beautiful in the same way the sea was beautiful. Strong, powerful, achingly dangerous, but otherworldly.

He nodded. "All right then. You will protect her until the very end, I see that now."

Manus glanced over his shoulder at his first mate who was staring up at the beast with mouth agape.

"First mate." His words lashed across the ship like the crack of a whip. "Fire the cannons."

"How is the babe?" a merrow asked. She swam close to where Saoirse and her daughter were tucked into the edge of a cliff. "It's not often we see a new one born in our pod."

"She is well." Saoirse lifted her finger, the baby's hand

wrapped tightly around it. "Already stronger than I expected she would be."

"She's quite beautiful. Like her mother."

"Oh, I think she's strong like her father." She looked down at the child and marveled at how much she looked like them. Manus's strong nose, her own dark eyes, the stubborn set of her jaw likely from both her parents.

The merrow reached out and traced a finger between the baby's eyes. Saoirse's daughter scrunched up her face, not crying yet but warning she might.

Both women laughed at her antics.

"She knows what she likes," the other merrow chuckled. "She will be a handful when she's older. The last merrow who did that when I touched her was Alannah's first daughter."

"Alannah had a daughter?" Saoirse asked in surprise.

"Yes. She lost her long ago. The girl's favorite pastime was deep sea hunting, she had scars on her back from the battles. A giant squid finally got her. They said it was a terrible death, but that she killed the beast on the way down."

"I'm so sorry to hear that."

"It's dangerous to live here." The merrow gave her a stern look. "Just as dangerous as it is to live above the waves."

"It does not surprise me. I lived in a cold water pod, at the bottom of the seafloor. There wasn't much danger there, but the journey to the surface was always tense."

"I suspect it was."

The merrow seemed to hesitate, and Saoirse wondered if she had something to say.

The other merrows had been strange around her for a while now. They swam close and opened their mouths, then closed them tightly as soon as another cast a glance in their direction. She recognized those who repeated this behavior.

"Do you have something to tell me?" Saoirse asked. "I'm sorry I haven't had time to get to know many of you. But I have seen you looking at me before."

"Saoirse, there are some of us who—"

"Ship!" The cry rocked through the waters. "Ship above!"

Merrows burst into a flurry of movement. Spears were passed between hands while feral grins spread across faces. Tails lashed into movement so quick they reminded her of the bean sídhe's eels.

Alannah raced towards her, pointing her finger and giving her a severe look. "You stay here. That babe's safety is the most important priority."

Saoirse gave a quick nod although she had no intention of staying.

Electricity raced through her veins as if she had touched a man-of-war. Manus was here. She knew it was him, no one else was mad enough to sail a ship into these cursed waters.

Her gills flared, and she watched the merrows leave with wide eyes. A few stayed in the depths, those who were not deemed fit to fight. Saoirse doubted there would be much fighting. The last guardian battle had ended with drowned men before the merrows snatched them up.

She had to see him. She had to *save* him.

Saoirse frantically held her daughter out to the merrow who had not left with the others. "Hold her."

"What? Why?" The merrow took the baby carefully, cupping her head and holding her against her shoulder. "What are you doing?"

"I cannot let them kill him. I won't let him die."

"No one can stop a guardian."

"I have heard tales there were ships allowed to stay in faeries waters. They could pass through without a guardian ever attacking them."

"I've never heard of such a thing!"

"There was only one ship, long ago. Mac Lir's ship." She pressed a kiss to her baby's head. "I need you to look after her."

A current buffeted her as other merrows swam closer. One folded her hands in front of her and blurted, "We want to help."

"You what?"

"We don't agree that all ships should be destroyed. Other merrow pods find husbands and bring them back home. We wish to do the same."

Saoirse stared out over the small number of merrows and marveled at their bravery. They lived in a pod of merrows who would sooner kill a human than allow them close. Yet these women wanted to go against their orders, against everything they were raised to believe, on the chance they might find a husband who loved them.

She knew exactly how they felt.

"In the legends, a guardian will allow a ship with a yellow belly to travel through our waters. That it is a marking of faerie approval."

"How will we do that? There is no way for us to paint a ship."

Saoirse reached out and grasped a small rock. She dug it into the soft flesh of her arm, letting blood flow into the water and press against the stones. Coral grew upon the rocky surface. Magic encouraged it to spread, vibrant colors blooming bright and vivid.

"We can control what grows," she said. "We will cover the ship with yellow coral and the guardian will stop its attack."

"And the other merrows?"

"They will not harm us." Saoirse looked up, meeting the gaze of each merrow waiting with bated breath. "Choose a sailor and keep them safe from harm."

"And bring them back?" a merrow asked.

"Only if they wish it."

The merrow holding her daughter cleared her throat. "Are you well enough for this?"

Saoirse wasn't certain how to answer. She was weaker than she had ever been before. Her spine ached, her heart beat sluggishly, and before this moment she had been staring at her daughter wondering when it would all end.

Now, she had a chance at life. A better life, and the one she had chosen.

She nodded. "I have to be."

Two merrows swam forward and took hold of her arms. It was embarrassing they had to do such a thing. She should be able to swim by herself, to save the man she loved. But Saoirse realized she would never make it to the surface without their help.

She let out a slow breath. "Take care of my daughter. If I do not come back, make sure she is given a life where her own choices are more important than the opinions of others."

The merrow nodded and smoothed a hand down the baby's dark green tail.

Saoirse didn't want to cry. She turned her eyes towards the surface and said, "We need to go now. The guardian will have reached the ship."

They raced towards her husband, clustered together in one mass of women determined to find those who loved them.

She was grateful for her people and wondered how many merrows in her previous pod thought the same way. Had her sisters wanted to free themselves from a future with a merrow man as a husband? Had some of them looked forward to living with the creatures?

Saoirse judged them harshly when she hadn't taken the time to get to know them. Even the women holding her arms were strangers to her.

There were many things she wished she had done differently in her life. She had always prided herself on kindness but had forgotten what kindness entailed.

Determination had her swimming faster than she thought possible. She would start a new life with Manus. They would never be parted, and she would never hide the truth from him again.

He would know what she was thinking, and she would hear his thoughts. They would understand where the other person was coming from. They would build a life based on trust and truth.

As they should have from the beginning.

Lightning cracked overhead, illuminating the ship hovering above them. A wall of merrows waited, each fierce warrior holding a spear and wearing a smile of hatred and anger.

"Stop!" Saoirse cried out. "Tell the guardian to stop!"

They were too late. Fire flashed on the side of the ship and something impacted the side of the guardian. It struck hard flesh shielded by magic and angered the beast.

The guardian roared in pain and anger. She brought her fist down on the ship and cracked the deck. The sound rocketed through the waters and pushed Saoirse down.

"We have to go now," she gasped. "We have little time left."

"Alannah will try to stop us."

"She won't have time. Let go of me, and swim as fast as you can to the ship. Grow the coral. I'll deal with the guardian."

They split up. Some burst through the rankings of the merrows and flattened themselves to the bottom of the ship. Others hovered in the waters to protect those who were working. They made the right choice as many of Alannah's merrows tried to pull them away.

The merrows were determined on both sides. Saoirse was certain they could grow enough coral to calm the guardian as long as she could capture its attention.

She sluggishly swam towards it, breathing hard and feeling as though her gills weren't working. She ran her fingers down the slits. They were open as wide as they could go, yet she still couldn't breathe in enough.

Saoirse slowed the more she swam until she was struggling to stay afloat. She wriggled in the water.

"Guardian," she whimpered. "Please listen to me."

A deep groan echoed from above the waves. "They hurt me."

"I know they did, and that was wrong."

"He wants to take you away from the ocean, again."

"And you want to protect me, I understand." She clawed at the water with her arms, tail falling limp and threatening to drag her down into the deep. "I need you to protect me now."

The guardian lifted her fist and grabbed one of the great masts. It snapped off in her massive hands and she gave a loud roar. "That is what I am doing."

"I need you beneath the waves! Forget the humans, I am dying, and I need you to be here."

Merrows shrieked as the two groups collided. Saoirse whipped around and watched as more blood filled the water. They did not fight with spears, a small consolation, but with their claws. Each dug at each other, shrieking their anger into the waves.

Alannah propelled herself away from the group. Anger marred her beautiful features, and Saoirse knew why.

If the matriarch reached her, then her plans would be for nothing. She would drag her back down to her child, or worse, lock her away forever. Saoirse would die in these waters and Manus would never know his child.

"Guardian!" She cried out. "Help me!"

For a moment, she feared the creature did not hear her. The boom of cannon fire drowned out her words and the angry cries of merrows filled the sea with rage. The waters boiled with blood and battle.

Just as Alannah reached for her, a giant hand moved between them. The guardian scooped her out of the water and brought her up to its chest.

Saoirse curled up in its palm. With her tail pressed to her chest, she shivered as salt water fell from her body and cold air chilled her skin. She was so near to death she could barely even speak.

"Thank you," she whispered.

"What are you doing, little merrow? Your place is here, with us."

"My place is with him. I wish to see him, guardian. My life and his are bonded for all eternity. I am willing to die in his arms if it is too late or live forever at his side if it is not."

"I don't understand why you would want to leave us. He will not let you return."

"We cannot speak for him. He has traveled all this way to find me, perhaps he has changed his mind."

The guardian looked down at her, thoughtful and kind. A cannon went off again and Saoirse felt its impact on the beast's great form. The guardian did not flinch.

"If you are certain, then I will place you at his side. But be warned, few of our kind think highly of a faerie who would stoop so low as to marry a human."

"Then I have no wish to know them. He is the greatest man I have ever met. And not because of his decisions." Saoirse grinned. "He makes horrible choices. But he loves me, and I love him."

She knew the concept was strange to a creature who could not understand what love was. Guardians were faeries, but they were entirely different from most beasts. Even normal faeries may never discover the blessing as Saoirse had.

"So be it," the guardian sang.

Saoirse held onto the guardian's thumb as she lowered her all the way onto the deck of the ship. Sailors scattered, shouting curses and raising their fists as if that might help.

The guardian deposited her in the center of the ship. "You have only a few moments before I will return."

"We painted the ship yellow," she called out. "Merrows

gave their blood to mark this ship as theirs."

"Your sacrifice is not in vain, I shall return to the depths. It was an honor to know you, little merrow."

"And you."

The ship rocked again with the grumble of the guardian as she slid beneath it. The men shouted and pointed. Perhaps they were shocked the beast returned to the deep. Perhaps they didn't understand the way faeries worked.

She wasn't a creature. None of them were. They could be reasoned with as long as they understood why the humans wanted what they did.

Now, Saoirse was alone. Perhaps the other merrows weren't finished yet, or still fought their own kind. She didn't have time to understand why the others weren't on deck.

She pulled herself forward on shaking arms, dragging her useless tail behind her. A sailor flinched away. His eyes were wide and wild with fear. He lifted a broken piece of wood up, brandishing it in front of him as if he needed to protect himself.

"Please," she begged. "Where is my husband?"

"Begone, siren! We will not listen to your cries."

"I will not hurt you. I want my husband."

"You won't find a husband here!" the sailor shouted. "None of us will return with you. We have no desire to find ourselves locked away in a cage far away from land and hope."

"You don't understand."

Why were they afraid of her? Didn't they know Manus was here for her?

Saoirse glanced around at all the men, their suspicious looks making her fear grow like a cloud of blood in the water. They didn't know who she was.

Could this be another ship? Was Manus not here after all?

"Throw her overboard!" One of the sailors shouted.

"Or better yet, kill it and send it back to the sea."

She whimpered and pushed herself back. Her tail wouldn't work, her heart pounded against her ribs, and pin pricks of energy made her hands shake. Saoirse had run out of time.

"Hold!" The shout pierced the air and pounding feet raced towards her.

Dark and swarthy, he raced towards her as if the Wild Hunt chased him down. Blood streaked across his face and splattered down his chest, but he was everything she desired and more. Her husband. Her life.

Manus fell to his knees and pulled her into his arms. "Saoirse," he breathed. "My love."

Relief poured through her body like cold water on a sunburn. "Manus, you have returned to me."

"I should never have left. I love you, Saoirse. I should have said it every single moment you were in my arms. I love you, I love you, *I love you*." He buried his face in her neck and whispered the words over and again.

Saoirse held him against her until his breathing slowed. He pulled back, brushed her hair from her face and pressed his lips to her forehead, eyes, cheeks. For the first time in months, Saoirse felt all her worries disappear. She lifted her hand and pressed it to his cheek.

"I should have told you everything that was happening."

"I should have loved you as you deserve." He pressed his lips to hers and she tasted salt on his tongue. "I will never leave you again."

Chains rattled, drawing their attention towards the side of

the ship. Merrows crawled up out of the sea. They launched themselves at the sailors and for a moment, she couldn't tell who they were. Saoirse held her breath until she realized the women were hugging the men.

They twined their tails around them, holding them in place, and pressing kisses to their necks. As soon as the sailors realized what was happening, stunned laughter spread across the deck.

"Saoirse." Manus's voice echoed in her ears. "What is going on?"

"They don't want to kill you anymore. They want to keep you."

One merrow she recognized. Webbed fingers spread wide over her daughter's back. The merrow pulled herself up with one arm and dragged her body across the deck towards them.

Manus stiffened and placed a hand on the knife at his side.

"Don't," Saoirse warned and held out her arms for her daughter. "It is our child."

"Ours?" The wonder in his voice made her look up in surprise. "Our child?"

"The leprechaun didn't tell you?"

"No, he said you left because you were dying."

"That is only part of the truth." Her tail melted into thin mucus. Saoirse plucked the baby underneath her arms and tucked her against her chest. "This is our daughter. She was born in the water as both her mother and father were. Now, the choice is yours where she grows up."

"Mine?" He stared at her numbly. "Why would that choice be mine?"

"If you wish me to return with you, then she shall live on

land. I will make my goodbyes to the sea, and we will search for some way for me to exist without you—"

He pressed his fingers to her lips.

"Say nothing more, wife. When I said I wanted you by my side, I meant in every possible way. I want to hear your laughter on the wind. I want to see your smiles every morning. I want to feel your skin against mine each night." He leaned forward and kissed her as she had never been kissed before. "I want to love you until the day I die."

Tears pricked her eyes. "And so you will."

EPILOGUE

Sunlight played across the quiet waves and danced across Saoirse's shoulders. She sat in a pool of warm water, sand heating her tail and waves cooling the sting. Fronds of kelp piled in heaps on her lap. She worked to weave them together, creating a strong rope that would last for a few weeks underwater.

"Máthair! Máthair!"

The bright voice calling out made her smile. There was never a day when the sound of her daughter's voice didn't make happiness bubble in her chest.

"Where have you been Orlaith?" she asked with a chuckle. "I thought you were lost in the heart of the isle!"

"There's no such thing, Máthair." The little girl plopped onto the sand. She held something in her grasp, but Saoirse was more concerned about the state of her daughter's hair.

"When did you last brush this?" She tried to run her fingers through the dark locks, but they tangled at her scalp.

"Pirates don't brush their hair."

"Then it's a good thing you aren't a pirate."

"Athair doesn't brush his hair!"

She would have to talk with Manus about that. Although she quite liked the dreadlocks on her husband, her daughter was another story. Saoirse wanted her hair to wave like sea fronds in the water. Not stick straight up like eels.

Orlaith sighed dramatically. "This isn't why I came here."

"Oh? Then why did you come running, my little clam?"

"Máthair!"

Her daughter hated the nickname which had stuck early on in her childhood. Manus claimed their daughter hadn't yet turned into a pearl but would someday become an incredible beauty.

Saoirse tugged on the tangled strands. "Fine, Orlaith. What is it you have?"

"Athair told me to give it to you." She handed a small, golden figure over. "He said you used to have a gold prince when you were little and that you might want this one instead."

She turned the figure over and grinned. It was a small golden pirate with his sword at the ready. It wasn't a prince, not even close, but it was exactly the kind of man she wanted to dream about each night.

"It's lovely, don't you think?"

Orlaith tucked herself underneath Saoirse's arm. "I think it looks like Athair."

"Do you? Why's that?"

"Because he looks fierce and strong."

"That he does." Saoirse held the figure up towards the sun. "Did you know your father fought off a guardian for me?"

"He did?"

"Of course! It was a long time ago, but he wasn't even afraid."

"Not even a little?"

"Well, you must ask him about that. But I remember he didn't even tremble."

She brushed a hand over her daughter's head and sighed in happiness. Her life finally came together. All the pieces she'd missed filled the spaces of her heart.

Waves splashed against the edge of a boat, thunking on worn wood. A secret smile spread across her lips and she looked down the shore to watch her husband navigate his boat towards them. He pulled the oars with strong arms, sun dancing off his caramel skin.

Manus reached them, jumping into the sea spray. "There's my two favorite girls. Are you ready to go?"

"Back to sea?" Saoirse asked. She nudged her daughter's back. "Go get your father."

"Are we actually going?"

"Looks like."

Orlaith stood, shucked her white linen dress, and sprinted through the water. Manus caught her with a bright smile, laughing even as her legs tangled together and merged into one dark green tail. "Hello, my little clam! Did you give your mother our gift?"

"I did! She thought it looked like you, too."

"Did she?" Manus met her eyes, heat reflecting in his. "I thought he was too handsome to look like me."

"You're handsome, Athair!"

"Am I?" He pressed a hand to his chest, hiking their daughter higher in his arms with the other. "Your mother never tells me anymore."

"Máthair!"

Saoirse burst into laughter. "Don't let your father convince you otherwise. He knows I think he's plenty handsome."

"Go get the boat for me, would you little one?"

"Okay!"

Orlaith wiggled from his arms and dove into the water. She was a better swimmer than Saoirse was at that age. She'd taken to her tail like a second skin and had no trouble switching between forms.

Saoirse was so proud of her. She was everything and more.

"Hello, wife." Manus's voice deepened, a husky whisper that sent shivers down her spine. "Are you finished with your work?"

"For now."

He knelt, waves kissing his thighs as he pulled her forward. "I have missed you."

Saoirse sighed as he cupped the back of her neck, pulled her forward, and pressed his lips to hers. He took his time, tasting her as one might a fine wine. His hands stroked the column of her throat while he plundered her mouth until she moaned.

Only then he did pull back, stroking her full lower lip with his thumb.

"I saw you yesterday," she said with a chuckle. "But I don't mind the welcome."

"How was your adventure with your daughter? She refused to tell me anything, only said that your adventures were for merrows to know."

Saoirse chuckled and rolled her eyes. "We found plenty of treasures."

"And?"

She loved it that he wanted more for them. It wasn't about money anymore. Their adventures were to enrich their daughter's life and give the entire family stories to tell at night.

"And we met an octopus who loved her. She still has tiny sucker marks on her shoulders, but he was gentle enough."

"She won't be disappointed coming back to the ship with me?"

"Manus, I think she loves being on the ship with you almost as much as she loves the water with me."

Her words seemed to ease her husband's worry. Manus constantly worried that both his wife and his daughter would leave him. The ocean was too tempting, he would say, how could a mere mortal man attract two equally amazing women?

Every time, Saoirse would tell him they loved him too much to leave. And it was true. No matter how far they traveled, she always wanted him by her side.

Manus pressed his forehead to hers. "Will you follow us in the water?"

"I'd like to stretch my tail for a while."

"Jump a few times for her. She likes knowing where you are."

"I'll let you know if there's any trouble up ahead."

"Trouble? In faerie waters? That's unlikely." He gave her a jaunty wink and splashed through the water towards their daughter. "Orlaith, did you catch that boat yet?"

Saoirse grinned at her adorable family. Manus tackled their daughter and wrestled her onto the small boat. She complained the entire time, saying she wanted to stay in the water for just a little while longer. But they both knew she wanted to get back to the ship.

Orlaith loved being aboard the Freedom. She raced across the deck, climbed the masts like a monkey, and teased the sailors mercilessly. They all adored her.

As her husband and child rowed away, Saoirse slipped under the waves. They had come to terms with the fact that she would always need to be in the water. It didn't matter that their bond was stronger than ever. She had to be in the water every day.

Manus didn't mind, and Saoirse took it as a sign they were growing together.

Schools of fish swirled as they streaked by her, their scaly bodies brushing against hers. A pod of dolphins chattered next to her, leaping from the waves and laughing as they splashed back down.

The deeper they traveled, the less she saw. Humpback whales eyed her on her travels, their song following her for miles.

She felt so good in the ocean. Strong, powerful, and incredibly free.

They sailed towards a faerie isle, one where supposedly the strongest women trained. Manus wanted to trade goods in return for a weapon that would grant them riches untold. He said a faerie had requested it, and she felt certain Declan was the one making the deals.

It didn't matter in the end. She was with the three loves of her life.

Her husband, her daughter, and the sea.

When the sun set on the horizon, Saoirse slowed her pace. The ship would travel slowly now that the stars were their guide. They would set their course for the rest of the evening and let the others rest.

She grasped the handholds Manus had installed on the side of the ship when they were last in Uí Néill. He wanted her to have something to hold onto, something to climb.

Hand over hand, she pulled herself up. Music started up, laughter spilling over the edges in a great wave of happiness and movement. She braced her arms on the railing and laid her head on her forearms.

Manus and Orlaith twirled across the deck. One of the sailors fiddled in the corner and a few of the sailors tapped their feet. Orlaith wore boy's clothing: billowy pants and a white linen shirt falling off her shoulders.

"Saoirse!" A sailor shouted. "I'll get your dress, lass."

They all knew her name and knew to be careful with it. Manus had filled his crew with trustworthy men and put the fear of god in them. He'd kill them if they ever disrespected her.

The sailor respectfully handed her the dress, turning his back to give her some privacy. She tossed it over her head, switching hands on the railing and shaking her legs to free them of mucus.

Manus handed off their daughter to one of the crew who whirled her into a wild jig. She shrieked with laughter and her feet raced across the floor.

Heat blossomed in Saoirse's belly as her husband stalked towards her. He was big, and real, and so powerful he made her shiver.

"Wife," he growled. His hands reached over the railing, surrounded her waist, and lifted her high over the edge.

She tucked herself into his arms with a peaceful sigh. "Husband."

He swayed back and forth, dancing her gracefully across the deck. "You know I love you more than all the stars in the sky?"

"And I love you more than all the fish in the sea."

AFTERWORD

I hope you enjoyed Bride of the Sea as much as I have! This was a journey and an unusual style compared to my other books.

I wanted to challenge myself with this one and create a story that I wouldn't usually write. And I am so incredibly pleased with this story that follows these two characters I love so much.

If you enjoyed this story, please leave a review! They help authors out so much.

<3 Emma

ACKNOWLEDGEMENTS

To all those who want to write, may you find the time to share your worlds with us.

ABOUT THE AUTHOR

Emma Hamm is a small town girl on a blueberry field in Maine. She writes stories that remind her of home, of fairytales, and of myths and legends that make her mind wander.

She can be found by the fireplace with a cup of tea and her two Maine Coon cats dipping their paws into the water without her knowing.

To stay in touch

www.emmahamm.com

authoremmahamm@gmail.com

CPSIA information can be obtained
at www.ICGtesting.com
Printed in the USA
LVOW11s1839070318
568993LV00001B/291/P